DANGEROUS INHERITANCE

*

In this novel we meet again not only the Duke de Richleau, hero of so many best-selling adventure stories by Dennis Wheatley, but also his friends and comrades from those same hair-raising escapades: Richard Eaton, Simon Aron and the American Rex van Ryn. Newcomers to the scene are Rex's son, and Richard Eaton's daughter—Fleur, who believes in all the freedoms, including that of sex. Interwoven with her adventurous love-life is the story of a strange inheritance which draws the whole party to Ceylon and into situations of terrifying danger . . .

BY DENNIS WHEATLEY

NOVELS

The Launching of Roger Brook
The Shadow of Tyburn Tree
The Rising Storm
The Man Who Killed the King
The Dark Secret of Josephine
The Rape of Venice
The Sultan's Daughter
The Wanton Princess
Evil in a Mask

The Scarlet Impostor
Faked Passports
The Black Baroness
V for Vengeance
Come Into My Parlour
Traitors' Gate
They Used Dark Forces

The Prisoner in the Mask
The Second Seal
Vendetta in Spain
Three Inquisitive People
The Forbidden Territory
The Devil Rides Out
The Golden Spaniard
Strange Conflict
Codeword—Golden Fleece
Dangerous Inheritance
Gateway to Hell

The Quest of Julian Day
The Sword of Fate
Bill for the Use of a Body

Black August
Contraband
The Island Where Time Stands Still
The White Witch of the South Seas

To the Devil—a Daughter
The Satanist

The Eunuch of Stamboul
The Secret War
The Fabulous Valley
Sixty Days to Live
Such Power is Dangerous
Uncharted Seas
The Man Who Missed the War
The Haunting of Toby Jugg
Star of Ill-Omen
They Found Atlantis
The Ka of Gifford Hillary
Curtain of Fear
Mayhem in Greece
Unholy Crusade

SHORT STORIES

Mediterranean Nights
Gunmen, Gallants and Ghosts

HISTORICAL

A Private Life of Charles II (*Illustrated by Frank C. Papé*)
Red Eagle (*The Story of the Russian Revolution*)

AUTOBIOGRAPHICAL

Stranger than Fiction (*War Papers for the Joint Planning Staff*)
Saturdays with Bricks

IN PREPARATION

The Ravishing of Lady Mary Ware (*another Roger Brook story*)
The Devil and all his Works (*Illustrated in colour*)

Dennis Wheatley

Dangerous Inheritance

ARROW BOOKS

ARROW BOOKS LTD
3 Fitzroy Square, London W1

HUTCHINSON GROUP

London Melbourne Sydney Auckland
Wellington Johannesburg Cape Town
and agencies throughout the world

First published by
Hutchinson & Co (*Publishers*) Ltd 1965
Arrow edition 1967
Second impression 1970
Third impression 1971

*Made and printed in Great Britain
by The Anchor Press Ltd.,
Tiptree, Essex*

ISBN 0 09 003920 3

For

S. and A.

with every kind thought

from their friend

DENNIS

CONTENTS

1

The Matchmakers

There can be few more beautiful places than the island of Corfu, and that was why the Duke de Richleau had decided to build a villa there in which to spend a good part of his declining years. Air travel made it easy for his friends to come out to stay with him, and in April 1958 he had four guests: the Princess Marie Lou, her husband Richard Eaton, their daughter Fleur and Rex Van Ryn's son Trusscott.

They had lunched under an awning at the south end of the sunny terrace, then moved for coffee and liqueurs to the north end, from which there was the best view of the enchanted lagoon, in which it was said that, long ago, Ulysses had been washed ashore.

Trusscott and Fleur refused liqueurs and, having drunk their coffee, walked away down the flight of broad stone steps that led to a garden of tall palms, candle-like cypresses and massed banks of many coloured flowers. The young American was very tall and Fleur's short-cut, copper-coloured hair barely came up to his shoulder.

As the three older people watched them go de Richleau turned to Marie Lou and murmured, 'Yes, it would be nice, wouldn't it?'

He was very old now. His hair was thin and white, his fine aquiline features lined with tiny wrinkles; but his grey eyes flecked with yellow, under the 'devil's' eyebrows, could still at times flash with brilliance and his mind had lost nothing of its swift intelligence.

She smiled at him. 'Dear Greyeyes, how like you to guess what I was thinking. It really would be lovely if they fell for one another, but I'm afraid there's not much chance of that.'

Richard was just on fifty. His brown hair with its widow's peak was flecked with grey, and as he ran his hand back over it in an habitual gesture he remarked, 'If they did, there's nothing would please me more. With taxes as they are in our Welfare State I've all I can do to keep Cardinal's Folly going; and I'd hate the old place to pass out of the family. But it will have to when I die unless Fleur marries money. For her to tie up with old Rex's boy would be the perfect answer.'

'But if she did marry him they'd live in the States.'

'For most of the year, perhaps; but with the Van Ryn millions they could well afford a place in England.'

'She might not want it,' mused Marie Lou. 'The problem of servants is becoming more and more difficult, and it would be no fun trying to run a rambling old house like ours without adequate staff.'

Richard shrugged. 'Given enough money that's no problem; and servants in England would still cost them less than they'd have to pay in America.'

'Perhaps; but Fleur is terribly modern in her tastes. She has no love for old things or country life. The friends she brings down to stay scoff openly at all traditions, and although she's too well mannered to say so in front of us I know she agrees with them. I really can't see her becoming the lady of the manor.'

'I fear you brought that on yourselves,' said the Duke quietly. 'By letting her go to London University what else could you expect?'

'I know,' Richard sighed. 'Ever since Harold Laski was the star professor there it's been a breeding place for Reds, and now it's full of blacks and browns who are anti everything we've ever believed in. It's no wonder that she looks on us as "squares". I was dead against it from the start, but like an ass I gave way.'

'We had to, darling.' Marie Lou laid a hand on his arm. 'She was set on it and old enough to know her own mind. The times are gone when parents could insist on their young leading the kind of life they would like them to. She's got too good a brain to waste and she wouldn't hear of Oxford or Cambridge. How could we stand in her way?'

Richard took her hand and kissed it. 'You're right, my sweet. I'm just an old fogey who still believes in Britain and regrets the passing of the Empire; so it riles me to hear Fleur's friends belittling all it stood for and see them going about like a lot of unwashed tramps. I suppose we should be thankful that, anyway, she still has a bath every day.'

'One can rarely have it both ways,' de Richleau's soft old voice came again. 'At least you can be proud of having a daughter with the brains and determination to get her M.A. And she won't remain in her present state for long. Someone once said that anyone who was not a Communist when he was twenty had no heart and if he remained one when he reached thirty he had no head. I, of course, never had a heart.'

He gave a quiet chuckle and went on, 'But that does apply to a great many people; particularly the young folk of today, who have been made far more conscious than their predecessors of the hunger and squalor that afflict the greater part of the world's population. I know Fleur took sociology with the idea of serving in one of those organisations that bring aid to backward peoples; but she's too attractive not to marry, and most women, bless them, are like chameleons in allowing their husbands to colour their beliefs and interests. All the odds are that, unless she marries some firebrand while she still has this crusading bug, in ten years' time she'll be as much a true-blue Tory as yourself.'

'I pray you may prove right, Greyeyes. But she's our only chick and it's going to be an anxious time waiting to see what she does make of her life. I'd gladly give five years of mine to have her happily engaged to young Truss before our visit here ends. How long is he staying?'

'I've no idea. Rex, very wisely I think, decided to send him to Europe for seven months before he starts at Law School in the autumn, and he's doing a modified version of the old Grand Tour; but, of course, unaccompanied by a tutor. I wrote that I hoped he would spare the time to look in on me here. Realising that anyone so aged as myself would be poor company for the boy, and recalling that he took rather a fancy to Fleur when he, his father and myself spent Christmas with you at Cardinal's Folly four winters ago, I mentioned as an attraction that you would be with me for a while from mid-April, and he wired me from Athens asking me if he could arrive today.'

'You wily old fox,' Richard laughed. 'But you're right, of course. The two of them got on famously that Christmas he spent at Cardinal's Folly and they both seem delighted to be together again. It's that which makes me rather hopeful.'

Marie Lou shook her head. 'By harking back to that boy-and-girl affaire you're building castles in the air, darling. Fleur was only just twenty then, and still in the stage when a girl will try her hand out on anything in trousers. While Truss, rising seventeen, would have not been normal if he hadn't been smitten with calf-love for her. But there is nearly three years between them and that makes a big difference now.

'Naturally she'll be pleased to have him as an escort while she's here, but she would have no time at all for a boy of twenty-one if there were an interesting older man about. And you can be certain that he hasn't the least intention of marrying anyone yet. With that ugly, attractive face, so like his father's, and any amount of money, he can get all the girls he wants. He'd be more of a fool than I take him for if he doesn't spend a few years sowing his wild oats before he settles down.'

'I suppose you're right,' Richard admitted, smiling at his lovely wife. For the thousandth time it crossed his mind how little she had altered since he had brought her out of Russia. Her heart-shaped face and big violet eyes seemed to have aged hardly at all. Although she was forty-seven most people would have put her down as still in her thirties. She was a very small woman, but her figure was perfectly proportioned and no one could lay a better claim to the appellation 'a pocket Venus'. After a moment, he added with a grin:

'Young Truss is the whale of a catch for any girl, though; and you may be wrong about Fleur not finding him attractive. If she does, whatever his ideas about sowing wild oats, if she had half your looks she'd get him.'

'I'll second that,' agreed the Duke, giving a low laugh.

'You preposterous darlings.' Marie Lou shook her head. Then, with a wicked glance at Richard, she said, 'But, after all, perhaps I could. If you'll divorce me I'm game to have a try. I'd love the chance to throw some of the Van Ryn millions about, and I bet a young Goliath like Truss would be good in bed. It's quite time I got rid of you and had a little fun.'

He gave a solemn nod. 'How right you are, and I'd divorce you tomorrow but for one thing. I happen to be a "square", so divorce is against my principles.' Standing up, he took her by the arm and added, 'That being so, there's only one thing for it. I'm taking you up to our room and you're not going to get much of a siesta.'

'Richard! How can you say such things?' Marie Lou had never got over blushing and as he pulled her to her feet she flushed scarlet, just as he had hoped she would.

'Off you go!' cried de Richleau gaily. 'I'll take my siesta here as usual.'

But he was not destined to doze for quite a while. Marie Lou, with Richard's arm about her, had only just disappeared into the villa when Petti, the white-coated houseman, emerged from it with a letter on a salver. With the low bow of a well-trained servant he presented it to the Duke.

Taking the letter with a word of thanks, de Richleau saw that the envelope was typed and carried a Ceylonese stamp. He knew no one in Ceylon and, as travelling friends usually sent only postcards, he could not imagine who could have written to him on any business matter from there. As he turned the letter over, the psychic sense with which he was endowed made him strangely reluctant to open it. Had he relied on his instinct and, without reading the letter, had it burnt, that would have been far better, for its contents were fated to bring pain and grief to his four guests and himself into great danger.

2

The Fateful Letter

The letter was from Messrs. Rutnam and Rajapakse, a firm of solicitors in Colombo, and signed by a partner, Anton Rajapakse. As de Richleau read it his forebodings that it might be the harbinger of misfortune were swiftly dissipated, and he became greatly intrigued by its contents.

He well remembered his cousin, Count Ivan Plackoff, an adventurous, courageous and autocratic noble, whom he had succeeded in rescuing from execution by the Bolsheviks during the Russian Revolution in 1917. When the Whites had been finally defeated and all hope of restoring a Czar to the Imperial Throne had gone, they had dispersed all over the world to make a living as best they could. Many of them had gone to China and to Constantinople, others who had money invested abroad had settled in the south of France, Paris and other European capitals. But Count Ivan, for some reason known only to himself, had decided to make his home in Ceylon.

During the twenties de Richleau had heard from him occasionally, so knew that he not only found life there agreeable but was well on his way to remaking his fortune. Ceylon is one of the richest countries in the world in gems and semi-precious stones, and the Count had acquired an estate that he had named after an old family property in the Crimea, Olenevka, in the jewel-mining area. Being a ruthless man who had inherited the views of his less humane forbears that serfs existed only to produce wealth for their masters, he had driven the Ceylonese natives he employed into making his mines pay an unusually high dividend. But after a few years he had ceased to write and de Richleau had no idea what had happened to him.

From the solicitor's letter it emerged that he had died in 1937 and, having no close relatives, was presumed to have left

Olenevka to his estate manager, a Mr. Ukwatte d'Azavedo, who, like many middle-class Ceylonese, claimed Portuguese descent. The will had been witnessed by one Pedro Fernando, the Count's butler-valet, another native who had inherited a Portuguese name from some remote progenitor, and his wife Vinala, who had been the Count's cook. In consequence d'Azavedo had entered unopposed on his rich inheritance.

But a few months previously Pedro, on being told by his doctor that he had only a few weeks to live, and being a Roman Catholic, had confessed to his local priest that he had known the will to be a forgery, and witnessed it only because d'Azavedo had bribed him and his wife to do so with a sufficient sum of money to keep them in comfort during their old age.

The priest had persuaded him that it was his duty to leave a signed statement to that effect, which he had done; and on his death the priest had sent it to Count Ivan's solicitors. The senior member of the firm had then recalled that the Count had some years previous to his death made a genuine will leaving everything to his cousin the Duke, in recognition of de Richleau having saved his life during the Revolution.

Now, the writer of the letter suggested that his firm should start proceedings on the Duke's behalf to claim his inheritance, and that he should come out to Ceylon to see the valuable property which would be his after the legal formalities had been observed.

It was a long time since de Richleau had travelled outside Europe and over thirty years since he had visited Ceylon. He remembered the island as an exceptionally beautiful place, so the idea of going there again appealed to him. Still toying with the idea, he dropped off to sleep.

Meanwhile Trusscott and Fleur had settled themselves in a belvedere at the far end of the garden, where its walks, bordered with flowering shrubs and orange and lemon trees in blossom, ended in a steep slope of rocky outcrop. Below them lay the Ionian Straits, an almost unbelievable blue. For many centuries they had been the scene of naval battles between Christians and Turks, for Corfu had been the last great bastion held in turn by the Knights and Venetians against the Infidel hordes in their attempts to conquer southern Europe; but now the placid waters were broken here and there only by the spreading ripples in the wake of half a dozen fishing vessels. Across the Straits, some ten miles away but in the clear air looking far nearer, lay the rugged coast of Albania. Beyond it rose the lofty snow-covered peaks of the Epiros mountains, their chain falling away to lesser heights towards the south where the tip of Corfu curved in almost to meet the coast of Greece.

The town of Corfu was about five miles to the north, but could not be seen from the villa owing to the high wooded peninsula of Kanoni that lay between them. Yet the view from the belvedere in that direction was breath-taking in its beauty. Far below, from the blue waters of the bay there rose two small islands on which stood ancient monasteries and tall cypresses; and the peninsula itself had the appearance of another, larger island, for, on its landward side to the south of the town, the sea formed a wide, mile-long lagoon.

As Trusscott had arrived only just before lunch it was the first time the two young people had been alone together and while walking through the garden they had exchanged only platitudes; so now Fleur said:

'I'm so glad you turned up. All this picture-postcard scenery is quite marvellous, I know, but I'm much more interested in people and I'm dying to hear what you've been up to all this time. Tell all with no holds barred.'

He smiled at her. 'There's not much to tell. Getting through college is no small undertaking these days. The standard gets higher every year and competition's fierce.'

Fleur made a grimace. 'You're telling me! I've been at it three years longer than you have. Work, work and more bloody work. There were times when I nearly threw my hand in.'

'But you didn't. And you got your M.A. You must be quite a blue-stocking.'

'Do I look it?'

He regarded her thoughtfully. She was taller than her mother but only of medium height. Her eyes were the same colour as Marie Lou's, but neither so large nor so vivid, and although her figure was good she was much slimmer. Her face was longer, ending in a round, aggressive chin indicating her determination to get what she wanted. A good straight nose and a full, beautifully modelled mouth were her best features.

Together with her violet eyes and copper-coloured hair, they made her decidedly good-looking.

After a moment he said, 'I can't answer that one. In the past blue-stockings were most always plain Janes, and these days there aren't any. Care of teeth, hair and skin in childhood and all the beauty aids available afterwards have put an end to the species. Contrariwise, now most girls have to get them a job, some of the prettiest have their little heads crammed full of facts and figures.'

She nodded. 'You're right about all the girls of our generation making the most of what they've got both in looks and brains. Being a natural honey-pot doesn't cut the ice it did; it's personality that gets the chaps steamed up about one.'

'Well, unless you've changed in the last four years you've plenty of that, and you're a good-looker into the bargain.'

'Thanks for the bouquet. But tell me about yourself.'

'As I said, I had to concentrate hard to make the grade, but I felt it was up to me not to let my old man down, and this seven months in Europe is the pay-off.'

'Where have you been so far?'

'Spain, Portugal and Greece; from here I'll do Italy. Then as the weather warms up I'll go other places further north: Paris, Brussels, Munich, Vienna; they've all got marvellous collections.'

'By the time you've done Italy I should have thought you would be sick of the sight of pictures. What were the night spots like in Spain?'

'Not bad; but I didn't go to many. The señoritas are a pretty poor lot as dancing partners.'

Fleur raised an eyebrow. 'Is that the only use you had for them?'

'Well, yes. Going places with that sort of girl in foreign cities can land one in a packet of trouble.'

'That doesn't stop the chaps I know. Evidently you're the faithful type and the truth is that you've got a sweetie at home. Some poppet you've been going steady with at your college.'

'You're wrong. Dartmouth is not co-ed.'

'What rotten luck that your father should have sent you there. One gathers that at most universities in the States it's a free-for-all and sex is counted part of the education.'

'Sure; but it was just as well there were no girls at Dartmouth. It was my own choice because I'm pretty good on skis. I was one of the college team in fact, and our team sends several skiers to the Olympic Games. For that you've got to keep real fit and girls and ski-jumping don't go together.'

'I see. But what about the hols? Surely you let up a bit then?'

He shrugged. 'Winters we go down to our old home in the South. It's a lovely place but miles from the nearest town, and I spend most of my time riding or fishing. Summers we spend at Cape Cod, and there's plenty doing there. The sailing and bathing are super.'

Fleur gave him a puzzled look. He was six foot two of splendid young manhood, broad-shouldered, slim-hipped, bronzed-skinned. His brown eyes held humour and intelligence; his very ugliness was of the kind that invariably attracts women. Suddenly she exclaimed:

'For heaven's sake, Truss, don't tell me you're a queer!'

His dark head went back and his big mouth opened wide in a great guffaw. 'Heavens no! Whatever gave you that idea? Just my not going whoring in Madrid? No, I'm as normal as they come, thank God.'

'But you don't seem the least interested in girls.'

'Oh, I wouldn't say that. But I don't get to know many except when we're at the Cape. There, of course, I dance every night, and I'm good enough at it to get more or less my pick of partners. I've nothing against necking either, for that matter. But being the heir to a mint of money has its liabilities. If I went too far with any of them they'd surely try to fix me, and I've no mind to get myself tied up yet. When the pace gets too hot I give them the polite brush-off. There's always plenty more to choose from.'

'So that's the form, and you really haven't got anyone in the States that you care about?'

'No. Keep it light is my motto, then there are no entanglements and no regrets. Naturally there have been three or four I got pretty smitten with, and several times I darn' near got seduced. But what with stacks of work and lots of vigorous play one can do without that sort of thing. And, after all, I'm only just on twenty-one, so I've lots of time ahead of me for leching.'

'Leching,' Fleur repeated. 'What a nice old-fashioned word. And, of course, I see your point of view. But it's very unusual these days. I mean, well, from what you've said I suppose you are still a virgin?'

'I am,' he nodded. 'And I see no reason to be ashamed of it.'

'No. Oh no, of course not.'

'Fine. And now let's hear about you.'

She shook her head rather sadly. 'I'm afraid you wouldn't approve, Truss. I'm not. But what girl is at twenty-four? As a matter of fact I lost it when I was seventeen, during my season. The first time I hated it and for quite a time it wasn't much fun, but I was madly in love with the chap so I let him go on; then I came to like it. But after a few months he was posted abroad. When he'd been gone for some time I began to crave for it. The tiger who's tasted blood, sort of thing, you know. But buried in the country down at Cardinal's Folly no one I liked enough came along. That Christmas you spent with us, if you hadn't been such an innocent you could have had me if you'd wanted, but we got no further than my teaching you how to kiss. Soon afterwards a friend of Daddy's made a pass at me and I'm afraid I didn't take much seducing; but it was a rather trying hole-in-the-corner affaire. We used to slip away from the hunt and have jollies in barns, which isn't a very satisfactory way of doing that sort of thing. Then I went to London U., and shared a flat with three other girls in the Cromwell Road. They were all as hot as mustard and the place was little better than a brothel. Perhaps that's an exaggeration and, of course, we didn't get money for it; but some of the parties we threw were pretty hectic, and we had to pay the old caretaker in the basement to keep her mouth shut.

'After a while I got sick of having to fight off men I didn't like when we were all half tight, so I moved to another place where I was on my own. While there I fell terribly badly for a married man who could get away for week-ends fairly frequently. As I was free to go and come as I liked we had some lovely times at country inns just outside London. But he wouldn't ask his wife for a divorce; so after eighteen months going steady with him I steeled myself to make a break. While I was working for my thesis I was a good girl. I simply had to be. Since then I've had two brief affaires, just physical attraction and the old craving rearing its ugly head again; but no more. And I suppose I'll do the same with the next man who attracts me. So there you have it, my dear. I'm no better than an old tart.'

'You mustn't say that,' Truss smiled. 'From that full rich mouth of yours anyone could see that you are passionate by nature. It was just your bad luck that you were seduced when still so young and that the only man you really cared about was married.'

'You're not shocked, then?'

'Why should I be? You are just a product of the age we live in. No better and no worse than those girls I used to team up with at the Cape. I doubt if many of them would have refused to sleep with me if I'd been prepared to play. I would have too if I hadn't been so scared that afterwards they'd swear I'd put them in the family way in order to force the issue and get their little claws on a share of the Van Ryn millions.'

'Thank you, Truss. I'm glad you feel like that. You see, when we had our boy-and-girl affaire I knew you thought a lot of me; so I felt I had to tell you the truth about myself. It wouldn't have been fair to let you believe that I'm anything but what I am.'

His brown eyes smiled into her violet ones. 'I give you full marks for that. How about us going someplace dancing to-night? I take it one of the hotels in the town runs a band?'

'I'd love it. During the five days since we arrived here I've been bored to tears. There's a big place called the Corfu Palace. We'll run down there after dinner.'

At dinner that evening de Richleau told his guests about the strange turn of fortune which, twenty years after it should have done, promised to bring him a jewel mine, and that he was contemplating flying out to Ceylon to see for himself his unexpected inheritance.

When the surprise, laughter and congratulations had died down, Marie Lou said seriously, 'We are delighted for you, Greyeyes dear, but you really must not think of going out to Ceylon. To talk to, no one would believe you to be a day over seventy but you must face the fact that you are eighty-three. You have kept yourself so fit that we who love you have every hope that you'll live to be a hundred. But you'll do that only if you continue to take great care of yourself. Such a long flight would prove too great a strain for anyone of your age.'

'Marie Lou's right,' Richard chimed in. 'Living quietly here for the greater part of the year is splendid for you, and an occasional trip to the South of France or England entails no great risk. But going to Ceylon is a very different matter. It's not only that after such a long flight you would arrive exhausted; but the conditions when you got there. From next month on the heat there will be terrific, and going from it into air-conditioned rooms you might easily catch a chill. There's the risk, too, that you might pick up one of those awful tropical diseases. Honestly, you must put this idea right out of your mind.'

The younger people supported their elders and after a while the Duke gave way. But he was so intrigued by the story of the forged will and about the property he had been left that he was eager to secure more particulars than could be sent in a letter. In consequence, as he could well afford it, he decided to cable the solicitor who had written to him and request that he should come to Corfu as soon as possible.

After dinner Fleur announced her intention of going down to the Corfu Palace with Truss to dance, and asked if they might have a car. In addition to the Duke's large car in which he sometimes went for drives, he kept a runabout for the convenience of his guests who wanted to make expeditions by the narrow roads up through the mountains. He said that by all means they could take it, and ten minutes later they were on their way.

The moon was not yet up so the lush vegetation on either side of the steep twisting descent to the coast road was veiled in darkness, but they were soon running past the airport at the inland end of the Kanoni lagoon and between scattered houses to the great sweep of Garitsars bay, south of the town, where the big luxury hotel was ablaze with lights.

It had been built only three years before and its spacious hall, broad staircase and the masses of exotic flowers in the big first-floor lounge were all impressive. As it was still early in the season there were only a score or so of people sitting about but at one end a three-man band was playing.

Although only a young man Truss's physique and well-cut tuxedo gave him the sort of presence to which head waiters always give a smiling welcome; so they were shown to a good table which Truss amply justified by ordering a bottle of French champagne. When he had approved the wine they went out on to the floor and, to his delight, he found that Fleur was a joy to dance with.

The three hours that followed passed all too quickly for

them both, and when the band played the Greek National Anthem they were surprised to find that it was one o'clock in the morning. By then they had consumed a second bottle, and when they went out to the car they were laughing together just a little hilariously.

A sickle moon was now up, high in a clear sky, its light so strong that by it they could see the outline of the age-old citadel on the big twin-peaked promontory of rock to the east of the town. It was said to have served as a refuge for the townsfolk during the Gothic invasion and, rebuilt by the Venetians, had, a thousand years later, defied the Turks.

Back at the villa they did not feel like bed so got themselves drinks, took them out on to the terrace and sat there breathing in the heady scent of the moonflowers. But it had now become a little chilly: so when they had finished their drinks Fleur stood up and said, 'I think now we'd better go in.'

Coming to his feet, Truss put his big hands on her shoulders, smiled down at her and replied, 'Surely. But when I take a girl dancing it's my custom to kiss her good night; and anyhow I'd like to show you I haven't forgotten what you taught me that Christmas.'

Fleur smiled back at him, lifting her face to his. 'Come on then, big boy. Just show me.'

Her full lips melted under his. Their kiss was long, moist and sweet. As he held her to him he felt her quiver slightly. When at length he took his mouth from hers he gave a little gasp and murmured, 'I could do with a lot of that.'

She was breathing fast and remained silent for a moment, then she whispered, 'Truss; as I told you this afternoon, I've been a naughty girl with quite a number of men. That at least gives me one advantage: I've learned how to take care of myself, and have never had a slip-up yet. You'd run no risk of putting me in the family way.'

His voice came huskily. 'You mean . . .?'

Gripping the lapels of his coat she went on tiptoe to give him a swift kiss. 'Yes. Why not? You've got to start some time, and I'm told most men are not too good at their first attempt. If you're not, knowing you've never done it before at least I'll understand. Whereas if you wait until it's with someone you're crazy about it may prove a bitter disappointment to you both.'

A sudden smile lit his ugly attractive face. 'It wouldn't take much to make me crazy about you. Come on, then; let's.'

With a swift gesture he put one arm round her shoulders and the other round her thighs. Picking her up without a trace of effort, he carried her into the house.

3

Happy Days in Corfu

Truss had arrived in Corfu on April 18th, and later he looked back on the eight days that followed as the happiest in his life. He was his own master with not a single thing to worry him: perfect health, ample money and time was his servant. As de Richleau's guest he lived in a household where long years of experience by its master decreed every possible comfort. His companions were intelligent and charming people, all of whom were fond of him. The French chef produced dishes of the first excellence and the Duke's cellar held wines which it would have been difficult to surpass. The island was an earthly paradise of shimmering mountains, dark olive groves and vistas of tranquil blue seas. Luxurious fruit abounded and on all sides the cottage gardens and woodlands were starred with flowers of every colour in the spectrum. Above all, for the first time in his life, he had a beautiful, interesting and passionate girl as his mistress.

Fleur's assumption that his excess of excitement at a first encounter might tend to spoil it had been correct; but Truss proved a quick learner. In his powerful body there lay the virility of a young bull, and out of her experience in the past six years Fleur soon taught him all she knew. After the first night they danced only until they could be reasonably certain that the rest of the household had gone to bed, and as the room next to hers was unoccupied they were able to romp and laugh in hers to their hearts' content. He had come to adore the feel of the satin-smooth skin of her slender body as a miser loves the feel of gold. She, having had other lovers, and being more interested in older men, felt no real love for him but accepted his caresses with eagerness and delight.

His pleasure in being with her in the daytime was exceeded only by the ecstasy that shook him during their hectic nights; for he left her only at dawn to go off with her after breakfast and revel in the surrounding countryside which was so different from anything he had seen in the States.

On their first morning she took him down to the town. It could hardly be called a city, as it had no more than thirty-five thousand inhabitants. The narrow streets twisted between tall old houses built in the Italian style, that were mostly blocks of flats. From their narrow iron balconies the Corfiotes hung their washing on lines suspended to the house opposite, which gave a pleasant shade. Some of the streets had arcades, while others consisted of a series of shallow steps leading up the hill. But as it was a Sunday the shops were shut.

To the seaward side of the centre of the town lay the Esplanade, a vast open space with a bandstand in the centre and in the southern half an avenue of chestnut trees in blossom that led to the slope down to Garitsars bay. Innumerable people were strolling there to the music of two bands, both of which wore uniform with plumed brass hats, and one of which was composed of women.

On the east of the Esplanade lay the public park beyond which was a deep canal spanned by a narrow bridge leading to the castles on the twin peaks dominating the promontory that juts out into the sea. In the park there were many statues, mostly of British Governors of the island who had administered it as a Protectorate for over fifty years during the past century.

At the northern end of the square stood the Royal Palace, that had been built as a Residence for these Governors. It was flanked by two great gateways named St. Michael and St. George and it was their propinquity which had inspired the title of the Most Distinguished Order of Chivalry bestowed upon so many famous British diplomats. Now, the Palace was an Archaeological Museum. It also housed an exceptional collection of no fewer than seven thousand five hundred pieces of Chinese and Japanese porcelain, lacquer, jade and precious stones.

Truss, like a good American, had read up on Corfu before arriving there and, guidebook in hand, was full of facts and figures. He wanted to go in to see at least the star pieces of Greek art that had been excavated from the foundations of the town: a Gorgon from the pediment of the Temple of Artemis, and an archaic lioness. But such things bored Fleur, so she dissuaded him and they sauntered across to the long arcades on the west of the square beneath which there were a number of cafés. These were known as the 'Listern' because in times past only the privileged, whose names were on a 'list' submitted to the British Governor, were allowed to sit and drink at them. By then Fleur was hot and tired, so they had cassata ices and sat there for a while before returning to the villa.

Over lunch the Duke asked them what they had seen. Then he said, 'Unfortunately Corfu has comparatively few interesting ruins because when the island was threatened by the Turks, before the famous siege of 1537, the town was still unwalled; so the Corfiotes pulled down most of the Greek and Roman temples and used the great stones to create defences.

'Even so, there remain quite a few traces of its chequered history. In Homer's day it was known as Phaeacia and at one time King Alcinous ruled here. It was his daughter Nausica who took pity on Ulysses when he was washed up on the shore, and after his many years of wandering sent him safely home to his own Kingdom, the neighbouring island of Ithica.

'Historically the first we know of Corfu was that it was colonised by the Corinthians about seven hundred B.C. Later the Kerkyarians, as they were then called, broke away and became independent. In due course the Romans conquered it, then it passed to the Eastern Empire of Byzantium. During the Middle Ages the Franks, Angevins, Naples and Sicily each held it for a while and Richard Cœur-de-Lion stayed here on his way to a Crusade.

'But most of the remains you'll see are Venetian. In the hands of the Serene Republic it remained for four hundred years one of the great bastions of Christendom against the Turk. When Venice fell Napoleon seized it by treachery, counting it his most valuable stepping stone to the conquest of Egypt and the East; but within two years a combined Russian and Turkish fleet wrested it from him.

'By the Treaty of Paris in 1815 it was awarded to Britain as a Protectorate, and for the first time for many centuries its wretched inhabitants were no longer plagued with wars and constantly ravished by pirates. For fifty years under British rule they enjoyed peace and a certain measure of prosperity. We gave them schools and hospitals and built all the roads so that one of their few great writers said of us, "If ever a State was prosperous, free and progressive under the dominion of another, that State was Ionia under the domination of Great Britain."

'Yet like so many other ignorant and primitive people they were led by so-called patriots, who are usually self-seeking politicians, to demand the casting off of the friendly yoke and to become re-united with Greece. Gladstone, that cheese-paring little Englander, saw a chance to save the few thousands a year the island cost to administer; so he let them have their way. As a result, from the sixties on, they sank back into poverty and still today the peasants go hungry half the year because their only means of support is their olive crop.'

'Thanks a lot, Duke,' smiled Truss. 'What you've said was most interesting; and you've certainly made a case for British colonisation in this instance.'

'I don't believe in it in any instance,' Fleur said quickly. 'It's fundamentally and morally wrong that any race should order another about.'

Richard laughed, not very happily. 'Now she's off on her hobby-horse. She conveniently ignores the immense good that superior races have done for backward peoples.'

'I don't, Daddy. But it was done the wrong way. It's right that countries that have the money and the know-how should help the poorer ones. In fact it's an obligation. But it's not right that they should take over the Government of a country that's not theirs and dictate how the people in it should live.'

'I'm with Fleur on that,' Truss put in. 'All peoples have the right to make their own laws; and it can't be denied that the great Colonial Powers exploited their subject races shamefully. The cruelties inflicted on the wretched natives of the Congo in the reign of King Leopold II of Belgium simply do not bear thinking about.'

'Every anti-colonialist raises that old hare,' Richard shrugged. 'But you're talking of a hundred years ago; and, anyway, it was an exception. There is abundant evidence that most of the countries that were colonised in Asia and Africa owe an immeasurable debt to Europe. We taught them methods of agriculture that greatly increased their crops, abolished famine by making them build up reserves of corn and rice, checked disastrous floods by building dams, opened up their countries to trade by giving them roads and railways, and altogether raised their standard of living.'

'But all that could have been done without inflicting on them the indignity of losing their freedom,' Fleur protested. 'It is being done still by loans which enable them to improve their countries for themselves, and by thousands of volunteers going out to help them better social conditions.'

'I know, dear,' Marie Lou put in. 'And we understand how anxious you are to take up that sort of work yourself. But the loans have no strings, so lots of the money goes on big houses and Cadillacs for unscrupulous politicians, and the volunteers have no power to enforce a better state of things. Just think of India and suttee. If the British hadn't put a stop to it the Hindus would probably still adhere to the awful custom of widows being burnt on their husbands' funeral pyres.'

'Not in these days, Mummy. And it would have been stopped by the progress of education if we'd sent them teachers instead of soldiers.'

'You may be right, but I greatly doubt it,' remarked the Duke. 'You overlook the part that soldiers played. Their presence ensured the continuance of a strong and benign Government; and that is the first essential for the maintenance of peace. Perhaps the happiest era the world has ever known was when the rule of Rome was enforced from the borders of Scotland to the frontiers of Persia and from the deserts of Africa to the Danube. The Pax Romana continued for nearly four hundred years, so that when at last the Romans withdrew from Britain, and the Danes invaded her, the people had come to regard a life of peace as their natural inheritance and no longer knew how to fight.

'The same applies to the Pax Britannica. Had the British not conquered India its history during the last century and a half would have been one long tale of wars between its many States. And what happened when India was given her freedom? The Hindus and Mohammedans resumed their age-old blood feuds. A million innocent people were murdered in the space of a few months. Think, too, what has happened in Indonesia since the Dutch withdrew, and of the blood-letting that is bound to ensue in Africa when those even more backward peoples are allowed to give free rein to their avarice and tribal hatreds. No, my child, whatever you and our American friends may think, there's a strong case for protecting the poor and humble from death and ruin by men of an alien and wiser race enforcing law and order. But at my age I know well that no argument will convince you; so let us talk of something else.'

As a result of their night of love-making, followed by their excursion that morning, both Truss and Fleur were feeling distinctly part-worn; so after lunch they went to their rooms and slept the deep sleep of youth so soundly that they had to be roused for tea.

Much refreshed by their slumber they then decided to go down and bathe. From the road below the villa a path led to the shore. There was no beach, but ledges of rock a few feet under water provided a shallow area until some forty feet out they ended abruptly and the water became many fathoms deep.

Fleur was a good swimmer and, having waded to the edge of the ledge, she struck out in a fast crawl. Turning on her back when she had covered a hundred yards, she saw that Truss, submerged up to his armpits, was still standing on the ledge.

'Come on!' she cried. 'What are you waiting for?'

He shook his head. 'Sorry I can't join you; I'll have to splash around close in.'

Swimming back to him, she blew the water from her mouth and asked, 'Why? Can't you swim? I thought you were a surf-rider.'

'Sure I am,' he smiled. 'But surfing is done over the waves when they break in shallow water. And I can swim well enough, but I've got a thing against going in deep.'

'What sort of thing?'

'I've had it since I was ten. It was one time when we were down in Jamaica. I was well out of my depth when I suddenly got cramp. A bunch of folks were playing with a big ball on the beach and kicking up a din, so no one heard my shout. I went under and was darn' near drowned. By luck my old man missed me and he's the tops under water. He struck out for the place he'd seen me last and near bust himself trying to locate me. He did, but only just in time. And don't you ever believe what they say about drowning being a pleasant death. That's all baloney. Ever since, I've been scared stiff I'd get the cramp again and there'd be no one handy strong enough to pull me out; so I've made it a habit to stay put in the shallows.'

To the south side of the place where they were bathing there was a rocky promontory crowned by the ruin of an old

Venetian fort. A narrow path led up the cliff face to it and when they had had their bathe they decided to explore the ruin. The way was steep and in places the drop from it sheer into deep water, but after a quarter of an hour of laboured climbing they reached the crumbling walls.

The spur of rock jutted out about half-way along the east coast of the island, so was a splendid vantage point from which they could see the whole sickle curve of Corfu from the north, where it approached Albania, to the south where it nearly touched Greece. They could also see, about a mile away, round the corner of the height on which the villa stood, a great white palace among tall cypress trees.

'That must be the Achilleion,' Truss remarked, 'the place the Empress Elizabeth of Austria built.'

'Yes,' Fleur agreed. 'Poor woman, she had a rotten life, what with such an old fuddy-duddy for a husband, her only son going nuts about a tart and committing suicide with her at Mayerling, then ending up by being stabbed to death by some awful anarchist in Geneva.'

'But Rudolph's girl friend wasn't a tart; she was a Czech Baroness.'

'What's the odds? That wouldn't have made it any less ghastly for his mother.'

'You're right in that. I gather that later the Kaiser bought this villa and used to spend his vacations here. I'd like to go see it some time.'

'All right. Since you're interested in that sort of thing we'll go tomorrow morning.'

But that evening they learned that for next day Marie Lou had planned an expedition. Except for the Duke they were all to drive across the island to Paleokastritsa on the west coast, and picnic there.

They could have gone more quickly by the main highway through Corfu town and then north-west, but to enjoy the finer scenery they elected to take the road inland and up through the mountains as even that meant a run of less than thirty miles. At first the way was bordered by the ubiquitous olive groves, interspersed with woods of oak and walnut trees, and many small acacias in blossom. Every meadow was carpeted between the ancient trees with a wonderful variety of wild flowers: purple anemones and honesty, yellow marigolds and buttercups, scarlet pimpernels, blue grape hyacinths, silenes, cranes-bills and bee orchis. Among them strapping peasant women were collecting the last of the fallen olives from the ground. The villages they passed through were silent, except for barking mongrel dogs, for every hand is needed to harvest the precious crop. Here and there along the rising ground were scattered farmsteads with vines, honeysuckle or wistaria half covering their white walls; many of the larger had small gardens gay with roses, carnations, stocks, wall-flowers and tree peonies.

Soon they reached a pass through which they could see the blue Adriatic sparkling in the sun. Turning north they ran for a while almost along the crest of the range then down through the Ropa valley to pass through olive groves again with swathes of iris, oxalis, narcissus, speedwell, mallow and shepherd's purse.

Presently, as they approached the rugged mass of Spartil, the ground rose again. Then they curved round the beautiful many-coved bay of Liapádon, that lay at the southern foot of the mountain, and so came to Paleokastritsa, with its ancient monastery of the Holy Virgin, perched on a spur of rock washed on all sides, but for a narrow causeway, by the sea.

After a glass of wine at the small hotel on the bay they visited the monastery. There was no sound but that of the waves and about the whitewashed buildings with their trellised vines there was an unbelievable atmosphere of peace which made the great cities of the world seem as remote as if they were on another planet.

Returning to the car they drove up the twisting mountain road to the village of Lákones for a bird's-eye view of the monastery—from that height looking no larger than a dolls' house set on a cardboard mound in a pool of dark blue water—then on for another few miles round the corner of the great headland to a hamlet where the road ended.

From there they walked some distance along a rocky track until they came in sight of Castel San Angelo. It stood on a small island separated from the mountain only by a deep cleft in the rock and other great rocks lay scattered in the sea as though once hurled there by Zeus in a fit of anger. Beyond the gorge the ground mounted in a succession of steep terraces seaward to a great broad promontory that, seeming to reach the sky, towered up a thousand feet. Circling the top like a diadem could still be seen the crumbling thousand-year-old walls of the once impregnable fortress.

Retracing their steps, they drove back to the entrance of the Ropa valley. In it, behind the hedges of prickly pear and wild roses, there were many meadows having here and there an almond, plum or peach tree in blossom, and carpeted in tall grey-green grass that in another few weeks would flower as swathes of silver asphodel. Selecting a pleasant spot they set about having their picnic. When they had demolished the strange langouste-like creatures that had flippers and orange-brown shells, and the April strawberries of Corfu, that Marie Lou had brought, they dozed for a while, then made their way home after a long and happy day.

Next morning Fleur and Truss did the Achilleion. Its garden, with the fine statues of Achilles, that gave the Palace its name, and the beautiful Rotunda, was a delight; and the lovely colonnaded gallery in which stood the statues of the Nine Muses gave a breath-taking idea of what the glory that was Greece must have been when Athens was in its heyday. But Fleur got a little bored of waiting while Truss took endless pictures with his cine-camera, and it was only with difficulty that she got him away from admiring the wall painting in the interior of the Palace of Achilles's triumph over Hector at the siege of Troy.

On the Wednesday at lunch de Richleau told them that he had received a reply to his cable to Anton Rajapakse, in which the lawyer said he was sending his son, a junior partner in the firm, who would arrive on the 26th.

Fleur at once said, 'We were talking about Colonialism the other day, and there's a case for you. The Sinhalese are a wonderful people. They were civilised long before we were and had splendid cities when London was only a collection of mud huts. But the Portuguese, the Dutch and then the British conquered and enslaved them. For the past three centuries they haven't had a chance. But since they were given their independence they've done absolute marvels. Ceylon is now a model for any self-governing state.'

De Richleau nodded. 'I believe you are right about that. They are an intelligent people, and they were lucky in having such an honest and dedicated man as Mr. Senanayake as their first Prime Minister.'

'He's dead now, though, isn't he?' Richard asked.

'Yes,' Fleur replied. 'Ceylon received her independence in 1948 and he remained Prime Minister until 1952. Then there was a tragic accident. He was injured by a fall from his horse and died the next day. After that his son, Dudley Senanayake, took over and at the next election the United National Party were again returned with a big majority. In 1953 Sir John Kotelawala became Prime Minister and kept the job until early 1956, but his Government ran into a lot of trouble.'

'You seem to be very well informed,' remarked the Duke.

She smiled. 'I had to learn the basic facts about the political development of Ceylon, and lots of other countries, when I was studying sociology. As I was saying, they ran into trouble because they reduced the rice subsidy, so there were a lot of strikes. And they didn't truly represent the people. Really it was the old British Raj continuing under the cloak of Independence, and they were much too far to the Right to be popular. They kept English as the official language and did all they could to support free enterprise.'

'And a darn' good thing, too,' commented the die-hard Richard.

'That's all very well, Daddy; but it's not right that the rich should be allowed to take all the jam of a country at the expense of the masses. Naturally the people expected to see real progress and an economy that would improve their lot; so the Socialists and all the other parties ganged up against the U.N.P. and the 1956 election was a landslide. The Opposition got in with an overwhelming majority. It was then that the present Prime Minister, Mr. Bandaranaike, came to power. He has made Sinhalese the official language, nationalised the 'bus service and the handling of cargo in the ports and started a whole range of social services, which is just as it should be in these days.'

'And where is the money coming from to pay for all this?' Richard demanded. 'From the docks and railways we built for them; and the British tea planters. If the planters decided to pack up, Ceylon would be bankrupt within twelve months.'

'Oh, you're incorrigible, Daddy,' Fleur flared. 'And you're wrong, too. The Ceylonese would take over the plantations and run them just as well.'

'I don't think it's quite such a rosy picture as you paint, my child,' said de Richleau mildly. 'Your father is right that they have been living on our fat so far. But time will show; time will show.'

During the week they made other expeditions: much further down the west coast to the bay of St. Gordis, and along the east coast as far as the pretty fishing village of Benityes. At every turn of the road new enchanting vistas opened for them: groups of nispros trees, their golden fruit looking like clusters of small oranges, pink and white magnolias, patches of blackthorn, laburnum and wild pear, and almost always with a background of rocky mountain against a pale blue sky, or cypress against the deeper blue of the sea.

Another pleasant afternoon was spent in visiting an historic property named Koukouritsa. The old house was situated in the centre of the island, surrounded by a lovely garden and on the summit of a hill, with splendid views in all directions, and of both the Adriatic and Ionian Seas.

De Richleau took them there to call upon two noble Corfiote widow sisters who were descended from Corfu's most famous son, Giovanni Capo d'Istria. As a diplomat in the service of Russia he had exercised great influence at the Congress of Vienna and later the Greek National Assembly had elected him as President of the infant Greek Republic when it was still fighting to gain independence from the Turks.

Over glasses of iced fresh orange juice, which tasted like nectar, the two ladies talked with admiration and affection of Queen Frederika. They maintained that her enemies took despicable advantage of the impulsive way in which she spoke her mind frankly. They recalled the courage with which, just after the war, their Queen had personally led a force of tanks to rescue two thousand of the many thousand Greek children forcibly deported by the Bulgarians to be brought up as Communists, and of her untiring labours to better the lot of her poorer subjects.

On the intervening days Fleur and Truss went off alone to bathe, laze in the sun with the sweet smell of the pines in their nostrils, talk interminably about setting the world to rights and, in secluded spots, make love.

Their delight in one another was so obvious that one evening towards the end of the week, when they had gone off to dance, Richard said to his wife and the Duke, 'Those two youngsters are bats about one another. I really believe now that it's going to come off and that they'll be engaged before we leave here.'

Marie Lou smiled. 'I do hope you prove right, darling. Anybody can see that he's got it terribly badly; but I'm not so certain about her. And, of course, she never tells me anything. Still, it does look now as if there's a chance.'

The Duke refrained from comment. Like most old people he required little sleep and, although his sight was still good, reading for more than an hour at a time tired his eyes; so for a good part of each night he lay dozing and toying with old memories. His hearing was still good, too, and three times during the past week he thought he had caught the sound of careful footsteps passing his door well before the servants would be up. He had also noted that on the days when Fleur and Truss were not out on a long excursion they both slept through the afternoons, which was unusual in healthy young people.

When young there had been many happy occasions when he had gone on tiptoe in the dark to be welcomed by a lovely lady in her bedroom; so he would have been the last man to condemn in others such a delightful way of passing most of the night, but in his day that sort of thing had never led to marriage.

Then, in the Parisian circle in which he had moved, it had been customary for marriages uniting good families of birth and money to be arranged, and only afterwards, while still maintaining most friendly relations with her husband, did the wife consider herself free to indulge her amorous propensities with lovers. Of course, among the peasantry in many parts of Europe the old institution of the *Probennacht* had been maintained for centuries, and after it, should the couple not enjoy themselves, either was free to repudiate the other. There was something to be said for it, and now that moral standards had declined it might be that in many cases young people resorted to the practice with every intention of marrying afterwards. But, somehow, he did not think that the sort of hectic affaire that he believed Fleur and Truss to be having led to wedding bells.

In the afternoon of Saturday the 26th, Mr. Douglas Rajapakse arrived. The Sinhalese are a small people, but he was above their average height and about five foot nine. His skin was dark but his features were Aryan. He had smooth black hair, a slightly curved nose, a sensitive mouth with beautiful white teeth, and fine eyes. His body was straight and slim and he was impeccably dressed in a brown suit that looked as if it had been cut by an English tailor. The Duke put his age down as a little under thirty.

After tea, he and de Richleau went into conference for an hour, then he was introduced to the others just before dinner. He showed neither the subservience that many coloured people display towards Europeans, nor its opposite: a brash self-assertiveness. His manners were charming and over dinner he talked well and fluently.

Soon Fleur got him on to the subject of his country and praised the progress it had made since receiving independence.

'You are kind,' he said, 'and in many ways we have been fortunate. Particularly in that the British left us such sound foundations to build on. We already had free education, of course, and a very good Public Health service; but there have been many other excellent developments in the past ten years. The great contribution of our first Prime Minister, Mr. D. S. Senanayake, was the reduction of malaria, which had been the scourge of a great part of my country for centuries. He also initiated the restoration of the ancient irrigation systems in the north of the island. These permanent gains will prove of far more benefit to us than many of the palliatives to popular opinion that have been brought in by our present Government. He was a fine man, and his loss was a great blow to us.'

'But Mr. Bandaranaike has done much more for the people,' Fleur said quickly.

'For some of the people, Miss Eaton.' Rajapakse's white teeth flashed in a swift smile. 'He came to power as the result of a vote-catching manifesto issued by the Mahajana Eksath Peramuna, which was a coalition of his own Freedom Party, Mr. Philip Gunawardana's Marxists and the Trotskyites. To retain the support of his extreme left-wing colleagues he has had to fulfil his promises to them, and you can hardly expect these policies to find favour with people like myself.'

'We're all in the same boat these days,' Truss put in. 'The taxes my father has to pay are astronomical. That the distribution of wealth for the common benefit is a world trend there's no escaping, and we've just got to face it.'

'I agree, Mr. Van Ryn. And the wealthier families in Ceylon are enlightened people. We are not at all averse to handing over a good part of our incomes for the public benefit, but that does not deprive us of the right to disapprove of the way in which our Government is spending it. Certain measures they are taking, too, are entirely contrary to the true principles of Socialism in which when younger I was a convinced believer.'

Fleur raised her eyebrows. 'So you were a Socialist?'

'Yes; and even in this company I am not ashamed to admit it.'

'Why should you be?' Her young voice was eager. 'I am one too. But in what way have they gone off the rails?'

'Since you are so well informed, Miss Eaton, you will probably know that in Ceylon there is a large minority of Tamils; some two million as against five and a half million Sinhalese out of a total population of eight million. One of the first principles of Socialism is equality, and the present Government has brought in laws which virtually make the Tamils a subject race. So you see it is not only the rich who have reason to feel that Mr. Bandaranaike is not giving them a fair deal.'

De Richleau nodded his white head. 'I read something in *The Times* last week about Bandaranaike having abrogated a pact that he had made with the Tamil leader, and that it was likely to lead to serious trouble.'

'You are right, sir.' Rajapakse gave a sudden grin. 'And it may prove, as you might say, "the last straw on the Tamil's back".'

Everyone laughed at his sally, then the conversation turned to other subjects. When Marie Lou stood up to leave the table, before Fleur made to follow her mother she looked across at Rajapakse and said:

'Mr. Van Ryn and I are going down to dance at a hotel in the town. Would you care to come with us?'

He smiled and bowed. 'Your suggestion is a most kind one, Miss Eaton. I should greatly enjoy that.'

A quarter of an hour later, when Truss had brought round the car, he put Rajapakse into the back seat, then hurried back into the front porch to waylay Fleur. When she came out he glowered at her and said in a low, angry voice:

'What, in God's name, possessed you to ask this fellow to come with us?'

She looked surprised. 'Why shouldn't I have? He's much more our generation than theirs. It would have been a shabby trick to condemn him to spend a dull evening with our elders. And, after all, we get plenty of time together on our own.'

'It's not that. He may ask you to dance with him.'

'Well; what if he does?'

'But damn it, Fleur,' Truss protested hotly, 'you can't dance with a coloured man!'

4

The 'Nigger' in the Woodpile

'So I can't dance with a coloured man,' Fleur repeated sarcastically. 'And why not, I'd like to know?'

'You ought to,' Truss snapped back. 'For a white woman to allow a coloured man to lay his hands on her is to demean herself.'

'Demean herself, my foot! Where have you come from; out of a cave in the woods?'

'No. I was brought up in the Southern States where we still know how to behave like gentlefolk.'

' "The land of the bollweevil, where the laws are mediaeval, and corn grows out of one's ears",' Fleur quoted Tom Lehrer's satirical song with an angry laugh. 'Be your age, Truss! This sort of nonsense went out before we were born.'

'Not with us, it didn't. And I'll not stand for seeing you make an exhibition of yourself in front of all those people down in the Corfu Palace.'

Fleur's firm chin stuck out. 'All right! Do the other thing. Stay here. I'll drive him down myself. He's waiting out there. We can't stay here arguing.' Pushing past Truss, she made for the car.

For a moment Truss hesitated, then he followed her and they got into the car together.

The evening was anything but a success, and it was due only to Douglas Rajapakse that it did not become catastrophic. He sensed that the other two were lovers and had had a quarrel; although, as he was used to mixing in Ceylon on equal terms with Europeans, it never entered his dark, handsome head that it was on account of his own presence. Truss's ill-concealed rudeness he took to be a not unusual manifestation of American self-assertiveness, and he made allowances for him. Fleur danced with them alternately, and in the intervals while Truss behaved like a surly bear, Rajapakse kept up a flow of amiable talk on trivialities which eased the tension. Just before they were about to go he left them for a few minutes and when Truss asked for the bill he was told that the Sinhalese had already paid it. To his frowning protest, Rajapakse replied with a smile.

'My privilege. Is it not customary at American universities when invited to join a group of any kind to, as they say, pay one's footing?'

Truss was furious, but Fleur thought it most amusing that he had been outwitted into accepting their coloured companion's hospitality and put in a position where Douglas, as she now called him, could reasonably expect to be asked to accompany them when next they went dancing.

Their good nights when they got back to the villa were formal; but half an hour later, still angry and determined to have the matter out with Fleur, in dressing gown and slippers Truss tiptoed along to her room. To his surprise and annoyance he found her door locked. Gently he tapped on it, but there was no reply. Several times he tapped again, but he dared not knock louder and there was still no response; so having hung about for ten frustrated minutes he made his way disconsolately back to his own room.

Next morning he tried, but without success, to get Fleur on her own. Then, after lunch, as it was Sunday, they all went to the little township of Gastouri, which was only a mile away, to see the dancing.

Partly from ancient custom, and partly now as a tourist attraction, the peasants still performed their national dances in the main street. The women wore bodices with full white sleeves under jackets of richly coloured velvet encrusted with gold embroidery. Their hair was most elaborately dressed over a double pair of semi-circular pads, decked with many gold ornaments and framed behind by an oblong of stiff, beautifully worked muslin. They danced sedately in a slow-moving, outward-facing circle, while the men, more soberly clad, leapt and gyrated with extraordinary vigour inside it.

As the Corfiote peasantry were still deeply religious, with few exceptions they attended the services held by their bearded, black-robed priests in the little white churches, each with its separate square belfry tower, on Sunday mornings; but after their midday meal they started to dance and continued, apparently indefatigable, till well into the evening.

Leaving them still hard at it, the party returned to the villa; then Truss and Fleur, accompanied by Douglas Rajapakse, went down to bathe. The hour they spent disporting themselves on the rocks and in the sea added fuel to Truss's anger, for Douglas proved to be an excellent swimmer; and while his lithe brown body streaked far out to lie floating near Fleur's pink one for what seemed to Truss an endless time, he was compelled to remain splashing about in the shallows on the submerged rock shelf.

It was not until after dinner, when the Duke took Rajapakse to his library to talk to him again about the inheritance, that Truss at last succeeded in getting Fleur to himself. As soon as they were alone, he asked:

'Why did you lock me out last night?'

'To teach you manners,' she replied promptly.

'Thanks; but I was taught those by my family.'

'Then they must be jolly disappointed with you as a pupil. Douglas couldn't have behaved better if he had gone to Eton, whereas you acted as though you'd been brought up in a slum. You ought to be ashamed of yourself.'

'Now listen, honey,' Truss said earnestly. 'I know you're full of advanced ideas, and I sympathise with most of them. After all, the Rights of Man has been our Bible in the States for generations. Who's rooted for equality and all it stands for, all these years, if not Uncle Sam? And look at the billions we hand out to help underprivileged peoples get themselves a better life. But this colour question is a thing apart. In the deep South, where I come from, it's become a real menace.'

'Why?'

'Because whites and niggers just don't mix. That's why. They're a different species, and no happiness comes out of mixed marriages. That's not a theory. It's hard experience.'

'Who's talking about marriage, anyway?'

'That's what the abolition of segregation leads to, inevitably. If you have nigger kids schooling with whites, by the time they're teenagers some of them are certain to start necking.'

'Douglas is not a nigger. And even if he were he would still be a human being with the same instincts, feelings and aspirations as you and me.'

'About that I don't agree. The psychology of blacks and whites is entirely different, and although he's not a negro he is an Asiatic; so his mind is utterly unlike ours.'

'You're talking nonsense, Truss. If one could change the colour of his skin he would pass anywhere as an English gentleman.'

'Pass maybe. But that's not the point. His mental processes are different, and the colour of his skin is the outward sign of that. A line has got to be drawn somewhere, and that line is colour.'

'You are for Apartheid, then; like those beastly whites in South Africa?'

'A form of it seems the only solution, anyhow in the U.S. The real trouble is that the niggers breed like rabbits and, if we concede them equal citizenship, in another three generations we'd have a negro President.'

'What's so terrible about that?'

'Sakes alive, honey! It's unthinkable.'

'Well, this isn't the States, and if I choose to dance with Douglas you can't stop me.'

'I know; I know. But don't you see that for any white girl to become familiar with a coloured man is letting the side down? Give them an inch and they'll take an ell. That's just what we're up against. As long as they were regarded as inferiors, which they are, everything was all right, and they were perfectly content. But in recent times so many misguided people have encouraged them to think they are as good as us that they are getting the bit between their teeth and demanding what they call their "rights".'

'They are their "rights",' replied Fleur angrily. 'The right of every human being to be regarded as the equal of all others. Anyway, until you are prepared to treat Douglas as your equal you needn't expect to sleep with me again.'

'Oh come, honey. You're not going to lock your door against me tonight. I want you, and want you bad.'

'I am. But not for that reason.'

'Then why, if I do my best to forget the colour of his skin?'

'For a perfectly good feminine one which you ought to be old enough to guess,' Fleur replied. And, turning, she walked rapidly away.

On thinking the matter over Truss derived a sop of comfort from the thought that, after all, this was Corfu, not Charleston nor, for that matter, anywhere else in the States where a girl of good family seen dancing with a coloured man would have been ostracised by her acquaintances. He then decided that if he was to regain Fleur's goodwill he must swallow the prejudice with which he had been brought up and make himself pleasant to the Sinhalese; so the following morning he suggested that they should take Douglas in to see the town.

On this occasion they went into the Metropolis, as the Greek Orthodox Cathedral is called, in which is enshrined the body of St. Theodora; then into the Church of St. Spyridion, Corfu's patron saint, whose body lies there in a great silver sarcophagus. Both buildings were rich with paintings in elaborately carved gilt frames, mosaics, ikons and chandeliers; and moving sedately about were numerous black-robed priests wearing their high, flat-crowned hats and with their hands clasped in front of them.

In St. Spyridion one of the priests gave them a smiling greeting and showed them round, then told them the story of the saint. His birthplace had been Cyprus and he had performed a miracle while attending the famous Council of Nicaea. He had died in the year 350 and a hundred and one years later, on sweet-smelling odours emanating from his grave, his body had been exhumed and installed in his church at Timython. When Cyprus fell to the Saracens the saint's body had been secretly conveyed to Constantinople, but that city also fell in 1453.

A priest named George Kalaichairetis had determined to save the body, together with that of St. Theodora; so he had stuffed both into sacks and loaded them, one either side, on a donkey. Pretending the sacks held only fodder, the courageous George had made his way through Infidel-held Greece and eventually reached Corfu. There, these holy relics had been received with due veneration and as, soon afterwards, the Corfiotes attributed the cessation of a plague to St. Spyridion, they made him their patron.

In his will George had left the body of St. Spyridion to his two eldest sons and that of St. Theodora to the youngest. After three generations the testaments of the brothers had led to St. Theodora becoming the property of the Church, but a niece named Asimene had inherited St. Spyridion and on her marrying a Corfiote noble named Bolgaris it had passed to that family, who had continued to own it and received the rich revenue in offerings that it brought right up to the present day.

On leaving the church, Fleur, Truss and Douglas drove out to the Castello, a fine crenellated pseudo-mediaeval building with a lofty tower, some miles to the north-west of the town, that had been turned into a hotel. While the waiter was getting them their drinks Truss remarked:

'What an extraordinary thing that a priest should have considered the bodies of two saints to be his personal property, and that a private family should still be making a big income out of one of them.'

Fleur shrugged. 'It's even more surprising that in this day and age hordes of people should still believe that they can do any good for themselves by paying good money to venerate a casket full of old bones.'

'Such beliefs die hard,' said Douglas. 'Many wealthy Buddhists in Ceylon who have been educated at universities continue to make rich gifts to the Temple of the Tooth at Kandy.'

'It is the Buddhists who are responsible for the persecution of the Tamils, isn't it?' Fleur asked.

He nodded. 'Yes, the Buddhists are a big force in the "Everything for the Sinhalese" movement. After years of sloth there was a strong Buddhist revival in the 1880s. They argued that when Ceylon was a Sinhalese kingdom Buddhism had enjoyed a privileged position, whereas under the British it had been usurped by the Christian religion. It is true, of course, that pupils educated in Christian schools got all the best jobs, because they were taught English.

'As long as British rule continued the Buddhists got no redress for their grievance, but when Ceylon received independence there came another great upsurge of Buddhist feeling, and in 1950 Buddhist leaders from all over the world assembled in Ceylon to inaugurate the World Fellowship of Buddhists. After that our Buddhists began to agitate in a big way for the official language to be changed. Neither Senanayake nor Kotelawala would give in but Bandaranaike got elected largely on that ticket, and two months later the "Sinhala Only" Bill was passed.

'Not unnaturally the Tamils began to kick. They organised strikes and riots in which quite a number of people were killed; so Bandaranaike reached a compromise with Chelvanayakam that a limited use of Tamil should be permitted in certain provinces, and various other matters. It is his having recently gone back on his pact that is causing the present trouble.'

'The Tamils are Hindus, aren't they?' said Fleur.

'Yes; they first invaded Ceylon from southern India many centuries ago, and there was a time when in the north of the island there were Tamil Kings. But there was another great influx in the latter part of the last century, and it still continues because Ceylon is a richer country than the part of India they come from, and our estate owners are glad to employ Tamils because they work much harder than the Sinhalese.'

Stubbing out a cigarette, Douglas went on, 'I should, perhaps, explain that there are two types of Tamils: those who are the descendants of the original invaders and the much more recent immigrants whom we call "Indian Tamils". Under the old constitution all Tamils had the vote and some of the up-country constituencies even sent Indian Tamils to Parliament. But Bandaranaike's Government has deprived them of their citizenship, which makes them virtually "stateless persons", and it has also brought in laws that deprive them of the right to own land. As there are nearly a million of them, that is a very serious matter; and naturally the Ceylon Tamils give them every possible support.'

That evening at dinner the Duke said to Richard, 'Mr. Rajapakse has now given me all the information he can about my unexpected inheritance so I expect his business commitments will necessitate his shortly returning to Ceylon. But before he leaves us I think he ought to see a little more of this lovely island; so perhaps you would care to take him for a run round it tomorrow.'

Douglas gave a little bow. 'You are most kind, sir. But I was due for some leave, and having come here at your request I can now think of no more enjoyable way of spending it than in Corfu. In the meantime, of course, my partners will be looking after your interests in Ceylon.' Turning to Richard he added, 'If it is convenient to you, sir, a trip round the island tomorrow would be delightful; then in the evening I will move down to a hotel in the town.'

Truss had been consoling himself with the thought that within a day or two he would be relieved of Rajapakse's unwelcome presence altogether, so he found this new development most displeasing. A moment later his annoyance was turned to silent fury, for de Richleau said:

'No, no. You will do no such thing. You make a most pleasant addition to our company. I shall be happy for you to remain here as my guest for as long as you like.' And Douglas gratefully accepted.

Next day, leaving only the Duke behind, they drove across the centre of the island and through a fertile plain watered by Corfu's only sizable river to Sidar, at the west end of the north coast. Near the little town, where the river enters the Adriatic, there are some remarkable formations of smooth, flat, tiered rocks that have been eroded into layers by the sea. They bathed from them, then picnicked and lay baking themselves in the sun.

Later in the week they made another expedition, through Corfu then along the poor but picturesque coast road that runs below Mount Pantokrator, the highest mountain in the island, right round the big gulf to the beautiful cypress-fringed bay of Kouloura. From there, in the crystal-clear air, the coast of Albania looked only a stone's throw away, and it was surprising to think that through all the centuries of strife the Infidel had never succeeded in crossing in force such a narrow strait.

On other days they went into the town, bathed below the villa and lay in hammocks in the garden. But wherever Fleur and Truss went Douglas went with them and, as time went on, Truss found it more and more difficult to continue being polite to him. It was not only that his presence prevented a tête-à-tête with Fleur but that it was the two of them who did most of the talking. Truss, being fresh from college, had little knowledge of the world. It was a passion for winter sports, acquired when young, that had led him to persuade his father to let him go to its Mecca for undergraduates, Dartmouth in New Hampshire. But his triumphs as a skier cut little ice with Fleur and apart from brief trips to England and the Caribbean he had never been outside the United States. Whereas Douglas, who was ten years older, not only knew London, Paris and Rome, but had visited India, Singapore, Rangoon, Bangkok and numerous other places in the East, and could talk most interestingly about them and their social problems, a subject to which Fleur never tired of listening.

Unhappily, but doggedly, Truss tagged along with them, inwardly seething with rage when Fleur placidly agreed to sightseeing that she had refused to do with him.

They spent one morning in the old Palace, where the Archaeological Museum was housed, looking at archaic Greek sculptures that had been dug up in the island, and the famous collection of Sino-Japanese art, upon which Douglas commented with interest and humour. Another morning Fleur, unprotesting, endured the long walk to the south of the town, along the peninsula of Kanoni, to catch a glimpse of Mon Repos, the present residence of the Greek Royal family when in Corfu.

Impatiently Truss waited till near the end of the week; then, by lying in wait for Fleur, he managed to corner her. With an eager grin he said, 'How about it, sweetie? Is everything all right with you now?'

She shrugged, 'I'm over the curse, if that's what you mean. But I'm not feeling like romps at the moment. We'll see next week.'

'Oh, come on, honey,' he protested. 'I could soon make you feel——'

'No!' She cut him short abruptly. 'You must learn, Truss, that you'll get no fun from pressing a girl when she doesn't feel like it.'

Sulkily he turned away, mentally cursing Rajapakse; for, although it was inconceivable to him that Fleur might have fallen for a coloured man, it was his arrival and presence to which he attributed the break between himself and her.

Richard and Marie Lou had also observed with growing concern the new orientation in Fleur's interest. That same night when in bed they discussed it unhappily.

'This fellow turning up when he did was the most lousy luck,' Richard declared. 'It really looked as if Fleur and Truss were going to make a go of it; now she's scarcely civil to him.'

'I know,' agreed Marie Lou. 'But it's quite understandable. Truss is hardly out of the egg, whereas Douglas is so much older and, one must admit, a polished man of the world. One can't wonder that she is attracted to him.'

'Attracted! God forbid! Surely you don't mean . . .?'

'Of course not, stupid. Anything physical between them is unthinkable. It wouldn't even cross Fleur's mind, and I'm sure he's much too much of a gentleman to make a pass at her. But they are both interested in things that Truss knows nothing about; so it's only natural that they should enjoy talking together and tend to freeze him out.'

'Well, it's got to be broken up somehow; so that Truss can

pick things up from the state they'd reached before this nigger got into the woodpile.'

'He's not a nigger, and far from it. But what do you suggest?'

'Of course he's not. He's a highly intelligent and charming little man. But I've been thinking. Truss is due to do Italy. How about our cutting short our stay here, inviting him to join us, going to Rome, hiring a car and the four of us making a tour of Florence, Siena, Perugia, Urbino and all those other places?'

'That's an excellent idea, and I'd love it. But it would be hard on Greyeyes.'

'I know. But he's the most understanding person in the world; and we could come back for another stay here with him in the autumn.'

As a result of this midnight conversation, Richard put the matter to the Duke the following morning. The old man, whose principal amusement these days was watching other people's reactions to changing situations, was well aware of the rift that Rajapakse had created between Fleur and Truss; so he said:

'My dear Richard, I sympathise with your hopes and fully appreciate your concern. In the circumstances the arrival here of our charming Sinhalese was most unfortunate. But having invited him to stay as long as he likes I cannot possibly get rid of him for you. Loath as I am to lose you and Marie Lou, your proposal at least offers a possibility of pulling the chestnuts out of the fire; so by all means adopt it.'

At lunch that day with kind but slightly cynical amusement de Richleau listened while Richard, with somewhat forced gaiety, put forward his plan for Marie Lou, Fleur and himself to tour central Italy, then invited Truss to join them.

Truss accepted with alacrity, but Fleur remained silent for a moment, her full mouth taking on a sulky line. Then she said, 'If you all want to go and stare at a hundred and ten Madonnas suckling an overweight infant, by all means do. But Grandpa Greyeyes invited us for a month and I'm staying here.'

5

It Could Have Been Murder

At Fleur's unequivocal declaration one of those silences that can be felt descended on those round the table. Marie Lou had long since given up the unequal struggle of arguing with her daughter and Richard, equally aware of the futility of endeavouring to persuade her to change her mind, forbore to comment. She was their only child, and for her he had the great fondness of a naturally affectionate man, but at times she drove him to a frenzy. With difficulty he suppressed an angry retort and concentrated viciously on the contents of his plate. And there, with the old Duke having difficulty in suppressing mild mirth at their discomfiture, the matter was dropped.

That evening Truss again managed to get Fleur on her own for a few minutes, and he said, 'Look, honey. I appreciate your not rating Italian Masters all that interesting, but how about us? Surely you must be feeling pretty good again by now, and I'm just aching to do this and that with you again. How about tonight?'

She shook her head. 'I'm sorry, Truss. Really, I am not in the mood. And, after all, you have no reason to complain even if we never do again. In fact you owe me quite a lot. I've initiated you into what are called the "mysteries of sex", and next time you feel like going to bed with a girl you'll be able to put up a good performance.'

'Do you . . . d'you mean,' he gasped, 'that you don't mean to let me again, ever?'

'I didn't say that,' she hedged. 'And we had great fun while it lasted, but . . . Well, at the moment my mind is on other things.'

'It's on Douglas,' he snapped, seizing her by the shoulders. 'That's the truth, isn't it? You've fallen for that slick Wog. Oh God, Fleur! How could you! Surely you wouldn't——'

'Of course not!' She broke away and glared at him angrily. 'But he's got a brain ten times the size of yours. And since you insist on the truth, you've become an unwanted third as far as going about with us is concerned. I want to find out much more about him; things he wouldn't tell me in front of you. Tomorrow I thought we'd hire a boat and go sailing. If you've any gratitude for what I've given you, you'll make some excuse to stay in the town and let us go off on our own.'

'Very well,' he said dully. 'If that's the way you want it. The sooner you've gotten over swapping life-stories with that so-and-so, the better I'll be pleased.' By mutual consent they turned and walked back in silence to join the others.

Next morning Fleur carried out her plan. With the best grace Truss could muster he said he wanted to have another look round the Museum, and the other two put off in a small boat into the blue bay. For a couple of hours he strolled listlessly about the galleries, regarding with unseeing eyes primitive stone carvings of lions and human torsos, broken pottery and beautiful Byzantine mosaics, while brooding about Fleur and wondering moodily whether the absorbed interest she showed in Douglas could really be explained in any other way than that she had fallen for him.

Admittedly they had said that the time of their return must be governed by wind and tide, but as it was a day of light breezes Truss expected them to be back for lunch; so from a little before one o'clock he began to haunt the water front. Half past and two o'clock came, but there was still no sign of them, so he bought a big punnet of strawberries from a vendor and ate them disconsolately without sugar while leaning against a bollard.

As the afternoon wore on his thoughts grew bleaker. He convinced himself that no girl like Fleur would want to go off on her own with a man for a whole day just to hear about his upbringing and to talk sociology. Mental pictures began to form in his mind of the two of them, having beached the boat in some lonely bay, lying in it necking. The thought was unbearable. He tried to thrust it from his mind but could not and, for the first time in his young life, he was seized with the pangs of a hideous jealousy.

It was nearly five o'clock before he sighted their boat and another twenty minutes before they landed. His stomach gave a nasty twinge as he saw that Fleur's hair was in disorder, but he tried to rid himself of his suspicions with the thought that it might have been blown about by the wind.

Stepping ashore, she greeted him gaily, 'Hullo! What have you been doing with yourself all day?'

'From one o'clock I've been waiting here,' he replied surlily. 'I'd expected you back for lunch.'

'Oh dear!' She hitched up her slacks, then ran a hand over her hair. 'I'm so sorry. I thought I said we'd get lunch somewhere. We landed at the end of the peninsula and had ours at the Kanoni Tourist Pavilion. It was heavenly on the water; we had a lovely day.'

Douglas had been busy tying up the boat. Joining them he, too, apologised with apparent sincerity, but Truss felt sure the real explanation for their lateness in getting back was because they had been enjoying themselves so much that they had decided to leave him in the lurch.

That evening he decided that he could not bear the sight of them dancing together so after dinner he said he did not feel well, and they set off on their own. As it was again a Saturday, it was extension night at the Corfu Palace, which meant that they would not be back before about half past one.

Having got to bed, Truss settled down to read but, after a while, he found that his mind was not taking in the story; so he put out the light and attempted to get to sleep. That proved equally useless. In vain he counted sheep or tried to make his mind a blank. Pictures of Fleur constantly floated into it; Fleur that first night in the moonlight suggesting that he should come to her room; Fleur naked, the nipples of her young breasts standing up hard from desire, the roundness of her hips a sight to make any man crazy; Fleur dancing with that damnable, good-looking, coffee-skinned Douglas. Then other imagined pictures of them that made Truss writhe.

At long last he heard footsteps outside in the corridor. As Douglas's room was opposite his, that meant they had returned. A glance at the luminous dial of his bedside travelling clock showed Truss that it was only twenty past one; so they would not have lingered on the way home for a necking session in the car. With a sigh of relief he turned over for the hundredth time and resettled himself with new hope of at last getting off to sleep.

He was just on the point of doing so when he became suddenly wide awake. The sound of a door closed gently had roused him. Then there came footsteps again.

With his heart hammering furiously, he sat up in bed. Those footsteps could mean only one thing. Douglas had changed into a dressing gown and was now on his way to Fleur's room.

For ten agonised minutes Truss wrestled with his chaotic thoughts. Fleur was free, white and twenty-one; those long-honoured qualifications in the United States for doing what one liked. If she wanted to give herself to Douglas she had the right to do so; and he, Truss, had no possible excuse for trying to prevent her. But hadn't he? Douglas was free and twenty-one, but he was not white. This could not be allowed to happen. However strong her infatuation for him, she must be protected against herself. If it did happen, Truss felt convinced that she would bitterly regret it afterwards. Sooner or later it seemed certain that she would marry, and Truss had been brought up in the belief that before marrying all decent couples told one another the truth about themselves. To admit to having premarital affaires was all right. Everyone had them these days. But how could she confess to a fiancé that she had allowed a coloured man to have her? And if she didn't she would always have it on her conscience, with the fear that, somehow or other, her husband would find out.

Suddenly throwing back the bedclothes Truss jumped out of bed and pulled on his dressing gown. He had convinced himself that it was no less than his duty to intervene before it was too late. And he would 'beat hell out of that bloody nigger'.

Shuffling into his soft shoes he pulled open the door and began to stride along the corridor. It then crossed his mind that Douglas might not be with Fleur, but had gone to the dining room to get himself a last drink. Changing his pace to an almost noiseless tiptoe he went ahead, but Douglas was not in the dining room. His worst forebodings renewed, the powerful young American, now seized with a fierce desire to get his big hands on the Sinhalese, proceeded quietly down the further corridor.

When he reached the door of Fleur's room he paused to listen. No sound of subdued laughter or muffled exclamations of endearment, such as he had expected to hear, came to him. Controlling his heavy breathing, he knelt down and put his ear to the keyhole. Still silence. In so short a time it seemed hardly possible that Fleur had undressed, made her toilette for the night and was already in bed dropping off to sleep; yet no streak of light came from beneath the door.

Perhaps, then, she was not there. During his visits to her they had always felt a slight uneasiness that in the night her mother might be taken ill or, for some other unforeseen reason, come along to her and catch them *in flagrante delicto*. It would have been bad enough had she been caught with him, but to have been found with Rajapakse in her bed would have meant utter disgrace and perhaps even a refusal to supply her with funds to go overseas and take up the welfare work on which she had set her heart. It seemed possible that rather than take the slightest risk of that she had told Douglas that they must make do with one of the big swing hammocks out on the terrace.

Grasping the knob of the door firmly, Truss turned it and pressed gently. The door opened a crack and made no sound. Opening it further, he peered in. Enough moonlight came through between the curtains for him to see that Fleur's bed had not been disturbed and that the room was empty.

Closing the door he padded softly back to the main hall of the villa and out on to the terrace. Bright moonlight made it as light as day, except where deep shadows were thrown by awnings and chairs. He listened intently but not a sound came to indicate that anyone was occupying one of the hammocks. Wondering where the devil they could have got to he advanced to the hammocks to make quite certain they were not lying silently embraced in one of them. Only then did he catch the subdued murmur of voices.

They came from below the end of the terrace. Stepping softly across to the balustrade, Truss peered over. They were sitting on a stone seat about twelve feet below him, a foot or more of space between them and not even holding hands.

Fleur's voice came up to him. 'As you already have Family Planning I could apply to go out there. It's the part of Welfare that I'm keenest on, and I'd thought of India when I start in the autumn on the Field Service I must do before I can take my Ph.D. But Ceylon sounds much more attractive.'

'It is,' Douglas assured her. 'Of course, it is utterly different from Corfu, but just as beautiful in its own way. In fact it's one of the most beautiful places in the world. You'd meet with a lot of opposition from the Roman Catholics, but you'd find that wherever you go.'

'Are many of the Christians out there Catholics?'

'Yes, the great majority. While the age of discovery lasted the Fathers were most zealous missionaries and they had a free run during the hundred years that the Portuguese were established in the island. Later, under the Dutch and the British, the Reformed Religion and the English Church never secured anything near the same number of converts.'

'The Buddhists are not anti-Family Planning, are they—or the Hindus?'

'No. In Hinayana Buddhism, which is dominant in Burma, Thailand and Cambodia as well as Ceylon, there is no authoritarian body, so each *bhikkhu* interprets the sacred texts according to his lights. None of the texts has any bearing on the subject of contraception, and there are no injunctions in them such as "Be fruitful and multiply". The question therefore boils down to, whether the prevention of conception amounts to the taking of life. If it does then the use of disinfectants to clean out dirty places must also be wrong, for that destroys the conditions which enable noxious insects to breed. That is the type of argument used by our more enlightened *bhikkhus*, who favour Planned Parenthood as the only means of keeping the population in reasonable proportion to the resources of the country, now that modern hygiene has so greatly reduced infant mortality. And the better educated Brahmins hold the same view. So it is only the Roman Catholics you would be up against; although even they have recently thrown a sop to modern opinion by advocating a system based on what's called the "safe" period of the month. But from what I've heard it's not very reliable; not to mention being a frightful bore.'

Fleur laughed. 'How right you are. Our clinics teach young women how to fit Dutch caps. That and the old French letter are the only things that are really any good.'

Truss had overheard enough. Enormously relieved that his fears had been unjustified, he reproached himself now for ever having thought that Fleur would allow her interest in a man like Rajapakse to affect her physically. Suddenly conscious that he ought not to be eavesdropping anyway, he was about to step back when he saw Douglas lean over, take Fleur's hand and say:

'I do hope that you will come out to Ceylon. We could have a marvellous time; especially if you come to stay with my mother with a view to what we talked about this afternoon.' Then he kissed her lightly on the cheek.

'I'll certainly think about that,' Fleur replied. As she spoke, she stood up.

Holding his breath, Truss backed away from the balustrade, turned and quickly moved into the deep shadow behind one of the big canopied hammocks. Two minutes later he saw the couple on whom he was spying come up the terrace steps and enter the house. After an interval he followed them, but not with any apprehension that they intended to go to bed together. The way Douglas had kissed Fleur had been too chaste for anything of that kind to be in the mind of either of them. But she had obviously not resented his kissing her. She had even leaned a little towards him and virtually presented her cheek. When Truss was back in bed, that gave him furiously to think.

Douglas had said that including the journey both ways he could afford to be away from his office for three weeks. That meant he could spend another eight days in Corfu. It appeared that Fleur had not yet fallen for him, but her acceptance of his kiss indicated that she was on the edge of the slippery slope. Given a few more long days alone with Douglas it seemed that she easily might. Then, should she accept his invitation to go out to Ceylon and stay with his mother, that opened a still more horrifying prospect. He would have a free field with her and, passionate as she was by nature, she might not only become his mistress, but remain long enough for it to become known and talked about. And that, to Truss's mind, meant that her life would be irretrievably ruined.

And he loved Fleur. She was the first girl he had properly kissed and, despite the years between, the first he had slept with. During this past week that she had denied herself to him the longing for her smooth, live body had given him an actual physical pain. But it was not only desire he felt for her. He had delighted in her companionship; admired her intelligence and forceful character. Even if she would have no more to do with him he wanted her to be happy, and was desperately anxious that she should not make a mess of her life.

Somehow he must put a spoke in Rajapakse's wheel; think of some way to make him show the cloven hoof of his coloured blood, or cause him to cut short abruptly his stay in Corfu. Yet how was either possible? Still wrestling with this seemingly insoluble problem Truss dropped into an uneasy sleep.

On the Sunday de Richleau decided to go for one of his occasional drives, so they all accompanied him in his big car along the winding roads fringed with acacia, walnut and eucalyptus trees. The others, as always on these drives, continued to draw one another's attention to the beauty of the countryside. During his first week there Truss, then feeling like a young god, had gloried in associating this earthly Paradise in his mind with the Paradise Fleur's kisses had opened to him. Now, he looked on these lovely sights with lacklustre eyes, and found the scent of acacia, orange blossom and tuberrose cloying, while continuing, on and off, to contemplate absurdly improbable happenings which might rid him of the hated Rajapakse.

Now that they were in mid May the day was very hot and its warmth lingered on well after sundown. As it was Sunday there was no dancing at the hotel; so after dinner the younger people remained with their elders sitting out on the terrace. For a long time the old Duke reminisced, lightly and with humour, about his adventures in the distant past, and the pleasant world as it was before the 1914–18 war, that youngsters of today would never know. He was a magnificent raconteur; so that as his gentle voice went on to tell story after story even Fleur was spellbound, and it was after eleven when they stood up to go to bed.

It was again a night with a splendid moon and as warm as a good August night in England. When Fleur had kissed her elders good night, she turned to Douglas and said, 'What about getting into out bathing things and going down for a swim? I'm sure the water will be warm enough.'

'Yes, let's do that,' he replied with quick enthusiasm.

Truss was still with them, and he put in, 'That's a great idea. I'll get out the car, then change and be ready to drive you down in, say, fifteen minutes' time.'

Fleur's glance, as she turned away, showed him that he was not wanted, but he ignored it. He had made up his mind that morning that, whatever Fleur might say, he was not now going to leave her alone with Douglas for even a few minutes if he could possibly help it.

A quarter of an hour later he had the car at the front door and the other two scrambled into it. They drove down through the woods which were gay with fireflies and noisy with the cheeping of cicadas. On reaching the rocks they threw off their bathing robes and went straight in, the water sparkling with cascades of phosphorescent drops as they struck out.

As usual, Fleur and Douglas swam several hundred yards and splashed about there for a time while Truss remained plunging and blowing on the shallow shelf of rock. But the water was not quite so warm as they had expected, so the two swimmers soon returned; then they all got out and dried themselves.

Disappointed that their bathe should have been so brief, Fleur suggested that they should go up the rock track to the ruined fort from which they could get a view of the whole coastline in the moonlight.

'Wouldn't that be a bit dangerous?' Douglas demurred. 'The path is very narrow and in places there is loose stone underfoot. It's safe enough in the daytime, but now the cliff is in shadow it's black as pitch up there and one of us might easily lose his footing.'

'Nonsense,' Fleur retorted. 'I've been up it half a dozen times and we're all wearing rope-soled sandals.' Turning, she led the way and the two men followed her, Douglas first and Truss bringing up the rear.

Douglas had been right in that they had to feel for each foothold, and once he slipped. Truss swiftly put out a hand and steadied him. Then the sudden thought came, 'Why the hell did I do that? If I hadn't, the coffee-coloured bastard might have gone over the edge.'

For the next few minutes his mind was in a turmoil. He had only to stumble himself and give Rajapakse a push and that would be that. The water below the track was deep and, although the Sinhalese was a good swimmer, they were now some way from the landing shelf; so there was a good chance that after falling from a height so much breath would be knocked out of his body that before he could reach the shelf he would drown.

'No,' Truss decided. That would be murder. It was unthinkable. He must put the awful idea right out of his head. But he couldn't. His thoughts ran on. With this damned coloured man out of the way he and Fleur would soon be back on the best of terms. She was not yet sufficiently in love with Douglas to be upset for long. After all, she had known him not much more than a week. He could not really mean very much to her; but he might if things were allowed to develop the way they were going. Now was the perfect opportunity to nip in the bud the dangerous attraction he seemed to have for her.

The temptation to give Rajapakse the necessary shove became almost unbearable. They were approaching a place on the track where it was very narrow and curved inwards above a sheer drop of some thirty feet to the sea. If, without warning, he fell from there the hope of his surviving would be slender. Truss shuffled his way up no more than two feet behind him. He felt that he had it in his power to put a sudden end to his detested rival as surely as though he had been an executioner leaning on his axe while Douglas was kneeling with his head on a block. But Truss could not do it. His instinct revolted at the thought of becoming a killer.

Then it happened. It was not Douglas but Fleur whose feet suddenly slithered on the loose shale. She lurched sideways. The Sinhalese made a grab at her arm. Before he could clutch it she had heeled over. His fingers closed on her bathing robe but she was wearing it only loosely over her shoulders. The pull on his arm very nearly took him over with her, but Truss seized him round the waist from behind. With a rending sound the fastening of the bathing robe tore and Douglas was left with the robe trailing from his hand. Fleur gave a single piercing scream and, head downward, her legs waving wildly, plummeted into the dark abyss.

There was a minute of awful silence, then they heard the loud splash as her body hit the water.

Next moment Douglas had dropped her robe, thrown off his own and dived in after her.

Truss continued to stand on the narrow ledge. A cold sweat broke out on his forehead. He knew that he, too, ought to take that terrifying plunge on the chance that he might be able to help in attempting to rescue her. But he couldn't. He positively could not face the terrifying fear that death lay waiting for him in the dark waters that washed the cliff face. The agony of cramp and the ghastly suffocation he had endured while drowning were still as clear in his memory as though they had been upon him yesterday. He would get cramp again. The cliff was sheer, with no projection he could cling to, even if near enough. If he went over, the dark waters would engulf him and he would die there. He felt certain of it.

A strangled sob broke from him. Peering over he could see the phosphorescent water churning. Perhaps Douglas had got her. But it was too dark to make certain. It might be only Douglas frantically splashing round in his endeavours to locate the drowning girl. Anyway, if either or both survived they would make for the bathing place. But whether they would have the strength left to reach it was another question.

Throwing caution to the winds Truss turned and scuttled helter-skelter back down the track. In a tenth of the time it had taken him to come up he was back in the little bay. Throwing off his robe, he waded out into the water as far as the edge of the ledge.

Five minutes passed; ten. In an agony of mind he waited, peering into the shadow cast by the cliff where it cut off the moonlight. Then, just outside the point he saw the wavelets breaking in a place where no submerged rock caused them ordinarily to do so. He let out a yell and started to shout encouragement. Slowly but surely the blob of heaving phosphorescence came towards him. Then he could see a dark head rising and falling. It was Douglas, swimming on his back and towing Fleur above him.

Hearing Truss's shouts, when Douglas got to within a few yards of the shelf he turned over and thrust Fleur's limp body shorewards. Truss stepped off the shelf, swam a few strokes and grabbed her. The sudden realisation that he was out of his depth almost petrified him, but with one arm under Fleur he kicked out violently. After only two frantic minutes, he found his feet again. With a gasp of relief he seized Fleur round the shoulders and half dragged, half carried her back into shallow water.

As he laid her down, still half submerged but with her head well above the lapping wavelets, he turned, expecting to see Douglas wading after him. But there was no sign of Fleur's rescuer. Leaving her, Truss swiftly waded out again, calling to Douglas as he did so. A faint cry, coming from fifty yards further up the little bay, reached him. He realised then that, almost exhausted, the Sinhalese had not had the strength left to come ashore and that the current had carried him some way to the northward.

Up to his chest in water Truss thrust his way with all the strength of his powerful limbs in that direction. He covered the fifty yards, and in the moonlight caught sight of Douglas's head. By then he had been carried a further thirty feet or more. Truss ploughed on after him.

Without warning his feet ceased to tread on anything. The shelf ended there and he had stepped off the edge. His weight carried him down and the water closed over his head. He came up spluttering. Panic again seized him. But he knew he could not turn back. He must swim out and, somehow, help Douglas to get to the rocks.

In a dozen strokes he reached him and actually grasped his arm. But it was slimy from the salt water and slid from his grip. Next moment Douglas went under. Truss knew that if he trod water the drowning man would, almost certainly, come up again. For inside of a minute he did so. Then the awful knowledge that he was out of his depth made his heart quail. He had, too, left Fleur half in, half out of the water. By this time the lapping waves might have drawn her back into it. That thought, added to his own fears, decided him. Turning, he struck out wildly for the shore.

To his relief he found Fleur as he had left her. But to all appearances she was a corpse. Dragging her clear of the surf he hastily turned her on her face and began to apply artificial respiration, pressing his strong hands rhythmically on her back to force the water from her lungs. After ten minutes he was dripping with sweat, but Fleur still showed no sign of life. In an agony of apprehension he turned her on her back and stared down into her face, now streaked with thick strands of clotted hair and made ugly by a slack and gaping mouth.

Grasping her fallen jaw with one hand and holding her nose with the other he pushed her head back then took a deep breath, put his mouth to hers and slowly forced the air down into her lungs. After repeating the process for several minutes he felt a slight quiver in her chest. Trembling now with renewed hope, he carried on until a shudder ran through her and she gave a low moan.

Thanking God that he had succeeded in bringing life back to her, he began to slap her limbs hard to restore her circulation. She started to whimper faintly and writhe under his slaps. Satisfied now that she would not relapse he wrapped his bathing robe round her, picked her up and carried her to the car.

As he laid her on the back seat his mind reverted to Douglas. For the past half hour he had not given Fleur's rescuer a thought. But now, for the first time he was brought face to face with the awful fact that, although he had had a fair chance of saving a human life, he had failed to do so.

Since the age of ten he had never ventured out of his depth from a beach, but he always went in neck deep and while at school had regularly gone with the other boys to swim in the baths, where his fine muscles had made him a strong swimmer. There were many occasions when he had swum, floated and trod water for a quarter of an hour or more without touching bottom, whereas just now he had not been beyond the rock shelf for more than a few minutes. In the baths, too, he had often swum under water.

He could, therefore, have dived after Douglas, or waited until he surfaced again, without the least danger of drowning and, as Douglas was quite a small man, got him ashore without any great effort. It was only the hideous fear of cramp that had caused him to leave the Sinhalese to die. He had to admit that now. To return in order to make certain that Fleur was safe had been only an excuse to palliate his own cowardice. Only her legs had been left in the lapping water and he had been away from her less than ten minutes. Even had the tide been rising she could not have been swept away in such a short time.

As he stood beside the car his conscience was stricken by these awful thoughts, and finally by the acid test. Had he left Douglas lying on the shore and it had been Fleur fighting for her life out there in the moonlit waters, would he have abandoned her? He knew that he would not.

Back to his mind then came the shocking memory that he had actually contemplated pushing Douglas off the cliff. How great a part, he wondered miserably, had that evil urge to rid himself of his rival played in influencing his impulse to leave him to drown? In those few wild moments as he struck out for the shore he had not been conscious of any satisfaction in the thought that his earlier wish had now been granted. Yet by not remaining to rescue Douglas he had brought about his death as surely as if he had thrust him over the precipice. Motive and opportunity were always said to be the forerunners of murder. He had had both; and, although the latter had been thrust upon him, subconsciously at least he had taken it.

Utterly appalled by this honest assessment of his act, he gave a low groan. Then, pulling himself together with an effort, he threw a rug over Fleur, got into the car and drove off up the hill.

On reaching the villa he found that although breathing stertorously she still appeared to be unconscious. Carrying her through into the big lounge hall, he laid her on a sofa then ran into the dining room and fetched the brandy decanter. Opening her mouth he poured some of the spirit down her throat. She shuddered violently and choked. When her coughing ceased he tilted the decanter again. She spluttered, opened her eyes and, lifting a hand, thrust the decanter away.

As consciousness returned to her she stared up at him for a long moment, then whispered, 'Truss. So . . . it was you who saved me.'

For a few seconds he did not reply. Evidently she must have already been unconscious when Douglas had found and grabbed her and knew nothing of what had since taken place. Douglas was dead; a flaccid body drifting in some current along the bottom of the bay. Truss alone knew the truth. He felt a terrible temptation to tell her that they had both dived in, then take the sole credit for her rescue to himself. But he resisted it.

'No,' he said. 'It was Douglas who went in after you. I only pulled you out.'

Struggling into a sitting position, she asked, 'Where is he?'

Truss hesitated. 'He . . . well, he got you round to our bathing bay and I was out there on the edge of the shelf. I took over then and he . . . well, he was pretty well all in by then . . .'

Her violet eyes opened to their fullest extent and she gasped, 'You . . . you don't mean . . .'

He nodded. 'I'm afraid so. I'm terribly sorry, darling; but there was nothing I could do.'

'Do!' she cried, suddenly becoming enraged. 'But damn it, you can swim! Why didn't you go in after him and help him ashore?'

'I had to get you ashore first. By the time I'd got you in he had drifted a good way off. I did go in then to try to rescue him. In fact I actually reached him and got my hand on his arm. But I lost my grip and he went under.'

'And then?'

'I turned back. I had to. I'd left you still half in the water. I . . . I was afraid you'd . . . you might be washed away.'

Fleur's eyes blazed. 'That isn't true! What little tide there is was going out. Everyone knows that anyone who is drowning comes up three times. Why the hell didn't you stay there and get hold of him when he surfaced?'

'I tell you I was anxious about you,' Truss protested miserably. 'And . . . well, I was a long way out of my depth.'

'So that's it!' she flared. 'You bloody coward! No; worse! You hated his guts so you left him to drown. You're little better than a murderer. Oh God! Oh God!' Flinging herself down on the sofa, she burst into a passion of tears.

'You're overwrought,' Truss muttered angrily. 'You don't know what you're saying. Stay put there while I get your mother.'

Leaving her, he strode off to the room occupied by Richard and Marie Lou. Hammering on the door, he cried, 'Wake up! Wake up! There's been an accident. We're in the hall. Come as quickly as you can.' Then he returned to Fleur, who was still weeping hysterically. Kneeling down beside her he patted her shoulder and made an awkward attempt to comfort her.

Two minutes later Richard and Marie Lou arrived in dressing gowns, still blinking the sleep from their eyes. Marie Lou lifted Fleur's head, sat down on the sofa and took her sobbing daughter in her arms, while Truss gave them the bare facts, making as much as he decently could of his abortive attempt to save Rajapakse.

Struggling free of her mother's embrace, Fleur sat up and cried, 'He's lying! He could have saved Douglas if he'd wanted to. But he didn't. He left him. He left him to drown.'

'He wouldn't do that,' said Richard firmly. 'I'm certain of it. And you mustn't say such things, Fleur.'

'Daddy's right, darling,' added Marie Lou. 'It isn't fair to Truss. This is an awful thing to have happened, I know. And naturally you are suffering from shock. But you'll feel better in the morning, and realise that Truss did his best to avert this tragedy.'

'I won't,' wailed Fleur. 'I won't, Mummy. You don't understand! You don't understand!'

Their voices had drowned the sound of approaching footfalls out on the terrace and, at that moment, Douglas appeared in the doorway.

He was wearing only his bathing trunks; his straight dark hair was matted, falling over his ears, and a wisp of it sticking to his forehead obscured one of his eyes; his lips had a purple tinge and his dark skin glistened slightly from the water that was still drying on him.

For a moment they all stared at him with distended eyes, for no one in a play could have better achieved the appearance of the ghost of a man who had been drowned. Lurching forward he grasped the back of a chair for support, gave a weak smile and muttered thickly:

'I thought I'd had it . . . But the current carried me along to the point and . . . and when I hit the rocks I managed to haul myself clear of the water. I must have fainted then. Anyhow it . . . it was quite a long time before I'd recovered sufficiently to walk up the hill. I'm sorry if you've been worrying about me.'

Jumping to her feet, Fleur ran to him. With a cry of 'Thank God! Thank God!' she flung her arms round his neck and kissed him fiercely on the mouth.

'Really, Fleur!' exclaimed Marie Lou. 'Of course, we're all delighted. But . . . but . . .'

Fleur swung round, her young voice shrill with emotion. 'Mummy, I told you you didn't understand. Douglas and I love one another. I'm going out to Ceylon with him, and we're going to be married.'

6

What's To Be Done Now?

It was a very subdued party that assembled for lunch on the sunny terrace the following day; and less by one, for Truss had left that morning.

Before his departure, Marie Lou showed her sympathy for him by kissing him three times. Richard showed his by pressing ten pounds into Truss's hand with the smiling remark that he hoped he was not yet too old to accept a tip. He thought that Truss was now probably far richer than himself, and he could not really afford to throw tenners about; but he had always held the belief that the enjoyment that could be bought with money steadily decreased with age; so he was habitually generous to young people, and that was one of the ways in which he had spoiled Fleur.

De Richleau had been told what had happened by Marie Lou first thing that morning. With his aptitude for assessing situations he had foreseen that Truss would not feel like remaining on at the villa; so he had at once set about writing half a dozen notes of introduction to friends of his up and down Italy. These he later handed to Truss, and smilingly expressed the hope that, should he at any time find his strenuous tour somewhat exhausting, he would not forget that while he was in Europe he had a home in Corfu.

Douglas Rajapakse appeared no worse for his narrow escape from death and neither by word nor manner indicated that it was no thanks to Truss that he was still alive. With smiling urbanity he had wished Truss 'Happy Landings' and added that, although it was unlikely that they would ever meet in the States, he hoped that one day Truss would come to Ceylon.

Fleur remained in bed all the morning, and Truss was in half a mind to leave without saying good-bye to her; but decided that he ought to. Having had a word with Marie Lou he had gone to Fleur's room. She had not done her hair and her face was not made up, but Truss did not even notice that. He saw only the girl that he loved so desperately and now had to leave in such unhappy circumstances. When he told her that he had come to say good-bye, she said:

'I'm sorry, Truss. I don't mean about your going. As things are that would be best. But about everything else. This last week must have been lousy for you. I behaved like an absolute bitch. I'm sorry, too, about last night. I said some horrid things to you; but I was all wrought up. I'm sure you would have saved Douglas if you possibly could.'

He shook his head. 'That's generous of you, Fleur. But, to be honest, I ought to have stayed around until he came up, and pulled him out. I realised that afterwards and felt like hell about it. If it had been you I would have; and I'll be thankful that all my life I won't have his death on my conscience.'

'Poor Truss,' she smiled. 'Don't think too badly of yourself. In emergencies like that it's generally more by impulse than judgment that people behave like heroes. Anyway, I'm not going to give it another thought, and you mustn't either. Wish me luck and come to see me in Ceylon.'

'Surely,' he nodded a trifle uncertainly. 'Bless you, honey, and . . . er . . . thanks for everything.'

When Richard and Marie Lou had got back to their room the previous night they had looked at one another in consternation, then he had muttered with a frown, 'What the hell are we going to do about this?'

'There is nothing we can do,' replied Marie Lou miserably. 'Fleur is no longer a schoolgirl. We can't take her home and lock her up, or even for a voyage round the world. She'd refuse to go. And after all our hopes for her! Not only about Truss I mean. But her wanting to marry this coloured man. It's awful; just too awful!' Marie Lou then burst into tears.

She sat down on the end of her bed. Richard was across the room in two strides and had his arms round her. 'There, there, beloved. Please don't cry. Naturally it's a ghastly shock for you; but you'll get used to the idea. We've just got to forget the colour of his skin. He's really a very decent chap; good manners, well educated and must have quite a bit of money. If only his pigmentation were a few shades lighter we'd be congratulating ourselves on Fleur having found herself a very nice husband. For her sake and our own we've just got to look at it that way and be pleasant to him.'

Marie Lou stiffened, choked back a sob and exclaimed angrily, 'D'you mean you'll let her go through with this?'

'If she is really set on it, what else can we do? You've said yourself that we can't stop her and, anyhow, it will be quite a relief to have her married to a decent respectable man.'

'What do you mean by that?'

He hesitated. 'Well, I didn't want to worry you, but after we'd let her go to London University I heard some rather shattering things about the girls she roomed with.' He refrained from adding that it was Fleur herself, in a moment of expansion when sitting up with him late one night, who had with youthful bravado made it pretty clear about the sort of fun they all indulged in. Having always enjoyed her confidence and not wishing to lose it for good, he had done no more than stress the dangers of promiscuity and add that men were worse gossips than women, so a girl who went in for wild parties soon got a label on her that she was liable to regret when she later fell in love with some decent chap and found him averse to marrying her.

'D'you . . . do you mean you think that while she was there she . . . she began to sleep with men?' Marie Lou faltered.

'I think she would be abnormal if she hadn't. You must know how contagious that sort of thing can be when a lot of young women in their early twenties are rooming together. And Fleur's outlook on life is so ultra-modern. For a long time I've dreaded that she'd fall for one of those clever professors who already had a wife, and make a mess of things for herself by going off and openly living with the bloody man. I'd rather she married Rajapakse every time.'

In consequence, when Douglas had waylaid Richard the following morning their talk had been smooth and affable. Rajapakse had expected violent opposition; but he did not resort to belligerence. He said with urbane and self-confident courtesy:

'Sir, I owe you a profound apology. Before asking Fleur to become my wife I should have asked if you would be willing to accept me as a son-in-law.'

Richard smiled. 'Then I'll credit you with the intention; although in these days it doesn't even seem to occur to most young men to ask the parents' consent before proposing to their daughter. But are you quite sure that it's really a good idea that you and Fleur should marry? After all, you've known one another only about ten days.'

'Those days, sir, we have spent together. The time was ample for us to realise how much we mean to one another. Perhaps you are unaware of it, but on Saturday we spent the day alone in a sailing boat. It was then we opened our hearts. I did not exactly propose to Fleur. I only told her that I felt a deeper love for her than for any woman I had ever met. And I suggested that she should come out to Ceylon to stay with my parents. But I did make it clear that if she then liked our way of life, and saw more of me in my normal surroundings, I hoped that she would decide to remain there as my wife.'

'That was fair enough,' Richard commented. 'In fact, entirely honourable. The only thing that worries me and my wife is the question of your being, well . . . of such completely different races and cultures. I find it difficult to believe that such a union could turn out happily.'

Rajapakse showed his white teeth in a swift smile. 'About that you must permit me to differ, sir. Of course, if Fleur contemplated marrying some Negro who had acquired a veneer of civilisation only yesterday, that would be very different. But, forgive me again if I mention that the élite familes of the Sinhalese, such as mine, enjoyed poetry and discussed philosophy, possessed libraries, dressed in fine raiment and took a bath daily, when yours were still painting themselves with woad.'

For the first time an indication that Richard considered himself one of the master-race showed in his voice, as he replied, 'How unfortunate for you that a handful of Europeans should have arrived in your country and imposed their more primitive ideas about civilisation on a great part of your people. Or was it that your own was simply falling into decadence, as most such early civilisations always did?'

No whit abashed, Rajapakse gave a laugh. 'You are right about that, Mr. Eaton, although the Kingdom of Kandy maintained itself for several centuries against both the Portuguese and the Dutch, and even in 1815 it succumbed to the British only because it had a bad ruler. Sinhalese independence was not finally extinguished until after it had lasted for over two thousand three hundred and fifty years, and not many other countries can claim that.

'However, what I was about to say was that, apart from my

love for Fleur, I can offer her more than most Englishmen can in these days. My firm is an old-established and prosperous one. My father is a wealthy man. I am his only son and shall come into his fortune when he dies. Fleur will live in a large house with every comfort. It contains many fine examples of Eastern art and has a pleasant garden. We should also go to a bungalow up in the highlands at Nuwara Eliya, where Fleur would live in pleasant conditions during the great heats. In Ceylon we have never had a colour-bar, and I have many European friends; so she would not be cut off from white society. She could have as many servants as she liked; which means that she would have plenty of free time to give to the work of Family Planning that she is so eager to take up. And, of course, while in Colombo there is dancing, tennis and wonderful bathing, which she would have ample time to enjoy.'

'Then you are right,' Richard nodded. 'That sounds a much more pleasant life than most young women in England can look forward to when they marry. Well, there it is. The only thing my wife and I are concerned about is Fleur's happiness; and if you are both set on marrying we must hope that it will work out.'

When Richard told Marie Lou of this conversation, she said, 'It all sounds marvellous, but for one thing. There is no getting over the fact that he is an Asiatic. They are different from us. As different as chalk from cheese. For a while, of course, they will be turtle doves and Fleur will cheerfully put up with all sorts of little things that she would otherwise resent. Then she'll begin to kick, then there will be trouble. She will become miserable and, as the wife of an Asiatic, she'll be no more than his chattel. Even if he sets her free, what then? The type of man we'd like her to marry is going to think twice before he takes on the cast-off of a coloured man. It's no good my talking to her, but I'm going to stop it if I can. I'll go and talk to Greyeyes. He's such a shrewd old darling, he may be able to suggest some subtle means of breaking this frightful thing up.'

She found the Duke in his room, but he did not prove very helpful. He, too, was of the opinion that such marriages rarely worked well; but, as he pointed out, Fleur having led her own life for several years it was impossible to job backwards and attempt to dictate to her. All he could suggest was that they should do their utmost to persuade her to agree to a long engagement.

'I mean to do that in any case,' said Marie Lou. 'If only we can get her back to England and keep her there for a few months, she may meet someone else and break it off with this awful man.'

'My dear, you must not think of him as an awful man,' de Richleau said gently. 'He is a very charming fellow, and you cannot blame him for having fallen in love with Fleur. But I was about to say that I think your chances of getting Fleur back to England are very slender. I doubt, too, if that would serve your purpose. Much better appear quite willing that she should go to Ceylon, provided she will agree to a long engagement. When she has spent several months there with Douglas as her constant companion their passion for one another may burn itself out. Again, it will give her a chance to see how different these people's private way of life is from ours, and when she has she may decide that an Englishman would make a more satisfactory husband after all.'

Marie Lou considered for a moment, then she said, 'I suppose you're right. But I won't let her go alone.'

'If you went with her it would mean your being away from Cardinal's Folly for most of the summer.'

'That can't be helped. In young Jeffson we are lucky in having an excellent bailiff. He is perfectly capable of looking after the herd and the crops without being overseen by Richard.'

'You would both go, then?'

'Of course. Except during the war and at other times when it's been imperative, Richard and I have never been separated for more than a few nights since we married. We couldn't bear to be.'

De Richleau nodded thoughtfully. 'In that case, I shall reconsider the decision I took when I first heard about my strange inheritance. You were right, of course, about it being too great a risk for anyone of my age to go to Ceylon on his own. But it is a lovely island. I'd like to see it again, and heat is good for my old bones. If you and Richard are going, I know you would look after me; so I think I will come with you.'

A sudden smile lit Marie Lou's lovely heart-shaped face. 'Oh, Greyeyes, we would love you to. We'd be terribly strict in seeing that you did not do too much, and take the greatest care of you.'

Thus, after all these comings and goings, lunch on the terrace was by no means the usual gay and carefree meal.

Fleur, knowing how strongly her parents must disapprove of her engagement, was belligerently on the defensive; while Marie Lou, who had never been good at hiding her feelings, found it difficult to be polite to Douglas. He, sensing her hostility, after one or two attempts to break it down fell almost silent in spite of Richard's rather too obvious attempts to be pleasant to him. The old Duke alone seemed completely at his ease and kept the conversation going on trivialities.

It was not until they were having their coffee that Richard took the bull by the horns, and said, 'Well, in view of what took place last night, hadn't we better make some plans? I take it, Douglas, you've no wish to rush things, and would be agreeable to just being engaged to Fleur for the time being.'

'Certainly, sir,' Rajapakse replied promptly. 'The last thing I would wish is to hurry Fleur into a marriage of this kind before she has got to know my family and the sort of life we lead.'

At that Fleur's mouth dropped, for he had taken the wind out of her sails.

'Fine,' said Richard. 'That's very sensible. Shall we say six months?'

'No, Daddy!' Fleur shook her head in violent protest. 'That's absurd. Long engagements went out of fashion ages ago. Besides, I'm twenty-four and not getting any younger.'

De Richleau laughed. 'That's a terrible age to be, my child. In no time at all you will be pulling out your grey hairs. But, seriously, you are proposing to make your home and live your life in entirely different circumstances from those in which you were brought up. In fairness to your future husband, if to no one else, you should satisfy yourself that you can make him happy there. To do so I suggest three months would not be unreasonable.'

Fleur hesitated. 'Well, all right Grandpa. That is provided that no objections are raised to my going with Douglas when he flies home from Rome on the 11th.'

'I've nothing against that,' Richard declared cheerfully. 'In fact, your mother and I felt sure you would wish to. The 11th is next Sunday, so we've got the whole week and I shouldn't think there are heavy bookings for Ceylon at this time of year. With luck, there should be places on the same aircraft for all of us. I'll telephone the B.O.A.C. office in Rome this afternoon.'

'For all of us!' Fleur echoed. 'But surely . . .'

'Yes, dear,' Marie Lou said quickly. 'You can't have thought we'd let you get married without a proper trousseau, and getting it ready will take several weeks.'

'That's sweet of you, Mummy. But you say you don't want me to get married for another three months, and assembling a trousseau won't take all that long. If you came out towards the end of July that would give you time enough.'

'It was my idea that we should all go out now,' the Duke put in smoothly. 'In the company of your parents I'll come to no harm. Douglas tells me that my late cousin made quite a fortune mining for precious stones. Parts of Ceylon are very rich in them, you know. We'll all go up to Olenevka and select enough jewels to deck you out like the Queen of Sheba.'

'Oh, Grandpa!' Fleur's eyes danced with delight. 'How terribly sweet of you.'

So matters were settled. The remainder of the week passed uneventfully, its halcyon days being all too short for Douglas and Fleur. On Friday the 9th, with the Duke's elderly valet, Max, in attendance, they left for Rome, and they should have taken off from there in the weekly Britannia service on the afternoon of the 11th for Ceylon. But they learned that the flight had been delayed; so they did not, after all, get off from Rome until the Monday morning.

Twenty hours later, after calling at Damascus, Bahrein and Bombay, they landed in Ceylon, thus arriving in the early morning of the 13th, a date long regarded by the superstitious as unlucky. For them it marked the beginning of a long series of anxieties and dangers, culminating in a desperate struggle to keep their freedom and their lives that they did not all survive.

7

A Rose with Many Thorns

They landed early in the morning at Katunayake, the great R.A.F. Base which, together with the historic Naval Base at Trincomalee, had been handed over to Ceylon only seven months earlier, marking the final withdrawal of British power.

It was surrounded by lines of coconut palms through which could be glimpsed the sparkling sea. Douglas's presence ensured them a quick passage through Immigration and Customs, and his father had sent two cars to meet them. By the time they set off for Colombo the sun was well up, it was pleasantly warm and the air balmy.

Fleur had never before been in the tropics, and during the hour's drive she could hardly have had a more pleasing sight of them. The road ran all the way through what had once been primitive jungle but was now a highly populated area. Along some stretches, palms, bread-fruit trees and frangipani, with almost bare branches but lovely flowers, grew in riotous confusion. Along others there were coconut groves alternating with broad belts of paddy fields; and all the vegetation was a startlingly vivid green.

Every few miles there was a village. Each had its school, either Buddhist or Catholic, and a dozen or more untidy, open-fronted shops, all of which seemed to offer the same goods—cotton garments, sweets, Coca-Cola and great heaps of tropical fruit and vegetables. The houses were small, and mostly wooden structures; but many were of brick covered with stucco and had absurdly elaborate porticos for their size. All of them had little gardens in front, gay with flowers, and even the most tumbledown shacks had a few pots of flowering plants outside their doors.

All the way there was a lot of traffic: many cars, mostly of ancient vintage and often piled high with produce, and here and there a slow-moving cart drawn by hump-backed oxen.

The people were light brown, small, slim, upright; the younger women pretty above the average, although their looks were often marred by protruding teeth. As it is an ancient custom to let the hair grow long, many of the men had theirs done up in big buns on the top of the head. The majority of both sexes were in native dress, the women in garments of several brilliant colours which never seemed to clash. Occasionally they passed an old man, nearly naked and carrying a tall staff as he made his way along the road, or a shaven-headed Buddhist priest wearing the yellow robe. There were, too, countless children of all ages, dressed in white European-style uniform, clutching a load of books, on their way to school.

After such sights Colombo, at first, was disappointing. There were no wide straight streets or spacious squares, but seemingly endless roads lined with decayed-looking houses and squalid shops. As they penetrated the city it seemed to be one vast slum. Then, at a snail's pace, the cars edged their way through a long narrow street jammed with traffic. On one side of it rose a high wall enclosing the docks, on the other were alleys that led to the fish market. The stench was appalling and every fifty yards or so a bedraggled old beggar lay asleep on the pavement.

But at length they got through to a few better streets in the district known as 'the Fort', and to the south of it came out on to a broad esplanade. Inland across a wide stretch of grass stood the imposing House of Representatives and other fine Government buildings and at the far end lay the palatial block of the Galle Face Hotel.

When Ceylon had been under British rule this had been considered one of the finest hotels in Asia, and Douglas said that although it was not quite what it had been he was sure they would find it comfortable. For the Duke he had secured a suite on the first floor, usually reserved for V.I.P.s. The rooms were vast, air-conditioned and looked out on the esplanade; but for the others he had been able to get rooms only in the further block, to which they had to walk through a quarter of a mile of passages. Having seen to it that they had everything they wanted, it was agreed that he should bring his parents to meet them at cocktail time, then he went off to his home. Tired after their long journey, they all had baths and went to bed.

When evening came they gathered in the long cocktail

lounge at the front of the hotel. Soon afterwards Douglas arrived with his father and mother. Mr. Anton Rajapakse proved to be a small bald man, wearing enormous tortoise-shell glasses; his wife was much larger and a formidable looking woman with a big hooked nose, from whom Douglas had obviously acquired his slightly aquiline features.

When the Duke offered drinks, Mrs. Rajapakse asked for a gin-sling; her husband said he was a teetotaller and would like tea. When it was brought Fleur was surprised to see the waiter set down a glass pint tankard that tinkled with ice and had slices of lime and sprigs of mint in it; but she was soon to learn that iced tea served in this way was a favourite drink in Ceylon.

After the first few rather awkward minutes Mr. Rajapakse laid himself out to be pleasant. He said that he had always been on excellent terms with the British, and greatly admired them; so he was very happy that his son should have brought home an English bride, and particularly such a lovely one as Fleur. Mrs. Rajapakse nodded agreement and showed her obviously false teeth in a smile; but Marie Lou formed the impression that Douglas's mother was by no means so enthusiastic about her son's choice.

For about half an hour they talked mainly of sights that the visitors must be taken to see while on the island, and it was arranged that they should dine with the Rajapakses the following night; then with handshakes and bows Douglas's parents departed.

Next morning Douglas came to the hotel and, leaving the old Duke in bed, they drove along to the Fort. As a shopping centre Fleur found its few streets disappointing. There was one big store called Cargills, but no little boutiques of the sort she had hoped to find. However, she was cheered up by Douglas taking her to a jeweller named Gunasena. It was a tiny shop but stocked with thousands of set and unset stones, mostly mined in Ceylon—sapphires of many shades, topazes, zircons, moonstones, garnets and catseyes. He also had diamonds but Fleur felt that for her engagement ring she ought to have a stone of the country, so she chose a beautiful square sapphire. Then Douglas insisted on also buying her a bracelet made up of a dozen fine semi-precious stones, each a different colour.

That afternoon they took their bathing things and drove out

the five miles to Mount Lavinia. A big hotel was delightfully situated there on the far point overlooking a charming little bay with both sand and smooth rocks, and the water was so clear that they could see the bottom many feet down.

When they were having tea on the terrace afterwards, Douglas had to drive off several large crows that were attempting to snatch the cake from Fleur's plate. Laughing, he told her that the crows in Ceylon were a positive curse, for they were as bold as brass and inveterate thieves; and, if she were not sleeping in an air-conditioned room, would come in at the open window and make off with any jewellery she had left on her dressing table.

De Richleau, still feeling the strain of the long flight, had asked to be excused from dining with the Rajapakses that evening; but the others accompanied Douglas to his parents' house. It was a large airy building with wide verandahs and a well-kept garden, out in the best residential suburb. The evening passed off pleasantly enough, although Fleur got no closer to Douglas's mother, and was somewhat disconcerted when she was asked if she knew the Queen, whom she did not. It then emerged that Mrs. Rajapakse and her sister—another bulky and formidable lady—who was present, had both been presented when Her Majesty had visited Ceylon in 1954, and had escorted her round the home for crippled children. There was, too, another awkward moment when Douglas's aunt expressed the fervent hope that Fleur would have at least six children, as she had definitely made up her mind that three was to be the limit.

Next morning the Duke felt sufficiently rested to hold a business conference with Douglas and his father. The latter, having stated that he had no doubts whatever about the justice of their claim, told de Richleau that it might not now be quite as easy to establish as they had at first believed.

On the Duke's instructions, the present occupier of the Olenevka estate and mines, Mr. Ukwatte d'Azavedo, had been served with papers. To have admitted his guilt would have been a confession of forgery and have led to a criminal action which would land him in prison; so, on his behalf, some days before his lawyers had sent in a formal repudiation of the claim.

That he would do so had been expected, but their case had appeared sound, resting as it did on the signed confession of

Count Plackoff's dead butler-valet, Pedro Fernando, and the anticipation that they would be able to produce the other participant in the forgery, Pedro's wife Vinala, in court as a witness. However, when Rajapakse had sent one of his clerks to Olenevka to take a statement from Mrs. Fernando, it was found that she had disappeared and no one knew where she had gone.

They had, of course, written to her earlier on the subject and assured her that, if she pleaded that her late husband had exerted pressure on her to witness the forged will, she would have nothing to fear; but it now seemed that she must have been so frightened at the thought of having to appear in court and confess to her act that she had decided to abandon her home and go into hiding.

When asserting d'Azavedo's innocence, his lawyers had stated that if the case went to court evidence would be brought to show that Pedro had had a long-standing grudge against their client; and if that could be proved it would weaken the value of his confession. Unless, therefore, the only living witness to the will could be found and persuaded to testify, the case would now rest largely on the evidence of handwriting experts.

On hearing all this the Duke was justifiably annoyed, as from the first account he had received it had appeared to be a clear-cut case; whereas it now looked as if he had been brought out to Ceylon on what might prove a wild goose chase.

The Rajapakses were most apologetic and the elder excused himself on the grounds that he had not received the Duke's instructions until the 30th April, it had taken several days to draw up the papers and the response from d'Azavedo's solicitors had not been received until the previous Friday. Moreover, they could not have foreseen either that Pedro's confession was to be challenged or that his wife would disappear. The question now was, did de Richleau still wish to proceed?

In favour of doing so were the points that d'Azavedo might be bluffing about Pedro and fail to show that he had any reason to seek revenge, that Mrs. Fernando might yet be traced and that, the inheritance being a large one, it was well worth an already rich man like the Duke gambling a few hundred pounds on the chance of securing it. Even more, de Richleau was influenced by the fact that now he was so old he could indulge in few amusements, and the endeavour to bring a forger to justice would provide him with a new interest. So, after some discussion, he told the Rajapakses to go ahead.

Their business being concluded, the elder Rajapakse took off his glasses, wiped them and said with a smile, 'Now, Your Grace, for more pleasant matters. Owing to your kindness Douglas has already enjoyed an excellent holiday in Corfu. But my partners and I can get on quite well in the office without him for a while. Your case will not come on for some time, and in these special circumstances I should be happy to give him a further week, so that he can show his charming fiancée yourself and Mr. and Mrs. Eaton something of the beauties of our country.'

De Richleau inclined his white head. 'You are very kind. Many years ago I spent some time in Ceylon. I should like to visit Kandy again and various other places; and the others, of course, would welcome such a tour, particularly since you could spare Douglas to be our guide.'

'It will be a pleasure,' Rajapakse replied. 'And it is just as well that you should go up-country for a few days, because the situation in Colombo at the moment is causing some anxiety.'

'So I gather,' said the Duke. 'I was reading the *Ceylon Times* this morning, and it looks as if there is going to be trouble.'

'I fear so. Ever since the death of our first Prime Minister, Mr. D. S. Senanayake, there has been a lot of unrest here. His son, Dudley, who succeeded him was a most respected man; but he was not supported by his colleagues and, unfortunately, we have a strong Communist element in Ceylon. The Reds engineered a national strike and riots which also seriously hampered his administration; so he resigned. Sir John Kotelawala also met with much opposition and it was during his administration that the agitation for Sinhala Only began, which is the cause of the present trouble. He visited Jaffna, the heart of the Tamil country, early in 1956 and promised parity of Tamil with Sinhalese. But a few months later came the landslide election in which his party was swept away, and Mr. Bandaranaike then put through the "Sinhalese Only" Bill. The Tamils, having been settled here for many centuries, naturally resented it bitterly and demanded the official use of their language in their own districts.'

'They are settled mainly in the north, are they not?' asked the Duke.

'Originally, yes. They arrived from southern India in a series of invasions dating from the eighth century and overwhelmed the old Sinhalese Kingdom of Rajarata there. Since then they have spread all over the island, mainly as plantation workers, but they keep to their own settlements and do not mingle with our village people. Many of them are now well-educated and clever men and, under the British Raj, held posts in our Civil Service. It was largely with the object of driving out both them and the British that Sinhalese was made the only official language.'

'You see, sir,' Douglas explained, 'we have a very large Civil Service and to enter it provides one of the best prospects in this country for an educated man to make a good living. These upper-class Tamils all went to schools, where English was taught, and competed on equal terms with the Sinhalese.'

De Richleau nodded. 'It is very understandable then that the Tamils should have created trouble when the Bill was passed that froze them out.'

'Indeed, yes,' Rajapakse senior agreed. 'And far greater numbers of them had still worse grounds for complaint. I refer to the more recent immigrants, the Indian Tamils, who have been deprived of their rights as citizens, and are now debarred from owning land. The situation looked so dangerous that Mr. Bandaranaike was forced to come to an understanding with the Tamil leader, Mr. Chelvanayakam, by which they were guaranteed certain rights. But under pressure from several of his colleagues he has now annulled the pact; so the Tamils are up in arms again, and I fear we are in for some very unpleasant disturbances.'

'That being so, it would certainly be best for us to leave the city for a while. Where do you suggest taking us, Douglas?'

'I thought we might go up to Haputale and Nuwara Eliya, then on to Kandy.'

The Duke agreed and, it being one o'clock, took his guests down to lunch.

On the Saturday de Richleau's party set off into the interior. For several miles the road lay through a thickly populated district of semi-cultivated jungle and paddy fields; but, as it mounted, groves of coconut palms gave way to rubber plantations and groups of paw-paws, then to great mango trees the size and shape of oaks. Even when they reached the highlands where the tea gardens began, there were still many villages and a lot of traffic. Owing to that and the constant twisting of the road as it wound its way up ever-steeper gradients, although the journey was less than a hundred miles it took them five hours.

At Haputale they were welcomed by British friends of Douglas's in whose bungalow they were to stay the night. The 'bungalow' was actually a big three-winged one-storey house, with a fifty-foot verandah on one side. It overlooked a well-tended lawn and a garden gay with many beds of English flowers. From it the view was breath-taking: a vista of fifty miles with range after range of mountains gradually melting into the far distance. Later, when they were sitting there having before-dinner drinks, they watched the sun go down in a vast aura of salmon, gold and purple.

Fleur was entranced and asked her host if all the interior was as beautiful.

'No,' he replied. 'That is Ceylon's great misfortune. It is only the south-west quarter of the island that gets both the south-west and north-east monsoons. The north and east get only the latter; so suffer severely from drought. In ancient times the Sinhalese got over that by the most wonderful irrigation works that the world has ever seen. Their first capital Anuradhapura, in the north centre of the island, was bigger than London in Victorian times; and to supply it they constructed a vast artificial lake thirty miles in circumference. They call these reservoirs "tanks" and there were a great number of them large and small, all connected by canals and controlled by sluices, so that every town and village had plenty of water. And they did all this while the Romans were occupying England.'

'What happened to their civilisation?' asked Marie Lou.

'The Kingdom of Rajarata in the north lasted for close on a thousand years. Then, after a long series of wars with the Tamils, the Sinhalese were driven out. But further south, in about 760, they built another great capital at Polonnaruwa, and another great system of tanks and canals. They maintained themselves there for another five hundred years, then the rot set in; partly owing to civil wars, but it is believed that it was due mainly to malaria undermining the health and vigour of the people. Anyway, all the great temples, palaces and waterways fell into ruin and have since been almost totally submerged by the jungle.'

'Parts of the area have now been reclaimed, though,' Douglas put in. 'That is one of the things we owe to Mr. Senanayake. You see, on account of the increase in population there is now hardly any cultivable land left to develop in the Wet Zone, and his pet scheme was to restore the ancient irrigation system in the Dry Zone, so that great numbers of landless peasants could be resettled there. At a place called Gal Oya, to the north of Polonnaruwa, they have built a big new town, and round about it there is now a flourishing area.'

Next morning their host drove them round the tea garden. It consisted of thousands of low camellia-species bushes set close together on the slopes of the hillsides with, here and there, tall spindly trees with bushy tops. The trees were to give the tea plants a certain amount of shade and were mimosa, but of a variety that had insignificant flowers with no perfume. Only the young shoots of the tea bushes are of any value and two leaves and a bud are picked from each stem every eight days. They had to be pruned only once in every four years, but to keep the weeds from springing up between them was a considerable labour.

After lunch they drove north, winding their way through the highlands, then down into a deep valley from which they ascended to even greater heights, arriving at the Club House at Nuwara Eliya in time for tea.

Here the country was very different and not unlike England. There were many fine houses in the neighbourhood, nearly all of which in the old days had belonged to wealthy British residents in Ceylon; for it was here, six thousand feet up, that they spent the hottest months of summer, among fine trees and meadows, on tennis courts, on the golf course and fishing.

At the Club they were given a good dinner and comfortable beds, and next morning they set off for Kandy. The mountain scenery on the way, as they wound down and down round bend after bend, was even grander than that they had seen the previous day.

The capital of the last independent Sinhalese kingdom lies on one side of a lovely lake, the other side being dotted with big villas set among great trees that cover the sloping hillside beyond; and this justifies its claim to be one of the beauty spots of Ceylon. They put up at the Queen's Hotel, which was pleasant enough, and stayed for two nights.

Marie Lou was anxious to see the Botanical Gardens, outside the town, which are said to be the finest in Asia, and she was not disappointed. The giant specimen trees were a magnificent sight, the beds with massed flowers beautifully kept and the orchid houses a feast for the eye of exotic blossoms.

De Richleau was more interested in the 'Temple of the Tooth', which contains the most precious relic in the Buddhist world; so Douglas made special arrangements for his visit and on their second evening in Kandy they went to see the ceremony at the Temple that takes place every day at 10 a.m. and 7 p.m.

Their guide first took them round the Temple, the interior of which is eight hundred years old and contains many shrines and cases of fabulous jewels sent as offerings from all parts of Asia by devout Buddhists; then up to a balcony at the end of which there was a square room housing behind protective glass and an iron grille a large beehive-shaped casket of solid gold, in which reposes the Sacred Tooth.

From the balcony they watched the yellow-robed Temple attendants down on the ground floor beating drums and blowing conch shells. Then the High Priest and his assistants made the offerings of milk-rice and jasmin, lotus and sal flowers, in the sanctum. Although the little congregation of kneeling devotees down below were not permitted to come up and enter the Holy of Holies, as an act of great courtesy distinguished visitors were allowed to do so; and when the ceremony had been completed, de Richleau's party crowded into a small room adjoining that in which reposed the holy relic. There they were presented to the High Priest, a little old man with intelligent black eyes set in a benign face.

He spoke English very well and for a few minutes the Duke talked to him about other Buddhist shrines he had visited in years gone by in China, Cambodia and Thailand. The High Priest, impressed by de Richleau's knowledge of his religion, then invited them to accompany him to his quarters.

The room surprised them by its furnishings, for they were of the most diverse ages. On a small altar there sat a primitive bronze Buddha that was probably two thousand years old, there was a vase of the Tang period holding a few flowers, a Victorian roll-top desk and a radio of the latest pattern.

While the others got bored and tried to hide their restlessness, de Richleau and the High Priest talked for over an hour of the life of the Lord Buddha, before they parted with many bows and cordial handshakes.

By the following afternoon, the 21st May, they were back in Colombo, and learned that the situation there had deteriorated during their absence. Harassed on the one hand by the Buddhist priests and Sinhalese extremists and on the other by the leaders of two million Tamils, Mr. Bandaranaike was shilly-shallying wildly. Although under pressure he had torn up the pact that had kept an uneasy peace for the past eighteen months, he still declared that he would introduce legislation to give the Tamils fair play. This had resulted in a storm of protest all over the country from the Sinhalese. In the south Buddhist *bhikkhus* were organising a boycott of Tamil-owned shops, in several villages in the centre and east Tamils had been badly beaten up, and in Colombo there had been mass meetings on Galle Face Green to call strikes.

At the hotel the Duke found a typed letter awaiting him. It was from Ukwatte d'Azavedo and read:

Honoured Sir,

The imputation made against me by your lawyers is false and it greatly distresses me. Also I believe you to be unaware of the true origins of Count Plackoff's fortune. If you would be so kind as to grant me an entirely private interview, at any time convenient, it would give me the opportunity to put the full facts before you. We might then come to some arrangement by which we could both save ourselves the heavy expense of a legal action.

Fleur and Douglas had gone to bathe in the hotel swimming pool, but de Richleau knew that as soon as they had dressed they would go to the cocktail lounge for a drink; so he went down there, ordered a Pimms for himself and placidly awaited their coming. When they arrived he showed Douglas the letter and asked him what he thought of it.

Having scanned it, Douglas said, 'This, of course, was drafted and typed in his solicitor's office and, I should say, is with the hope of tricking you in some way. It is never sound policy, sir, for principals to meet when an action is pending, because one or other is apt to commit himself inadvisedly; but, of course, you must do as you wish.'

'I think I'll see him,' replied the Duke. 'It would be interesting to hear what he has to say; and, anyhow, I'd like to have a look at the fellow. Whatever he has up his sleeve you need not fear that I'll agree to anything without first consulting you.'

In consequence, the following midday Mr. d'Azavedo was shown into the Duke's sitting room, and with him he brought his son, Lalita.

Mr. Ukwatte d'Azavedo proved to be an unusually big man for a Sinhalese. He was dressed in a white tropical suit, which bulged in the region of his stomach, had wavy grey hair and a slight cast in his left eye. De Richleau put him down as about sixty and suspected that, while his blood might be mainly Sinhalese, it had a strong Arab strain and his name was the only thing about him that was Portuguese. The son was smaller, slimmer and his somewhat flamboyant clothes were typical of the native dandy. Thick-lensed glasses showed that his eyes were weak and he had a pendulous lower lip. He looked to be about thirty.

It was soon obvious to the Duke that the elder d'Azavedo was a rough diamond, a man of little education but forceful personality, whereas the younger was typical of the new middle-class intelligentsia, subtle-minded and glib of speech; although the English of both left much to be desired.

Having asserted that if the case came to court they could show that Pedro Fernando's confession was inspired by malice, they put forward two hypotheses. First: assuming that Ukwatte was guilty, morally his crime would have been justified by the fact that it was he who had discovered the jewel-bearing strata near Ratnapura and had worked it. Count Plackoff had done nothing but buy the land and provide the money for its exploitation, and he had always promised to make Ukwatte his heir. Second: if Ukwatte was innocent, as he averred was the case, it would be a terrible injustice if, after a lifetime of hard work, his property were taken from him.

It was then admitted that Fernando's confession gave the Duke a basis for his claim and that it was possible the case would be decided in his favour. Should that happen de Richleau would not only come into the value of the property Count Plackoff had left, but one four times its value, owing to the profits that d'Azavedo had ploughed back into Olenevka during the past twenty years. Therefore, rather than risk losing everything, he was prepared to compromise and made the following suggestion.

As de Richleau already knew, the Plackoff inheritance consisted, in addition to the estate of Olenevka and the mine, a small office-cum-workshop in Colombo. While Ukwatte ran the mine his son, Lalita, lived in rooms adjacent to the office, over the workshop, and was responsible for activities there. The gem-bearing quartz and precious pebbles were sent down to the city, cut and polished in the workshop, then sold on the market.

But the market fluctuated considerably, according to world demand; so it had been the d'Azavedos' policy to build up a big stock of cut gems which constituted their capital and, from time to time, release only a portion of these when the market was most favourable.

They estimated that this reserve stock was worth about four hundred thousand rupees—some thirty thousand pounds—and their proposal was that these cut stones should be handed over to the Duke in full settlement of his claim to the Plackoff inheritance.

For some minutes de Richleau thought this over carefully. The estate and mine were estimated to be worth half a million rupees; so with those jewels the total value of the inheritance should be about nine hundred thousand. The d'Azavedos' offer of nearly half of it might, therefore, be taken as a sign of weakness. On the other hand, in a similar situation he might have considered insuring himself against the loss of his whole fortune by making such an offer.

If Ukwatte was innocent, the last thing the Duke would have wished to do would be to rob him of everything on the false confession of a man who had a grudge against him. Even if he were not and he had told the truth about his discovery of the mine and Count Plackoff having promised to make him his heir, it would be hard on him to lose the whole proceeds of a lifetime's work. Last, but not least, there was the possibility that, the Duke's case not being a very strong one, he might lose it.

At length he said, 'I appreciate your having put matters to me so frankly, and your offer. But for the moment I am not prepared to commit myself. I should first like to see the property and any accounts you may have which will show the increase in its value since my cousin's death.'

Lalita leaned forward eagerly. 'We most willing you do that, sir. Coming here my father say, "Let us invite noble gentlemans to our home. He see then for self many new working of mine we open in last twenty year." House is large one. Plenty rooms for you and all friends of you. All accounts open for inspection. Please to come. Most welcome. When you wish?'

'Thank you,' the Duke nodded. 'As the situation in Colombo at the moment is far from pleasant I should be glad to get out of it again. Shall we say the day after tomorrow?'

That being agreed, it was settled that they should set out for Olenevka on Saturday afternoon and that the d'Azavedos should pick up the Duke and his party at three o'clock. With many expressions of goodwill the visitors then left.

When de Richleau told Douglas about this meeting, over dinner that evening, he agreed that a settlement out of court was well worth considering; but he was averse to the proposed visit to the mines. He said that for one thing the whole country was now in a state of unrest and that for another both d'Azavedo and his son were said to be tricky customers. The latter had political ambitions and was a close friend of Mrs. Bandaranaike, who had considerable influence and was much more to the Left than her husband. Douglas added that he would have been happier if he could accompany them on this trip, but after his month's absence from his office he had too much work with which he had to catch up.

On the Friday the situation had worsened still further. At the new settlement north of the old capital of Polonnaruwa a number of Tamils had been set upon and murdered and their women raped. There were also rumours that the Tamils at Jaffna and Trincomalee were banding together in great numbers and threatening to invade the south. But Ratnapura was even further south than Colombo and a good two hundred miles from the centres of disaffection; so the Duke saw no reason to change their plans, and on Saturday afternoon his party set off with the two d'Azavedos.

8

A Desperate Situation

Lalita d'Azavedo had managed to arrange matters so that the Duke, Richard and Marie Lou travelled with his father in the larger car and he had Fleur to himself except for de Richleau's man, Max, in the back of the smaller one.

Fleur had not been at all keen to come on this expedition; but had she insisted on remaining in Colombo, now that Douglas was fully occupied in his office she would have been able to be with him only in the evenings, and as the party were to be away only two nights she had been persuaded to come.

Now she was rather glad she had, because she found Lalita much the most interesting person she had met since arriving in Ceylon. Douglas had told her that when younger he had been a Socialist but further discussion had revealed that he was now, at most, a very pale pink Liberal, and his parents were so reactionary that they gave the impression that they regretted that their class no longer owned slaves.

Lalita, on the other hand, had what Fleur considered the right ideas. To begin with he had been extremely cagey about giving his own views on Ceylon's social problems to an English girl of the upper class; but when she had shown her colours he let himself go and they began swapping with gusto the old phrases, about liberty, equality and fraternity.

He was, however, a highly intelligent man and advanced reasons which were new even to Fleur for abolishing the capitalist system; but he naturally refrained from telling her that such money as his father and he might have to disgorge by way of additional taxation under a Government much further to the Left, he hoped to more than make up for by graft when his friends got into power and gave him a good job.

When they had covered some thirty miles they came in sight of Adam's Peak. As they approached the mountain, Lalita stopped talking politics and began to tell Fleur about it.

'Sacred Footprint on rock at summit said to be the Buddha's. Hindus claim to be Siva's, Mohammedans say Adam's, Eastern Christians say St. Thomas'. Officially, of course, is Buddhist shrine. But peoples of all religions, all races, make pilgrimage here from all parts Asia.

'We educated ones,' Lalita went on, 'know such pilgrimage waste of time. Soon we teach ignorant masses that. But now, still come. Half starve on long journey, then climb rugged mountain.' With a little snigger he added, 'Even street girl refuse gold to be prostitute on way here. For superstitious silly can you beat, eh?'

Some twenty miles further on they came to a rest house at the foot of the mountain, and there the party stopped for tea. Over the meal the Duke told them that on his earlier visit to Ceylon he had made the climb. From where they were sitting, almost at sea-level, it was over seven thousand feet to the top. In parts the mountain was thickly wooded, in others there were over-hanging cliffs down which still hung the stirrup-shaped links of enormous chains by which, at one time, it had been the only way to reach the summit. More recently a tortuous path fifteen miles long had been cut through the jungle, and it had taken him a day and a half to come down that way to the Ratnapura road. He had gone up from Maskeliya on the mountain's other side, as the altitude there was already four thousand five hundred feet, and a steep flight of steps had been cut out from the rock to make the ascent easier.

He went on to say that although the trip was a most fatiguing one it had been well worth it. Owing to the great amount of rain attracted by the mountain the jungle on the steep slopes was very dense and full of wild life. Sambhur, jackals, monkeys, hawk-eagles could all be seen and their baying, chatter and screeches made a discordant music against the background sound of the many streams rushing down through rocky runnels. There were, too, many caves, some having inscriptions in ancient Sinhalese, Sanscrit and even Chinese characters, carved on their walls by long-dead hermits who had once dwelt in them.

Of the shrine itself, he said that it was a very simple one; no more than a tile roof supported by four pillars over the six-foot-long footprint; and, although the title 'High Priest of the Peak' was one of the highest in the Buddhist hierarchy, so remote was the possibility of anyone desecrating the shrine that it was deemed necessary to have only a few monks in attendance on it.

As the Olenevka property was this side of Ratnapura, they had only another fifteen miles to go, so reached it in time for a rest before dinner.

The house was hideous, as it had been built in mid-Victorian times by a coffee planter in the days before the blight *Hemileia vastatrix* had ruined the coffee industry with the result that tea had replaced it as Ceylon's principal export. Presumably Count Plackoff had bought it because it was the only sizable house within easy reach of the area he was about to mine.

Ukwatte, it transpired, was a widower, and the visitors were received by his housekeeper, whom he introduced as Mrs. Mirabelle de Mendoza. She showed no signs of having European blood, neither had she the portly form usually associated with housekeepers. She could not have been more than thirty, was pale coffee in colour, had big, widely spaced, slumbrous eyes, an excellent figure, was dressed in rich silks and moved with a languorous, slinky walk as she came out on to the porch to greet them.

The furnishings of the house proved to be a strange mixture of West and East. It seemed that the Count had felt a strong nostalgia for his native Russia, so had gone to some trouble to collect the chattels of his nation. Several portraits of long-dead Czars and Czarinas hung on the walls, and a fine collection of ikons, but much of the furniture was bamboo and all the fabrics were of native handicraft.

After they had been refreshed with gin-slings, Mirabelle took Marie Lou and Fleur up to their rooms. The tired and dusty visitors then discovered to their annoyance that the house had only one bathroom, and the stove that heated the water was unlit. Max, the most perfect valet when serving the Duke in his normal surroundings, but pathetically helpless when removed to any other sphere, did not attempt to hide his shocked disapproval. But they made do as best they could, then came down to dinner.

There were a table and chairs in the dining room, but also at the far end of it three piles of cushions with small tables in front of them, which suggested that the d'Azavedos and Mirabelle normally ate their meals crosslegged on the floor. The fact that she dined with them made the visitors more than ever inclined to suspect that, although she might fill the role of housekeeper, she was also Ukwatte's mistress.

Dinner consisted of an unidentifiable soup, a huge dish of very hot curry and a splendid selection of tropical fruits. During it, they were intrigued to find that Mirabelle made a gracious hostess and evidently came from a social stratum superior to that of the d'Azavedos. Up till then she had said very little, but she spoke better English than they did, and it became obvious that she had both a sound intelligence and the basis of a good education.

Afterwards they went into the lounge-room and listened to the English broadcast, which followed the one in Sinhalese. The news was far from good. Many riots were reported in which small Tamil communities had been mobbed and, in some instances, killed. Sinhalese agitators, among them Buddhist priests, were inciting the people to further violence, and there were more rumours that the Tamils in the north were preparing to march on Colombo and exact vengeance. But the Government had not yet taken any steps to restore order.

Excusing themselves on account of tiredness the visitors went early to bed, but they had a far from comfortable night as their mattresses were unsprung and the mosquito nets, which had probably been there since Count Plackoff's time, were riddled with holes.

On the Sunday morning Marie Lou urged the Duke to get through his business as soon as possible so that, making some excuse, they could beat a retreat to Colombo that afternoon. De Richleau would gladly have done so; but the d'Azavedos excused themselves from taking him to the mines that morning, because the men would not be working them. So, with Richard to assist him, he had to make do with going through the financial records of the mine; and it was evident from them that since the Count's death Ukwatte had greatly increased the value of the property.

When they assembled on the verandah, after sleeping through the heat of the afternoon, Lalita suggested taking Fleur for a walk; so they went out together along one of the paths through the jungle. For a time they flogged their favourite subject: the Rights of Man and Equal Opportunity for All. Then he switched the conversation to personal problems, and paid Fleur a number of fulsome compliments that, as she was not in the least attracted to him physically, made her distinctly uneasy. Soul-mates they might be, politically, but she had given her heart to Douglas and had no time at all for such attentions from anyone else.

After dinner that night, while the others were again listening to the radio, he offered to show her some of the gems that came from the mine. Having no plausible excuse for refusing, she accompanied him to his father's work room. There he unlocked a large safe. The greater part of it contained rugged lumps of quartz and pebbles, which he told her would be sent in to Colombo and cut to the best advantage to show their glittering cores. Then he opened a drawer and took out a small tray of many-coloured stones that had been prepared for marketing.

'These,' he said with a grin, 'we keeps here for show tourist who visit mine. Silly fool think they get cheap because buy at source. But not so, and we makes bigger profit.'

The roseate fires of the stones, sparkling and scintillating under the lamp he held over them, would have fascinated any woman. A sidelong glance at Fleur told him that she was no exception and he said softly:

'You like, yes? I like see fine gem on pretty girl, not rich old womans. Per'aps you kind to me, eh? If so I give. You take pick.'

Instantly Fleur stiffened, thrust out her hand with the square sapphire on it and said, 'I thought you knew that I was engaged to Douglas Rajapakse.'

He shrugged. 'I hear that, yes. But what it show? Confirm you not high-hat; mean what you say 'bout coloured men good as white. You not wife of Rajapakse yet. He not know. Come! Take choice of gem, then give me little kiss.'

Fleur gave one look at his watery eyes behind the thick-lensed spectacles and his pendulous lower lip. Then in a swift gesture she knocked the tray of glittering gems out of his hand so that they scattered all over the floor. 'You bloody swine,' she said and, crimson with anger, marched out of the room.

It was as a result of this encounter that on the Monday morning, when they were getting ready to go to the mines, Fleur took her father aside and said, 'Daddy, please fix it that I don't have to go in Lalita's car. The little so-and-so made a pass at me last night.'

'Did he?' Richard showed swift concern. 'Darling, I'm sorry. Oh, hell! This just shows the sort of thing to which you are exposing yourself by . . . No, I didn't mean that. For two pins I'd break his bloody neck. But we mustn't quarrel with these awful people while we are their guests. Anyway, don't worry. You get in the car with the others and I'll go with him.'

In consequence, much to Lalita's annoyance he was quickly manœuvred into taking Richard as his passenger instead of Fleur. Then, with Ukwatte leading in the big car, they set off along a rough track through the jungle.

After they had crossed a valley the ground rose again then, a mile further on, they came out on to an open hillside sloping down to another valley through which a fast but narrow river ran. The road descended for a further half-mile along one side of the valley to end at a cluster of wooden buildings and palm-leaf huts. On its other side the ground rose steeply forming a barren cliff in which there were the dark entrances to a score or more of man-made caves; obviously the mine workings in the alluvial deposits of sand and gravel from a time when, centuries ago, the river had been much deeper and broader.

Connecting the village with the far bank there was a wooden bridge, and as a short cut to the nearer workings a single plank spanned a narrow gorge some fifteen feet deep through which the water hissed and tumbled.

To Richard's surprise, at the top of the rise instead of following his father's car down the slope, Lalita braked and halted his car.

'What's the matter?' Richard asked.

'I do not like,' Lalita murmured. 'The Tamils, they not working.'

Richard had already noticed a group of some sixty natives who had been squatting in the compound and who, on seeing Ukwatte's car, had all stood up.

'So they are Tamils,' said Richard uneasily. 'I hope there's not going to be trouble.'

Ukwatte had pulled up at the bottom of the hill, about four hundred yards short of the cluster of buildings. The Duke, Marie Lou and Fleur got out, then he drove on for a further two hundred yards, to a place where the road widened, and turned in it so that the car was facing up the hill. Meanwhile the Tamils were walking towards him. Pulling up again he stood up in the car, turned round so that he was facing them and began to shout at them in their own language. The Tamils halted for a moment, then gave an angry shout.

'This looks bad!' Richard exclaimed. 'Quick! Drive down and we'll pick up the others.'

'Not'ing to worry,' Lalita assured him. 'My father only tell them get back to work. But hothead per'aps throw stone. That why he dropped others little distance.'

As Ukwatte continued to harangue the Tamils they screamed abuse at him. Then suddenly the whole mob started forward in an ugly rush.

Before they could reach the car Ukwatte sat down, pressed the starter and ran the car forward. Swiftly its pace increased and, ignoring his passengers, he came charging up the hill.

'Good God!' Richard exclaimed, levering himself up in his seat. 'Your father must be crazy to have left the others there. Come on, man! We've got to get them.'

Lalita already had his car in motion, but instead of running down the hill he gave the wheel a swift turn so that the vehicle nosed into the jungle. A moment later Ukwatte's car roared past behind them.

'What the hell are you up to?' yelled Richard, seizing Lalita by the arm. Shaking off his grip Lalita reversed the car, then began to turn it to follow his father.

Half standing, Richard, now frantic with anxiety, was still watching the scene below. The Tamils had not halted as Ukwatte drove off, but, with threatening yells, were now heading for de Richleau and the two women. They had turned and, evidently having decided that they could not reach Lalita's car at the top of the hill, were running towards the plank that spanned the narrow gorge across the river.

'You bloody coward!' Richard cried, striking Lalita a back-hander across the face.

The car halted with a jerk. But Richard realised that there was no time to force Lalita to reverse again, or throw him out and take the wheel himself. Flinging open the door, he jumped to the ground and set off down the hill at a furious pace.

As his flying feet struck and slithered on the loose pebbles of the road, he saw that the situation was desperate. He had about three hundred yards to cover and the screaming Tamils were about the same distance behind the others. The plank bridge was only a hundred yards ahead of them and, with the lead they had, they should have reached it easily but, fit as he was for his age, the Duke was too old to run any distance.

Richard's eyes were fastened on them in an agony of fear.

Even as he prayed, 'Oh God, don't let those devils get them,' de Richleau stumbled and fell. Fleur gripped him by one arm and Marie Lou by the other. Pulling him to his feet they dragged him along with them, but their pace was slowed and the howling Tamils were rapidly gaining on them.

His lungs nearly bursting, Richard hurtled on down the slope. When he reached the flatter ground his pace increased still further by leaps and bounds. As his beloved ones staggered up a little rise that led to the near end of the plank, the Tamils were upon them. Fleur gained the plank, pulling de Richleau after her. Marie Lou, a small courageous figure, turned at bay and hit out at the nearest native.

The Tamils were bigger men than the Sinhalese and not, like them, Aryans. They were a much darker, more primitive people. These miners were the lowest caste of their breed and their uncouth faces were filled with rage and hate as they surged about the plank head.

The man Marie Lou had struck gave back a pace, then sprang forward. Seizing her in his arms, he lifted her and turned to carry her off. Sick with horror at the thought of what they would do to her, Richard hurled himself forward. Grabbing the man by the hair, he jerked his head violently backward. The man gave a strangled gasp and dropped her. As she stumbled to her feet another of them ran at her; she dodged him, but a third grasped her by the wrist and began to drag her away.

Richard was fending off two assailants, so could not go to her help. De Richleau, white-faced and shaken, was half lying on the far side of the plank, holding a hand to his chest as he laboured to recover from his unaccustomed exertion. But Fleur ran across to aid her mother. In her hand she held a stone the size of a cricket ball. From a distance of only four feet she hurled it into the man's face. With a scream of agony he let Marie Lou go. Lurching away from him she staggered across the plank.

Before Fleur could turn and follow her a huge, half-naked Tamil seized her round the waist. But Fleur was no Victorian maiden, and now her knowledge of the facts of life served her to good purpose. Thrusting down a hand she clutched the sweating native by his testicles and squeezed them with all her strength. His eyes started from their sockets. He let out a screech that echoed down the valley then, as she let go, reeled away vomiting. Swinging about, she dashed across the plank to join her mother.

Richard could not have survived for two minutes had the Tamils been armed, but Ukwatte's arrival had taken them by surprise while sitting in their compound holding a palaver. As things were, having been a good boxer in his youth he would have been a match for any one of them with his fists, but with four or five of them trying to overwhelm him he had all his work cut out to fend them off while holding the near end of the plank over which the others had reached temporary safety.

From blows he had received his mouth was bleeding, his left eye was half closed and every time he hit out with his right fist he was racked by a stabbing pain from having wrenched his shoulder. He dared not look behind him, even for a second, to make sure where the end of the plank was, and feared now that if he retreated further he might miss it and go over backwards into the deep gully. His three-hundred-yard run had already left him breathless when he entered the fight. He was now almost at the end of his tether.

Then a stone whizzed by on either side of him. One, thrown by Fleur, struck the man on his right on the ear, the other aimed by Marie Lou caught the man on his left in the chest. For a moment only the Tamil immediately in front of Richard continued to be a menace. Feinting with his right, Richard landed a blow on the native's sparsely bearded chin. As the man rocked back Richard turned and, swaying drunkenly, crossed the plank before the others could rally to continue their attack on him.

At its far end he turned, and not a second too soon. A scrawny fellow with gleaming white teeth protruding from his black face was coming after him. Fleur halted the man with another big stone, but only for a moment. Yet that was just enough for Richard to gasp in a breath and get a firm stance. As the man came at him again, he ducked a blow from him and hit him hard in the stomach. He doubled up, heeled over sideways and fell from the plank into the ravine.

But the far bank now swarmed with glistening black bodies. From scores of throats came howls of abuse in a high-pitched tongue. A hundred eyes, their whites showing in strong contrast to the dark faces, glared hatred. On seeing their comrade hurtle into the rock-strewn torrent below the nearest Tamils had given back, but those behind were forcing them forward. Two had already been edged on to the plank. The foremost was only six feet from Richard. Although he would now have to take them on only one at a time he was terribly aware that his strength was ebbing. Soon his blows would be too feeble to ward them off. One of them would rush him and bear him to the ground, then the whole pack would tear him limb from limb. Yet it was not that thought that harrowed him. It was what these human beasts would do to his wife and daughter.

It was the Duke who now temporarily saved the situation. On the slope below the caves several broken pit props and other mining debris lay scattered about. Stumbling to the nearest short length of timber, he snatched it up, ran the few steps back and thrust it into Richard's hand. Now that he had a weapon a new surge of hope revived him. While the Tamils were hesitating to attack him again he had had a short breather. Then, gathering his remaining strength, he took a pace forward and swung his rough cudgel at the nearest man's head.

The Tamil threw up a knotted arm to fend off the blow. The rough wood cut savagely into his muscle. He gave a whimpering cry, stepped back, missed his footing and, his arms and legs whirling, plunged into the gulf below. Again Richard struck out. His second victim was not even quick enough to raise his arm. The cudgel struck him fairly on the head. He collapsed without a sound, blood seeping through his matted black hair as he rolled off the plank.

The aged Duke, although no longer capable of taking part in a fight, still had an eye for a tactical situation. 'Now's our chance,' he shouted to Richard. 'Come back and we'll pull the plank in.'

Fearful of meeting the same fate as his predecessors, the nearest Tamil was stoutly resisting the efforts of his companions to thrust him forward. While they struggled there Richard beat a swift retreat. Marie Lou and Fleur, regardless of their nails, were already frantically digging away the earth in which the end of the plank was embedded. Richard was hardly past them when they had their fingers under it.

'Heave!' cried the Duke. 'Lift, then pull on it.'

Exerting all their strength, the two women raised the end of the plank a few inches. Richard stooped, grasped it and added his weight to theirs. Suddenly the far end of the plank came free. They all went over backwards, but the plank tilted sharply then, wrenching itself from their grasp, shot downwards to land with a splash in the river.

For a couple of minutes, while the thwarted Tamils continued to yell at them, they remained where they had fallen, striving to get back their breath, and unutterably relieved at the thought that they had escaped from their enemies. But the moment the Duke saw that they had partially recovered he roused them to fresh action. Standing beside them he had been anxiously watching the Tamils on the far bank. Their excited chatter had suddenly ceased. As one man they turned away and the whole mob began to run down the road towards the mining village. Instantly he guessed their intention and cried:

'They are making for the bridge down there. In ten minutes they'll be across and swarming up this side. We can't stay here or they'll get us yet, and we'll all be murdered.'

9

Within an Ace of Death

As Richard, Marie Lou and Fleur got to their feet, the Duke pointed to the cliff behind them. 'The mines! To get into one of them and hold it is our only chance.'

The nearest cave-like entrance to a mine was only fifty yards away but the path that led up to it was steep and littered with loose stones. De Richleau had to be helped as they made their way up, and when they reached it he panted, 'The entrance is too wide. We'd not be able to keep them out. It's worth a few minutes to find a stronger situation.'

Quickly they traversed a twenty-foot-wide ledge along the cliff face, on to which a number of the mines opened. As they came to the fourth Fleur, who was leading, cried, 'This is a good one! It's not very wide and there are some boxes and things with which we can barricade ourselves in.'

They were still short of breath from their recent climb and without exchanging a word they set to work, knowing that their lives again depended on their exertions. The mining material Fleur had seen consisted only of a few wooden cases, some bundles of pitprops and a roll of wire netting. Hastily they made as good a barricade as possible with them across the ten-foot-wide entrance to the cave. The few boxes made a barrier only two feet high with small gaps between them. The ground was too hard to drive the pitprops into it and they had no nails to fasten the wire netting to them; but by wedging the props as best they could then tying them criss-cross with some pieces of cord they came upon, and weaving the wire netting in and out, they succeeded in making a breast-high palisade.

These poor defences were scarcely completed when the sound of many tramping feet, coming from the opposite direction to that by which they had reached the cave, announced the approach of the murder-lusting mob. As the leaders caught sight of the barricade they halted, giving yells of triumph, and their followers surged up behind them until the broad shelf outside was packed with screaming Tamils.

Three of the foremost launched themselves forward, grabbing at the loose wire to tear it away. But Richard, Marie Lou and Fleur had armed themselves with pit-props and with them jabbed at the ferocious black faces. Fleur got one man in the mouth, Richard another in the eye and Marie Lou got her man in the neck. With howls and groans the attackers staggered back, but only to be replaced by others seemingly berserk and urged on by the taunts of their women.

For ten awful minutes the fracas raged. A part of the barricade was torn away but none of the Tamils succeeded in penetrating it. The sun was now high in the heavens and the heat in the cave almost intolerable. Its defenders—dirty, dishevelled, wild-eyed—were streaming with sweat. When, at last, the attack ceased they could hardly believe that they had succeeded in beating it off.

Although no more of the Tamils seemed inclined to risk punishment, the men remained crowded outside while the women led off their wounded. After a short while they turned to one another and began to chatter like monkeys, evidently debating some means of more successful attack. Then, as though by common consent, they all moved away and in a matter of seconds the broad rock shelf in front of the cave became empty.

Still keeping a sharp eye on the now deserted space, the inmates of the cave sat down to take a desperately needed rest. But not for long. Ten minutes later the Tamils appeared again, now carrying broken pit-props, branches of trees and other pieces of useless wood. One by one they flung their burdens down outside the barricade. De Richleau, grimly watching them, said in a low voice, 'The devils are preparing a bonfire. They mean to smoke us out.'

Only a sally could have prevented the steady increase of the heap of wooden debris, and had they attempted it they would have been torn to pieces. With growing apprehension, they looked on as the pile steadily grew higher. Twenty minutes later the Duke's foreboding proved right. The Tamils set the heap alight.

There was no means of putting the blaze out, and the green branches that had been mixed with the old wood gave off a dense smoke. The inmates of the cave began to cough and splutter. Their only remedy was to retreat further into the low tunnel. Even there the smoke penetrated, making their eyes water and rasping their lungs. It would not have been quite so bad had they had a little water in which to soak torn-off parts of garments to cover their mouths and nostrils, but they could only hold their hands over their faces while retreating still further into the airless cave, fearing as they did so that in the darkness they might stumble headlong down a mine shaft.

Suddenly there was a roar like thunder. The earth shook, small pieces of shale rattled down from the roof of the cave, a searing blast of hot air struck them and they were thrown to the ground.

Richard was the first to pick himself up. Groping through the darkness he located de Richleau and found, to his great relief, that the old Duke was badly shaken but not seriously injured.

'What happened?' gasped Fleur. 'That terrific explosion and blinding flash at the end of the tunnel. Surely they can't have bombs to throw in at us?'

'No,' Richard told her. 'There must have been some explosives for blasting in one of those boxes. The intense heat would have set it off. Anyway, it must have taught those swine a lesson.'

For a while the acrid fumes of the explosive made it impossible to advance but, when they could do so without being seized by violent fits of coughing, they cautiously made their way back to the entrance to the cave. Their barricade had been blown to smithereens. Only a few charred sticks of it remained. Outside a dozen black bodies, their rags burnt away by the flash, lay dead with grotesquely twisted limbs, or were writhing in agony. With wails of lamentation other Tamils were returning to carry away those who still lived. Ten minutes later, apart from dead bodies, the rock shelf outside was empty.

Soon afterwards Richard went out to make a brief reconnaissance.The plank by which they had retreated was now at the bottom of the gully, and too far down to be recoverable. At either end of their side of the valley sheer cliffs made exit from it impossible, except to a skilled climber. The only other way out was by the bridge that led direct to the village and there the Tamils were congregated, making a hideous din as they mourned their dead.

When Richard returned, he shook his head dolefully. 'I'm afraid there's no way out. We're trapped here.'

'Help must reach us soon,' Marie Lou declared optimistically. 'Although those wretched cowards deserted us, they must know we'd be attacked and will at least have telephoned the nearest police station.'

'I don't suppose there is one nearer than Ratnapura,' Fleur said gloomily, 'and it would take hours for the police to get here.'

'Even if they are on their way,' Richard added with a bitter laugh. 'It's my opinion that old d'Azavedo deliberately planned this pretty little party.'

'What?' Marie Lou's big violet eyes opened to their fullest extent. 'You can't mean that he left us hoping we'd be murdered?'

'Not you and me and Fleur, darling. We were just expendables and he didn't give a fig whether we lived or died. It was Greyeyes that he wanted his Tamils to do in. Anyway, I lay long odds that that was the big idea.'

'You mean to scotch the claim to this property?' Fleur said slowly. 'But if he had, someone else would have inherited it under Greyeyes's will.'

'No doubt,' her father replied. 'But as things are at the moment the claim is not a very sound one; so an heir might not feel inclined to risk his money fighting it.'

'I think Richard is right,' put in the Duke. 'At least with me out of the way there would have been a long delay before my heirs brought a case against him; and they might well have decided that he was not worth powder and shot. I think, too, that several things point to this having been an attempt to rid himself of me. He must have been aware that his Tamils were already in a state of unrest. In fact the reason he gave for pulling up and asking us to get out of the car was that he would have to be a bit sharp with them and they might react unpleasantly. What he said to them I don't know, but I gained the impression that instead of trying to reason with them he gave them deliberate provocation. Before that, even, he had turned his car round in readiness to make a quick getaway. That shows that he expected them to become violent. Then when they made a rush for him and he drove off he had an ample lead to have slowed down and pick us up. But he shot past without even giving us a glance.'

'It all adds up,' agreed Richard. 'So does the way that rotten little blighter Lalita behaved. He wouldn't have stopped his car on the hill-top if he hadn't known what was going to happen. When the outbreak started he had ample time to run down the hill and you could have clambered into his car while the Tamils were still a couple of hundred yards off. But not a bit of it. The moment they began to shout at his father he started to turn his car about. I had to slog him one in order to pull him up so that I could get out. He was just waiting there for the balloon to go up, and he's in this damnable plot up to the neck.'

For half an hour they sat nursing their hurts, then Richard went out again to make another reconnaissance. On his return he gloomily shook his head. 'The majority of the Tamils are still down in the village. But a little group of them are squatting on this side of the river, only about a hundred yards away, keeping watch on the cave. As soon as they saw me they got to their feet; so we daren't attempt to ford the river or they'd attack us again.'

It was still not midday, but the sun was blazing down so that at the entrance to the cave it became unbearably hot and they had to withdraw well inside it. They had no torch and Marie Lou and Fleur had lost their handbags when first attacked, so the only means of exploring the mine was by Richard's lighter and a box of matches that de Richleau carried for lighting his long Hoyo de Monterrey cigars. With this faint light Richard penetrated as far as he dared, hoping that he might come upon another entrance that would give them a better chance of escaping the Tamils; but the cave sloped straight down into the hillside, and when his lighter petered out he felt again that it would be dangerous to go any further in case, in the pitch darkness, he fell down some hidden shaft.

After his abortive foray they reasoned that, although the d'Azavedos seemed to have deliberately abandoned them, they would not dare leave it at that. To save their faces they must give to the nearest police and also to Max some version of what had occurred. He had been the Duke's personal servant for close on forty years and was devoted to his master. Although he was a very shy and timid man he was no fool, and was not likely to allow himself to be fobbed off with some dubious explanation for the party's failure to return. It seemed, therefore, that in another hour or two help must reach them; so they reconciled themselves to waiting, with the best patience they could muster, for their state of seige to be relieved.

Yet throughout the afternoon their situation remained unchanged and during it they began to feel hungry and thirsty. None of them had any means of satisfying their cravings and about the Duke the others were greatly worried. The physical strain from the time he had had to run for the plank until they had reached the cave must have been terrible for a man of his years. He was sitting with his back propped up against the side of the cave and when, from time to time, they asked him how he was feeling he endeavoured to reassure them. But during the long hours he spoke very little and was obviously suffering from extreme exhaustion.

It was just on sundown when, without a murmur, he slid sideways and fell over on his face. With a cry of alarm Marie Lou threw herself on her knees beside him and lifted his head on to her lap.

'Oh God!' she gasped. 'Greyeyes, dear Greyeyes! For God's sake speak to me! You mustn't die. We couldn't bear it.' But his mouth hung slackly open and his eyes remained closed.

Richard thrust a hand under de Richleau's shirt. After a moment he exclaimed with relief, 'His heart's still beating! He's not dead. He's only fainted.'

'It's this stifling atmosphere in here,' said Fleur quickly. 'And the fumes left by the explosion. It's water we need. If only we had water we could bring him round.'

'You're right!' her father declared. 'I'll have to get some.'

'No!' cried Marie Lou. 'No, Richard. If you go out the Tamils will murder you.'

'I must!' he retorted sharply. 'We can't risk his dying for lack of it. There's a place not far off where I could get down to the river. Both of you collect as many stones as you can carry. If we can keep the Tamils off even for five minutes that will be long enough for me to scramble down the bank and up again.' As he spoke he quickly began to snatch up some of the larger stones that littered the floor of the cave.

Without a word the two women followed his example, thrusting the rough stones hurriedly into their shirts.

'Now,' said Richard. 'Everything depends on speed. We've got to run at them hell for leather. And remember the old dictum. Don't fire until you can see the whites of their eyes.'

Leaving the cave together they raced straight for the little group of squatting Tamils. There were five of them and, coming to their feet, they stared in amazement at the three figures dashing towards them.

When the attackers were within thirty feet, Richard yelled 'Fire!' and three rocks hurtled through the air at the dark-skinned natives. Two hits were scored. Taken off their guard by this sudden attack the Tamils gave way. Pulling up, Richard and his companions delivered another volley, scoring two more hits. One of the Tamils was struck in the face and went over backwards. The others turned and ran.

While Marie Lou and Fleur continued the bombardment, Richard slithered down the bank, took off the panama hat he was wearing and filled it with water. Then one of the Tamils looked back over his shoulder. Seeing that the two women were now alone he shouted to his companions and halted. The other four pulled up, then turned and all five began to run back towards the place where they had been squatting. But they had covered some seventy yards and by the time they were nearing it Richard had succeeded in getting up the bank again.

Marie Lou and Fleur gallantly held their ground until Richard shouted to them to retreat. Fleur's last stone rendered another Tamil *hors de combat* then, with her mother beside her, they made for the cave.

Richard was some way ahead of them, carrying the precious water. For fear of spilling it he dared not run all out; so they reached the cave mouth together. The three remaining Tamils were only a dozen yards behind them, but Fleur and Marie Lou snatched up more stones and threw them as they backed into the entrance to the mine. Realising that their prey had now escaped the natives pulled up, stood there yelling abuse for a few minutes, then beat a retreat.

Still panting, but triumphant, Richard said, 'You two behaved like heroines; but . . . to quote Wellington . . . it was a damned close-run thing.'

Kneeling beside the Duke, Marie Lou again took his head on her lap while Fleur dribbled some of the water into his mouth and bathed his face with it. To their heart-felt relief he opened his eyes and, after a few minutes, murmured, 'Never fainted before . . . the . . . the heat . . . Sorry to have been a bother. I'll soon be all right.'

But they knew him to be far from all right, and continued to be desperately afraid that he might collapse before help reached them.

After taking a few sips of water themselves, they put aside for him what remained. Then, to their joy, Marie Lou produced from inside her shirt four bananas. She had seen them at the spot where the Tamils had been keeping watch; then, when they had been driven off, she had run forward and snatched up the fruit.

Fleur laughed for the first time in hours. 'Douglas told me that here in Ceylon if they want to disparage a person they say, "He's a banana", and apply the word to anything so cheap that they can get it for next to nothing; but these are worth their weight in gold.'

They fed one of the bananas slowly to the Duke, divided two between them, and kept the fourth to give him later in the night. For darkness was now falling and they feared that if help did not come soon a rescue party would fail to find them until the morning.

Before long they were to suffer still further cause for dread. About two hours after Richard had fetched the water a stone whizzed without warning into the cave and clattered on the floor. It was followed immediately by a volley of a dozen, one of which struck Richard on the side of the face, gashing it badly. Under cover of the darkness the Tamils had crept up to within close range and in this new attack were seeking revenge for the casualties they had suffered.

A swift retreat further into the stuffy cave was the only course open; yet as they made it they feared that was just what their enemies wanted, so that they could rush the entrance, then overwhelm them. As soon as they had carried de Richleau to safety, Richard grabbed up his cudgel and Fleur and Marie Lou threw stones back at the attackers. But in the first scramble what remained of the precious water was spilled and the last banana trampled underfoot.

For desperate minutes they crouched staring out into the darkness, but no attack matured and after a while the bombardment ceased; although only to be renewed again with odd stones and sudden volleys, from time to time, for over an hour.

The strain of remaining constantly on the *qui vive* was appalling, and they now felt they would never be able to stick it out till morning. De Richleau lay unmoving at full length and Marie Lou was near collapse. Then there came the sounds of distant shouting. Wild cries suddenly rent the night outside the mine. There was a patter of naked feet and odd stones ceased to ricochet from the sides and roof of the cave.

After a few minutes Richard cautiously advanced to the entrance to see if he could discover what had caused the stampede. He gave an excited cry, 'The village is on fire! Come out and see! What the devil's happening?'

The women joined him and Fleur said, 'It must be the Sinhalese. It was said on the radio last night that they were attacking the Tamils all over the island.'

That seemed the only explanation, and for the next half-hour they watched the awful spectacle of a small community becoming the victims of the ferocious hatred of a much larger mob. The wooden houses and palm huts caught fire like tinder and by the lurid light of the flames they could see small dark figures running about, struggling together and being trampled on.

At length the blaze died down and the place where the village had stood could be located only by scattered piles of glowing embers. They then debated whether to make their way to the village and ask the help of the Sinhalese to secure transport for the Duke to the nearest house where he could be put to bed; but decided against it. Shrill cries of agony and terror were still coming up from the jungle across the river, where solitary Tamils were being hunted down and their women being raped. It was against probability that any of those peasant Sinhalese would understand English; and maddened by blood lust as they were, it would have been too great a risk to count upon their not proving hostile.

The small amount of water they had sipped up from Richard's panama had only temporarily quenched their thirst, and a craving for more had been afflicting them for many hours; so, now the coast seemed clear, Richard made three more journeys to the river, while Fleur stood on guard nearby with a stone in her hand ready to throw if any natives suddenly appeared. The three hatsful enabled them to drink their fill as well as again temporarily reviving the Duke; but soon afterwards he became comatose.

The night hours seemed interminable yet, desperately tired as they were, they did not sleep. They were all far too concerned for de Richleau and sent up prayer after prayer that the old man would live.

At last dawn streaked the sky and, with the rapidity of the tropics, soon afterwards it became fully light. Another half-hour passed, then three police cars came speeding down the road towards the now deserted village where bodies lay sprawled among the charred remains of the burnt-out buildings. Richard was sitting hunched in the entrance of the cave. Standing up he gave a hoarse shout and began to wave. He was seen at once. Ten minutes later four policemen had crossed the bridge and were approaching him.

Their leader was a big man who introduced himself as Inspector van Goens. Fleur, who had been reading up the history of Ceylon, recalled that the name of one of the Governors of Ceylon during the Dutch supremacy had been van Goens; so, although the Inspector obviously had some Asiatic blood, he was a 'Burgher', as the numerous descendants of Dutch colonists were termed.

Having got the gist of Richard's story, the Inspector proved quick, efficient and kindly. He said they had been notified the previous morning that four Europeans had been left stranded among rioting Tamils; but before the operator could get the name of the village where they were the line had gone dead, so they had supposed it to have been cut. Then, only an hour earlier, a report had come in that there had been a massacre at the Olenevka mine.

Richard made no comment at the moment, but smiled sardonically at the thought of how clever the d'Azavedos had been. They could not now be accused of having failed to notify the police that a party of whites were in danger, but by refraining from giving their name or the place had sabotaged any hope of the party being rescued.

Expecting that there would be casualties in the village the third police vehicle was an ambulance. A stretcher was brought up and the Duke carried down to it. The others walked, but were so exhausted by their ordeal that they had to be helped along the stony way. Thermos flasks of iced tea and flasks of brandy were produced to fortify them for the time being. Then the ambulance set off and, a little over an hour later, delivered them at the hospital in Ratnapura.

They were still greatly concerned for de Richleau. When he had been carried out of the cave the light had shown his face to have turned an ugly shade of violet. Marie Lou, breaking down at last, had burst into tears and, holding his unresponsive hand, wept all through the bumpy journey. But, after a brief examination, the doctor in charge at the hospital said that the Duke's heart was as sound as a bell and that as there was nothing physically wrong with him, there was a very good chance that he would pull round.

Greatly comforted, Richard had the wound in his cheek dressed while Marie Lou and Fleur had their bruises treated. Then, utterly exhausted, they were put to bed, given sedatives and slept the clock round. By the evening de Richleau's state had improved and the others had recovered sufficiently to eat a hearty meal. Inspector van Goens came to take a more detailed statement from Richard, then he said:

'Old d'Azavedo is as crooked as they make them. That's well known in these parts; and his son is no better. From what you tell me of this inheritance I've not a doubt in my own mind that they planned to get your old gentleman killed. We have questioned some Tamils who escaped and d'Azavedo undoubtedly provoked them. He told them that they were dirty scum, sacked the lot and gave them three days to quit; so it's no wonder they acted as they did. When I went to the house he refused to see me. That lush young woman of his said he was in bed and prostrate with distress at having panicked and left you people at the mercy of the Tamils. The Duke's manservant confirmed that. Of course they told him that they had telephoned the police, so a rescue party would have started out to find you; but the poor old boy sat up all night worrying himself sick and silly. I left him packing your clothes and we are sending a car to fetch him this evening.

'Young d'Azavedo had gone off to Colombo, no doubt to stir up more trouble; because that's just what the political gang to which he belongs wants. It was he who phoned the police, and conveniently forgot to give his name or let us know from where he was speaking. But we can't bring a case. There isn't one they couldn't knock the bottom out of in ten minutes. D'Azavedo had a perfect right to sack his Tamils if he wanted. It's no crime to panic and desert people who are supposed to be your pals. The telephone line was cut, and there's no proof that a Tamil didn't cut it.'

Richard gave a grim smile. 'So that's that. Anyway, we're

lucky to have escaped with our lives. How are things at the moment?'

'Bad. Damn' bad. And they will continue to be as long as we are saddled with this weak-kneed Government. To curry favour with the Buddhists they've curtailed the powers of the police, and we'd be fired if we laid a finger on one of these monks who are preaching murder up and down the country. Yesterday there were serious riots in Colombo. Still, that may be all for the best. Our Governor General, Sir Oliver Goonetilleke, is a good and strong man. He's had enough, and this morning he took over. He has proclaimed a State of Emergency, which cuts the ground from under these dirty vote-catching politicians, and now we may have a chance of restoring law and order.'

By midday on the 28th all of them except the Duke were fit to leave the hospital; so Richard went to the Rest House to secure rooms, but the Sinhalese manager told him in a surly manner that he had none that were free. Richard then went to the police station in the hope that van Goens might be able to tell him of suitable accommodation.

The Inspector grinned at him and said, 'The old swab has plenty of rooms. It's the fact that you are British. Maybe you haven't realised that this "Sinhalese Only" agitation isn't aimed only at the Tamils, although they are the principal target. They want to get the last of the British out too, and the Dutch burghers like myself, and what we call the "Moormen", who are Indian Mohammedans settled on the east coast. The Sinhalese want the whole country for themselves; and when they get it, God alone knows what an unholy mess they'll make of it.'

Nevertheless, van Goens proved very helpful. He offered to take Richard and Marie Lou into his own house and find a room for Fleur with friends of his. And Richard gladly accepted his offer.

By the 30th, after four days of complete rest, the old Duke's splendid constitution had fully restored him; so, having taken grateful leave of van Goens and his plump kindly wife, they hired two cars and drove back to Colombo.

The State of Emergency was beginning to take effect. Now that troops and police were free of Bandaranaike's wavering hand they were arresting, and even shooting, Sinhalese as well as Tamils whom they caught attempting to kill one another.

This led to further outcries by the Sinhalese, egged on by the Marxists and Trotskyites, who were aiming to pull down the Socialist government. Even at the Galle Face, the staff had become slack, inefficient and rude to Europeans, whom they regarded as the secret enemies of their attaining absolute mastery of their island.

In consequence, after the Duke had been back there for twenty-four hours he called the others into conference and said, 'My friends, this is not good enough. Surly waiters, ill-cooked food, long delays in fetching drinks. I am too old to put up with this sort of treatment. If we are to remain in Ceylon much longer I favour renting a house up at Nuwara Eliya, where we shall be free from this unpleasant atmosphere.'

The others agreed, so that evening after dinner Douglas was consulted. He deplored the state things had reached, praised Sir Oliver Goonetilleke for the strong measures he was taking, then agreed that for the time being they would be much happier at Nuwara Eliya and said he knew that his father would gladly let them have the use of his bungalow there.

Although he did not say so, de Richleau was averse to accepting prolonged hospitality from the Rajapakses, so he enquired of Douglas the number of rooms available. On learning there were only three bedrooms, apart from servants' quarters, he pointed out that three would not be sufficient for Douglas to come up to stay and be with Fleur during weekends; then asked him to find another house with more ample accommodation that they could rent for two months.

Eager to please the Duke, Douglas returned next day with the news that he had found a large furnished house that should prove suitable. De Richleau at once instructed him to take it, and on June 4th the Duke and his party moved up to it.

Many of the British officials who had habitually spent their summers at Nuwara Eliya had long since left the island, so there was little society at the Club, except for tea planters and their wives who occasionally dropped in. There were fishing, tennis and golf, and the Duke was content to sit placidly in the sunshine; but, with few companions available to join them in their sports, after a week Fleur and Richard became distinctly bored.

As Ceylon abounded in game Richard would have liked to go on safari, but it would have been poor fun to go on his own; so on most days he haunted the Clubhouse in the hope of picking up a partner for a game of golf.

Fleur, meanwhile, grew daily more moody. She could now see Douglas only when he came up for week-ends, could find nothing to interest her at Nuwara Eliya and was longing to get married. At the end of a fortnight she tackled her mother and asked that her engagement should be shortened by a month.

Marie Lou took the opportunity to plead with her again to reconsider if she really wanted to make her home in Ceylon, where there was endless trouble, a Socialist government that at any time might become Communist, and the British, except by a minority and the Sinhalese upper class, were heartily disliked.

To all this Fleur turned a deaf ear. She was madly in love with her handsome Douglas, and her one desire was to become his wife.

Postponing the issue for the moment, Marie Lou privately consulted the Duke. On the advice of the Rajapakses his case against d'Azavedo had been put off until the autumn session, in order to give them a chance to trace Mrs. Fernando, so that she might be produced as a witness; and he was now anxious to get home. But he would not have allowed that to influence him in his advice to Marie Lou.

After some thought he said to her, 'My dear; the object of persuading Fleur to agree to a three months' engagement was so that seeing the conditions under which she would have to live if she made her home in Ceylon, she might find them so uncongenial that she would break off her engagement. But while she remains up here at Nuwara Eliya we are defeating our object. If she lived here a year she would still know little more about life as the wife of a Ceylonese. Either you must let her go down to Colombo and stay with her prospective mother-in-law, or accept the situation and allow her to marry Douglas in a few weeks' time.'

Faced with this dilemma, Marie Lou pondered for a while, then she said, 'The saying that "absence makes the heart grow fonder" is nonsense to my mind. If I let her go down to Colombo and she sees Douglas every day she'll become madder about him than ever. I think . . . yes, I think now we'd better let them marry and be done with it.'

Fleur was naturally delighted. A large quantity of linen that Marie Lou had already ordered from England was due to arrive any day and, Marie Lou having once taken her decision, mother and daughter found a new camaraderie in getting down at once to planning the trousseau.

The following day was a Friday and Douglas arrived for the week-end. Glowing with happiness Fleur told him her good news, then said, 'We must set about finding a house at once.'

He looked blankly at her and replied, 'But, darling, we don't need a house. We shall naturally live with my parents.'

Fleur's mouth fell open. 'Are you mad?' she exclaimed. 'I wouldn't dream of it! I must have a house of my own.'

'But it's the custom here,' Douglas protested. 'It's a large house. There is ample room. What do we want another house for? You are being absurd.'

'Live in the same house as your mother!' Fleur cried angrily. 'Be overlooked in everything I do and dictated to morning, noon and night by that old . . . old lady. Never! Never! I'd sooner give you back your ring.'

Douglas was a man of character and convictions. He felt that he had every right to insist that Fleur should accept the same conditions of marriage as other Ceylonese wives. And he said so in no unmeasured terms. They had a blinding row, which ended in Fleur flinging her ring at him and running upstairs in floods of tears to her mother.

As she sobbed out this awful situation Marie Lou's heart was deeply touched; but she could not help but feel a secret elation.

After having consoled Fleur as best she could she helped her to undress and go, still weeping, to bed. Returning to her bedroom she found Richard had come up and with a heavy sigh she said:

'Poor Fleur. The child is heartbroken. But we've won, darling. Douglas wants her to share that big house with her mother-in-law; and, quite rightly, she's flatly refused. So the whole thing is off.'

But it was not off. Next day Douglas gave way and agreed that Fleur should have a house of her own. They were married three weeks later.

10

Enter Simon Aron

It was more than two years later and autumn in Corfu, but in that favoured island there was no sign of approaching winter. As was usual, during the long hot summer, drought had dried up the few shallow streams and the lush vegetation had been burned to a brittle pale gold, yet within a week of the first rains an amazing transformation had taken place.

At first only a faint sheen of green appeared beneath the dried-up leaves of spring; a few days later thousands of buds were bursting on stems and branches, then a new glory of colour pervaded woods and meadows. By the third week in September bushes and plants on every side were gay with their second blossoming; broom, incense plants and wild narcissi scented the air, clusters of marguerites, autumn crocuses and sea-lavender sprouted like weeds through the recently parched grass, and amongst the crisp, russet leaves of the vines hung tight clusters of grapes ranging in colour from greenish gold to bluish black.

Like every estate owner, large or small, de Richleau had his own vineyard, and on this sunny morning he had walked the half mile to it on the arm of his old friend Simon Aron, who was now staying with him.

To those who knew the old Duke and the middle-aged Jewish financier only slightly it might have appeared a strange friendship. But, despite their difference in age and race, appearance and tradition, they had many tastes in common. Both loved beauty in its many forms and could linger happily over a jade carving or a page of prose; and for well over a quarter of a century they had enjoyed a pleasant rivalry in producing for each other meals that were masterpieces of the culinary art and classic wines of the finest vintages. It was as lovers of wine that they derived a special pleasure from watching for an hour the vintaging that had begun the previous day.

A line of girls and women in gaily coloured clothes laughed and chattered as they swiftly cut the bunches of grapes from the vines and dropped them into big baskets; then, splendidly erect, carried the baskets balanced on their heads to tip the cascades of grapes into deep panniers on the sides of patiently waiting donkeys. Young boys led the donkeys back to the cool dark 'magasin' which lay below the terrace of the villa, and there the men took over. For several days past they had been working on the vats and butts, repairing and scouring them in readiness for making the wine.

Knowing the intense prejudice of a backward peasantry against modern scientific methods, de Richleau had refrained from importing any machinery; so the grapes were pressed in exactly the same way as they had been for three thousand years and more. A strong young man, naked except for a shirt, the tails of which were knotted between his legs, worked his way down through the grapes in a vat that was taller than himself. As he trod the fruit, must gushed out of a spigot into jars standing in a long wooden trough, until nothing could be seen of him except his juice-stained hands clutching the rim of the vat.

Having watched a pressing, the two friends went up on to the terrace. There, on a table under the striped awning, a bottle in an ice-bucket had been set ready for their refreshment; but it did not contain a wine of Corfu. The Duke had the wine made for his dependents, only sampling each vintage when it was ready to drink; although he did occasionally enjoy one by-product of it. This was *mustelevria,* a delicious jelly made from boiling down fresh must with a little semolina and spices, then sticking the paste so made with almonds.

Simon took the bottle from the bucket, glanced at the label and poured the wine. It was a rich golden Anjou from a famous vineyard that made only a limited cuvée. Lowering his bird-like head with its thin, Semitic nose over his glass, he sniffed the wine appreciatively and said in his jerky fashion:

'Good to drink this again. Don't often see fine Anjou. Favourite wine of Athos, wasn't it?'

The Duke nodded. 'And of myself, except for Hock. But I doubt whether the Musketeers ever had the good fortune to taste German wines.'

'Appropriate though. I mean that you should rate it high. Remember the old days? How we used to rag one another—

joke about being modern Musketeers with you as our noble Athos?'

'Indeed I do. And a fine team we made! The mighty Rex as Porthos, level-headed Richard as D'Artagnan and yourself as the subtle-minded Aramis; pitting our wits and weapons against every variety of rogue half-way across the world—from Russia to Haiti and Poland to Spain. What marvellous fun we had.'

'Fun?' echoed Simon, giving a little titter and raising a slim hand to half-cover his full-lipped mouth. 'May have been fun for you, but I was scared stiff most of the time.'

'Nonsense, you were as brave as any of us. Of course, we did get into a tight corner now and then . . .'

'Now and then! For months on end I thought I'd never live to dig a spoonful of foie gras out of a Strasbourg Pie again.'

A gentle smile lit up the Duke's fine aristocratic face, then he sighed, 'Well, we survived, and it's all over now. It is getting on for two and a half years since I was last in danger of coming to a violent end; and I don't suppose I ever will be again. I count Father Time no enemy, and now that I'm eighty-five his coming for me cannot be very long delayed.'

'It's you who're talking nonsense now. You'll see a hundred, I'd bet a dozen of my Cognac des Tuileries on it. But you were referring to that nasty business when the Tamils nearly got you, Richard, Marie Lou and Fleur. How's your mine out there doing?'

'Far from well. As you may recall, it was only after seventeen months of appeals and legal wrangling that I got possession of the estate; and I don't think the man who's been running it for me since is much good. His reports are full of excuses about labour difficulties and other troubles. Anyhow I've seen no money from it yet. I expect I told you, too, that I lost the stock of cut gems that were in d'Azavedo's workshop in Colombo, and which were said to be worth thirty thousand pounds.'

'Ner.' Simon used the curious negative habitual to him. 'Didn't know about that. How? Did the old crook make off with them?'

'I think it highly probable, but there is no way of proving that he did. It was just about this time last year that they should have been handed over. Then on September 25th Mr. Bandaranaike was assassinated. A Buddhist monk with a grouse emptied the contents of a revolver into him at point-blank range, and he died the following day. As there were half a dozen political factions intriguing for power, both inside the Government and out, the Prime Minister's sudden death provoked an open clash. Agitators incited the mobs to violence and a number of buildings were looted and burned. That in which d'Azavedo's workshop was situated was one of them.'

'But the jewels,' Simon objected. 'Must have been in a safe. Salvage people should have recovered it. Couldn't have melted in the fire—only fallen into the basement.'

'It did; but was found to be open and the gems had gone. D'Azavedo's explanation was that the looters had forced his foreman cutter to give away the combination, then rifled its contents before setting fire to the building. That may be so, but it's equally probable that the whole thing was a put-up job.'

Simon's dark eyes narrowed behind the heavy tortoiseshell-rimmed spectacles he always wore. 'As you knew the approximate value of the stock, must have been a list. When he comes out of prison and starts disposing of the stones, police should be able to identify them.'

'He never went to prison. At least only for a few weeks.'

'But the fact that you got a verdict. That proved him to have forged the will. I'd have thought he'd get three years at least.'

'He might have, had his crime been a recent one and there had been a cast-iron case against him. But I got my verdict only after several juries had disagreed, and then only on the evidence of handwriting experts sent out from England. Moreover he was being tried for an act committed over twenty years earlier. He pleaded "not guilty" and continued to protest his innocence. Naturally the Sinhalese were biased in his favour, and there was quite an agitation on the lines that, guilty or not, he had suffered quite enough by losing the results of his life's work. So, although the court had to find him guilty, he was given only a nominal sentence.'

'Still, if he did make off with the stones—police should have been able to trace them as soon as he started to unload.'

De Richleau shook his head. 'No. My estimate of the value of the stones is theirs of the reserve stock they offered me as a compromise before inviting me up to Olenevka, and somewhat vague confirmation extracted from their foreman cutter after the fire. Even if d'Azavedo were caught with a bag of jewels, it could not be proved that they came out of the safe. After all, for many years he worked as Count Plackoff's manager at quite a handsome salary. In such a situation a thrifty man who could buy uncut gems at source might well have accumulated a private hoard to which his right could not be questioned.'

'You're stymied, then. Doubt if you'd stand much chance of winning a case against him anyway, now. Whole island's going to pot. The Bandaranaike election started it. Then his death really sent the balloon up. Although he'd already ousted his Communist colleague Philip Gunawardena, the rest of them fought like a pack of alley cats. Fellow who took over as caretaker P.M. either sacked or arrested half his Cabinet. Even so, he didn't last long.'

'No, but long enough to suppress the freedom of the Press and start stealing British businesses under the guise of nationalisation. That was W. Dahanayake. At least, though, he had the sense to repeal the Act by which they had suspended capital punishment.'

Simon violently shook his narrow head. 'Taking life's wrong in principle.'

'Yet sound in practice,' smiled the Duke. 'That is when the person concerned has been proved to be a dangerous enemy of society. Whether it is actually a deterrent to crime is, just possibly, arguable; but it is unreasonable that a part of the taxes paid by law-abiding citizens should be used to keep alive for years brutal or unscrupulous men, who have either murdered others or have been instrumental in provoking riots that have caused the death of innocent people.'

'We'll never agree on that. Anyhow, reverting to Ceylon. The electorate threw Dahanayake out and Dudley Senanayake, the grand old man's son, was brought back for another term of office. Poor fellow didn't have a hope against such a gang of crooks. He did manage to set up a Bribery Commission, though, that convicted some of the ex-Ministers.

'Had that in mind just now when I said I didn't think you'd stand much chance even if you had grounds for bringing a case against d'Azavedo. Not since the election last July, when Senanayake's brief term ended and Bandaranaike's widow became P.M. She's the perfect figurehead for the crazy crooked gang who're ruining the country. Maybe she doesn't realise what's going on, but ousting the last of the British and the

Dutch burghers from the Civil Service and Police has left openings for scores of unscrupulous clever-dick Sinhalese. They've got their chance now to make a real killing. Under Mrs. B. the place has become virtually a dictatorship. We all know what that means: corrupt officials taking bribes to do all sorts of dirty work; and a Lalita d'Azavedo is in a position to pull pretty well any strings he wants.'

De Richleau gave his friend a puzzled look. 'I had no idea you knew that d'Azavedo had a son, let alone that he was mixed up in politics.'

Simon's full lips parted in a wide grin. 'D'Azavedo is an unusual name. Saw it in a secret report sent me a week or so ago. Thought he must be some relation to your old forger. He is now a Colonel in the Security Service.'

'Is he indeed! May one enquire the reason for your interest in Ceylon's Secret Police; and, for that matter, how you come to be so well informed about political developments there?'

'Well now, I'll tell you. For many years my firm has financed one of the biggest tea planters when they needed additional capital to buy estates that came into the market. Quite a lot of properties on offer now. Owners getting cold feet about what may happen if Mrs. B. continues her ultra-Socialist activities. Our friends maintain that no Ceylonese Government would be quite so crazy as to take over Tea; so they want to buy. But Ceylon is in a muddle—a really nasty muddle. And the possibility of an immense loss of income has never yet prevented a dictator Government from cutting off its nose to spite its face if it's set on living up to Marxist ideals. So it was decided that I should go out and take a look at things personally before we agreed to risk our mun.'

'Your what?' enquired the Duke.

'Our money.'

'Of course. It's so long since I heard you use that expression I had forgotten it. When are you going?'

'Next month. In the meantime I called for all the information available about the place. And the sort of people we merchant bankers employ to get us that sort of thing are pretty good. They have to be.'

'As you are going to Ceylon, you will be seeing Fleur.'

'Um. Very fond of Fleur.'

'I know. I remember those fabulous toys you used to bring down to Cardinal's Folly for her, every time you went there when she was a child. I don't wonder she always looked on you as her favourite "Uncle".'

Simon wriggled his narrow shoulders. 'Had a lot of fun seeing her little face light up. Probably gave me more pleasure than the toys did her. It was fun, too, taking her to dinner at the Savoy Grill when she was older and studying in London. Vechelli and most of his waiters knew that I was an old friend of Richard's and that she was his daughter. But we must have looked a queer couple to people at other tables. She used to laugh about that and say, "Let's lead them on a bit—pretend you're a rich old so-and-so and keeping me in a flat in Maida Vale!" Then she'd insist on holding hands across the table.'

De Richleau laughed. 'By then she had become a real little Don Quixote, delighting to tilt at all moral conventions and denounce her class as parasites battening on the masses. But I imagine that as you've always held such strongly Liberal views you were not greatly shocked at finding that she had become a red-hot Socialist?'

'Ner,' Simon grinned back. 'I listened to all the old clichés as seriously as if she'd been Moses with the Tablets. And I'd rather the young became Communists than Nazis any day.'

'That's very understandable in your case, dear Simon. But if you ever get caught up in a revolution it's quite certain that you will be shot. The Pinks always pay the penalty for their ideals. Only the Reds or Blues have any chance of surviving and coming out on top.'

'How's Fleur's marriage going? Heard anything lately?'

'Not for some months; but well, as far as I know. The man she married, Douglas Rajapakse, struck me as a very decent fellow: warm-hearted, intelligent, civilised. Were it not for the colour of his skin he would be accepted anywhere as one of us. But there was no escaping the fact that Fleur would have to adjust herself to becoming a member of an Asiatic family, and when she found their way of life to be so different from our own she might feel that she had made a terrible mistake. Naturally Marie Lou and Richard were intensely worried about her future; but as the marriage has survived for over two years, it looks as though she is happy with her husband and means to remain with him.'

'Hard luck on old Richard and Marie Lou,' Simon commented. 'I mean, her living so far from them. Expensive trip to Ceylon, and Richard can't get even half the cost for the two of them tax-free, as he could if he were a business man.'

'I know,' the Duke agreed. 'About nine months after Fleur was married they went out to see how she was getting on. That was in the spring of '59, and Richard told me afterwards that they couldn't possibly afford to go every year. I've gathered since, though, that there is a plan for them all to spend a holiday together in Beirut or somewhere in the Eastern Mediterranean this winter. I should think Douglas could afford to bring Fleur to England every other year, and you may be sure she would be happy enough to flaunt him about the place; but I can't see Marie Lou enjoying presenting a dusky son-in-law to the County; so for them to meet half-way seems a good idea from every point of view.'

Simon rubbed a finger up and down the arc of his large Semitic nose and his weak eyes squinted a little through his glasses as he said, 'Would be if it weren't for Mrs. Bandaranaike and her boys. They're formulating legislation to prevent Ceylonese subjects taking money out of their country. Jolly tough ones, too. I'm told they'll be permitted to take out only one hundred and fifty pounds once in every seven years.'

'But that is iniquitous,' exploded the Duke. 'The worst possible form of Socialist tyranny.'

'Hard on people who've been used to coming to Europe now and then. Bad for Ceylon's external relations too. Anyway, however well-off Douglas may be this is going to scotch his bringing Fleur to meet her people in the Med. The currency restrictions in Ceylon have been getting worse for quite a time. No firm is now able to import anything into the country without a permit. If machinery breaks down and an incompetent Civil Service delays granting a permit to bring in the parts needed to get it going again, the firm is in a muddle. Sort of muddle that can cause a serious loss of profits. That's one of the things that is worrying Rex and me.'

'Rex? What has he to do with this?'

'Well now, I'll tell you. Since the nineteen-thirties, as we are both bankers, Rex and I have been into quite a lot of things together. Our London–New York tie-up has proved very useful. Anyhow, among other things in which we've shared risks was financing the estate purchases of these tea planters I was telling you about. Now they want more mun; if we decide to give it them, it will come fifty-fifty from us again. So Rex is going to meet me in Ceylon and we'll take a look at things together.'

'That will be pleasant for you, Simon; although I should have thought that either of you could have relied on the other's judgment. For both of you to go looks to me suspiciously like a holiday on your expense accounts.'

Simon's head came forward and he tittered into his hand. 'Well, you're right in a way. But old Rex hasn't been very well lately. Nothing serious, thank God—just felt a trip through the sunny parts of Asia for a few weeks this winter would do him good. He'll look in on his contacts in India, then come down to meet me in Ceylon. Afterwards I'll fly on with him to do a little business in Singapore, Bangkok, Manila and Hong Kong. From there I'll turn back, while he heads for home across the Pacific.'

'I take it Rex will be travelling in the aircraft that his bank bought for him to make his trips to Europe. I wonder if he will feel up to flying it himself?'

'Flying's always meant a lot to Rex. Expect he'll fly her part of the time anyway. But he usually has his Captain do any night shifts. She's a lovely thing. Beds for six passengers, and every comfort laid on.'

'Yes. The idea of this trip makes me envious. I wish I were coming with you.'

'Why don't you, then? I'm planning to leave about October 24th. I could go via Rome and you could meet me there. For that matter, I could leave a little earlier and pick you up here. That would be best. I'd be on hand then to look after you all the time.'

De Richleau shook his white head. 'Thank you, Simon; but I don't think I ought to. Although I must confess I'm greatly tempted. In these days I need sunshine to warm my old bones, and here it can become quite chilly in the winter. It is dull, too, as no one ever comes here during November and December.'

'Um,' Simon nodded his narrow head up and down like a toy china Mandarin. 'Same as the South of France in the old days. Square in front of the Casino at Monte looked like an empty film set all through October, November and December. People just couldn't be persuaded to go south till the New Year. Then almost overnight the Café de Paris became like the Tower of Babel.'

'Yes, I remember. Well, in a more limited way it is like that here. During the spring and early summer I could fill the villa with friends three times over, and from after Christmas or during high summer there are plenty of people I like to have who are happy to come out to stay. But not during those last months of the year. It's not that I want to have people staying all the time. I enjoy a quiet week now and then, just browsing in my library. But I do get bored if for several weeks at a stretch I have no one here to talk to.'

'Then why not come out to Ceylon with me?' Simon urged. 'Even if you are eighty-five, you're as fit as a fiddle. And I'd be on hand if you did fall ill.'

'No, Simon; no. If it were just to Ceylon and back I might. But you will be going on with Rex to Singapore and those other places. A series of long flights would prove too much for me; and I wouldn't like to risk flying back from Ceylon with only Max. He is a dear faithful fellow and one could not have a better valet, but he would be no use whatever to me in an emergency.'

At that moment Petti announced lunch, and as they moved along to the far end of the terrace—where they were still enjoying their midday meal out of doors—no more was said of the matter. But that night after dinner, as they lit two of the Duke's long Hoyo de Monterrey cigars, he raised the subject again.

'While resting this afternoon, Simon, I was thinking over what you told me before lunch about Ceylon. I had particularly in mind your secret intelligence to the effect that Mrs. Bandaranaike's Government intend to introduce legislation which will prevent capital assets, or money earned in the country, from being sent out of it. If you are correct that means that I shall never receive any money from the proceeds of my mine, even if it were being worked competently and they were considerable.'

'Um,' Simon agreed, waving the lighted end of his cigar under his big nose to sniff its fine aroma. 'You won't see a penny after these new laws go through, which they may any time after the New Year. That is, unless you take to smuggling; and that might land you in a muddle.'

'Then it seems my wisest course would be to sell the mine.'

'You mean in the next month or two, so that you can get your money out while the going is still good?'

'Yes. Do you see anything against that?'

'Only that other people must know what's in the wind. That means no well-advised European or U.S. jewel-mining company would make you an offer. Limits your market to the locals. You'd probably get a much better price if you hung on until the muddle in Ceylon sorts itself out and pressure of one kind or another forced them to alter their policy.'

'Sound advice, Simon; but that may not happen for another ten years, and I'd wager against my having that long to live. In any case the mine has proved more or less a white elephant. When d'Azavedo had it the Olenevka property was estimated to be worth half a million rupees—that's getting on for forty thousand pounds. I imagine it is worth considerably less now; and, of course, these new laws will further reduce its value. Fortunately, I'm in the happy position where it would not cause me the loss of a wink of sleep even if Ceylon had a Marxist Government and they stole the mine from me; but as I did receive this inheritance I may as well get what I can out of it.'

'You'd like me to dispose of it for you then, while I'm in Ceylon?'

'No, I don't wish to saddle you with that; and no doubt there will be numerous papers to sign, so I'll handle it myself.'

Simon's full mouth broke into a happy grin. 'You mean you've decided to go out there with me after all?'

'Yes. It provides a good excuse to enjoy a few weeks' sunshine. But I shan't go on with you and Rex to Hong Kong. I shall remain in Colombo. Fleur will take care of me there. One thing, though, I do mean to ask you: that is, instead of flying direct from Hong Kong to London, you should return via Ceylon; so as to pick me up and see me safely back here.'

'Of course I will. Only too delighted. And how pleased old Rex will be when he hears that you'll be with me in Colombo.'

De Richleau smiled. 'I'm so glad that this affair has come up. I had only Prince Voralburg and his daughter coming to stay for a week early in October, then no one until the Osbornes and the de Brissacs come here for Christmas. Now this trip will fill in my autumn splendidly. I could leave any day in the last week of October, so just arrange matters as suits you best.'

It was on the 21st October that Simon returned to Corfu to collect de Richleau and his man Max. After a night at the villa they flew via Athens to Rome, and next day caught the Comet that was to take them to Ceylon. The old Duke appeared hale and hearty, and was in excellent spirits. It is probable that he would have been just as cheerful even had he known that it was to be the last long flight he would make in his life.

11

The Trap

When the Duke and Simon arrived at Katunayake airport early on the morning of October 24th they found Fleur there to meet them. Douglas, she said, sent his apologies for not being there too; but the previous day he had had to go up to Kandy and would not be back in Colombo till that afternoon. Her bronzed skin showed up her violet eyes to perfection and made her more attractive than ever. Embracing them in turn, her laughter and kisses showed how delighted she was to see them.

But their reception by the officials at the airport was far from being so welcoming; and it was clear that many of them now regarded white people, particularly the British, with scarcely veiled hostility. Health, Immigration and Customs men all asked innumerable unnecessary questions and, to the Duke's fury, the latter insisted on opening every one of the air-tight tins in which he had brought a supply of his Hoyo de Monterreys thus, by premature exposure to the humid atmosphere of Ceylon, spoiling the cigars.

Even Fleur's expostulations in Sinhalese had proved of no avail and when at last they got away in her car she said:

'I'm terribly sorry about this, but most of these people are new to their jobs, and having been given a little power it has gone to their heads.'

The hour's run to Colombo, through semi-jungle, paddy fields and villages, had lost nothing of its beauty; the vivid greens of the vegetation, the gay costumes of the women, the yellow robes of the Buddhist monks and the many flowers made it as colourful as it had been for the past two thousand years. But on entering the city de Richleau saw that a considerable deterioration had taken place. On his last visit he had thought that it had an uncared-for appearance; but now the paint was peeling from shops and buildings even in the Fort quarter, and there seemed to be many more beggars in the streets.

When the Duke had written to Fleur to let her know that he and Simon were coming out, she had at once replied inviting them to stay; but he had declined on the grounds that he now spent a good part of his time in bed and it would be much easier for Max to look after him at the Galle Face.

After they had registered at the hotel it was agreed that they should spend the day resting, then she and Douglas should come to dine there with them that evening. Up in their rooms they found that she had arranged big vases of beautiful flowers for them and dishes of tropical fruit. She had also left a selection of drinks and tins of biscuits. Simon, who had a special liking for digestive biscuits, was touched to find she had remembered that for, although the biscuits in his bedside tin were a not very attractive sort of softish sponge, she had slipped in a note which read, 'Sorry, no digestives, not allowed to import them any more.'

When Douglas arrived with her that evening, de Richleau thought him as good-looking as ever, but somewhat distrait and lacking his old gaiety. Over their drinks Fleur remarked that the food in the restaurant had gone off shockingly compared with what it used to be, but that it was still good in the Mascarilla, as the hotel's night-club was called; so they had dinner there. After sinking three cocktails and drinking his share of two bottles of indifferent but expensive red wine, Douglas became more cheerful but he deliberately changed the conversation every time Simon asked him about recent developments in the island.

Next day the visitors lunched with Fleur and Douglas at their home. It was a pleasant two-storey house in one of the broad, tree-lined roads out near the Racecourse, and had been built in the early 1900s. A semi-circular drive bordered by flower beds led up to a broad flight of steps at its entrance, beyond which a row of spacious lofty rooms, with fans set in the ceilings, opened into one another. Several smiling white-coated servants attended on them and the observant Simon formed the impression that they liked their mistress; but it was not until luncheon was over that Douglas said to him:

'Mr. Aron, I'm afraid you must have thought me very cagey last night in fobbing off a number of your questions about how things are going in Ceylon; but the fact is that people like myself find it wiser not to give our honest opinion about our government in public any more.'

De Richleau raised his white 'devil's' eyebrows. 'Surely you don't mean that Ceylon has actually become a Police State?'

'No, I wouldn't say that,' Douglas replied. 'But there are plenty of signs that, like Ghana, it might easily become one. Since the assassination of Mr. S. W. R. D. Bandaranaike there have been a considerable number of arrests made on one pretext or another, mainly of people known to be strongly opposed to the Government, and there have been unorthodox delays in bringing some of them to trial. That sort of thing naturally makes one cautious about being openly critical of our lady Prime Minister's régime.'

Simon nodded his head up and down. 'Very understandable. But between four walls . . .'

'That is another matter. Among friends I readily admit that people like myself are greatly perturbed by the way things are going. You will have seen for yourselves how dilapidated the city is becoming, and the same thing is happening throughout the whole island. If you go up-country you will find that your car has to go very slowly and cautiously over the smaller wooden bridges that span culverts, because the roads are no longer being repaired adequately. Air conditioning plants and other machinery that breaks down can no longer be repaired, because the Government cannot afford to import spare parts, let alone replacements. The docks have fallen into a hopeless state of inefficiency, because they are now run largely by people who have never been trained to administer such concerns. Cargo ships often have to lie off our harbours for several days before they can be brought in and unloaded. In the past the traders in Colombo made a lot of money out of tourists coming ashore for the day from luxury liners; now the ships of many lines no longer call, because it is uneconomic to give the time needed to formalities before they can land their passengers. There are scores of other ways in which through ignorance and prejudice the new Sinhalese officials are ruining their own country; but I won't bother you with them.'

'And the taxes,' added Fleur. 'The way they have increased them is absolutely iniquitous. If things go on like this we may have to move to a smaller house.'

De Richleau smiled at her. 'You used to favour a policy of soaking the wicked rich.'

'I still do.' She countered the mild jibe without hesitation. 'That is, in reason, and provided the money obtained really benefits the masses. But this isn't in reason; and so much of it is squandered by Government hangers-on giving themselves a good time.'

'To what other uses do they put it?' asked Simon.

'A large part of it goes on education,' she replied, 'and one can't grumble about that.'

'Oh yes, one can,' Douglas took her up. 'To teach every child the three Rs and give them a good general grounding, then enable the brighter ones to pass on to a higher education, is only right. But the cranks who are now responsible for education here have the pipe-dream that every little backwoods Sinhalese boy and girl might later qualify as an accountant, musician, lawyer, radiologist or in some other highly technical capacity. So at great expense they are all being crammed with odds and ends of knowledge that in ninety-nine cases out of a hundred will never be the least use to them.'

'Every child has a right to an equal chance with the rest,' Fleur retorted, doggedly maintaining her old convictions.

Simon tittered into his hand. 'Won't be much good to them if their country goes bankrupt.'

'And it will,' Douglas averred, 'if the Government continues its present policies. The ignorance and stupidity of the people whom Mrs. Bandaranaike is allowing to run the country are almost beyond belief. They have decided that revenue could be increased if Ceylon manufactured her own brandy, gin and rum; so they are planning to build a huge distillery where they will crush cane and by adding various chemicals produce a variety of spirits. But the idiots have failed to take into account the fact that Ceylon grows enough sugar only for her ordinary needs. As they will have to buy the cane from abroad to supply the distillery, instead of helping our own agriculture it's going to put us further in the red.'

'Bad show,' remarked Simon. 'But I suppose one can't blame a people who have recently won their independence for wanting to stand on their own feet in various ways.'

'There would be a case for that if we could afford such expensive experiments, but we can't. Still worse, these fanatical nationalists have such a hatred of the Western world that they are throwing away some of our best assets simply out of spite. To have antagonised the British by robbing them of many of their big commercial undertakings here was bad enough. Now they mean to treat the Americans the same way. Their latest bright idea is to withdraw the concession by which Shell and the American companies supply the greater part of the island's petrol and give it instead to the Russians.'

'Yanks won't like that. Shouldn't be surprised if the Americans cut off the aid they're giving you.'

'You're right, Mr. Aron. And what makes it so tragic is that Ceylon is potentially a rich country. It could well support its people in reasonable prosperity if it were administered by an able Government that, instead of squandering capital, protected it and encouraged the foreign investment which we need to develop our industries. But as things are, just the opposite is happening. People are selling up and sending their money out.'

'Won't be allowed to much longer, I'm told.'

Douglas gave Simon a quick glance. 'Where did you hear that?'

Simon shrugged his narrow shoulders and grinned. 'Well, I'm a banker; and bankers hear things, you know.'

'I hope you are wrong, but that certainly ties up with a rumour I heard a little time ago,' Douglas said with a frown.

The Duke then told him that this threat to freeze capital was his reason for having come out to Ceylon and asked his opinion about disposing of Olenevka.

As the mine had failed to show a profit, and no change of Government could be hoped for in the foreseeable future, Douglas agreed that it would be sound to sell, provided they could get a reasonable offer. So, after lunch, they drew up a suitable advertisement for insertion in the *Ceylon Times*; but de Richleau said that before finally deciding to sell and sending the advertisement in he meant to have a talk with the manager of the mine, for whom he had sent to come to see him the following morning.

The manager was a Sinhalese named de Zoysa and had been chosen for the post by Douglas from a number of applicants, soon after the court had decided the case for possession in de Richleau's favour. The Duke had asked Simon to remain with him for the interview; so when de Zoysa's name was sent up they were together in de Richleau's private sitting room.

De Zoysa proved to be a thin, angular man with a nervous manner. Although his employer urged him to be at ease, he sat throughout on the edge of his chair and fiddled uncomfortably all the time with a soiled panama that he held between his knees.

When asked why Olenevka had shown no profit during the past year, he explained that that was due largely to the state in which d'Azavedo had left it. Owing to the massacre of the Tamils the mine had been left for many months unworked. Then, when d'Azavedo had at length succeeded in collecting a skeleton labour force, he had been under the shadow of a High Court action which might still deprive him of the property; so he had not exerted himself to get the mine fully operative again. Later, when the verdict had been given against him, although it would have been difficult to prove that he had actually sabotaged the best workings, de Zoysa was of the opinion that he had done so. At all events they had been left in such a state that it had entailed months of work to get them going again. Now, too, they had to rely on Sinhalese instead of Tamils. The former were not such good workmen, and under the Bandaranaike Government labour was receiving much higher wages than it had in the past.

Most of this de Richleau already knew from the written reports he had received. He had sent for de Zoysa only to assess his personality and judge whether it would be a good long-term bet to retain the mine with the possibility of its increasing in value under his management and proving a handsome legacy to leave Fleur. He glanced at Simon.

Not a muscle of Simon's face moved but behind his thick spectacles his dark eyes flickered swiftly from side to side. It was a silent signal that had often caused his partners to refuse a loan of many thousands to applicants who appeared to offer good security. De Richleau knew it of old and read it as, 'This fellow's no good. Not enough guts to make a go of it. Much better sell.' Turning to de Zoysa, the Duke said:

'As the immediate prospects of the mine are not very good I am minded to dispose of it. Since you have managed it for over a year I feel it only fair to give you the first refusal, should you care to make me a suitable offer.'

De Zoysa swallowed hard, shook his head and replied, 'Sir, you are very kind. But I have not the capital. No way either to raise it.'

The Duke stood up and extended his slender hand. 'Then it only remains for me to thank you for the work you have put in and to assure you that you will receive full compensation for the termination of your contract.'

When de Zoysa had awkwardly bowed himself out, Simon telephoned to the *Ceylon Times* the announcement that Olenevka was for sale, then he and de Richleau went downstairs to lunch.

On his previous visits the Duke had seen all the sights Colombo had to offer so he was content to spend most of his time in the precincts of the hotel dozing in the sun over a book; but Fleur was determined that Simon should see everything of interest and she had arranged to call for him that afternoon in her car.

They took the road out to Mount Lavinia and after a quarter of a mile she pointed out to him on the left a wall about a hundred yards long but only about four feet high. Immediately behind it was a thick hedge of higher shrubs. As he glanced at it he was amazed to see that wedged into the hedge at intervals of only about ten feet stood a line of bored-looking soldiers, each of whom held a Sten gun.

'Behind that hedge,' said Fleur, 'lies Temple Trees, Mrs. Bandaranaike's residence.'

'No, really!' exclaimed Simon. 'Poor woman must be properly scared to keep a dozen gunmen standing about in her front garden.'

'She has reason to be,' Fleur replied. 'She is known as the "wailing widow" because she got herself nominated a Senator and the leader of her husband's Party after his assassination by making capital out of his death and going round every village weeping over their children. Since then the men she has allowed to run the country have set everyone by the ears: the Sinhalese élite, the Press, the merchants, the Catholics, the Hindus, the Mohammedans, the Dutch burghers, the British. There are scores of people who would put a bullet into her if given half a chance.'

Four miles further on they turned off to the left and pulled up outside the Zoo. It was said to be one of the best in Asia. There they spent a happy two hours looking at the animals and a wonderful collection of tropical fish in the Aquarium, then watching the elephants perform in a natural amphitheatre shaded by fine trees. Afterwards she drove him back to her home for tea and, just before they reached it, she pointed out a fine building standing back from the road, with several tennis courts.

'That,' she said, 'used to be the British Club, but the Government commandeered it as a playground for children.' Then she added with a laugh, 'But the children have turned out to be government officials and Civil Servants.'

Over tea Simon asked her about the sort of life she led, and she told him that, apart from the fact that Douglas was constantly worried about the way things were going and that she did not get on with her mother-in-law, she had nothing of which to complain. They had many friends, both British and Sinhalese, she was on the committees of several charities and spent four mornings a week at the Family Planning Clinic, where she felt she was doing really worth-while work.

Simon said 'Ner' and 'Um'd and nodded his birdlike head while she talked freely but, he thought, a shade too quickly and cheerfully about her activities; so that when he left her he had the impression that she had not been entirely frank with him, and he was a little depressed by the thought that their talk had not resulted in a resumption of their old intimacy.

When he got back to the Galle Face he found a cablegram from Rex. It had geen sent from Delhi to say that a fault had developed in one of the engines of his aircraft and that, instead of arriving in Colombo on the 27th as planned, he would be delayed until the 30th, and not to book rooms for him as he would be staying at the American Embassy.

As the Duke and Simon had been greatly looking forward to having Rex with them within the next twenty-four hours they were naturally disappointed; but it made no material difference to Simon with regard to his business in Colombo. Rex's financial contacts there were mainly American agents, whereas Simon's were associated with London, and he had already made a number of appointments with tea planters, land agents and other people he wanted to see.

Next morning, Thursday the 27th, de Richleau's advertisement appeared in the *Times* and Fleur came to lunch with him. In the evening she returned with Douglas and his parents, who came to pay their respects. While they were having drinks Simon, who had been out all day, joined them and later the two friends dined quietly together.

On the Friday Douglas arrived unannounced just before

lunch, to find the Duke enjoying a glass of champagne on the glassed-in verandah at the front of the hotel. He was carrying a brief-case, which he put carefully between his legs as he sat down at de Richleau's table then, when a glass of wine had been poured for him, he said:

'I have a buyer for your mine; but I'm a bit doubtful if you will be willing to accept his offer.'

'Why?' asked de Richleau. 'Is it a very poor one?'

'No. On the contrary, I consider it very good. That is, as things are at the moment. Mr. Aron's intelligence service must be quite exceptional to have picked up several weeks ago a rumour that the Government might decide to put a ban on money being sent out of Ceylon. The secret can have leaked out here only quite recently. But since we talked of it at lunch on Tuesday several people have mentioned it to me. In consequence, no foreign-owned company will now put money into anything until the situation clarifies, and we've had no enquiries at all about the advertisement from quarters from which we might expect them. That being so, I'd certainly advise you to accept this one; but you may not wish to do so, because it comes from old d'Azavedo.'

'What! That rogue!'

Douglas smiled. 'Yes. And what is more, he is offering to buy back the mine with assets that we have some reason to suppose he stole from you.'

'Well, I'll be damned! Of all the barefaced impudence. Tell him to go to the devil.'

'I thought you would feel like that about it; but as I am acting for you it was up to me to transmit his offer to you.'

At that moment Simon appeared, mopping the perspiration from his sloping forehead with a silk handkerchief. De Richleau greeted him with a laugh. 'Come and listen to this, Simon. Would you believe it? That villain d'Azavedo has had the audacity to make an offer for Olenevka.'

'Has he?' Simon sat down, signed to the waiter to bring another glass and added, 'How much?'

'I neither know nor care. The fellow did his best to have me and our friends murdered. I wouldn't let him have the mine back for all the tea in China.'

'I'd part with most things for that,' Simon grinned. 'Lot of tea in China.' Then he looked across at Douglas and repeated, 'How much?'

'About twenty-four thousand three hundred pounds, more or less.'

'Why "more or less"?'

Douglas took a drink of champagne, then replied, 'D'Azavedo and his son came to my office first thing this morning. He said he wanted to buy back the mine, largely for sentimental reasons, because Olenevka had been his home for most of his life. He added that on account of the past, His Grace might be reluctant to sell the mine to him, so he was prepared to pay a bigger price than we were likely to get elsewhere now that properties have suddenly become difficult to dispose of.' Pausing for a moment Douglas opened his briefcase, took from it a flat leather zip-up folder about twelve inches long by six wide, laid it on the table and said, 'This is what he offered.'

While the others looked at him in some surprise, he unzipped the folder and turned back its leather flap, revealing the shallow bottom which was divided into scores of tiny compartments. Very nearly all of them held a cut precious stone large enough to make a valuable ring, and the effect of the whole as they blazed in the strong sunshine was positively dazzling.

'Phew!' Simon whistled, craning forward his head. 'Must be worth a packet.'

'There are more than four hundred of them,' Douglas told him, 'and at least a third of them would fetch over three figures on the market. D'Azavedo put their value at twenty-five thousand pounds, but he asked me to have an independent valuation made of them in his presence; so I sent for Gunasena, whom I know to be trustworthy. It took him and an assistant the whole morning to weigh and assess them, then he signed a statement that at auction they should fetch approximately twenty-four thousand three hundred pounds. When d'Azavedo was running the mine it was probably worth about forty thousand pounds. But it has deteriorated a lot since, and with this threat of a currency embargo I've been advised that we'd be lucky to get fifteen for it today; so this is an exceptionally good offer.'

'Funny, d'Azavedo making his offer this way,' Simon remarked. 'Why couldn't he sell the stones, bank the money and pay by cheque?'

'To dispose of them to the best advantage would take time,'

Douglas replied, 'and he is anxious that the deal should go through quickly.'

'Then he has been counting his chickens,' said the Duke. 'He proposed a deal of this kind originally and I was prepared to accept it. Then in a most unscrupulous manner he endeavoured to bring about the death of myself and my friends. I'll have no truck with him.'

Simon's dark eyes flickered from side to side. 'Now, wait a minute. Great mistake to mix personal relationships with business. Argument about him being a crook doesn't hold water anyway. You believed him to be a forger from the beginning, yet you were ready to do a deal with him.'

'A forger is somewhat different from a man who has tried to commit murder.'

'No real proof that he didn't lose his nerve. But let's agree that he tried to do you in. Doesn't make this lot of sparklers worth a penny less. Mine's no good to you. Doubt if you'd ever get anything out of it as long as that chap de Zoysa is running it. Put in another manager and the odds are he'll do no better. Even given you get one who is a fire-ball and dead honest, you won't be able to take out of Ceylon any profits you make.'

De Richleau shrugged. 'We have been over that already. It is my reason for deciding to sell. And, as I have told you, since I have an ample income already, I should not be greatly disappointed if, from beginning to end, I got nothing out of Olenevka.'

'Um, I know that. But you'll admit that it is now of no value to you unless you do sell.'

'Certainly. But Douglas says I might get fifteen thousand from some other source.'

'Hang it all! That's nearly ten thousand less than you are being offered.'

'True; but by a man with whom I do not desire to have any dealings.'

Simon's agitation at the thought of throwing away such a sum was apparent. 'You mustn't let personalities enter into this,' he insisted. 'Or look at it another way. Odds are most of these stones are the stock that was in d'Azavedo's safe before his workshop was burnt out. If so, by rights they're yours. He's offering to let you have them back. And for what? For something you want to get rid of anyway.'

Douglas passed a hand over his smooth dark hair. 'Mr. Aron is right, you know. It is a hundred to one that these are the stones that should have been handed over to me for you last year. Anyway, assuming that the mine is worth fifteen thousand pounds, and I greatly doubt if we could get more for it, by accepting d'Azavedo's offer you would be making an extremely handsome profit.'

Occasionally Simon made jokes against his own race and now, spreading out his slender hands, he said with a heavy Jewish accent, 'And der man vot takes a profit don't never go broke. For God's sake be sensible. However rich you are, take the man's offer. If you don't want the money you can always give it to someone else.'

The Duke smiled and shook his head, but not very firmly. Then Douglas said, 'There is one aspect you may not have considered. Owing to the state into which the mine has been allowed to fall, and labour difficulties, d'Azavedo will be letting himself in for a packet of trouble before he can hope to make it a paying proposition again. In fact, it's a gamble which he may have reason to regret later. As you have no cause to like him, why not leave him holding this somewhat dubious baby?'

'That is the best argument for accepting that has yet been put forward,' said de Richleau. 'All things considered, perhaps the two of you are right and I should be a fool not to take the fellow's money, or rather these gems.'

Having noticed a waiter eyeing the blazing array of stones with fascinated amazement, Douglas had already zipped up the leather cover of the shallow case. Now he slipped it back into his brief-case and said, 'Very well, then. I'll prepare a contract of sale. It should be ready by Monday.'

As he stood up the Duke invited him to stay to lunch but he shook his head. 'No, sir. Thanks all the same; but I'm temporarily responsible for this lot. D'Azavedo insisted that I should bring them to show you. He probably thought the sight of them was more likely to tempt you than just a description of them. I brought one of my clerks with me in the car and I've got a gun on me. All the same, the sooner I've handed them back to d'Azavedo the better I'll be pleased, and he's waiting for me in my office.'

The rest of that day and Saturday and Sunday passed uneventfully, except that on Sunday morning Simon had a telephone call from Rex. On the flight it had emerged that the mechanics in Delhi had failed to put the faulty engine of his aircraft one hundred per cent right; so he had thought it best to come down at Trincomalee. He had Truss with him and they were motoring down to Colombo, but they did not expect to get in until late that night; so would not come to the Galle Face until Monday morning.

Simon was out for a good part of the week-end, but Fleur called every afternoon to spend a couple of hours with de Richleau and twice had meals with them. On Sunday evening Simon had been invited to dine with a Mr. Chandrasekera, the chairman of one of Ceylon's largest insurance brokers, and as Fleur and Douglas had a long-standing dinner engagement for that evening, the Duke was left on his own.

Max always shaved him in the morning and helped him to dress; but he never kept his man up late, as he was perfectly capable of putting himself to bed and invariably did so on Sundays when Max had his evening off. On this occasion he went straight to bed after dinner and settled down to read. Then, at a little after ten o'clock, his telephone rang.

When he answered it a high-pitched male voice said, 'I speak wiv Mistair Aron, no? Hotel desk say he out. Say you also friend Mistair Missus Rajapakse. They have accident. Cars crash. Both hurt. Missus Rajapaske hurt very bad. They ask friends at Galle Face come quickly. Very urgent. They in my house. I send car fetch you. Ten minutes, yiss. You come pliss. No time for lose.'

Quickly the Duke asked for further particulars, but received only a jumbled repetition of the facts that Fleur and Douglas had been injured in a car smash and that a car was being sent to fetch him. Then, before he could ask the address of the house into which they had been taken, the man rang off.

From the urgency of the summons he gained the impression that Fleur's injuries were so serious that she might be dying. The moment the line was clear he rang Max's room, hoping he would be there to come along and help him dress more quickly, then come with him; but there was no reply, so evidently Max was still out. Panting a little he got into his clothes as swiftly as he could; then, as he did not know where to get hold of Simon, he scribbled a note telling him what had happened.

Down in the hall, as soon as he spoke to the night porter he was told that a car had just arrived for Mr. Aron and himself. He gave the man the note for Simon and a good tip to ensure that it was given to him immediately he came in, then hurried out to the car.

It was a dilapidated Citroën and its driver a bearded Indian wearing a turban and thick glasses. From that, as there were quite a number of Indian merchants in Colombo, de Richleau assumed that it was into the house of one of them that Fleur and Douglas had been taken. As soon as he was seated in the car he began to question the driver; but the man only smiled, shrugged and shook his head; so it seemed obvious that he did not speak English.

The car ran inland, rounded the southern end of the lake then turned north, first through a seedy district then a more open area where here and there medium-sized houses stood a little back from the road in their own gardens. Some ten or twelve minutes after leaving the hotel the driver swerved his car sharply through an open gateway, up a short drive and pulled up with a jerk before a double-fronted two-storey house.

As the Duke scrambled out the driver sounded his horn twice, then followed him. Mounting the three steps to a narrow verandah, de Richleau advanced towards the front door over which a light was showing. It swung open to reveal a big man with a heavy paunch, but against the light the Duke could see his features only vaguely. Next moment he felt a sharp prod in the back and the silent driver said in English:

'Keep quiet. Go straight in. I press a gun against your backbone.' At the same second de Richleau recognised the big man who was holding the door open as Ukwatte d'Azavedo.

Drawing a sharp breath, he did as he was bid. Closing the door behind him and the driver, d'Azavedo smiled and said, 'A surprise for you, eh? Better perhaps than to find young Mrs. Rajapakse in state you expected. I think that bring you here. And very necessary. We have some business to transact.'

As he spoke he led the way into a room on the left of the fairly wide hall. It was a shabbily furnished sitting room. On a bamboo table in its centre the Duke saw some papers and the flat leather case in which Douglas had brought the jewels to the Galle Face. Behind him the driver said:

'We have not said good evenings yet. You, I hope, remember me.'

Turning, he saw that the pseudo Indian had thrown aside his beard and turban, and was pulling off a loose cotton garment. It had hidden a smart belted uniform, and its owner added with a laugh, 'Colonel Lalita d'Azavedo of Ceylon Security Police at your service.'

'Good evening . . . Colonel,' de Richleau replied quietly. In spite of his eighty-five years his brain had lost none of its swiftness and in a matter of seconds this revelation made a number of things clear to him. As a senior secret police officer the younger d'Azavedo would have special facilities for checking up on people's movements and, as Mrs. Bandaranaike found it necessary to keep a score of armed men in her garden, it was certain that her Government would have placed spies in every hotel and as servants in the houses of scores of people who were believed to be disaffected. By these means d'Azavedo could easily have found out that the Rajapakses and Simon were all dining out that evening and had seen to it in some way that Max should not return to the hotel before the telephone call was put through.

After a moment he said, 'May I ask the reason for your having lured me here?'

'Very simple,' Ukwatte replied, pointing to the documents on the table. 'Here two copies of contract by which you return Olenevka to me, in exchange for twenty-five thousand pounds' worth cut stones. We bring you here for sign.'

De Richleau gave a puzzled frown. 'I have already agreed to the transaction, and Douglas Rajapakse is getting out a contract which will be ready tomorrow. Why have you gone to all this trouble to get me to sign it tonight? That is if the terms of the contract you have drawn up are straightforward, and there is no catch in it.'

'No, terms are same as they would be in Rajapakse's.'

'Then why . . .?'

'That my business,' d'Azavedo cut him short roughly. 'Come! Pen there. You sit down, sign.'

Taking up one of the documents the Duke read it through. He could see nothing wrong with it, except that the signatures of the two witnesses had already been written below the still blank space where the contracting parties were to sign; but common sense told him that the d'Azavedos would not have kidnapped him like this unless they intended to trick him in some way.

'How about the jewels?' he asked.

'Here are jewels.' Lalita unzipped the flat leather container, and the four hundred sapphires, rubies and topazes shimmered and glittered with a thousand rays of coloured light. 'Soon as you have signed we hand over.'

'What then?' enquired the Duke, his grey eyes sharp with suspicion. 'Will you let me go free, and arrange for me to be driven back to my hotel?'

'Yes. I drive you back myself,' replied Lalita cheerfully.

De Richleau could not possibly believe that they were being honest with him. Tapping the contract he said, 'I see no reason for this extreme urgency to settle our business. What can a few hours matter? I have promised to sign and I have never yet broken my word. But I prefer to sign an agreement drawn up by my own solicitor.'

'You going to sign here and now,' declared Ukwatte harshly.

'What if I refuse?'

The big man took a step towards him and his eyes held open hatred. 'Then it be very bad for you. Two years ago you do best to ruin me. For me very great pleasure to give you beatings-up. For me it suits that you sign tonight. Sign then you had better. You are very old man. Beatings-up very bad for you. Refuse to sign would be good excuse for me to lose temper.'

Leaning on his malacca cane, de Richleau's gaze never faltered as he held the eyes of the big, rough-looking, paunchy man who confronted him. But he knew d'Azavedo was right. At his age a single blow could kill him. After a moment his lips twitched in a smile. He made a little bow and said, 'Very well. You win.'

Sitting down at the table, he took up the fountain pen that was lying there and wrote his name at the foot of both copies of the contract. Ukwatte did likewise and gave one to Lalita, who put it in his pocket; the other he slid under the soft leather flap of the jewel case then, with a grin, zipped it up and handed it over. Slipping it into the big inner pocket of his heavy camel-hair overcoat de Richleau stood up, wondering with some apprehension what was going to happen next.

It came to him as no surprise when Ukwatte said, 'You not leave yet. I tell now what I plan.'

'I thought there was a catch in it somewhere,' replied the Duke calmly.

'Catch, yes.' The big coarse-featured man stared at him with hard malignant eyes. 'I not suppose you so big fool to think we got you here only to sign contract. But you were fool to think I give you stones worth seven-eight hundred thousan' rupees to get back Olenevka. Also by return to Ceylon you signs your own death warrant. You is going to die.'

'I have been expecting to die for some time.' De Richleau's voice never quavered. 'I am only interested to know in what way you propose to bring about my death.'

Ukwatte leaned forward. His lips parted in an ugly grin, showing his yellow teeth, and the Duke was unpleasantly conscious of his bad breath.

'Death planned for you is very painful. Unfortunate but no way to avoid. Lars' year death penalty reintroduce here. I take no risk—or of many years prison. Your death must look as accident. In back room here I have king cobra. We put you in room and leave rest to my snake.'

For the first time de Richleau paled slightly. A cobra's bite meant an agonising death, and he had always hoped that his end would be a relatively painless one. Moistening his lips, he said:

'You won't get away with this. The telephone call that lured me from the Galle Face will be traced. This contract that you have forced me to sign will be useless to you unless you have it ratified by the courts. Many people in Colombo know that you have grounds for wishing to be avenged on me. It will all add up. If you kill me it is a five to one chance that you will be tried for murder. Why take such a risk? You have got your contract. You would be on a much better wicket to keep the jewels and let me go.'

'No.' Ukwatte shook his dark head. 'You miss biggest-ever point. For contract to be valid you must receive stones. At least, for people to believe I give you. If not, you go to law on me for not fulfilling contract.'

'If you propose to bring about my death before I leave this house how can you possibly convince people that I did receive the jewels?'

'I have work that out,' Lalita put in with a sly grin. 'That you were willing to do deal on these lines has been known by several people for past few days. Rajapakse's office clerks, they draw up contract. One of my agents had good luck to see stones being shown you at the Galle Face Friday morning.

Why my father wished to complete deal quickly may be asked. For that we have explanation. He has to go up to Jaffna tomorrow. Call quite unexpected but on business very urgent. May be detained there some days; so not'ings much extraordinary that he telephone and ask you to come here to sign contract tonight. Just as you go to leave house you have bad luck to tread on serpent in garden. Sort of misfortune not unusual. Happens in Ceylon somewhere maybe once a week.'

'Very clever,' snapped the Duke sarcastically. 'But unless you leave the jewels on my dead body there will be no proof that I ever received them. And you will still be suspected of having arranged my death in order to retain them.'

'No,' Ukwatte snapped back. 'Cobra bite kill fast. Soon after he bite you, while you still alive but can speak no more we put you in car and Lalita drive you back to Galle Face. Jewel case will still be in pocket of your coat, but stones no longer in it. Lalita give help to get you up to your room while doctor is sent for. Tomorrow morning empty case found in your pocket, also your copy of contract signed by both party. Everyone then think that while you unconscious and dying a servant found case and stole stones. To make this all sure, Lalita has made arrangement. Floor waiter on your floor at Galle Face, he in our pay. Man will not know why, but for good big sum he ready to leave for a village long way upcountry. That he disappears make everyone think him be thief.'

For a moment de Richleau remained silent, striving to find a flaw in this damnably clever plot made possible only by d'Azavedo having offered jewels in payment for Olenevka instead of a cheque. Then he said, 'No, it won't wash. If everything had happened as you mean to represent it, and the whole affair been above board, your son would have come to fetch me openly, in the sort of car a Colonel would use. But he did not. To get me here he had to use a disguise. Apparently I am picked up by an Indian who cannot speak English. An Indian cannot take me back and give all the necessary explanations about how I came to be bitten by a snake. The Colonel must take me back as himself. But where has the Indian got to? People will want to know, and you won't be able to produce him. Once the Colonel appears on the scene he will have involved himself. But he still has a chance to keep out of this,

No one can prove that he was here tonight. If I were in his shoes, I would back out while there is still time. The best thing he can do is to run me back to within a quarter of a mile of the Galle Face, drop me there and make himself scarce.'

Lalita's dark face suddenly took on a greyish tinge. His eyes looked enormous through his thick spectacles. Turning to his father he exclaimed, 'Gautama defend me, he is right! We fail to foresee that when Indian driver cannot be found suspicions will be arouse. If I take Duke back someone perhaps guess it was I dress as Indian who pick him up. No! I not show face at the Galle Face tonight, or I will be in it up to neck. We must think; find some other way of disposing of body.'

Standing up, Ukwatte broke into a harsh tirade in Sinhalese; Lalita replied with equal anger. As de Richleau had hoped, he had set the son against the father, and for several minutes they quarrelled bitterly. Then it became obvious that Lalita refused to be coerced. At length he turned to de Richleau and exclaimed in English:

'You clever devil! I wish very much now my father let me do as you ask, so we are rid of you. But he say "No". Me, I get out. No one be able to say I am Indian who pick you up, or prove that in all this I take any part.' Turning on his heel he marched out of the room, slamming the door behind him.

De Richleau gave a heavy sigh. He had won half the battle for his life but he knew that he was very far from being out of the wood. To the glowering Ukwatte he said with a confidence he was far from feeling:

'When rogues fall out good men come into their own. So it remains only for me to point out to you that if you proceed with your idea of murdering me your chances of getting away with it are now more slender than ever. The contract that I have signed will prove completely valueless to you unless you admit that I came here tonight to sign it. Now that your son has ratted on you, how do you propose to get my still living body back to the Galle Face unless you drive it there yourself? And remember, the Indian who brought me here will still remain unaccounted for. You really would be well advised to keep the jewels and let me go.'

For a full minute Ukwatte remained silent, then he said, 'No. You would bring action to get them. To fulfil contract I have to give. Then I would be at great loss.'

'What if I gave my word not to bring a case?' suggested the Duke.

'I would not take. Once free you feel only urge to get back on me.'

With a calmness that he was not feeling, de Richleau shrugged. 'Without your son's help, how can you possibly hope to kill me and not be found out?'

Ukwatte stuck out his big chin. His black eyes were relentless. 'I have the cobra bite you as I planned,' he said thickly. 'I say the Indian have been a casual driver who was passing and I send for you. They fail to find him; what matter? You came here, signed contract. I say we leave house so I take you back to Galle Face in car. Then outside house you are bitten by snake. I wait little while. When you are past talking I telephone for doctor. No proof possible that in dark you did not step on snake.'

'It must take some time for the poison to take effect. The doctor will know that and, as you have a telephone, want to know why you didn't call him in at once.'

Ukwatte shook his head. 'No. Death from cobra bite quite quick; much quicker than from other snakes.'

'The jewels?' argued de Richleau desperately. 'Now that your son is out of this your plan about them breaks down. You won't be able to make it appear that I ever had them.'

'Yes, yes, I shall. They take you away with empty case in pocket. Nobody think to examine till morning. Inside will be copy of contract we both sign. But no stones, no. Everyone say then someone at hospital stole stones during the night.'

In vain the Duke racked his tired brain for further arguments that might deflect d'Azavedo from his awful purpose. If the worst came to the worst he was determined to make a fight for it. Better to be struck down and die of a heart attack than suffer the agony of a cobra bite. When younger he had been a fine swordsman and he grasped his malacca cane firmly, hoping that, if attacked, he might summon the strength and agility to lunge with it and plunge its end into one of d'Azavedo's eyes.

Suddenly the big paunchy man stood up. Exclaiming, 'Come! I put an end to this!' he lurched towards de Richleau. The Duke rose at the same moment, his cane came up but his aged limbs had lost their swiftness of action. In one fierce swipe d'Azavedo knocked the cane from his grasp, then seized him by the shoulders, swung him round and propelled him towards the door.

Out in the hall a faded velvet curtain hid the back of the premises. De Richleau was pushed through the division in its middle. Still grasping him with one hand d'Azavedo opened a door on the right. It gave on to a room that was not in complete darkness. Through slatted blinds moonlight lit it faintly, showing that it was empty except for a big wicker basket standing near the centre of the floor.

D'Azavedo gave the Duke a shove that sent him sprawling; then, taking a few steps forward, he gave the basket a violent kick that sent it over. A loud angry hiss came from it. Springing back he ran to the door, slammed and locked it.

As the Duke came to his knees he saw that the snake had emerged from the basket. The fact that it was about twelve feet long showed that it was indeed a king cobra, for the more common species rarely attains half that length. The bite of such a snake is so deadly that no antidote except vaccine has ever been found for it, and even that has to be injected quickly. The serpent's body, thick as a medium-sized hawser, slithered on the floor, swiftly forming into a coil. Its head reared up and the flat hood behind its neck distended. In the moonlight de Richleau could plainly see the strange white marking, like a pair of spectacles, on it. For a moment the evil head swayed from side to side while the brute's thin, forked tongue flickered in the distended jaws. The Duke was standing now; but only six feet from it. With another furious hiss the cobra drew back its head to strike and pour its deadly venom into the veins of its victim.

12

Simon Seeks Revenge

Simon did not get back to the Galle Face until after eleven, but the night porter recognised him at once and gave him the note that de Richleau had left for him. As he took in its contents he was filled with shocked concern. Then he saw that the Duke had scribbled a time at the bottom of the slip of paper—10.15. That meant he had been gone for the best part of an hour; but where? Next moment it occurred to Simon that in the past hour someone would have telephoned to the Rajapakses' home to let their head boy know about the accident that had befallen his master and mistress. Hurrying over to the porter's desk he picked up the telephone and got on to Douglas's house.

To his amazement it was Fleur who answered. For a few brief sentences they talked at cross purposes; then they got matters straight. She and Douglas had just got back from a pleasant dinner party; they had not been involved in any car smash and she had no idea who would have hoaxed the Duke, or why.

'Enough for now,' said Simon tersely. 'Coming round. Be with you shortly.'

People who had been dining out were still returning to the hotel; so Simon had to wait only a few minutes before the night porter was able to get him a taxi, and Douglas's house was not much more than a mile from the Galle Face. By half past eleven Simon was running up the steps to the verandah where Fleur and Douglas, having heard the engine of the taxi, were waiting at the open door to meet him.

'Who could possibly have played this filthy trick on dear Grandpa Greyeyes?' Fleur asked indignantly.

'Haven't a clue,' replied Simon a little breathlessly. 'And if you haven't I doubt it's being a trick. Joke I mean. Now I'll tell you. Seems to me more like dirty work.' Turning to Douglas, he added:

'Greyeyes is pretty rich. Worth holding to ransom. You must know the types of crime carried on in Colombo. Any local gangs who go in for the snatch racket?'

Douglas shook his sleek dark head. 'No. There's been a big increase in crime recently, owing to the deterioration of the police. Plenty of cases of robbery with violence. Mostly in the streets at night. Murders, too, in the poorer quarter. But it is primitive crime for immediate gain. Not the organised kind that is needed for kidnapping.'

'Then this is personal. Someone with a grudge against him.'

'Oh, come! Greyeyes hasn't an enemy in the world,' Fleur protested.

'He has,' Simon countered promptly. 'The d'Azavedos.'

'But the hatchet has been buried between them and him,' Douglas reasoned. 'He's agreed to sign the contract they want; so what would they stand to gain by getting hold of him like this?'

Simon made an impatient gesture. 'How should I know? But something. Fact that they tried to get him killed last time he was here shows they've no scruples. If they have got him this is a muddle, a really nasty muddle. Got to find out—and fast. Where do they live?'

'I don't know,' Douglas replied, 'but if they're on the telephone we'll soon get their address.'

As he spoke he ran back into the house and began to flick through the leaves of the telephone directory. A moment later, he cried, 'Here we are. D'Azavedo, Ukwatte. Jetavana, Timbirigasyaya Road. That's inland off the main road to Mount Lavinia. From the Galle Face we're half-way there already. It's not much more than a mile from here.'

Simon had kept his taxi. His eyes flickered towards it, then he said quickly, 'We'll go in your car. Might prove awkward having a witness.' They ran down the steps together, Douglas to get his car out of the garage, Simon to pay off his taxi. As Simon turned away he saw that Fleur was pulling on a coat that she had snatched from a stand in the hall.

Running back to her he said with a shake of his head, 'Ner. Can't have you in on this, ducks. Might be dangerous. But we'll want a torch. And Douglas's gun. He brought one to the Gale Face on Friday. Know where he keeps it?'

Fleur knew that there were times when Simon could not be argued with. After only a faint protest she hurried into Douglas's study and, a minute later, returned with a revolver and a large torch.

Simon took both, handling the gun gingerly as though it might bite him. He hated firearms. By then Douglas had brought the car round. As Simon turned towards it, Fleur suddenly pleaded:

'Oh, let me come! Please let me come! It's not fair to leave me here. I'll be in agony until I know that dear Greyeyes is safe.'

'Ner,' he said firmly. 'Sorry. Can't be done, duckie. Let you know the moment we find out what's been going on.'

Douglas had the door of the car open. Scrambling in, Simon handed him the revolver, keeping the torch himself. Next moment they were off.

The drive took them only a little over five minutes. Bright moonlight showed up the houses in Timbirigasyaya Road so clearly that the names on their gates could be seen. As Simon spotted Jetavana he said, 'Drive on a hundred yards before you pull up.'

Getting out, they hurried back to the house. There was a light over the front door and streaks of light came from a curtained bay window on its left. Tiptoeing up the short drive they tried to see into the room but there was no crack between the curtains large enough. The centre window was open at the top and for a couple of minutes they stood there listening intently, but no sound broke the silence.

Taking Douglas by the arm Simon drew him back then, still on tiptoe, led the way round to the rear of the house. There, a French window opened on to a small, untidy garden. Behind the window a Venetian blind had been lowered but its slats were only partially closed. Stepping up to the window, Simon endeavoured to peer between the slats but he could at first see only bars of moonlight on a bare floor, some of which streaked across what looked like a shapeless bundle. Putting his hands on either side of his face to concentrate his gaze he continued to peer at the dark hump. Suddenly he realised that it was a body.

'Oh God!' The cry came from his heart. 'The Duke! Those devils have killed him.'

Next moment he had thrown all his weight against the

French window. Its flimsy lock gave under the impact and he stumbled into the room. As he flashed on his torch, before he could focus it on the sprawled body its beam lit on the overturned basket. There came a loud angry hiss and the cobra reared up from beneath it.

Douglas was just entering the door. Over Simon's shoulder he saw the snake. 'Look out!' he gasped. 'It's a cobra.' Seizing Simon by the arm he dragged him back, then hastily shut the door.

'Let me go!' panted Simon. 'Let me go! De Richleau may still be alive. I've got to go in and get him.'

'You can't.' Douglas grasped Simon by the shoulders and held him back. 'He's dead already. A cobra's bite is fatal and kills quickly. You can't go in. I won't let you. It would be suicide.'

'Where's your gun?' Simon demanded. 'Give it me and I'll shoot the snake. He may not be past help. I've got to go in! I've got to!'

'I won't,' Douglas declared firmly. 'Unless you are a crack shot you wouldn't have a hope of hitting it. To try would be madness. A cobra can move like lightning. Its bite would kill you before I could reach a hospital and get back here with a serum.'

Tears were running down Simon's face. 'Oh God!' he sobbed. 'Just to think of it! My splendid friend. Dear, dear Greyeyes murdered by those fiends.' But he had ceased to struggle, and allowed Douglas to lead him back round the side of the house.

When they reached the drive Douglas said, 'We must get the police. They'll deal with the d'Azavedos. That is, if they are still in the house. I think they must be; or if not they'll return shortly. They'll not dare risk leaving the body to be discovered where it is, so will have planned some means of disposing of it before daylight.'

Suddenly Simon ceased sobbing and gulped. 'You're right. All the odds are they're there and only waiting till it's certain that de Richleau's dead. But to hell with the police. This is my affair. I'm going in to get them.'

Douglas's coat hung open and the moonlight now glinted dully on the butt of the revolver, which he had thrust into the top of his trousers. Simon had caught sight of it and, snatching the weapon, turned towards the house.

Again Douglas seized him by the arm. 'No! For God's sake, man!' he pleaded urgently. 'Think what you'd be letting yourself in for.'

'What do I care?' Simon's eyes were black with anger and he was trembling with emotion. 'They killed my friend. The finest man I've ever known.'

'But they are probably armed. Maybe they'll get you. At best, if you kill one or both of them it will be murder. That they killed the Duke will be no defence. Your grief has driven you crazy. It's lunacy to risk throwing away your life like this when the police can get them for you.'

'The police!' Simon sneered. 'Young d'Azavedo's pals. They're no better than the Nazis. They'll cover up for him. If I don't get them, no one will. And I mean to. Now you keep out of this.'

When driven to it Simon could be a very tricky customer. In one swift movement he wrenched himself free and shot out his left hand. It caught Douglas on the chest and the violent push sent him sprawling backwards into some bushes. Next moment Simon had mounted the verandah steps and was at the front door.

Instinctively he grasped the knob and turned it. To his surprise the door was not locked. Easing it further open, he peered inside. A single low-power bulb in a cheap glass shade lit the hall rather dimly. It was about seven feet wide and fifteen deep. There was a door on either side and at the far end a pair of worn velvet curtains shut off the back of the premises. Stepping cautiously into the hall he pushed the front door to, but not quite shut, behind him, then advanced a few paces almost noiselessly. Ahead of him the door on the left was ajar and the room beyond it lit. It must, he knew, be that with the bay window. Holding his breath, he listened. Still no sound came from it.

Seething with inward fury as he was, and obsessed with the idea of avenging de Richleau at the earliest possible moment, his mind remained clear. He was acutely aware that he was pitting himself against at least one extremely dangerous man, and perhaps two—if the son had aided his father in bringing about the Duke's death—and that either of them was likely to prove more able than himself in handling weapons. Therefore, his chances would be less than even unless he could take them by surprise.

Soundly, he reasoned that while waiting for de Richleau to be quite dead they would not have left the house, but have gone upstairs to their rooms and were probably lying there on their beds. If so he might catch one of them napping and shoot him before he had a chance to get to his feet. The sound of the shot would bring the other running but, with luck, he might be ambushed from behind the door and shot as he entered the room.

To get upstairs without being heard was going to be the difficulty, because it was unlikely that they would be sound asleep. The first obstacle was the velvet curtain, as the staircase to the upper floor was obviously behind it and it hung on brass rings which, if moved incautiously, would make a clatter. Simon decided that he must risk that, and that if he was very careful he could ease his way between the curtains without the rings making more than a faint tinkle. Again he advanced on tiptoe, but when he came opposite the door from which the light was showing, he halted.

It had just occurred to him that the man or men he meant to kill might not be upstairs but in there dozing. If they were and he chanced to stumble in the dark behind the curtain as he started up the stairs they might hear him, come out and take him in the rear. To insure against that he had to make certain that the room was empty.

Cocking the revolver he held it at the ready. He would have liked to thrust the door wide open, but dared not in case it gave a loud creak and roused anyone upstairs. His mouth was dry and his heart hammering wildly from the realisation that in the next few moments he might have to kill or be killed. But his resolution never wavered. He gave the door a gentle push. To his relief it swung open a couple of feet quite noiselessly and no sound of sudden alarm came from inside.

As a large part of the room became swiftly revealed to him he suppressed a gasp of mingled excitement and triumph. At the far end of the room some twelve feet from where he stood there was a high-backed armchair, It faced away from him but in it lay sprawled an elderly man, evidently asleep. Only the top of his head could be seen, a bald patch surrounded by some long whitish ruffled hair, and one arm that hung limply over the left arm of the chair. Simon had never met Ukwatte d'Azavedo but he had not the least doubt about the sleeper's identity, and he now had him at his mercy. It now seemed fairly certain, too, that he had only one enemy with whom to deal. Lalita might be upstairs, though it was more likely that he would have remained with his father; but perhaps he had left the house, or had not even been there and had had no hand in the foul plot to do away with de Richleau.

The thought of taking human life had always sickened Simon. In the past the Duke had never sought to disguise the fact that he derived pleasure from hunting and killing people who, if given a chance, would have killed him; Rex had maintained that one was justified in ridding the world of evil men; and Richard, with practical good sense, had often said, 'I don't want to die yet; so if anyone gets in the way of a bullet from me, that's his look-out.' But Simon had never got over his revulsion at the thought of taking human life.

Even now, with raging hatred in his heart, he felt his stomach turning over at the idea of shooting d'Azavedo in his sleep, from behind and in cold blood. Yet, as he visualised again the tortured end of his friend, writhing for minutes that must have seemed endless as the venom of the cobra boiled in his blood, he steeled himself to go through with this awful business.

Raising the revolver he took careful aim at the bald patch on his enemy's head. But his hand was shaking and his spectacles misting over. Impatiently he shook his head. Whatever happened he must not make a mess of things. If he missed and d'Azavedo was armed he might yet be shot himself. To make more certain of his aim he took two cautious steps forward.

Doing so gave him a fuller view of the sleeping man's arm dangling over the side of the chair. He could now see the hand. It was not brown, but white, slim, long-fingered, fragile and had a gold signet ring on the little finger.

Simon's mouth fell open, but no cry came from it. Dropping his gun, he ran forward. The hand could only be that of de Richleau. Next moment he was kneeling beside the armchair, clutching the awakened figure in it and sobbing wildly:

'Oh God, you're safe! I thought they'd murdered you. But you're alive! Alive! Thank God! And I was about . . . about to shoot you. If I'd pressed the trigger I . . . I'd have killed you myself. Oh, thank God! Thank God!'

'Simon, dear Simon,' de Richleau put one arm round his friend's shoulders and with the other stroked his dark hair. 'Calm yourself, my son, calm yourself. Yes, I've had a very narrow escape. But why were you about to shoot me?'

'We guessed you were here,' Simon blurted out. 'Rajapakse and I. We broke into the back room, saw a body on the floor. Thought it was you, then were driven off by a snake. I came round the front. Meant to get those bastards even if I swung for it. Only saw the back of your head and jumped to it that you were old d'Azavedo.'

The Duke gave a low laugh. 'So you came in to avenge my death. And you are always telling people that you lack courage. What nonsense, dear Simon. But where is Douglas?'

'Left him outside,' Simon replied. 'He's still there, I expect. Must let him know you're safe.' Getting to his feet, he ran from the room and out to the front door.

Against the possibility that Simon might need to make a quick get-away, Douglas had collected his car from further along the road and was now sitting in it outside the house. On seeing Simon he pressed the self-starter and called, 'Praise be you didn't use that gun. Come on! Let's get out of this.'

'Had no need,' Simon called back, halting on the verandah. 'The d'Azavedos aren't here. But de Richleau is and, believe it or not, I found him asleep. Come along in.'

Scrambling out of the car, Douglas hurried up the drive and asked, 'If the Duke is safe, whose body did we see in the back room?'

'Don't know, but de Richleau may,' Simon replied, as he led the way back into the sitting room.

When Douglas had expressed his delight at the Duke's being safe and sound, he said, 'Mr. Aron was convinced we would find you here; but as you had agreed to the d'Azavedos' proposition about Olenevka I've been puzzling my wits in vain for a reason why they should have wished to get hold of you.'

De Richleau told them about the d'Azavedos' plot to secure the mine without giving up their jewels, then how he had partially upset their plans by scaring Lalita but that had not saved him from being pushed by Ukwatte into the room with the cobra.

At that, Simon exclaimed, 'Heavens! Even you can't often have been nearer death. How in the world did you save yourself?'

'Old soldiers never die,' quoted de Richleau with a smile. 'I owe my survival in this case to having once been a soldier; although the use of physical weapons did not enter into it. I must long ago have told you how, as a young officer in the French Army, owing to my having come upon proof that Dreyfus was innocent I attracted to myself the enmity of the Minister of War[1] who would have been ruined had the truth come out. In consequence I was sent to do garrison duty on Madagascar and remained in exile there for over two years.'

Simon nodded. 'I remember. And you found life in that primitive island so utterly boring that you made friends with the witch-doctors. Took up magic and made a serious study of it.'

'Yes. The Malagesy, being largely of Polynesian extraction and partly Negro, enjoy knowledge of the secret arts as practised both in the Pacific and in Africa; so they have a greater understanding of what we term the supernatural than any other occultists in the world. Among other attributes their medicine men have inherited the means of exerting power over snakes, and that was among the things I learned from them.'

'So you managed to charm the snake?'

'Hardly that. I had so little time that I really thought my end had come. But an angry snake can be calmed if one has the courage to extend one's hand with two fingers pointing downward over its head. Why that gesture should have such an effect I have no idea. No doubt willing the snake not to strike is the real secret. But that is what I did, and it worked. For a few minutes the reptile continued to sway its head and hiss at me, then it relaxed, sank down and went to sleep.'

'And then?'

'I too lay down. Knowing that d'Azavedo would return to collect the jewels and dispose of my body, I shammed dead. In due course he came in, threw the cobra a chicken, then bent down over me. Having mustered all my strength, I reared up and struck him a single judo blow on the neck with the side of my hand. It was well aimed and got him right on the jugular vein. He collapsed on top of me. I heaved him off, succeeded in pulling him to his knees and gave him a shove that sent him backward right on top of the cobra just as it had begun to lick the chicken. Then I stumbled from the room and locked him in.'

'So it was his body we saw.'

De Richleau chuckled. 'Yes, and I'm glad to have your

1. See *The Prisoner in the Mask.*

confirmation that the snake bit him. I felt pretty sure it had because if it hadn't he would have come round after a few minutes and I'd have heard him trying to break out. By now he must be as near dead as makes no matter and it gives me considerable pleasure to know that he met with the terrible end he intended for me.'

'But why,' Douglas asked, 'having outwitted them, did you remain here?'

'Alas, I'm not the man I was, my friend. I'm no longer strong enough to walk the two or three miles it must be back to the Galle Face. And so late at night there would be very little chance of my getting a lift.'

Simon pointed to the telephone that stood nearby on a small, hardwood table. 'You could have telephoned me. Why on earth didn't you?'

The Duke shook his head. 'No, my son. You would have come out here in a hired car. We would then have been faced with a most unpleasant dilemma. Either we would have had to go straight to the police and tell them the whole story, or risk d'Azavedo's death being followed by an enquiry, and my being suspected in connection with it, owing to the driver reporting that he picked me up here in the middle of the night.'

'As your lawyer I must advise you to go straight to the police anyhow,' said Douglas firmly. 'Ukwatte's death has no relevance to the fact that the d'Azavedos lured you from your hotel on false pretences, then used threats of violence to force you to sign a document. Your proper course is to bring an action against Lalita, as the surviving partner in this criminal conspiracy.'

De Richleau shook his head. 'No, thank you. The fact that you found me in this house is no proof that I was lured here. It is known by several people that I had already agreed to sign such a document and I have the jewels which were to be my consideration for so doing. As a Colonel in the Security Service Lalita must have considerable pull with all sorts of influential people. Such an action against him would get us nowhere. It would serve only as an admission that I was in this house at approximately the time Ukwatte met his death.'

'Concerning that you have nothing to fear. The natural assumption will be that Ukwatte left you in this room and went to give his snake its meal, then it bit him.'

'I would you were right,' the Duke gave a tired sigh. 'But if a full inquiry is started a very different picture will emerge. It will be seen at once that Ukwatte has a big bruise on his neck, owing to the congestion of blood in his jugular vein from the judo blow I struck him. No fall or accident could have caused that; only a human agency. Once we admit that I was here tonight, Lalita will declare, and quite truthfully, that he left me alone with his father. The odds are that on leaving here he went to some place where he has friends or acquaintances who will vouch for his presence with them for the remainder of the night. In any case there is no reason why he should not be believed. Who else then but myself could have struck Ukwatte unconscious and left him at the mercy of the cobra? It is true enough that he planned to kill me, but the fact is that I killed him; and I've no wish to be tried for murder.'

Simon's head bobbed up and down like that of a nodding china Mandarin. 'Um, I get you. Got to keep the police out of this. No way we could explain away that bruise on Ukwatte's neck. We'd be in a muddle, a really nasty muddle. But what did you intend to do?'

'Doze here till daylight, when there would be people about. Then go out and walk as far as a main street where I could pick up some form of transport. No one except Lalita would then ever have known that I had been near this place. And unless he was prepared to divulge that he had participated in a criminal conspiracy he would not dare say that I had. Even were he prepared to face that, it would be only his word against mine.'

Douglas still looked worried and he said, 'These things have a nasty way of coming out unexpectedly. Honestly, I feel you would be wiser to let me ring up the police, tell them the whole truth, enter an action against Lalita and plead that while you were struggling with Ukwatte to save yourself from the cobra he tripped and fell on the snake.'

A gentle smile twitched the Duke's lips. 'I'm sure, Douglas, that you have my best interests at heart. But you must leave me to be the judge of how to protect myself against a charge of murder. I killed Ukwatte as surely as though I had put a bullet through his brain; and at my age I could not stand up to hours of grilling by detectives. To escape that I must get back to the Galle Face. If the question of my having gone out soon after ten o'clock ever arises, I could say that by arrangement I went to meet Simon, as I will be returning with him. But all the odds are that, unless Lalita is so ill-advised as to accuse me, no one will even think of connecting me with his father's death.'

'You're right,' agreed Simon. 'Sooner we get out of here the better. I wonder though that you didn't make yourself scarce immediately you'd dealt with Ukwatte. If Lalita had come back and found you still here, you'd have been for the high jump.'

The Duke gave an abrupt laugh. 'I had little fear of that. I had made him too scared of becoming involved in my murder. There is every reason to assume that he will allow ample time for his father to devise some means of disposing of my body; so it is most unlikely that he will return until tomorrow.'

They all stood up and, with de Richleau leading, walked out into the hall. The front door was still ajar, as Douglas had left it. He drew it open. With sudden shock it impinged on his mind that de Richleau's statement a moment before might be counted among '*famous last words*'.

Outside on the verandah Lalita was standing. The moonlight glinted on the thick lenses of his spectacles and in his hand he held a heavy automatic.

13

Battle of Wits

As Douglas pulled the door open he had stepped aside for the Duke, and Simon was only a pace behind de Richleau, so the three of them were bunched together. Lalita stood pointing the gun at them from about six feet away; too far off for there to be any hope of rushing him. His slack mouth broke into a grin and he said:

'I catch you nicely. Recognising Mr. Rajapakse's car tell me that he, and perhaps others, come to rescue the old gentlemans. How lucky that I come back with new plan regarding him. I have only to wait here for you come out. Hands up, all of you, and inside. Be quick.'

As he spoke, he thrust forward his pistol. Under the threat they retreated to the middle of the hall. Following them he pushed-to the door behind him, then snapped, 'Now, form line. Turn round. Backs towards me.'

When they had obeyed him he jabbed his weapon against de Richleau's spine. 'You move, or your friends, and I shoot.' With his left hand he quickly frisked the Duke, and from the way he did so it was clear that since he had become a Security Officer he knew his business. While repeating the procedure with the other two, he removed Douglas's revolver from Simon's trouser top and thrust its barrel inside the belt of his uniform tunic.

His next orders were, 'Advance now to curtains. Turn to face me. Hands you may put down.' When they had obeyed him he walked forward until he was within two paces of them, so that he could look into the sitting room. Seeing that it was empty he said:

'My father? You catch him off guard, eh? Then tie him up. Where you put him?'

It was de Richleau who replied, 'You will recall that it was his intention to put me in the back room with the cobra.'

Lalita's eyes narrowed. He was making no admission before witnesses, so he said cautiously, 'This is strange statement you make.'

'Well,' said the Duke, 'he did. But instead of biting me it bit him.'

'Aiee!' Lalita's mouth dropped open and from it there issued a strange wail of mingled grief and shock. His muscles tautened as though he had been hit, then suddenly relaxed, causing the hand that held the heavy automatic to droop. Seeing that the pistol now pointed toward the floor both Douglas and Simon seized their chance. Before Lalita had time to recover they simultaneously threw themselves upon him.

The ensuing struggle was so brief that it was over in a matter of seconds. Douglas flung his arms about Lalita. Simon grabbed his gun hand, gave his wrist a sharp twist and tore the weapon from him. Thrusting him against the wall, Douglas then recovered his own revolver and, seeing that Simon had Lalita covered, struck it back in his trouser band.

De Richleau had taken a few steps towards the door. Turning, he said to Lalita, 'It is your turn now to listen while we talk to you. Get over there with your back to the curtain.'

'My father!' gasped Lalita, still panting from the recent scrimmage, as he moved over. 'Oh, what have you do? Is he . . . is he dead?'

The Duke nodded. 'As he was bitten at least half an hour ago he must certainly be beyond aid by now. But if you wish to make sure we will put you in there with him.'

'No! Please! No; no!' Lalita wailed. 'I meant no harm. I do nothings against you. I refuse help my father. Leave house. You know it.'

'Yes. You ratted on your charming parent. But only to save your own skin. It was you who lured me from the Galle Face.'

Lalita rallied suddenly. 'You cannot prove. I make no admissions I was ever here.'

'Naturally.' A cynical smile twitched de Richleau's lips. 'And you were very wise to have backed out of assisting your father to murder me. Had you remained and done so, instead of him tripping up and falling on the cobra it might have been you who met with such a fatal accident. But you have been very foolish to return. Although it might be difficult to trace the telephone call you made to me and identify you with the Indian who picked me up, if I liked to charge you with having abducted me, both Mr. Aron and Mr. Rajapakse can now swear to it that they found me in this house, and that later you arrived and held the three of us up with your pistol.'

'I should say it mus' be my father who telephone. That I know nothings of it. That I come to see him, find you here and thought you was burglars.'

'Very clever. But I still feel I could make a case that you would find difficult to answer. However, it is your good fortune that I am averse to involving myself in a criminal action which might lead to my being detained in Ceylon for some time as the principal witness. So we will draw a veil over this night's work. It remains only for you to throw a hearty meal to the cobra then, when it is sleeping it off, remove your father's body, tell your neighbours that his pet snake bit him and make arrangements for his funeral.'

Lalita nodded dully. 'Yes, that I mus' do. For he is dead, dead! To realise is hard yet.' For a moment he remained silent. Then suddenly his dark eyes behind the heavy spectacles lit up and he gave a pale smile. 'But he made you sign contract. I inherit. Olenevka is now mine.'

'Don't be too certain. Where is your copy of the contract?'

'In safe place.' Lalita's smile deepened. 'You see my father give me, to take away. I take to my office and put in safe. Contract already witness by two mens very reliable to me. All in order. No use you demanding back. I claim deeds; firm of Rajapakse have to give.'

'To that I can see no objection,' remarked Douglas tartly, 'or what you have to look so pleased about. Your vile plot was aimed at getting both Olenevka and keeping the jewels. Instead you are having to give up the jewels and you have lost your father.'

'Aiee!' The strange wail came again from Lalita. For a moment his features were contorted with hate and rage, then he cried, 'My father! Yes! That he is dead, the shock drives all sense from my head. The contract was never meant to be fulfil both ways. The stones were bait only. Shown only so that later people believe we give them you as paying for Olenevka, but they worth more; much more.'

Simon tittered into his hand. 'Case of the trickster tricked, isn't it?'

'You think very funny,' snarled Lalita. 'But I not sit down for this. Stones are property of d'Azavedos. Now myself. You leave house with them and I charge you with theft.'

De Richleau shook his head. 'They are not the property of the d'Azavedos, and they never have been. They are the stones that should have been handed over to my representative after a verdict was given against your father in the Court of Appeal. The very fact of your father possessing such a hoard shows the story of their having been looted at the time your workshop was burned out to be a pack of lies. In fact he admitted that tonight and boasted to me of the clever trick he had played in order to retain them.'

'And why not?' Lalita sneered. 'It pleased him, I guess, to have last laugh at you; although idea of using riots for purpose of keeping our fortune in stones was mine.'

Actually, Ukwatte had made no mention of the fire and the Duke's saying he had was just a clever bluff by which he had hoped to secure an admission from Lalita. And it had come off. Glancing at his friends he said, 'You see. He admits that the stones are my property.'

Lalita gave a quick shrug. 'No matter. What has been said here makes nothings different. Word of you and your friends against mine; no proof. No proof whatevers. As for contract I not use now. I tear up. Olenevka I lose; but stones of much greater value I keep.' The case showed as a large oblong bulge at the left side of the Duke's overcoat. Pointing to it, Lalita added, 'You have stones there. Give me back. Then you all go and much riddance.'

'No,' replied de Richleau. 'I'm keeping them as a small remuneration for their having very nearly cost me my life.'

Again Lalita shrugged. 'Then you behave very foolish and ask for much trouble. How you get stones, eh? Not as payment for mine. Contract I scrap. Come. You hand over or I go to police. Charge you as thief and you go to prison.'

'Not so fast,' Simon put in. 'There's the other copy of the contract. The one that's with the jewels. Tear yours up if you like; but you can't wriggle out of the deal that way. His Grace's copy is all that's needed to prove it took place.'

For a moment Lalita appeared to be nonplussed; then his dark face took on a sly look. 'Witnesses who sign blanks are my men; very reliable. You produce contract, I say witnesses who are they? Describe please. Duke has never seen, so cannot. Then I say, he get hold of these men's names and for bad ends forge them. Police send for men, very reliable. They say as I tell them. These writing very like ours, but not. Never seen contract, never seen Duke. These forgeries.'

Douglas gave de Richleau an unhappy look. 'I'm afraid we are up against it, sir. I don't doubt he's got a score of men under him who'd swear to anything he told them to. We know the jewels are yours by rights, but we can't possibly prove it; so if you go off with them——'

'Neither can he prove that I took them,' the Duke cut in sharply. 'Nor that any of us have ever been here tonight. He dare not go to the police at all without risking the part he played in the conspiracy to murder me coming to light. No, I have the jewels and I mean to keep them.'

Turning to Lalita, he added:

'Moreover, should you attempt to make use of the contract your father extorted from me, I warn you I shall contest it; and I've good reason to believe that the case will go in my favour. You may count yourself lucky that I'm not bringing a charge against you for kidnapping. And now, since there is nothing else to discuss, we will be going.'

Simon had been holding Lalita's automatic at the ready ever since he had secured it. Now, he thrust it into his trouser top and, together with the Duke and Douglas, turned towards the front door.

At that moment a woman's voice came from behind them, 'One moment. I've got you covered. Stay where you are and put hands up.'

Taken entirely by surprise, all three of them halted in their tracks as though momentarily frozen. Then they slowly raised their hands and looked over their shoulders. The velvet curtains near which Lalita was standing had parted and between them stood a tall, good-looking woman in a blue and gold sari. She was pointing a small, nickel-plated revolver at them. De Richleau recognised her immediately as the coffee-coloured beauty with the widely spaced eyes who, when he had been up at Olenevka, had played the part of housekeeper, and whom he had believed to be Ukwatte's mistress—Mirabelle de Mendoza.

She spoke swiftly to Lalita, 'Get their guns. They snatch your gun so quick, too late for me to come to your help then. And after, I not risk to show myself while the Jewish one had your own pistol pointing at you. But now we've got them; and I have much to tell you.'

Lalita gave a cry of triumph. 'Mirabelle! Oh, blessings! Now I have witness that they try to rob me. One moment only while I get the stones back; also my pistol.

'O.K., *ma belle*!' he went on gleefully, as he stepped forward, relieved Douglas of his revolver and stuck it in his belt. Then he took his own automatic from Simon and, keeping it in his right hand, pulled the jewel case out of de Richleau's pocket with the other. Glancing at Mirabelle, he said, 'What now? What have you to tell me?'

Instead of answering him she addressed the others. 'You may put your hands down now. Turn round and all go into sitting room. I have been standing behind this curtain long time, and I wish to sit down.'

As they obeyed her and filed past Lalita into the room, de Richleau gave her an uneasy glance. He had a shrewd suspicion about what she might be going to tell Lalita and, if he were right, a new and extremely dangerous situation would result. One of Simon's favourite phrases came into his mind: 'We're going to be in a muddle; a really nasty muddle.'

Lalita, gesturing with his automatic, lined up his captives at the far end of the room. With the slinky walk that de Richleau well remembered, the lady swayed gracefully to the armchair in which Simon had found the Duke, sat down and relaxed. As Lalita had them covered, she laid her small revolver down on the lower shelf of the small table on which stood the telephone, then helped herself to a cigarette from a box that also stood on it. After taking a few puffs she said in a lazy voice:

'These people tell you lies, Lalita. Poor Ukwatte did not die through accident. He told me to go to bed soon after ten o'clock, and stay there. As always, I obey him. I ask no questions and soon I am asleep. My room, you know, is above that in which Ukwatte have put his cobra. Presently I awake. I hear sounds of breaking in below me. I think, whatever Ukwatte intend to do this is not part of it. I get up, put on my sari, get my little gun from the drawer and come downstairs to find out what happens.

'From behind the curtain I hear voices, but not that of Ukwatte. Also they speak in English. I strain the ears to listen and I hear what they say. I learn with shock that Ukwatte has been bitten by the cobra; that he is dead. I was, you know, quite fond of your father.'

Mirabelle paused a moment, then her rich lips parted in a smile and she went on, 'Do not mistake me. I had not love for him as I have for you. But I am much upset. I listen then still more intently with hope to hear how this accident happens and why these men break into our house. They are talking of your father's death. The Sinhalese gentleman—it must have been him from sound of his voice—he wishes to call for the police. But the others would not let him. The old man—he is the great English Lord, you remember, who come to Olenevka—he said, "No, if the police come they will find out that I killed him." '

'What you say?' Lalita exclaimed. 'This cannot be. He is so old; very feeble. He has not the strength.'

'It was not in a fight. He is a clever one, and dangerous; a *bhikkhu* with mystic powers. For your father he prepared a cunning trap. This is what he tell his friends. Ukwatte left him with the cobra. He charmed it into sleep. Then he lays down and make sham that he is dead. When Ukwatte return to take away his body he rouse up, strike him violent blow on neck, push him onto the snake and run from the room. The blow have leave a bruise that will betray him. That is why he says "We must not have police here. If we do I shall be charge with murder." '

Lalita's dark face glowed with excitement. His voice came in a trembling whisper of unalloyed triumph. 'Murder! Murder! And you have heard him admit.'

Mirabelle nodded. 'The bruise will give proof of it.' She stretched out a hand to the telephone. 'I will get the police.'

'Wait, madame!' cried the Duke. 'Wait, or you may regret it. Things will not go as smoothly as you think. You said just now that you loved Lalita d'Azavedo. His father tried to murder me. Lalita too was in the plot. I shall plead self-defence and, whether I am judged guilty or not, he will not escape. You will be condemning the man you love to several years in prison.'

'That is true,' Douglas added quickly. 'If you bring the police here they will make a full inquiry. They will take statements from Mr. Aron and myself. How did we come to be here? We came because we had reason to believe that His Grace was here and being held against his will. Why did he come here? We can produce his copy of the contract and will state that he was forced to sign it under duress. The telephone call by which he was lured from his hotel can perhaps be traced. Who brought him? An Indian driver who cannot be found. Where was Lalita d'Azavedo between half past ten and half past eleven tonight? Has he an alibi? How did His Grace get into the room with the cobra? No! The whole thing reeks of conspiracy. Unless you wish to see your friend condemned for complicity in attempted murder you dare not call the police.'

Faced with this potent argument, Mirabelle's forehead creased in an anxious frown; but Lalita's eyes were glowing with an almost insane hatred, and he snarled, 'These are all supposings. I am not fool. The telephone call to hotel will not be trace; I make from box. And I have alibi. How Duke got here no matter. Motive quite clear. He come here to steal stones shown him on Friday. Then surprise by my father and murder him. Also I have influence; much influence. I am Colonel of Security Police. People believes me, not you.'

'No,' Simon countered. 'In some things, perhaps; but not all. Too much mud for some of it not to stick.'

'Then I take risk. Odds all with me. I not give up chance to avenge my father.'

De Richleau needed no telling that he was in one of the worst corners that he had ever been in in his long and adventurous life. Mirabelle had overheard even more than he had thought likely of his conversation with Simon and Douglas, and as she had told her story his fears for himself had steadily mounted. Feeling confident that, if it came to a trial, he could show himself to have been trapped by a plot, he did not believe that he would be convicted of murder; but he might be of manslaughter. Even if he got off altogether, to have to face such a trial was an ordeal to be dreaded, particularly at his age. In consequence, while he was still determined to do his utmost to get the better of Lalita, he felt that it would be wiser to throw 'a sop to Cerberus' rather than to leave him minded to seek revenge whatever the risk to himself. So he said:

'If you have me brought to trial it is quite possible that I shall be found "not guilty". And you may be certain that I shall leave nothing undone to prove that you planned my murder. For such a gamble do you really think it worth the risk that you may ruin your career and instead become a convict? Cannot we reach a compromise? What if I agreed to make you some compensation for your father's death?'

The fury drained from Lalita's eyes and cupidity took its place. Slowly he nodded. 'You buy me off? Give blood-money like ancient custom, eh?'

Simon, also realising the great danger in which de Richleau now stood, nodded vigorously. 'Um. Much the best way to settle this.' Then, knowing that the Duke set no great store by retaining the mine, he added, 'How about your claiming Olenevka and His Grace refraining from revealing that the contract was extorted from him?'

The Duke made no comment on this suggestion. He had been prepared to part with a few thousand pounds as the price of getting out of his dangerous situation; but for a reason he could not disclose at the moment it would have suited him much better if Lalita, excited and overwrought as he still was by his father's death, failed to spot the snag in Simon's offer and accepted it.

But in that he was to be disappointed. A sudden frown again crossed Lalita's sloping forehead, and he exclaimed, 'But no! Is not good for me. To make contract valid I must give stones. More, much more than Olenevka is worth. You try to make fool of me. Not'ings doing. We leave stones out of this.'

After taking the jewels from the Duke, Lalita had laid the case down on the table and, had he fallen into the trap, de Richleau had not intended to draw his attention to it by attempting to walk off with the jewels there and then; but he would have been able to sue Lalita for their return, with a good hope of getting them back later. Now, he could only protest:

'They are my property. You have admitted that you and your father withheld them by a criminal act.'

Lalita shook his head. 'No matter. Possession they say nine points of law. Use contract and give you right to them, not likely. You find some way I have Olenevka as blood-money, no strings attached. If not I call police.'

They seemed to have reached an impasse; but Douglas, now convinced that for the Duke to allow himself to be charged might have most terrible results, stepped into the breach with a suggestion, 'I think that could be arranged. His Grace could make Olenevka over to you by a Deed of Gift.'

Simon was equally anxious to see the Duke out of it, whatever the cost. Eagerly he nodded, 'Um. Good idea. Very good idea.'

'Maybe yes; maybe no.' Lalita's eyes narrowed. 'People's not make big gift without good reason. Father, relative, rich patron, yes. But Duke not like this to me. Without good reason perhaps he repudiate later.'

Douglas shook his head. 'In law a deed is a deed. No motive is required for it, and it could not be repudiated afterwards.'

'I am not lawyer. In you why should I trust? No fear. We do this, yes. But only with good reason, to make all seem right.'

The Duke gave a contemptuous laugh. 'As soon raise your father from the dead as find a good reason why I should present you with a fortune. You can go to hell.'

De Richleau's apparent blindness to his peril filled Simon and Douglas with the utmost perturbation. Both of them racked their brains in vain for some means of meeting Lalita's demand. While tense moments drifted by the silence could be felt.

Then Mirabelle, who had been following the conversation with lazy interest, said quietly, 'It was the will that start all these troubles. The English Lord say it was forged. He goes to the law and wins; so we are turn out. But perhaps he was wrong from beginning. Say he finds out that he make terrible mistake. Great injustice done d'Azavedo family. As honest man he wish to put right.'

'Um,' Simon acclaimed her idea enthusiastically. 'Lady's got something there.'

Douglas, too, seized on it eagerly and turned to Lalita. 'Yes. His Grace could send a letter to that effect to the papers and that would put you in the clear. There ought to be some mention in it, though, about where this new evidence has come from that the will was not a forgery.'

After thinking for a minute Lalita said, 'That I provide. To the will there was two witnesses: Pedro Fernando and wife Vinala. He is dead, she disappear. Not heard of since. She long time make home in some jungle village, I expect, under other name. Never come back from fear of trouble. You say she writes letter telling she now dying. No address but just telling that Pedro was liar. Will not forged but all proper.'

Simon and Douglas both sighed with relief. 'That would do,' said the latter. 'Couldn't be better. Now if you have some paper I will draft the Deed of Gift and His Grace will sign it.'

'No,' declared the Duke firmly. 'I will not. That is unless the jewels are returned to me. I will give up either the estate or the jewels to make an end of this business. But I'm damned if I'll let this rogue get away with both.'

Lalita rounded on him furiously. 'It was you who first suggest give me blood-money. What then? You leads up garden path by let your friends talk, talk, talk. Arguments no more. I will not have. Rajapakse writes Deed of Gift. Now at once. You sign, and your friends witness. This you do or I send for police.'

'Now wait a minute,' Simon said urgently, grasping de Richleau by the arm. 'He's got us. You must let Douglas draw the deed and put your signature to it. No other way out.'

'Oh yes there is,' the Duke retorted. 'Let him call the police and I'll face the music. He's in this thing up to the neck and he knows it. I'm going to call his bluff.'

'You daren't! You're crazy. If he isn't bluffing you wouldn't stand a chance.'

'I don't agree,' de Richleau turned to Douglas. 'You are my legal adviser. What is your opinion?'

Douglas gave him an unhappy look. 'The charge would be manslaughter, not murder. If the circumstances were normal I think we'd get you off. But they are not. Public sympathy would be with him, because he is Sinhalese, and he has a lot of pull. So you would be taking a big risk. As far as he is concerned I have no doubt at all that we could get him a heavy sentence for conspiracy. But that wouldn't do you any good if a verdict of manslaughter were given against you.'

Simon's eyes were flickering wildly. 'That's just it. Of course you'd like to land him in the bin; but to do it would mean cutting off your nose to spite your face. Besides, you can't have realised what you'd be letting yourself in for. Once you're charged they'll put you in prison. Perhaps Douglas could get you bailed, but perhaps not. Anyhow, even a night or two could prove too much for you. At your age you couldn't stand up to being in gaol. Not even an English one, let alone one here in Ceylon. To go through with this would be signing your own death warrant.'

De Richleau had already thought of that and had no intention of letting himself be taken off to prison. But he had been a fighter all his life and he still believed that, if he maintained his bluff, Lalita would give in rather than go to law and risk a conviction for conspiracy. Shaking off Simon's hand, he said to Lalita:

'I agree that we have talked long enough, and apparently we have one thing in common. Neither of us is concerned about his future. Since you are determined to ruin your life, as I have nothing to look forward to I am quite willing to gamble mine. Go ahead and call in the police.'

For a long moment Lalita hesitated, then he took a step towards the telephone.

'Stop!' cried Simon. 'I'll not let this happen. You want blood-money. You shall have it. Instead of your getting Olenevka I'll pay you five thousand pounds.'

Lalita turned and stared at him. 'You mean this?'

'Um.'

'You pay ten.'

'Ner.' Simon shook his head. 'Would if I'd got it,' he lied. 'But I haven't. Five thousand. Good night's work for you. Jewels still yours as well and you're out of trouble. Better than going through with this and finding yourself in prison.'

'You pay me now?'

'Um. Haven't got a cheque book on me. But give me a piece of paper and I'll write you an I O U. Rajapakse will witness it and I'll redeem it tomorrow.'

'O.K.,' said Lalita. 'I take offer.' Then he walked over to an oak desk in the other side of the room.

'Really, my dear Simon, I cannot allow you to do this,' de Richleau protested vigorously. 'I'm certain that the fellow is only bluffing.'

Owing to an act that he could not disclose to his friends in front of Lalita, he had good reason to believe that he had outwitted Ukwatte and that, if the contract were presented, he could render it invalid. Hence his refusal to substitute for it a Deed of Gift. But, counting the contract out, that would still leave Lalita in possession of the jewels, and the thought that he should receive five thousand pounds in addition riled the Duke exceedingly. Desperately he sought a way to prevent his enemy from achieving such a triumph; but in vain.

Simon, determined to save him from himself, pigheadedly rejected his protest. Yet Fate still had a card up her sleeve to produce a new situation.

To get the piece of paper from the desk Lalita pushed his pistol back into its holster. As he opened the desk a cheerful voice said, 'Hello, folks! What's going on here?'

None of them had been looking in the direction of the door.

But now the eyes of all of them swivelled towards it. For the third time that night someone had unexpectedly come on the scene. In the doorway stood a huge man. A smile was on his face and in his hand he firmly held an automatic.

It was that big, ugly, attractive American—who in the nineteen-thirties had been the most sought-after bachelor between Long Island and Juan les Pins—Rex Mackintosh Van Ryn.

14

The Battle Continues

Lalita had two weapons within a few inches of his right hand: his own automatic in its holster and Douglas's revolver thrust through his Sam Browne belt. But it was at him that Rex's big pistol was pointing, so he dared not make a grab at either. Mirabelle might still have given trouble had she been sitting sideways on to Rex and swiftly snatched up her little nickel-plated weapon from the lower shelf on the telephone table. But her chair had its back to the door; so, automatically, on hearing Rex's voice she jerked her head right round. Before she could do more than give a gasp it was Douglas who had snatched up her pistol.

Rex's smile broadened into a grin and he said to Simon, 'Better relieve our friend in uniform of his artillery; then we can talk.'

As Simon moved sideways towards Lalita, so as not to obstruct Rex's line of fire, de Richleau chuckled, 'My dear Rex. How good to see you. Your arrival could not have been more opportune. It enables me to secure twenty-five thousand pounds' worth of jewels which are my property.' As he spoke he picked up the leather case from the table.

'No! They are mine!' Lalita expostulated violently. But Simon had already taken his automatic from its holster and with it gave him a hard jab in the ribs.

'Hold your tongue,' he snapped, 'or it'll be the worse for you.' With his free hand he drew Douglas's revolver from Lalita's belt and passed it to its owner. Then to Rex he said:

'Greyeyes is right. Your turning up couldn't have been better timed if we'd planned it. 'Nother couple of minutes and I'd have signed away five thousand pounds to this dirty crook. But what sort of miracle enabled you to pull us out of this muddle?'

'Yes,' added the Duke. 'How did you learn that we were here and involved in an extremely unpleasant business?'

Now that both Lalita and Mirabelle had been disarmed, Rex casually tucked his automatic away in an armpit holster and advanced into the room. Had Lalita attempted anything, the American was so big and strong that he could have strangled him with one hand. Shrugging his mighty shoulders, he said:

'It's quite simple. Truss and I . . . I think I told you I'd brought Truss along on this trip . . . didn't get in from Trinco' till round eleven o'clock. When we'd checked in at the American Embassy and had a wash I called you at the Galle Face, but only to be told that you were both out. We had drinks with our host and nattered till well after midnight. Then, assuming you'd have got back, I called the hotel again. Still no dice. Knowing Greyeyes doesn't keep late hours these days I became a bit puzzled. After that I made quite a nuisance of myself trying to find out where you'd gone.

'They gave to the effect that Greyeyes came down from his room round quarter after ten and went off in a private car with an Indian driver, which seemed pretty queer to me. Then that you, Simon, got back a bit past eleven, but went out again in a mighty hurry. At the risk of rousing young Fleur from her beauty sleep I decided to call her. By then it was close on one, but it didn't take long for her to put me in the picture. The poor child was near hysterical with worry, so I sent Truss off to hold her hand till I'd found out what was cooking.

'I've not carried a gun for the whale of a while, but I thought it best to come armed, so I borrowed one, and a car, from the Embassy. After a few false casts the driver located his street and I left him at the end of the road. The front door of the house was ajar; so I gumshoed in and listened in the passage for a while to the decidedly acrimonious conversation going on in here. Through the crack on the hinged side of the door I could see a section of the room; and when our friend in the natty uniform put his gun back in its holster I judged it was time to make my bow to the assembled company. That's all there is to it. Now, let's have your end of the story.'

Between them, de Richleau and Simon told him what had taken place. He already knew about the Duke's inheritance and the attempt by the d'Azavedos to get him killed during his previous visit to Ceylon; but as he heard of the plot to have him bitten to death by the cobra, the American's big open face grew darker and darker. When they had done, he said tersely:

'For sheer unadulterated villainy this beats all. But now we've the game in our hands I see no complications. Let the punishment fit the crime. This little Nazi-type so-called Colonel can weigh no more than a sack of potatoes. I'll just sling him over my shoulder and bung him into the back room to keep his father and the cobra company. All the odds are he'll be either dead or a loony come morning. But that's not going to cost any of us a wink of sleep.'

'No!' screeched Lalita, wringing his hands. 'No; no! You cannot do this! You say punishment fit crime, yes. But I have no hand in attempt to murder. I wish to keep stones—lifework of my father—and become owner of Olenevka; very natural. But no more; no more.'

De Richleau contemplated him for a moment with angry contempt, then said:

'You had murder in your heart when you brought me here tonight. To be thrown to the cobra is the punishment you deserve and nothing would give me greater pleasure than to see you disposed of in that way. But, unfortunately, my friend is not right in assuming that if we did so there would be no complications.'

His glance had fallen on Mirabelle and Simon had had the same thought. 'Certainly would be,' he agreed, 'as soon as the lady went to the police. She wasn't in the murder plot; so we've nothing against her. And she's nothing to fear from them. What is to stop her from charging us with having done in her boy friend?'

Mirabelle smiled at him. 'Thank you for not holding against me that I come to Lalita's help. And you are right. Harm him you dare not, for I have whip hand of you.'

With the same swift resilience that he had shown previously when matters turned in his favour, Lalita exclaimed, 'You see! We still have best of you. Arrival of your big friend make no difference to situation. You give back jewels and sign I O U five thousand pounds. If not, soon as you gone I ring for police. Mrs. de Mendoza swear you break in and cause death of my father. I come later and find you here. But you hold me up, take stones and get away.'

'Not so fast, sonny boy,' said Rex laconically. 'You're

wrong about my arrival on the scene making no difference. Before, you had the drop on my friends and could have held them here while you called the cops. But now it's I who have the drop on you. We can quit this place when we like and by the time the cops come on the scene there'll be nothing to show that any of us have ever been here.'

'You not get away with that,' Lalita declared angrily. 'No, not when I make accusation. How you prove you not been here? Past three hours where you all been? How you make alibi?'

It was the subtle-minded Duke who provided the answer. 'The flaw in your case will be the fact that you cannot produce the Indian driver who brought me here. That is unless you own to his having been yourself. To do so would be to admit that you were here tonight before your father's death, and so involved in the plot to murder me.'

After a moment de Richleau went on, 'There is, too, a way in which we can provide ourselves with a perfectly satisfactory alibi. We shall say that on Mr. Van Ryn's arrival in Colombo tonight, he was anxious to hold a conference on urgent business with Mr. Aron and myself. It was he who telephoned me at the Galle Face and we decided that the most suitable place to hold this conference was at the house of my solicitor, Mr. Rajapakse. Mr. Van Ryn then sent a car, the driver of which cannot be traced, to pick me up and take me there. As Mr. Aron was dining out, I left a message for him to follow me as soon as he came in, which he did. We shall be able to produce the taxi driver who took him there, and no one will ever be able to prove that it was not there that all of us spent the past three hours.'

'Oh, damn' fine cheat,' Lalita scowled. 'But lies, lies, lies. And your word only against Mrs. Mendoza and mines. We trip you up somewhere. You see. Cars outside here all night. How explain? Police no fools. They go into this very thorough. I see to that.'

Douglas gave the Duke an anxious look. 'I'm afraid we are back where we started—or rather where we were before Mr. Van Ryn came on the scene. His having actually telephoned the Galle Face much later and asked for you could upset the alibi you suggest. Then the case against you would look very black. If the police are going to be called in I'd much prefer that we did it ourselves and came clean.'

'That,' retorted the Duke sharply, 'is out of the question. And I have already told you why.'

Mirabelle gave a low laugh. 'You are wise, old gentleman. You have not forgot I hear you confess to Ukwatte's murder. Much better leave jewels with Lalita and go home to good sleep in bed. Police station is bad place.'

'And I O U five thousand pounds.' Lalita was grinning now. 'Rajapakse say right. We back where we was. You leave both and I keep quiet. Otherwise . . .'

'I'll be damned if I do!' De Richleau, taking up the fight again, cut him short.

'Then you very foolish. I make report. Tomorrow inquiry start. Soon you is committed for trial and see inside of prison.'

Simon and Douglas again became extremely perturbed and as Rex followed the argument he had ceased to smile. Lalita might also be imprisoned while awaiting trial on counter charges, but that would not help the Duke. Through their minds ran swift thoughts of cells, damp and dark—or perhaps like ovens owing to the sweltering heat outside—anyway filthy, lice-ridden and horribly uncomfortable; of food, barely fit for human consumption and certainly nauseating to anyone who had been accustomed to living well; of warders, uncouth, brutalised by their work, and now inclined to be deliberately vicious against any prisoner of the old ruling class. De Richleau's friends knew that a week of such a life must prove fatal to him, and that even a few hours of it might be sufficient to bring about his death.

The Duke knew that, too, but it went utterly against his nature to leave Lalita in complete possession of the field, and he still believed that Lalita would not gamble his whole career simply to spite an enemy, so he said calmly:

'If Mr. Aron is foolish enough to make you a present of five thousand pounds I cannot stop him. But I am keeping the jewels.'

For a moment Lalita was silent. Behind the thick lenses of his glasses his dark eyes went from one to another of the faces of the people round him, then he declared, 'Five thousand too little. Must be more; much more. Twenty-five. The value of jewels.'

De Richleau hid his sudden elation. Since Lalita was willing to give up the jewels, he had been bluffing. He would never have agreed to do that unless he had grave fears for himself should the whole matter be brought into the open. Now determined to press him further, the Duke said:

'Mr Aron has already told you that five thousand is the most he can raise.'

For Lalita to be willing to surrender the jewels on terms had also revealed to the astute Simon his reluctance to make trouble; so, anxious as he was to make a deal that would place de Richleau out of danger, for the moment he refrained from raising his bid.

But Rex, now as fearful as the others that the Duke might be sent, even temporarily, to prison, sprang into the breach. 'If it's a question of money,' he said quickly, 'I'll find——'

'No, Rex!' de Richleau cut him short. 'You are not a rich man and you have a large family to support. I forbid both you and Simon to impoverish yourselves on my account.'

Rex had difficulty in keeping his face from expressing amazement. Simon's mouth was, as usual, a little open, but his eyes did not even flicker. As Rex was a millionaire with only one son, and Simon was very rich, both realised at once that the old fox from Corfu must be playing one of his deep games.

It was Lalita who broke the short silence that followed. Hammering on the top of the oak desk with his fist, he cried, 'I will not be made monkey of! I am injured party. My father dead, you take stones and I am offer only five thousand pounds. Police make trouble for everyone, self included. That I know. Death for Duke if he go to prison, yes. But bad business for me too, I admit. Both sides tell many lies. Some on both sides found out. Who wins? No one; like atom bomb war. That we make deal is sense. But only if fair. You give me blood-money. Good blood-money. If not I face what come to self for sake of revenge, and old Duke die.'

To the surprise of his friends de Richleau nodded. 'You are quite right. If either of us discloses what has happened here tonight he is going to suffer severely for it; so we should be wise to come to some arrangement. I think it would be best, though, if we forget all this business about I O Us and Deeds of Gift by which I should make over Olenevka to you as an act of restitution for injustice. Instead why should we not adhere to our original contract as though your father had no ulterior motive when he suggested it? The estate and mine are worth fifteen thousand pounds. You have a copy of the contract duly signed and witnessed. You can see for yourself that for me to contest it by declaring that it was extracted from me by threats would mean bringing about the police inquiries we both wish to avoid. Use it to claim Olenevka and, as per contract, I take away the jewels.'

After a moment's consideration Lalita replied, 'The idea is good. But it is not enough. Also I must have I O U five thousand pounds.'

'No!' said the Duke firmly. 'You get Olenevka or nothing. Refuse my offer and I'll take Mr. Rajapakse's advice and call in the police myself. I am still strong enough to stand up to a short time in prison. Mr. Rajapakse will then get me out on bail. And I can't be charged with murder. At worst it will be manslaughter. If I disclose this whole business to the police now I'll have a better case than you have, and I'll get you for complicity in attempted murder.'

'The old Lord is right, Lalita,' Mirabelle put in, after a puff at a newly lit cigarette. 'He look very frail I know. But to fight you all this time he must inside be very tough. I think you come off worse than him in long run if you challenge him with police. Olenevka is good place. We be very happy there. You take and we forget altogether this bad night we have of much argument.'

Lalita gave her a long look then turned and nodded to the Duke. 'O.K. I agrees. I settle for Olenevka.'

Frowning at him, Douglas said sharply, 'You can consider yourself lucky. As a lawyer I am convinced that we could have torn to pieces any case you brought; and had it not been for the danger to my client, at his age, of spending even a few days in prison I am convinced that I could have got you a really stiff sentence.'

'You disappointed, eh?' Lalita scowled at him. 'And think I come out of this well. But I do not think. I have Olenevka but he have stones; so I get bad end of stick. Ten thousand pounds of bad end. Perhaps much more as Olenevka not working good these days. This I not forget. Soon your British friends go from Ceylon. But as Sinhalese with business here you stay put. For help you give these peoples sometime, not too long distant, I make you pay.'

With a shrug, Douglas turned to the others. 'We had better not go off with their weapons. He's quite capable of issuing a search warrant and, if they were found in the possession of one of us, bringing a charge of theft.'

De Richleau nodded. 'As we leave you can throw them into the bushes in the garden, where it will take some time to find them.' Then he pushed the jewel case into the pocket of his overcoat, picked up his Malacca cane, made a little formal bow to Mirabelle and led the way from the room.

A quarter of an hour later he and his friends were back at the Galle Face and assembled in his sitting room. Douglas was telephoning Fleur to let her know that all was well and that he would be home shortly, while Simon and Rex were mixing brandies and soda for them all. The Duke was slumped in an armchair, now looking very grey-faced and limp after the many hours of ordeal and strain he had been through.

Simon brought him a drink and, looking very concerned, said:

'Place for you is bed. You can have your drink there. Come on. I'll give you a hand to undress.'

'No,' replied the Duke. 'There are one or two things we ought to settle. I'll drink this here.'

Simon shook his head. 'Plenty of time to hold an inquest on this filthy business tomorrow. Or later today, rather. You're not to get up, though. We'll all meet in your bedroom after lunch.'

'Thanks for your concern, my son; but we must talk for a few minutes now. It's about the Olenevka estate.'

'What about it? Lalita will have it now, and good riddance. You always said it didn't mean a thing to you, anyway.'

'It doesn't. Even so, I am determined that my would-be murderer shall not enjoy it.'

'I don't see how you can prevent him from doing so now,' Douglas remarked. 'That is, unless you mean to go back on your word and contest the contract on the grounds that it was improperly witnessed.'

'Oh yes, there is a way.' The Duke raised a tired smile. 'All I promised him was that I would not contest the contract on the grounds that I had been forced to sign it. But I can, and mean to, on another count. I wrote my name on the contract but it was not my usual signature. Without having to disclose any part of what has happened tonight, I have only to declare the document to be a forgery. And as he had had it witnessed in advance by two of his stooges who have never even seen me, he won't have a leg to stand on.'

'Well, I'll be damned!' exclaimed Simon. 'And there was I

offering good money in the hope of getting you out of your muddle.'

Rex's big mouth spread in a grin almost from ear to ear. 'I'll say the old fox has lost none of his cunning. What a laugh on that horrid little man in the natty uniform.'

'*Grâce de Dieu*,' shrugged the Duke. 'Having been born with a few wits it would be flying in the face of those who create one not to use them against one's enemies.'

But Douglas frowned and said, 'This is all very well. But unless you allow Lalita to ratify the contract you will have no title to the jewels.'

'That is true,' de Richleau replied calmly. 'But unless Lalita is prepared to go to the police and invite a full inquiry into tonight's events he cannot produce Mirabelle as evidence that I walked off with them. As they are morally mine by right I should feel fully justified in declaring that they had never been handed over. However, in his position, he could fake up some excuse, such as that Simon and I are evading the currency regulations by buying rupees on the black market, and have our quarters here searched in the hope of recovering them. It is that I wish to guard against, and the sooner the better.'

The leather case was lying on a chair beside him. Picking it up, he handed it to Rex and added, 'I'm sure you will not mind taking charge of this for me.'

'I must warn you,' Douglas said quickly, 'that if you are thinking of asking Mr. Van Ryn to fly them out for you in his private aircraft he will be taking a considerable risk. The export of jewels from Ceylon without a permit is illegal.'

Rex had pulled back the zip and was admiring the dazzling contents of the case. 'Holy smoke!' he exclaimed. 'The very cutest of babies would be nice to Daddy if they found this lot in their Christmas stocking.' Then, taking in Douglas's warning, he replied to it with a smile. 'Don't worry about that. If one owns an aircraft there are plenty of places in her where a little clutch of stones like this could be secreted and the Customs boys wouldn't locate them in a month of Sundays.'

'About that we'll see,' replied the Duke. 'For the moment all I want is that you should deposit them in the safe at the American Embassy.' Drawing his signet ring from his little finger he went on, 'Do them up in a parcel and make five seals on it with this, then leave instructions that the parcel is to be handed over only to a person who produces a piece of paper with five of the same seals on it. You can let me have my ring back tomorrow.'

'I'll do that,' Rex said, and Simon nodded vigorously. 'Good idea to cache them right away. Those stones are going to be red-hot as soon as Lalita learns that he's not going to get Olenevka.'

'How right you are,' Douglas agreed gloomily. 'And I don't like any of this at all. Naturally it goes against the grain to see a crook get away with an estate worth fifteen thousand pounds. But I'd rather that he did than see us put ourselves on the wrong side of the law with such a slippery customer.'

'I view the matter differently.' The Duke's voice held a trace of asperity. 'It is against my principles to let a rogue get away with anything. We secured the jewels tonight, and on account of that we have nothing to fear as long as they remain in the safe at the American Embassy. But I wish also to ensure that, however many false witnesses Lalita may bring, he will never succeed in establishing a legal claim to Olenevka. To that end, Douglas, I wish you to draw up a deed by which I make over the estate to Fleur as a free gift. You will pre-date it as though it were signed by me last week. If I had signed such a document then it would make nonsense of any other concerning the estate signed later; and would double-back my contention that my name on Lalita's contract is a forgery. Please bring me a Deed of Gift to sign tomorrow afternoon.'

Simon would have much preferred to let sleeping dogs lie, and for Lalita to have Olenevka, but with de Richleau in that mood he knew that there was no more to be said; so, among a chorus of 'good nights', he helped his old friend off to bed.

Rex and Douglas went downstairs to their respective cars. The big American was one of those happy-natured people who never waste their time speculating about possible future troubles; so he had already brushed Lalita from his mind. Instead, having never previously met Douglas, he said how pleased he was to do so after hearing such a lot about him as Fleur's husband. He then enquired after Fleur, whom he had known from her childhood, and said how much he was looking forward to seeing her again.

Douglas replied with his usual politeness and they arranged that Rex should come to lunch to see Fleur's home on the coming Tuesday. But Douglas's mind was by no means fully occupied by these social exchanges. The greater part of it was visualising the rage and malice with which Lalita would be seized when he learned that he was to be done out of Olenevka.

On Fleur's behalf, Douglas had naturally expressed his gratitude at the Duke's decision to make the property over to her. But as his wife was to enjoy it instead of Lalita it followed that he would be credited with having inspired the gift. Lalita had already declared his open enmity and, while Douglas would not ordinarily have feared him, he could not help being apprehensive of the powers he wielded as one of the blue-eyed boys of the Bandaranaike Government. And now that he had lost the jewels and Fleur was to be made the means of depriving him of what he no doubt looked on as the other part of his rightful inheritance, it seemed likely that he would stick at nothing to avenge himself on those who had benefited by his discomfiture.

In consequence, as Douglas Rajapakse drove himself home he was considerably perturbed by this prospect of future trouble. But, had he only known, trouble from the malice of Lalita d'Azavedo was not the only kind that was boiling up for him.

15

The Unexpected

Truss Van Ryn had arrived at the Rajapakse home about half an hour after midnight. On learning that the Duke was believed to be in trouble, Truss had wanted to accompany his father but Rex had said:

'I don't want you mixed up in this. Maybe I'll have to use a gun and get pulled in for that. If so, you'll then be more use to me outside, calling on our friends at home to pull every wire in Washington in support of our Ambassador here to wave the big stick. And young Fleur sounded near frantic with worry; so you go and administer the smelling salts to her.'

As Truss and Fleur had made it up before he left Corfu they had since exchanged Christmas cards and very occasional letters. On both sides the letters had been comparatively brief, as they led such different lives and had few mutual acquaintances to write about. Judged by a disinterested reader the letters from both would have been regarded as cordial, but there was no suggestion in them of past intimacy or anything to imply that their writers had ever been closer than, possibly, cousins.

Therefore, on this night near the end of October, when Truss was driven in one of the American Embassy cars to Fleur's home, he had no idea at all of how she felt about him; although, with the prospect of spending a week or more in Ceylon, he had recently thought about her a good deal.

He had expected that their meeting would take place at a large luncheon party where they would by an exchange of platitudes easily break the ice of renewing their friendship. Now, contrary to anything he could possibly have foreseen, he had been pitchforked into going to see her in the middle of the night during an emergency that had made her semi-hysterical. That seemed an odd twist of fate but one that, if he handled the situation rightly might, he felt, turn out for him extremely well.

As the car drew up and he got out, he wondered anxiously if he would be called on to use slaps and vinegar to restore Fleur to a reasonable degree of normality. He need not have feared. She was waiting for him inside the front door. Her face was tear-stained but she had full control of herself. Kissing him lightly on the cheek, as she might have any old friend, she said:

'How nice to see you, Truss. It was good of you to come. I'm worried stiff about what may have happened to Greyeyes. Being left here alone was terrible. But now you're with me I'll be able to bear the suspense better till we hear if Douglas and Simon have found him. Come in, and I'll get you a drink.'

She led him into the lofty sitting room, mixed him a whisky and soda and brought it over. He noted that she already had one and, from its colour, judged it to be pretty strong. Sitting at the two ends of a sofa they looked at one another.

She registered the fact that two and a half years had altered him considerably. He had always been tall but he had filled out and now, at twenty-four, was almost as powerful-looking a man as his father. His hair was no longer crew-cut, but of a respectable length and neatly parted. He was wearing light tropical clothes but his jacket and trousers had the unmistakable cut of a good English tailor.

He realised that he was not seeing her to the best advantage. Her fine eyes were slightly swollen from crying and her hair was rumpled from lying down. He noted, too, that although she was wearing evening clothes her whole turn-out appeared very provincial compared with those of the girls who made up his own set at home. But in all essentials she was the same: the rich full mouth that could give such luscious kisses, the sylph-like figure, now even improved by a slightly larger bust, and the long slender legs. She had, too, acquired a tan that made more vivid than ever the colour of her expressive eyes.

For a few minutes they exchanged hurried sentences of concern for de Richleau, who was regarded by both as a grandfather of whom they were extremely fond; but their speculations about what could have become of him were soon exhausted, so they fell almost silent until Fleur said:

'Now tell me about yourself. I was glad to have your letters, but they didn't really say very much, and two and a half years is an awful long time.'

Truss gave his ready laugh. 'It certainly is, and during that time I've done plenty. Far more than I would have if I hadn't staged my rebellion. But I wrote you about that.'

'Yes; when you got back from your trip round Europe you refused to go to Law school. That must have needed some guts, and I take my hat off to you.'

'Thanks. Anyway, it was the best thing I ever did. Every little hick from Hickville wants to get into Law school these days and all the cleverest make the grade. I've no grouse about my mental abilities. They're good enough to cope with most problems that come up in a business man's life from day to day. But they're nothing special and I knew they wouldn't get me a high place in competition with those hand-picked clever-Dicks. So I said to my old man, "Look here." '

Truss broke off to light a cigarette. 'I said, "What's the point of my sweating my guts out with law books when the Corporation can hire as many guys as it wants who'd be better at the job than I would? They've got to be, poor sods, because it's their only chance to pull down a five-figure income. But you're no lawyer and neither was Grandad Channock; yet there's no sounder name in banking than Van Ryn. So why the urge to make me waste my time? Instead of paying out dollars to no good purpose, let me start right away to earn some. I'll empty the wastepaper baskets, or do any durn' thing you want; only put me into one of the branches of the bank so I can start to learn what makes it tick." '

'Good for you, Truss. And you got your way.'

'Surely. The old man put me through the mill, of course. He wouldn't give me a job in our own organisation. Said it would upset the staff and lead to favouritism. But he fixed one for me with a subsidiary of the Chase Manhattan, and arranged for them to change my job time to time so I'd get maximum experience. The whole of the first year I spent in small towns out in the back of beyond. That was pretty dreary; but later I was posted to cities and given work that was worth while. Six months ago my old man pulled me out and I was put through a grilling all afternoon by four of our top executives. Seems I made the grade. In fact I know I did. I wouldn't be here else.'

'Well done, my dear. But what has being here to do with it?'

'Making this trip with my old man is part of the pay-off. He was so pleased at the way things have turned out that he aims to give me the chance to meet our principal contacts here, in Singapore, Hong Kong and other places is the sort of break fellers don't normally get till they're a good bit older. He says that if I don't go off the rails he'll have me made a Vice-President time I'm thirty.'

'Truss, that's marvellous. But how about the rails? Do you feel an inclination to go off them now and then? Or are you still sticking to the straight and narrow, like you were when we met in Corfu?'

'It depends what you mean by "rails",' Truss smiled. 'In my old man's sense it's playing the market with money you haven't got, taking to drink or dope, or getting hitched up to some little gold-digger who's right outside the social orbit. I don't think there's much likelihood of my doing any of those things; though better fellers than me have come a cropper before now through meeting the wrong kind of dame. I got myself in bad that way during the first year I was on my own, and it took the lawyers to get me out of it.'

Fleur's face showed her concern. 'You . . . you don't mean that some bitch trapped you into marrying her?'

'No, it didn't come to that. This was during my second assignment. I'd been sent to a bank in a god-forsaken dorp in the corn belt. While at college I'd had my buddies, the winter sports and all that. In the vacations there were always lots of jolly people, fishing, riding and other things to do. But at Drover's Springs there was nothing. The folks were kind enough but they just didn't talk my language. Most of them thought their little town the tops, had never been anywhere and didn't want to go. After a fortnight I was near blowing my top with boredom.'

'So you began to take an interest in the local blonde?'

'That's it. She worked in the drug-store on the corner. Her name was Esmée and she was as near a cretin as makes no matter; but she had chocolate-box colouring and the right sort of curves.'

'Poor Truss. I thought you were frightfully choosey, and would never have fallen for that sort of thing.'

'Ah!' Truss held up a finger. 'Time was when I wouldn't have. And I'd have been too scared of her trying to inveigle me into marrying her to have gone further than a necking party.

But the previous year I'd been on a trip to Europe, and there I'd met a girl. Maybe you've forgotten what you once said to me about a tiger who's tasted blood?'

Fleur stared at him aghast. 'Oh, Truss! Please don't tell me that it was because I . . . because of what happened in Corfu that you got into this trouble.'

'Good Lord, no!' he laughed. 'If it hadn't been you it would have been someone else, and it was quite time I grew up. The fact that it was you was the sort of break that very few fellers are fortunate enough to get. I've often thought of that week and what heaven it was; but, pretty naturally, after the tiger had once tasted blood he wanted to see it on the menu pretty frequently.'

She frowned. 'So at least I'm answerable for your becoming an habitual lecher.'

'I'm not. And even if I were it wouldn't be your fault. As a healthy man I wouldn't have stayed a virgin all my life. But after I left Corfu I didn't turn up my nose quite so much at the prettiest dance hostesses in the night spots. Of course, I found them disappointing after you, but going back to their apartments with them filled my need for the moment; and I was always hoping that I'd find something better. When I got back home I had plenty of nice girls to choose from, and I'd gotten over my belief that the one idea in all their pretty heads was to nail me for a husband. With a few I had to be a bit wary, but most of them didn't have to go after money and were just out for a good time. Well, by then I'd about gotten over you, and I was feeling on top of the world; so for a few months I gave it them, and plenty.'

'That sounds like the period I put in at that awful place in the Cromwell Road,' Fleur commented, 'when the girls I was living with talked of practically nothing else and none of us could have enough of it.'

Truss nodded. 'I remember your telling me, and that after a while you quit. Me too. It's a sort of fever that's got to be worked out of the blood, and it ended with me when I was sent off to my first assignment in a little backwoods town. For quite a time I was really thankful that I didn't have a date to sleep with anybody.'

'But that didn't last?' Fleur smiled.

'No. Time I got to Drover's Springs I was thinking girls again. And I don't mind admitting you figured pretty large in the programme. By then I'd had fun with plenty others but you had the whole works. With you I was happy; real happy until that——' Truss broke off and gave a rueful grin. 'I'm afraid I was going to say that so-and-so Douglas came along—forgetting that he is your husband. I suppose, too, he wouldn't much like us to be exchanging this sort of confidence?'

Fleur shrugged. 'There's no need for him to know. And, after all, why shouldn't we? We've been friends from childhood. Go on. You had just paid me a very charming compliment.'

'What, that I've always thought of you as the tops in bed—and out of it, for that matter? But we were talking of Drover's Springs and Esmée. It wouldn't be fair to say she really made a play for me. She hadn't the wit. But she did know that I was a Van Ryn and her ma and pa knew it too. On that account, no doubt, no objection was made to my taking treble time to transport her home after the Saturday-night local hops. Time came, of course, when I persuaded her to let me have her. God help me, it couldn't have been more disappointing; her body all tensed up, no warmth, no response. Then tears and lamentations. But I'd done it, and pretty soon the bill came in. She had told her ma, and her pa sent for me. Drover's Springs had grown out of shot-gun marriages; but only just. Esmée's pa wanted an assurance that having ruined his daughter I meant to do the right thing by her. I stalled, of course—said I'd have to communicate with my folks. And I did. I wrote off post-haste to my old man; gave him a full account of the whole miserable business.'

'How did he react?'

'Like the grand guy that he is. He arranged for me to be transferred from Drover's Springs within twenty-four hours, and sent his attorney down to talk turkey to Esmée's pa. He warned me, though, that seducing unmarried girls nearly always leads to trouble and that I'd be wiser in future to blow off steam with women who were just as eager to play as I was.'

'That was certainly sound advice. I hope you took it.'

'I did; although it was not all that easy to follow as long as I remained out in the wilds. Small towns never seem to have such a high percentage of good-lookers as the cities; and the few who are worth having an affaire with, even if they're willing, tend to hide their lights under bushels. They have to, for fear of gossip. The local lads know the form, of course; but to find a willing girl friend isn't easy for a stranger.'

'Poor Truss.' Fleur's tone held a shade of mockery. 'So you nobly resisted temptation for fear of burning your fingers again.'

'Well, yes. The Esmée affair resulted in my reverting to the line I used to take with girls before our affaire in Corfu. I'd become scared again that one would try to hook me by saying I'd put her in the family way, or a husband would suddenly come on the scene and cite me as co-respondent.'

'Then you can't have felt the urge to go to bed with a girl very badly.'

'Oh yes I did. Not as an obsession, of course, but now and then. Occasionally there were nights when I'd have given everything I possessed to have that week with you in Corfu over again.'

Colouring slightly, Fleur said, 'Truss dear, it's a charming compliment that you should have felt like that; but really it's a bit embarrassing for you to tell me so. I do hope, too, that since you came out of the backwoods you have had other affaires that you can look back on just as happily.'

'Well, to be honest, not quite. But soon after I was posted to San Francisco I had a break. She was an artists' model named Sally: as pretty as they come and no strings attached. All she wanted was an apartment of her own, a guy to take her about and plenty of loving. We got on famously and I was real sorry when I had to leave her to go to a branch of the bank in Denver.'

'Did you have any luck there?'

'Not much, and Sally had been pretty demanding; so I was quite content to concentrate on my work for a while. Towards the end of my stay I got to know a call-girl who was a very decent kid, and now and then spent a night with her. But you couldn't call it an affaire. I had another lucky break in Boston, though. She was the wife of an officer in the Navy and his ship was way off with the Sixth Fleet. In her own way she was the faithful type. She had two young children, really cared about her husband, and wouldn't have divorced him even if I'd been so mad about her that I'd have implored her to, or have let anyone lay a finger on her as long as he was within call. But she was very highly sexed, and when he was at sea for long spells she just had to have a man: someone she liked and could trust, and I happened to fill the bill.'

'You were lucky, then,' Fleur remarked, 'and I don't think one can blame her. I'd feel the same if my husband had to leave me for months at a stretch; and all the odds are that he was having his fun in foreign ports. After Boston who was your next?'

Truss smiled. 'That was my last post. And you can imagine what New York is like. Now I'm back in circulation I could go to bed with a different girl every night if I liked. I don't because too much of that sort of thing would be bad for my work. But I get all the fun I want. How about yourself?'

She looked away quickly. 'Oh, I'm in quite a different category. I'm married.'

'Sure; but so were five out of the seven lovelies I've had brief affaires with in New York during the past six months.'

Fleur shrugged. 'They couldn't have got away with that here. In Colombo if a wife makes one false move she's finished; and she simply wouldn't dare take the slightest risk because she's spied on the whole time by a houseful of native servants.'

'That's just too bad. D'you mean you've had no fun on the side at all, then?'

'Certainly not,' she replied a shade sharply. 'And I've no desire to.'

'Oh come, honey,' Truss grinned. 'Leopards don't change their spots. After all you told me about yourself in Corfu I just can't believe you would have kept to the straight and narrow all this time if you'd seen a chance to do otherwise with a fellow you had a yen for.'

'You're wrong; entirely wrong. No woman could have a better husband than Douglas, and I'm devoted to him.'

'What, after two and a half years? You're kidding. At least I hope you are.' Truss leaned right forward and stretched out a hand to lay it on hers. 'You're lovelier than ever. And you're the attraction that made me jump at the chance of coming to Ceylon. I was counting on we two getting together again.'

Suddenly Fleur's eyes narrowed, she drew her hand from under his and smacked him with it sharply across the face. Then her voice came, half choked with indignation. 'So that's how you thought of me, eh? As someone who'd be only too willing to deceive her husband for you and become your mistress for a week or two, then be waved a cheerful good-bye when you flew off to scavenge Singapore and Hong Kong for other likely bitches to amuse you.'

A bright red patch showed on his cheek, but he only blinked and did not draw back. After a moment he said quietly, 'That's just about it. Time was when I would have liked to have you for keeps, but you didn't even wait till I was leaving to wave *me* good-bye. And you'd made it clear from the beginning that you had no scruples about going to bed with anyone you took a fancy to. Well, that goes for me, too, these days. How was I to know that you were still nuts about Douglas? I've never yet tried to get a woman who was still in love with her husband. But it isn't normal for a girl who's kicked up her heels with a score of men before she was married to remain faithful to one for two and a half years afterwards. As I see it I was quite justified in hoping that we might again have some good times together with no hard thoughts about one another afterwards. But I was wrong. All right. I apologise.'

The anger had drained from Fleur's face, and she said, 'I'm sorry, Truss. I shouldn't have done that. It was . . . well, I've been awfully wrought up tonight about what may have happened to Greyeyes. And . . . and nobody has made a pass at me for years. No Sinhalese would think of doing so, out of respect for Douglas, and although some of the men among the white residents might like to, they never get a chance. You see, if the servants hadn't already gone to bed when Simon arrived here, our head boy would still be about. For me to be alone with a man at this hour of night is something quite exceptional.'

He nodded. 'Let's forget it.' Then he added on a lighter note, 'It's quite an amusing situation, though. In Corfu you were the scarlet woman who seduced the innocent lad, and here I've taken the role of the unprincipled lecher trying to seduce the chaste wife. It would make a hit play if only we could think of a good third act.'

'You could kidnap me,' she suggested, welcoming the lighter lead. 'We'd have a terrific scene with me kneeling on the ground clinging to your knees begging you to spare my honour. But you'd refuse and rape me just the same. Then Douglas would appear at the critical moment and shoot us both.'

'Censor wouldn't pass it, even in these days. At least, he'd insist on our being shot before we got any fun out of the rape.

But, talking of kidnapping, I wish to God we did know what was happening to Greyeyes.'

For some minutes they indulged in further futile speculations, then Fleur mixed them fresh drinks and, when they had settled down again, Truss asked, 'Tell me, just what sort of a life do you lead here in Ceylon?'

Fleur drew on her cigarette. 'It's not very exciting but it is pleasant. Running the house is not much trouble. Even the best of native servants are not very dependable, and however well trained are apt to forget a well-established drill at times; so I have to check up on them quite a bit, especially before parties, but there's no question of my ever having to do anything for myself. Even in the garden, where I spend quite a lot of time, I'm never allowed to soil my hands; only to say what is to go in here or there. Then I'm on several charity committees and I spend four mornings a week at the Birth Control Clinic.'

Truss nodded. 'I recall that you were always set on going in for Family Planning.'

'Yes; and I'm sure we do a lot of good. Douglas is terrifically anti the present Government, but at least they are behind us in that; and the women are unbelievably grateful at being saved from having eight or ten pregnancies before they are thirty. Then during the great heats we go up to the hills. At least I do, and Douglas comes up for long week-ends. We have a very nice bungalow at Nuwara Eliya. We must motor up there one day so that you can see it.'

'I'd love that.'

'Then there is the social round. We have many friends, both Sinhalese and Europeans. Having lots of servants makes throwing parties easy, both for them and us. And between times Colombo has a lot to offer for anyone with leisure. There are dances at the Galle Face every Saturday, the bathing at Mount Lavinia is as good as you would get in the South of France, I play quite a lot of tennis and recently I've taken up golf. So you see I've hardly a free moment.'

As she rattled it all off Truss listened attentively. He had not Simon's subtle perception to suggest to him that Fleur was drawing too bright a picture for it to be quite true, and when she had done he said:

'Well, Fleur, seems to me you're to be envied out here in your lovely tropical backwater. At twenty-six or -seven—

which you must be now—half the young women in the States are worrying themselves silly about how long their marriage is going to last or, if they get their divorce, how much alimony they'll be able to get their claws on; or are taking to drink or drugs because the feller they have a yen for has left them flat and is sleeping with their best friend. I tell you, it's a jungle; and some of the animals in it are more vicious by a long sight than those in the forests of Ceylon.'

'Yes, I'm lucky,' Fleur agreed, 'very lucky. After all, contentment is what really matters in life, and I have it here. Enough to do to keep me occupied but never so much that it becomes a wearisome chore. I've friends, my gardens here and up at Nuwara Eliya, a heavenly climate, ample money to buy anything in reason that I want, and a devoted, intelligent husband. I've not the least desire ever to see Europe again.'

For half an hour longer she talked on in the same strain, in all else giving Truss to understand that she had not a worry in the world. Then the telephone rang.

It was Douglas, speaking from the Galle Face, reporting that the Duke was safe, that all was well and that he would be home within a quarter of an hour.

When Truss had heard the good news, he said, 'Thank God for that. Now you'll forgive me if I don't stay on to say how-do to Douglas. I've had one hell of a long day. We made an early start from Trinco', but owing to a temporary breakdown we were held up for some hours; so it was after eleven before we got in, and now it's well into the small hours of the morning.'

'Of course,' Fleur agreed. 'It was sweet of you to come and keep me company during this anxious time. You get off now. I'll ring you tomorrow about a date for lunch, and I do want to see as much as possible of you while you're here.'

He gave her a cheerful wave, cried, 'Thanks a lot. I'll be seeing you,' and went through the wire gauze doors. The car that had brought him was parked a little way off with its coloured driver asleep at the wheel. Truss walked down the steps from the verandah. He had only just set foot on the drive when there came a flurry of skirts and a cry behind him. As he turned Fleur flung herself into his arms.

'Oh, Truss! Truss,' she sobbed. 'What I told you is all lies. Lies, lies, lies! I'm not happy here. I might as well be in prison. I hate every moment of it. If I don't get away from here I shall go mad. I was crazy to marry Douglas! Crazy! For God's sake help me to get free or I'll have ruined my whole life.'

Truss was nearly a foot taller than Fleur. As he held her trembling body to him he looked up at the stars, made a slightly comical grimace and, patting her back, murmured, 'Don't take on so, honey. It may not be too late to pick up the pieces.'

16

The Duke Refuses to Compromise

At lunchtime on the Monday Simon telephoned the others to say that de Richleau had woken in fair shape but would benefit from another sleep during the afternoon; so he proposed that they should not meet until six o'clock. At that hour they assembled in his private sitting room and he joined them wearing a dressing gown. While they were helping themselves to drinks their conversation was naturally of the previous night's events and the extremely narrow escape from death that the Duke had had. After some minutes he called for their attention, and said:

'I owe you all my warmest thanks. Had you not come to my rescue it is pretty certain that on his return Lalita would have done me in, and quite certain that I would not have at last secured the whole of the property left me by my late cousin.'

Simon tittered. 'I was scared stiff for you; but I take my hat off at the way you dug in your toes about the jewels, and fooled those crooks by not putting your usual signature to the contract.'

'That would not have invalidated it if the witnesses had actually seen you write your name,' Douglas commented, 'and Lalita may still get them to swear that they did.'

'Exactly,' smiled the Duke. 'Hence my request that you should draw up an ante-dated Deed of Gift by which I make over Olenevka to Fleur.'

'I have the deed here.' Douglas took a paper from his brief-case, then with a worried look continued, 'I must tell you frankly, though, that I am most opposed to all this; and if it were not for my personal attachment to you, sir, I'd have no hand in it. I realise, of course, that we are combating a crook and endeavouring to protect property which is yours by right, but that does not justify putting a false date to a legal document; and if it ever comes out, you, myself and whoever witnesses it will all be in serious trouble.'

'Unless what we propose to do is given away by one of us—which is unthinkable—it cannot possibly come out. But I appreciate your professional scruples as a lawyer, Douglas, and if you wish to withdraw . . .'

'No, sir. You are in no position to get this done by any other solicitor. And, in view of your generous intention towards Fleur, I could not possibly refuse to carry out your wishes. Even so, I beg you most earnestly to reconsider the situation. If Lalita does bring false witnesses to swear that you signed the contract, and that you did so after making the Deed of Gift, you will be liable to prosecution on the grounds that you endeavoured to obtain the jewels under false pretences.'

'I agree your premises. But last night Lalita admitted that if he brought any charges against me he could not avoid facing one himself of conspiracy with intent to murder. That still holds good. He dare not make any move which will bring this affair into the open.'

'Yet the fact remains that by invalidating the contract and retaining possession of the jewels you are guilty of a felony. It is that which worries me so greatly. If by some unhappy chance it emerged that you had them you would certainly receive a prison sentence.'

'I have taken precautions that it will not emerge.'

'Even so, I beg you to allow Lalita's contract to stand. Letting him have Olenevka will give you a legal title to them.'

'No. My mind is made up,' the Duke replied stubbornly. 'I've got the best of that murderous rogue and I'll not let him have any part of my inheritance. Come, give me the Deed of Gift.'

With an unhappy smile Douglas gave him the document. He signed it, Simon and Rex witnessed it, then it was handed back.

Fleur, who had accompanied her husband to the conference, kissed the Duke lovingly and said, 'Dearest Greyeyes, I can never thank you enough for this magnificent present. But what Douglas has said worries me a lot; and if there is any trouble, at least you know that you have only to say that Olenevka must after all go to Lalita and I'll make it over to him at once.'

He patted her cheek. 'Thank you, my child. I had always

intended that Olenevka, or the money from its sale, should go to you. And there will be no trouble. Lalita is far too scared for himself to make any.'

'In that I'm afraid you are wrong,' Douglas remarked despondently. 'I'm not thinking now of the contract or the jewels. But when Lalita discovers that he has been deprived of both he is going to be wild with rage. You may be sure that he will do his damnedest to get his own back on us in some way or other.'

'How?' asked Rex. 'What do you figure he could do?'

'It's difficult to say, but as a senior officer in the Security Service he has plenty of thugs who will take their orders from him and ask no questions. It's quite possible that he might arrange for an attack to be made on the Duke, and afterwards say he had been mistaken for some dangerous criminal.'

'Don't like the sound of that,' Simon said in a worried voice. 'Especially as Rex and I will be away from Colombo for quite a while on our trip to the Far East.'

'When do you go, and for how long will you be away?' asked de Richleau.

It was Rex who answered. 'Another two days here will complete my business, and Simon has already got through his; so I'd have liked to fly out on Friday. But I put through a call to Trinco' this morning and my pilot's still not happy about that faulty engine. He wants to be dead sure it's one hundred per cent O.K. before we make the long hop to Singapore, so I've agreed to postpone our take-off until Monday. As that gives us three extra days in Ceylon, Simon and I thought we might use them to visit the ancient capitals in the north on our way up to Trinco'. But now I'm not sure we ought to leave you.'

'Nonsense, my dear fellow. Of course you must. I visited them years ago. Both Polonnaruwa and Anuradhapura are fascinating. But you'll need a good guide if you are to get the best out of your trip.'

'Yes; a good guide is essential,' Douglas agreed. 'I only wish I could take you but, unfortunately, I have too many business commitments.'

'Why shouldn't I be your guide?' Fleur suggested. 'I've been up there twice with Douglas and I've read lots of books on the history of Ceylon.'

Douglas nodded. 'That's an excellent idea. And Fleur could drive you up, which would be much more comfortable for you. Most of the hire cars are on their last legs these days, with their springs sticking through the seats.'

'Thanks a lot,' Rex accepted. 'We'd love to have Fleur take us on this trip. That is, if we make it; and I must say I'm now concerned at the thought of leaving Greyeyes.' Turning to the Duke he added:

'Simon tells me you came here only for the change and to explore the possibility of selling the mine. There's nothing to keep you here now. How about heading for home sometime this week?'

De Richleau shook his head. 'No, Rex. I hate to admit it but old age dictates my movements now. I wouldn't care to risk so long a flight with only Max as a companion. He's a good chap, but if I did have a collapse it would probably prove the end of me, unless there were someone like Simon or yourself at hand to ensure the aircraft landing at the nearest base available so that I could be rushed to hospital. I must remain here till Simon gets back. How long do you expect that to be?'

Truss, who had so far been a silent spectator of the scene, pulled out his wallet, took a slip of paper from it and read out their itinerary:

'7th/11th Singapore, 12th/16th Bangkok, 17th/21st Manila, 22nd/29th Hong Kong. From there Dad and I fly home via Honolulu and Uncle Simon should be back here on the 30th or 31st.'

'Then, as I supposed, he will be away three weeks. That being so, three more days visiting the ancient capitals can make little difference.'

'It's not the three days we're worrying about,' Simon said. 'It's leaving you here on your own at all.'

'My dear fellow, you really have no cause for anxiety. Were I forty years younger and likely to go out at night with the object of discovering what diversions the city has to offer, Lalita might find a good chance to have me slogged on the head. As it is I am quite content to read and doze either here or in the sun lounge; so I doubt if I will leave the hotel even in daytime, except to visit Fleur and Douglas or to go for a drive now and then.'

'You should be safe enough while in the hotel,' Rex agreed, 'although about even that one can't be certain; and I don't at all like the idea of your going for drives on your own. If only we were in the States we could hire some reliable strong-arm man to go about with you. But I doubt if we could find anyone here we'd care to trust.'

'I know one that we could,' Fleur put in quickly. 'That is, if he is free.' Turning to the Duke, she went on, 'You remember that nice Police Inspector, Nicholas van Goens, who took charge of things after our terrible experience at Olenevka? I ran into him again only a few weeks ago. Like nearly all the senior police officers who were trained under the British, things were made so unpleasant for him that he was virtually forced to retire, and he moved down to Colombo where he is doing his best to make a living as a private detective.'

'Sounds just the man,' said Simon. 'Think you can get hold of him?'

It was Douglas who replied. 'Yes. After he met Fleur he sent me a line asking me to put in his way any business I could. And we couldn't get a better chap. His knowing about the d'Azavedos' earlier activities will be a great advantage, too. It means we can tell him everything; except, of course, about the Duke having got the jewels.'

There being no other matters to discuss, de Richleau said that he was going back to bed. Simon had already asked Rex and Truss to dine with him downstairs, and he invited the Rajapakses to join them. Fleur would have liked to accept, in the hope of finding some excuse to have a private talk with Truss afterwards; but Douglas, as well as having been up a good part of the night, had had a long day at his office; so he refused for both of them. In consequence, as they were about to leave, she said to Truss:

'Are you going to be hard at work tomorrow or would you like me to pick you up in the morning and run you out to Mount Lavinia for a swim?'

'I'd love that,' he smiled. 'Just for once I'll give Dad a treat, and let him handle our appointments without me.'

Rex gave him an indulgent smile. 'O.K., son. I hope the time will come when I can land you with all of them.'

Next morning Fleur duly picked Truss up at the American Embassy, but on the drive out to Mount Lavinia they refrained from saying anything about the matter that was uppermost in both their minds. It was not until they had changed in two of the cabins on the terrace of rock below the hotel, had a brief swim and came out to sunbathe that Fleur broached the subject.

'I want to apologise,' she said, 'for my outburst on Sunday night. I was terribly wrought up, and Douglas arrived on the scene before I had a chance to explain myself.'

Truss gave her a sidelong look. 'Are you trying to tell me that you were just in a fed-up mood and didn't really mean that you'd ruined your life by marrying him?'

'I wouldn't say that . . . altogether. But at the time I did give you to understand that I was absolutely desperate—shattered by the mess I'd made of things. And you very nobly offered to pick up the pieces.'

'Let's be accurate,' he said a shade coldly. 'What I actually said was that "it might not be too late to pick up the pieces". I didn't say that I was the guy who was going to do the collecting.'

'Oh!' her mouth drooped a little. 'I got the impression that you were still in love with me.'

'Maybe I am . . . in a way. I've always thought of you as the Number One girl in my life. When we were in Corfu I'd have given anything to have had you for keeps. But that's two and a half years ago, and you know how things ended. As soon as Douglas came on the scene you showed that going to bed with me hadn't meant more to you than playing a game of skittles.'

'I know, Truss; I know. I've often thought since of how shockingly I treated you. But I just couldn't help myself. To say that Douglas was the snake and I was the bird would be a gross distortion of the situation. There is not a trace of evil in him. But that's how I felt. Just fascinated by and drawn to him beyond my power to resist. I became insensitive to every other feeling. It was obvious to me from the beginning that he'd fallen for me; but there was that awful barrier of the colour-bar. And he is too decent a man ever to have taken me as a mistress. So it had to be marriage or nothing. To get him I had to be brutal to you and ride roughshod over my mother and father and everyone. Can you understand?'

'Yes, I think so. But it hasn't paid off. That's the long and short of it.'

'It did to begin with. To some extent it does still. Douglas is the kindest and most considerate husband any woman could ever have. But Mummy was right in saying that it wouldn't work out. It's having become a member of an Asiatic family that has got me down. They are different from us; utterly different. Their minds don't work the same way as ours. They don't look on women as individuals who have minds and ambitions of their own. For them women are only a superior sort of servant whose job it is to produce children. For some reason I can't; at least, not by Douglas. It may be his fault; but, of course, his family put it down to me. So my mother-in-law and those awful aunts regard me as a sort of criminal who snared Douglas into marriage under false pretences. They hate my guts and have me spied on the whole time, then retail to Douglas every little thing I do of which they think he might not approve. I've plenty of acquaintances but no real friends with whom I can let down my hair. No Sinhalese woman would have the least sympathy for me. She just wouldn't understand. And the European women that I know would sympathise too much. Their pity for one of their own kind who had been idiot enough to marry a coloured man would be quite unbearable. So I'm trapped, and go round and round like a squirrel in a cage.'

Truss threw a pebble into the surf, and asked, 'Well, what do you intend to do?'

'God knows! Having made my bed I must continue to lie on it, I suppose. Anyhow, I'm thankful now that I didn't land on you any feeling that you were under a chivalrous obligation to get me out.'

'We'd better qualify that. I've a pretty soft spot for you, you know. I made no secret of the fact that when coming to Ceylon I hoped that, having been married for a couple of years, you'd be game for a little fun on the side. You made it pretty clear that that wasn't on. But later you threw yourself at me and asked me to get you out of this mess you've landed yourself in. Naturally, that made me think again. In the past two and a half years I've grown up quite a bit, and your life has been very different from what it was when you lived in England. I asked myself, could we bridge that gap? You see, when I do marry I want it to be for keeps, and not just to pull someone of whom I'm fond out of a hole, with the possibility that she may ditch me again later.'

'Yes, Truss. I appreciate that. As far as I'm concerned I feel that I sowed all the wild oats that I'm ever likely to want to before I married Douglas. So if I did marry again, a man I loved, I'd be a faithful wife. But even if you wanted to I wouldn't like to rush you into anything.'

For a few minutes he remained silent, then he said, 'I'll be here for another week. If you come up to the ancient cities as our guide we'll be seeing a lot of one another. Before I fly out we might have another talk and see how we feel about things then.'

Fleur's eyes were full of tears and she looked away quickly as she said, 'It's . . . it's good of you, Truss, even to think of this seriously—much more than I deserve. I must be honest, though. I've got to consider Douglas. Perhaps a short break of this kind may be what I need—to enable me to go on with him; as I ought to do. In any case, even if you asked me to run away with you, I couldn't. Ceylon is not like England or America where wives can go off with other men and no one gives a second thought to what they've done. Here, among the Sinhalese, for a wife to leave her husband would cause him a most terrible loss of face. If I ever do decide that I simply can't stand things here any longer I'll have to go home to England, wait for a few months then write to Douglas that I don't mean to return.'

Truss smiled at her. 'I get the situation, and it's O.K. by me. Let's leave it that neither of us is committed either way. If at the end of the week you feel resigned to staying here and making the best of things, that will be that. And if I feel we've grown too far apart to plan a future together you'll understand.'

For a little while they remained silent, then they went in for another swim. When they came out Fleur said, 'Whatever we may decide later, while you are here I want to spend as much time as possible alone with you. Young married women don't normally go about with unattached men in Colombo; but fortunately the Rajapakses look on Greyeyes as though he were the head of a family of which we are all members.'

'That's not surprising, seeing we both refer to him at times as "Grandpa Greyeyes" and speak of each other's dad as "Uncle." Anyhow, it's lucky for us. Tomorrow and Thursday I'll have to give a couple of hours both mornings to going round with my old man meeting the local financial big shots, and I can't get out of a dinner party that's being thrown for him at the Embassy tonight. But, apart from that, my time's all yours.'

'Then when you and your father lunch with us today, I'll say that I've promised to show "Cousin Truss" the sights. We have six other people coming and giving them the impression that we're related will serve to check any scandal that might get round if we are seen frequently together.'

As a result of this measure Fleur was able to spend that afternoon and the greater part of the next two days with Truss. They saw no sights, but drove out to deserted beaches where they talked interminably. It was so long since she had been able to disclose her thoughts freely to anyone of her own kind and generation that the days seemed all too short to her; and now that Truss was older she found him a much more interesting companion than she had in Corfu.

When there it had been mainly sexual attraction that had drawn them together but now, while he was very conscious of her lovely golden body masked only by a bikini, he was content, for the time being, to restrain his impulse to attempt to seduce her and, instead, delight in seeing the strain she had been under gradually replaced by natural, carefree laughter.

On the Wednesday, Douglas brought Nicholas van Goens to see the Duke and the ex-Inspector expressed his willingness to undertake the role of bodyguard. A room near de Richleau's suite was secured for him, and on the Thursday he moved into the Galle Face.

That night the Duke gave a final dinner party and afterwards, upstairs, they held a last conference about possible developments which might arise from their dealings with Lalita d'Azavedo.

Douglas reported that he had, the previous day, received a letter from the Land Registry Office concerning the transfer of Olenevka. He had replied that he was much surprised as he had no knowledge of any such transaction, and he would like to see the document on which it was based. When it reached him, which might be the next day, he would repudiate de Richleau's signature as a forgery. The balloon would then go up and they must be prepared for trouble. Lalita would again become the legal owner of the jewels; and, naturally, he would do his utmost to get them back. In an attempt to do so it was quite probable that, on a trumped-up charge that de Richleau was implicated in some sort of illegal activity, he would secure a warrant to search the Duke's rooms.

At that the Duke laughed and remarked, 'Then he'll have his trouble for nothing.'

'Yes,' Douglas agreed. 'You must send for me at once, of course, and van Goens will be here. They won't dare do you any harm in his presence, and in this the law will be on our side; so I can require that you should not be further inconvenienced without due cause first being shown.' Turning to Rex, he added:

'There's another thing. By now Lalita is certain to have learned that you have a private aircraft at Trincomalee, and will shortly be leaving Ceylon in it. He'll naturally jump to the conclusion that you will be taking the jewels out with you for the Duke. As it is illegal to export precious stones without a licence, you must be prepared for him to come on the scene with his men and make a thorough search of your aircraft before you are allowed to take off. And if he finds them you will be in very serious trouble.'

'He won't,' grinned Rex. 'The Duke foresaw such a possibility and refused to allow me to take the risk. For the time being the jewels are staying put.'

Douglas wondered for a moment if it had been agreed to tell him that only to save him from becoming an accessary before the fact to an illegal act; but he nodded and said, 'I'm very relieved to hear it.'

An hour later, as the party was making an early start the next morning, Simon, as well as Rex and Truss, said good-bye to their old friend. Both the former had, at first, been decidedly dubious about leaving him; but, talking it over later, they had decided that, with van Goens and Max in the hotel, Douglas who could be rung up at once and, if need be, the British High Commissioner, who could be called on to make serious trouble with the Government if one of its officials interfered with the well-being of a distinguished British citizen, he would be adequately protected. Fleur, too, would be back in Colombo in less than a week, and looking in every day to see that he lacked for nothing.

But if they could have foreseen what was in store for them during the next few weeks the Duke and Douglas would have accompanied the others to Trincomalee and got out of Ceylon in Rex's aircraft while the going was good.

17

Of Ancient Cities and Modern Love

Next morning, with Truss beside her and the two older men in the back of the car, Fleur took the main road north-east, which cuts the island diagonally in half and ends at Trincomalee. The road was straight, more or less flat and the countryside uninteresting with hills in the distance. After two hours they passed through Kurunegala and, an hour later, entered Dambulla, an old town in the very centre of the island.

It was here that they passed from the 'wet' zone into the 'dry' zone, and so striking was the change in the scenery that they might have entered an entirely different country. In the former thunderstorms and cloudbursts bring the rain sheeting down at a higher rate in a month than the whole of the rainfall in London during a very wet year; whereas in the latter the rain is barely sufficient to keep the vegetation alive and, when it does come, so hot and baked is the earth from months of cloudless skies and torrid sun that much of the rain ascends again in steam.

This extraordinary contrast in conditions in the two parts of the island makes it seem strange that Ceylon's ancient civilisation should have been confined to the dry plains of the north, now very sparsely populated, instead of developing in the mountainous south where in modern times all the wealth, industry and great bulk of the population has become concentrated. Yet it explains the vast irrigation system created by the early Sinhalese Kings; for only by conserving the heavy falls of rainwater in innumerable reservoirs could the crops be grown to support their people.

From Dambulla onwards all the vegetation was parched and many trees and bushes had lost their leaves; so it was easy to see for some way on either side into the jungle, which seemed to hold even more wild life. On the side road they had taken they caught sight of several kinds of deer and monkeys, bears, snakes and once a leopard drinking at a distant water-hole, before they had covered the last twelve miles of their morning's run which brought them to Sigiriya.

After a good lunch at the rest house there they explored this strange natural formation that a powerful and evil man had so amazingly conquered for his own protection. It was a vast column of granite six hundred feet in height and on its broad circular flat top there were the remains of what had once been a splendid palace.

It had been built in the fifth century A.D. by King Kasyapa. He had murdered his father by burying him alive and, fearful of the vengeance of his brother Moggallana, had selected the top of the rock as the perfect place in which to fortify himself. There he had reigned for eighteen years, to leave behind a memory so potent with evil that for fourteen centuries no one had dared go near the rock, and even in recent times archaeologists had found difficulty in persuading natives to work for them excavating the ruins of the palace.

But now Sigiriya had become recognised as one of the marvels of the ancient world, not only for the incredible feat of building a palace on its summit, but also because in caves in the rock there are frescoes and inscriptions testifying to the extraordinarily high state of Sinhalese culture in the distant past. The paintings are of women and depict two types which might well be of different races: jewel-bedecked beauties with pale golden skins toying with flowers, and much darker ones who were evidently their attendants. The inscriptions on the 'Mirror Wall', so-called from the lovely sheen that time has given it, are love poems in praise of these ladies and as delicate in sentiment as any written by the mediaeval troubadours of Europe many hundreds of years later.

In the branches of the forest trees near the huge rock pile they noticed a number of great balls up to four feet in diameter, and Simon asked Fleur what they were.

'Hornets' nests,' she replied, 'and when Douglas first brought me to see Sigiriya he told me a strange story about the hornets in this neighbourhood. Very little sugar cane is grown in Ceylon and the peasants have never been able to pay for imported sugar; so they have always used honey to sweeten things. Yet they have never learned to keep bees; they rob the nests of the wild ones. There are many kinds of bees, from tiny creatures up to the big *bambara*, which make the best honey. They make their nests in high places under overhangs of rock where they are protected from the wind; so you can imagine what a suitable place Sigiriya was for them. In the old days there were hundreds of swarms here. Then, quite recently, sometime in the twenties, the hornets, which had lived for generations at peace with the bees, suddenly declared war on them. Why, nobody has ever discovered, but for weeks on end the most terrible battles were fought in which tens of thousands of insects were engaged. The *bambara*'s sting is nearly as poisonous as that of the hornet; but the hornets won and wiped out the entire population of bees in the area.'

From Sigiriya they accomplished the twenty-mile run to Polonnaruwa in ample time to spend the late afternoon among the ruins of Ceylon's second most ancient capital. From as early as the fifth century A.D. northern Ceylon had been invaded by Dravidian races from southern India and, for a time, Tamil Kings had even succeeded in establishing themselves in Anuradhapura. In spite of this the old Kingdom of Rajarata, apart from short periods, had maintained itself in power and splendour until near the year 1000, when dissensions among its ruling caste made it unable to resist further the waves of invasion by the darker-skinned people.

Yet the retreat of the Sinhalese to central Ceylon was very far from being a rout; it was in the nature of a long-term strategic withdrawal. Realising that it would be impossible to grow enough crops to support their people unless enough water could be made available, the Sinhalese Kings entered on immense labours over a long period of years before finally abandoning their old capital of Anuradhapura. In the neighbourhood of Polonnaruwa they created artificial lakes, some of which are over thirty miles in circumference, and many smaller ones. These so-called 'Tanks' were connected by a network of canals and locks so skilfully planned that for efficiency they rivalled the system of aqueducts by which the Roman engineers supplied with water the great cities of their Empire. Then, in due course, they built their great new capital, covering many square miles with streets, palaces, courts and temples.

The heyday of this great city had been during the reigns of the Norman Kings in England. Then early in the thirteenth century internecine wars had led to its abandonment and gradual decay. For six hundred years jungle had encroached upon it, the swelling roots of trees in time bringing down tall statues of the Buddha and thick creepers prising apart sections of once solid wall; so that now it was a great area of tumbled ruins emerging here and there from a sea of vegetation.

Yet those ruins still displayed a wealth of intricate carving, and enough of them remained comparatively undamaged to give an idea of the city's ancient grandeur; among them the Vatadage, once a great shrine, and the twenty-five-foot recumbent statue of the Buddha at the Gal Vihare.

As Truss, who had relieved Fleur at the wheel for the afternoon, drove them slowly along the dirt tracks that wound in and out among the masses of crumbling brick, thick tangles of jungle and the remains of ancient waterways, they became even more fascinated by the teeming wild life that abounded on every hand, than in the ruins.

Many of the Tanks, owing to the decay of their embankments, had long since become no more than dry jungle-covered depressions, but others in the past fifty years had been restored. In their shallower parts innumerable crocodiles could be seen basking on mud-banks, herds of elephant and wild buffalo were enjoying their evening bathe, flocks of flamingoes and pelicans skimmed the surface seeking fish, while among the palms, talipot trees and dense bush that fringed the water hordes of monkeys chattered, birds with plumage of every hue flitted from branch to branch and, occasionally, a bear or leopard could be glimpsed making its way through the undergrowth.

The reclaiming of the 'Tanks' had been with the object of making a great new agricultural settlement for the landless, so in the neighbourhood of Polonnaruwa there was again a population of many thousands. But it was a poor and squalid area of shacks the sight of which depressed them.

However, the rest house in which Douglas had booked them accommodation for the night—like the great majority of the hundred and more that have been established by the Government to the great benefit of visitors to Ceylon—proved everything they could have desired. The food was plain but excellent, the rooms clean, the servants polite and obliging. As Fleur remarked, it was only the minor officials with Communist leanings who were officious and offensive to the

British; the Sinhalese people as a whole were kind, generous and most friendly.

After they had dined they went out on to the screened verandah and, when they had ordered drinks, Fleur said:

'If you're to get the best out of what you are seeing, now is the time for me to tell you something of the history of the island.' Then as they settled down, she went on:

'From ancient times throughout the East, Ceylon has been known as Lanka, and the Sinhalese race derives its name from *sinha* which is the Sanscrit for lion. Unlike their neighbours in southern India they are of Aryan descent, as is shown by their features, comparatively fair skins and, in many cases, blue eyes. Their recorded history goes back for two thousand four hundred years and there is ample evidence to show that they once had a civilisation that could have rivalled those of Egypt or Babylon at the same period; so they have a past of which they are justly proud and must never be thought of as an ignorant people.

'They are known as the Lion race owing to the myth by which they account for their origin. It is said that some time during the millennium before Christ there lived an Indian princess who made her parents very unhappy because she was a nymphomaniac. Having quarrelled with them, she ran away with a caravan to a distant part of the country then, as men could not satisfy her, she tamed a lion and went to live with him in his den. By him she had twins, a boy and a girl. At the age of sixteen the boy, whose hands and feet resembled the paws of a lion, broke out of the cave, carried off his mother and sister, and later killed his father, the lion. For this feat he was offered the Kingdom of his grandfather, who had just died; but he refused it, made his mother Queen there, became King of the country in which he was born and married his sister. The poor girl is said to have borne him twin sons sixteen times, and the eldest of them was named Vijaya.

'Vijaya was a thoroughly bad hat, and so enraged the people by the depredation that he had a great band of his followers made on them that, at last, his father was forced to send him and his seven hundred toughs into exile. He landed with them in Ceylon in 504 B.C. on the very day that Gautama Buddha died, and the last decree of the Buddha was that Vijaya should be protected by the gods and make Lanka for ever the stronghold of his religion.

'In that lies the root cause why through all the centuries the Sinhalese have displayed such unswerving loyalty to Buddhism. But they were fortified in their belief by other happenings. In 307 B.C. the great Indian Emperor, Asoka, sent his son, the Prince-Priest Mahinda, on a mission to spread further Buddhism in Ceylon; in 288 B.C. a branch of the sacred Bo-Tree, under which Gautama attained enlightenment, was sent here and planted at Anuradhapura, and he is said to have visited the island himself three times, the last occasion being when he set foot on Adam's Peak.

'Of course, as with other religions, there have been schisms and, occasionally, heretic Kings; but neither time nor conquest has lessened the pride which the Sinhalese feel in being a chosen people; and still, today, they look on the Sacred Tooth at Kandy as the talisman that guarantees the divine protection of their race.

'The greater part of what we know about early Ceylon is due to the *bhikkhu* Mahanama, who lived in the fifth century. In a chronicle called the *Mahavamsa* he left us a history of the first thousand years of the Rajarata Kingdom and its splendid capital, Anuradhapura. It not only records the doings of warrior and saint Kings like Dutugemunu, who was both, and killed the great Tamil King, Elala, in single combat then buried him with high honours, but also describes the development of Buddhism. It has an extraordinary similarity to the Old Testament, and goes a great way to explain why the Sinhalese, like the Jews, should look on themselves as a unique and chosen people.

'In ancient times the wealth and culture of the Sinhalese Kingdom was recognised throughout the whole of the then known world. It was famous as the "Land of Jewels". Chinese, Greeks and Romans all came here to trade for its precious stones, spices and beautiful woods. How long that commerce lasted you may judge when I tell you that the coins of twenty-five Roman Emperors have been dug up here by archaeologists, and there are hundreds of Chinese inscriptions on the walls of caves in which lived hermits who came here because it was the favoured country of the Buddha.

'The Rajarata Kingdom lasted for twice as long as the Roman Empire and even when, in the time of our William the Conqueror, the Sinhalese withdrew from Anuradhapura to Polonnaruwa their ruling caste continued to live here for a further two hundred years in a luxury that rivalled that of the Indian Princes.

'It was not until the beginning of the thirteenth century that a decline suddenly set in for which two explanations are possible. King Parakrama Bahu I, who ruled during the latter half of the twelfth century, was as great a builder as the early Pharaohs. The works this tyrant decreed should be undertaken were so vast that a great part of his people must have been employed upon them as slaves. That may have led to agriculture being neglected to a point where the nation fell a victim to famine and exhaustion. On the other hand it is possible that for the first time the *anopheles* mosquito arrived here bringing malaria and the disease devastated the population. Probably it was a combination of both.

'One thing is certain: malaria has been the curse of Ceylon for the past six or seven centuries. Many thousands of people died from it every year and its ravages debilitated the whole nation. No effective means of checking it could be found until the discovery of D.D.T. Then, during the war, when Ceylon became Britain's main base in Asia and Earl Mountbatten's Headquarters, the Imperial Government launched a great campaign to stamp it out. In five years the number of cases was brought down from over three million a year to a little over one million, and since Independence the Ceylonese Government has continued the war against the mosquito with marked success, greatly reducing the death rate.

'At the date Polonnaruwa was abandoned the Roman Empire had already ceased to exist for eight hundred years; so from that time the Arabs became the principal traders to the island. Then in 1505 the Portuguese, under Francisco de Almeida, first landed here. Twelve years later they erected a fort at Colombo, and became the undisputed masters of several of the coastal areas for the next hundred years.

'But the Sinhalese Kingdom had continued to survive with its capital at Kandy, and early in the seventeenth century the King of Kandy asked the aid of the Dutch to check the inroads of the Portuguese into his territories. By the middle of the century the Dutch had ousted the Portuguese and for the next hundred and forty years all Ceylon's trading posts remained in Dutch hands. Then, in 1795 the British sent a strong expedition against the Dutch and in less than a year had totally defeated them.

'The penetration by the Portuguese and the Dutch gave the British, who succeeded them, mastery over a large part of the island but, even so, the Kandayan Kingdom maintained its independence for another twenty years. It was not until the excesses of a tyrant King led to the British taking full possession of it in 1815 that, after nearly two and a half thousand years, the people of the Lion race finally lost their independence.'

Fleur ceased speaking for a moment, then she concluded, 'I hope I haven't bored you; but I did want you to appreciate that, whatever the faults of their present government, the Sinhalese are a great people and should be regarded by us as in every way our equals.'

'You certainly haven't bored me,' declared Rex heartily. 'Most of what you've told us I'd never heard before, and I found it fascinating.'

Simon smilingly nodded his appreciation, and Truss added his thanks; but while Fleur had been giving them the history of the country of her adoption his mind had not been altogether on the subject.

His eyes had never left her face, the contours of which were made still more beautiful by the subdued light out on the verandah, except, now and then, to dwell on her long legs and supple body.

When they went off to bed his mind was still full of her and excited by the sort of craving that he had learned to know very well. In vain he tried to get to sleep, but memories of the nights he had spent with her in Corfu chased one another through his mind as vividly as episodes in a recently seen film.

During the past five days they had, by tacit agreement, refrained from tempting one another to become lovers again; but to resist such an urge on a deserted beach behind the cover of rocks was one thing, while to do so when they were in bedrooms separated by only about thirty feet was, he felt, quite another.

At length, after twisting and turning for an hour, he decided that, whatever her decision might be about the future, he must at least once again hold her lovely body in his arms before they parted. Getting out of bed, he slipped on his dressing gown and cautiously opened the door of his room. As they had sat up late the other visitors at the rest house had gone to bed before them. It was now quite silent and the verandah only dimly lit. Treading carefully he made his way along to Fleur's room and quietly tried her door. To his relief it was not locked; so he gently eased it open and slipped inside. The room was almost in darkness but, through the jalousies, the moon gave enough light for him to see that Fleur was sleeping peacefully.

On tiptoe he approached her bed, slid an arm beneath her shoulders and, bending, kissed her on the mouth. It opened to savour his kiss. Only partially aroused from sleep, she threw an arm round his neck to draw him down on to her.

Suddenly, becoming fully awake, she tore her mouth from his, put her free hand on his chest and thrust him violently away. Then, giving a gasp, she sat up.

'Honey! It's me, Truss!' he strove to reassure her. 'I just had to come along. All evening the sight of you has been driving me crackers. I've got to have you! I've got to!'

'No!' She shook her head. 'Please, Truss! Please don't try to persuade me. God knows, I'm tempted to let you. But not yet! Not yet! Until I've made up my mind about the future I want to remain faithful to Douglas.'

'Oh, damn Douglas,' he retorted angrily. 'You know that he's gone stale on you and you don't really love him any more. Haven't the past few days meant anything to you? It's brought us closer together than ever before. You can't deny yourself to me just because in a crazy fit you got married to him.'

'It was not a crazy fit,' she protested. 'I knew perfectly well what I was doing. And if it weren't for his bloody relatives and their archaic ideas about a wife being a sort of favourite slave without any individuality of her own, I'd be happy with him still. That . . . that is . . . if you hadn't come on the scene.'

'But I have. And you've got as big a yen for me as I have for you. Come on; admit it. Time's come, Fleur, when you've got to make up your mind what you mean to do.'

'Not yet.' Again she shook her head and pushed him away. 'Anyway, if I do decide to leave Douglas it's got to be a clean break, and I'll not let you sleep with me till then.'

Agonised frustration led him to say sharply, 'You're putting him before me and I take that hard, honey. Maybe I'll have second thoughts about wanting a wife who's still so attached to her first husband.'

Tears sprang to Fleur's eyes. 'Oh please, Truss. Try to understand. It's not that I wouldn't love to have you sleep with me. It's simply a matter of principle. I know that in the past I behaved like a slut, but one doesn't have to remain one all one's life. I only want to do the decent thing by him until I've made up my mind whether I really must make a break and leave him.'

'And when will that be?'

'I'll let you know when we reach Trincomalee. Honestly I will. Please bear with me till then. If I have decided to leave him, and you feel you don't want me after all, I can always go back to England and try to start a new life there.'

Releasing his hold on her he took a step away from the bed, and said a shade ungraciously, 'O.K. Have it your own way. But your holding out on me like this doesn't indicate that you've the feelings for me that I'd hoped you had. And I'm not the guy to play second fiddle to Douglas Rajapakse just because you don't hit it off with his family.'

'Oh, Truss!' she cried, stretching out her arms. But he had already turned on his heel and, without a backward glance, he walked out of the room.

The following morning the party spent two hours visiting more of the most interesting remains at Polonnaruwa, then set off on the sixty-odd-mile drive to Anuradhapura. They passed many of the smaller 'Tanks' and two that were the size of great lakes. Here and there on the bright blue surface floated big patches of red lotus, open in the midday sun; wild pigs wallowed in the mud of the banks, herons and kingfishers skimmed the waters.

The area covered by the ruins of Anuradhapura is of even greater extent than that at Polonnaruwa for the city measured more than eight miles from side to side. After lunching at the rest house they went out to see some of its staggering remains.

Of these the four great *dagobas* are the most impressive. They are huge white domes rising direct from the earth and crowned with a spire, which were built to hold relics of the Buddha. Their vastness can be imagined from the fact that the largest was higher than the dome of St. Paul's Cathedral and that it has been estimated that with the bricks used in it eight thousand houses could have been built, forming a town the size of Ipswich.

But Anuradhapura had many other unique sights to offer. Among them were the Sacred Bo-Tree grown from the branch sent from India and said to be the oldest tree in the world; the

Eight Places of Worship to which thousands of pilgrims come every year; the Queen's Pavilion with its beautiful carvings; the enormous Elephant Stables, and the Brazen Palace, built by the great King Dutugemunu.

This last was a monastery. It rested on one thousand six hundred granite columns in forty rows each forty columns long. It had nine storeys and in each of them were one hundred apartments. The outer walls were plated with silver, the roof covered with copper tiles, and it was embellished both with jewels and festoons of leaves made of gold that tinkled in the breeze. The upper storeys, being made of wood, had disintegrated, but the forest of twelve-foot-high granite pillars still stood to be marvelled at.

They slept at Anuradhapura on the Saturday night and, there being so much to see, did not leave on their eighty-mile drive to Trincomalee until five o'clock on the Sunday afternoon. Then, when they were still twenty miles from the city, misfortune overtook them. On coming round a sharp bend in the road they came face to face with a herd of buffalo. Truss, who was driving, braked hard then swerved sharply to one side in an attempt to avoid the animals. He got past the nearest, only scraping its side, but he had had to run partly off the road and the car was brought to an abrupt halt by hitting an old tree-stump submerged in the coarse grass. When he attempted to back away it was found, to their consternation, that the stump had broken a steering rod.

Three-quarters of an hour elapsed before a motorist came by who promised to have help sent to them from a garage in Trincomalee; then for another hour and a half they kicked their heels impatiently until at last a mechanic arrived in a small van. As it would take a day or more to repair the damage, they decided to leave the car to be towed in next day and, crowding into the mechanic's van, had him drive them into the city.

They had expected to arrive there at about half past seven but, as a result of the delay, it was not until half past ten that, tired and hungry, they reached the Welcome Hotel. By the time they had had a wash and a drink and eaten the ham and eggs that the manager had knocked up for them in lieu of dinner it was getting on for midnight; so the obvious move was to bed.

Although Truss had not made any actual arrangement with

Fleur he had intended to take her for a walk after dinner, and she too had expected that evening to be able to tell him of the decision she had come to; but they now had no option but to go upstairs with the others.

Nevertheless, when Fleur got into bed she had put no night cream on her face, and made no attempt to go to sleep. Instead she kept her bedside light on and tried, without much success, to concentrate on a book. Three-quarters of an hour later, when the hotel had become entirely quiet, her expectations were realised. The door opened and Truss slipped into her room.

Smiling, he walked over to the bed, sat down on the side of it, took one of her hands in his and said in a low voice:

'Now; have you made up your mind, honey?'

She returned his smile. 'Yes. Have you made up yours?'

'Sure. For me you've always been the tops in women—ever since I was a kid. This week with you has brought it all back, and stronger than ever. You've dealt yourself a rotten deal so far. Now, you've just got to let me take you away and make it up to you.'

'Dear Truss.' Her eyes were shining and she put up her free hand to stroke his face. 'I'm so glad and that's what I want. You are right, too, about this week we've been together. I couldn't go back to Douglas and life in Colombo after that—even if you didn't want me.'

He gave a low laugh. 'Bless you, sweetie. You must get free of him just as soon as you can. Then we'll have great times. Start life again all bright and new, as though we were a couple of eighteen-year-olds.'

'You mustn't be too impatient,' she said seriously. 'It's not as though I were leaving a husband who had been mean and beastly to me. I couldn't bear to hurt him more than I have to.'

'Yes, he's a decent guy,' Truss admitted. 'Though he ought never to have asked you to marry him in the first place. He was old enough to know there was a big risk that it wouldn't work out. Still, there's no point in going into that again. We won't have much chance to talk in the morning, and we've got to make some sort of plan.'

'As fas as I'm concerned it's made already. When I get back to Colombo I mean to tell Douglas that I feel that I must have a holiday in England; then when Uncle Simon returns from this trip he is going on with you I shall get him to take me home when he leaves with Greyeyes. Directly I get there I shall write to Douglas, tell him that I have definitely made up my mind not to return to him and ask him to send me evidence that will enable me to divorce him. He may not want to, but he will realise that, if I don't mean to come back, the only way he can keep face with his family and friends is not to admit that I've run away from him, but lead them to suppose that I found out that he has been having an affaire with someone else while I was away on holiday.'

Truss nodded. 'Clever girl. That's certainly doing the best you can for him. Now, what about us?'

She smiled. 'That's up to you, darling. Both England and the United States are a long way from Ceylon. No one here is likely to learn how I was behaving myself in either. So if you like I'll willingly become your mistress until the divorce comes through.'

'Thanks a lot, honey. That's fine by me, and I'll just love showing you the high-spots in New York. I mean to be mighty careful of your reputation, though. Still, that's no great problem. I'll fix it for you to stay as a guest in the apartment of a middle-aged widow I know. She's been left badly off, but she's a good sport and will be glad of the money to act as a complaisant chaperon.' For a moment he was silent then, with a grin, he added:

'But do I have to wait until you get to New York?'

'Darling, no! Why should we?' Fleur threw back her head and laughed up at him. 'From now on I'm all yours to do as you like with. Take off your things and hop into bed.'

As he cast aside his dressing gown, she pulled her nightdress off over her head.

Just four minutes later the door opened again, and Lalita d'Azavedo walked into the room.

18

The Sword of Damocles

At the sound of the door opening Truss pulled away from Fleur. Both of them sat up in bed. Giving a gasp of dismay she swiftly jerked the sheets up to cover her naked breasts. For a moment they stared at Lalita, who had been followed into the room by a woman and a sergeant; then Truss roared:

'Who the bloody hell are you? Get right out of here!'

'Security Police,' replied Lalita. Turning, he pushed the Sergeant out of the room and shut the door. Then his thick lips forming into a grin that extended almost from ear to ear, he said:

'Very surprising, this I come on. Mrs. Rajapakse make out she like Caesar's wife, even before married. Cold like icicle. Now I find in bed with big American friend.' Suddenly his expression changed and he added viciously, 'For me how good. With what pleasure I see face of husband Rajapakse, who ruin me, when I tell him wife unfaithful.'

Only then did Fleur recognise him as the man who, two and a half years before at Olenevka, had tried to buy her kisses by offering her a jewel, and the woman behind him as Mirabelle de Mendoza. In a hoarse whisper she said to Truss, 'This is Colonel d'Azavedo. You have heard Greyeyes and the others talking about him.'

'I certainly have!' Truss cried. 'So this is the dirty little crook who's been trying to cheat the Duke out of his inheritance.'

'Have hold on your tongue!' snarled Lalita, pulling his pistol from its holster and pointing the weapon at Truss. 'It is he who have cheat me. I learn this yesterday. He say my claim to Olenevka is forgery. Also he have my jewels. To get back I come here. Your father plan to smuggle out in aeroplane; is it not? Aeroplanes private owned can have many hiding places. But he not risk sending jewels through post for one of crew to hide; that certain. No, he bring with. I come to hotel tonight;

make search of whole party. One of you have them. Soon I find out which.'

'You'll have no luck here,' Truss snapped. 'Nor with the others. We haven't got your jewels and don't know a thing about them. You can search till you're blue in the face.'

'You tell lies. One of you has stones. I find; then prison for all as gang of thieves. Also I make mocking stock for every-ones of lawyer Rajapakse by telling his wife found in bed with big American.'

'No!' cried Fleur. 'No! I beg you not to. You have nothing to gain by doing that, and it would hurt him terribly.'

Lalita grinned. 'For me pleasure to hurt. All blame he become my enemy his. If he not start trouble Olenevka still property of my father, and he alive. Also we robbed of hims lifework; fortune in stones. This most good luck opportunity to make lawyer Rajapakse eat mud before family and all peoples known to him. English wife proved bitch. No honour. Whore to white man who says lie down on back for him.'

Fleur's face, already red, went almost scarlet as though she had been smacked hard on both cheeks, and she lowered her eyes. Truss had gone white with rage at these insults to her. He was prevented from jumping out of bed and attempting to strangle Lalita only by the fact that the automatic was pointed at him, and the knowledge that the villainous little man would not hesitate to use it because he could say afterwards that his victim had resisted arrest. Striving to control his fury, Truss sought desperately to think of some way to help Fleur save both herself and her husband from this horrid scandal. After a moment he swallowed hard, and said:

'Surely there's a way we can settle this? You say you've been robbed of your fortune; so you must need money. How much do you want to forget that you caught us here tonight?'

The scowl faded from Lalita's face. 'Now perhaps we talk,' he said in a quieter voice. 'I learn yesterday that Olenevka made present to Mrs. Rajapakse. She give me back and all forgotten.'

'You must be crazy!' Truss cried angrily. 'The estate is said to be worth nearly two hundred thousand Ceylonese rupees.'

'No matter. That my price.'

'Then you can go to hell! I had in mind offering you a thousand or two to stop you wagging your tongue. But this colossal blackmail—not on your life! I'd see you damned before I'd allow Mrs. Rajapakse to agree to it.'

Fleur, now feeling terribly guilty at having exposed Douglas to what he would regard as indelible shame, and anxious to protect him at almost any cost, hesitantly said to Lalita, 'I . . . I couldn't make Olenevka over to you anyway. How could I possibly explain my doing so to my husband? But I might be able to arrange for you to receive a share of the profits from the mine when it starts to pay again.'

'How you manage to do without your husband find out, eh?' Lalita asked dubiously.

'I . . . I don't quite know . . . but there must be some way I could do it. I have my own bank account. When the profits start coming in from Olenevka I could tell him that I've decided to save them and instead send a sum every few months to you.'

Lalita shook his head. 'Not good enough. If Olenevka belong me I make mine pay. As long as it is run by de Zoysa no guarantee it ever pay.'

'Very well, then,' Fleur replied desperately. 'I've a little money of my own. I'll pay you something every month out of that.'

'No!' Truss cut in sharply. 'Fleur, I'll not let you commit yourself to anything like this. You'd never be free of a millstone round your neck. And a time might come when you couldn't pay. Then he'd expose you and you would have been through months of hell for nothing. This will be hard on Douglas, I know; but that just can't be helped. Far better face up to the worst now than have the constant fear that it may blow up on you at any time in the future.'

Turning to him she began to speak in rapid French. 'But don't you see that it's not as though we were trying to buy some incriminating letters from him? He can produce this woman any time as a witness to how he found us. And if he had taken your offer of a cash payment down we would have had nothing but his word for it that he wouldn't double-cross us, and vent his hate against Douglas as soon as he gets back to Colombo. Even if he didn't it would only be because he hoped to squeeze more money out of me later. Do you understand what I'm saying?'

Truss nodded. 'Yes. I got the gist of it.'

'Very well, then,' Fleur went on in French. 'My paying him a monthly sum will keep him quiet for the present, and won't prove very costly. It's not as though I mean to remain in Colombo. By the time I join you in America I can stop paying it. What I'm anxious to do is to protect Douglas until it becomes common knowledge that he is letting me divorce him. Then it won't be half as bad for him if this comes out. He can save his face by saying that I did it to avenge myself because I'd already found out that he was having an affaire with another woman. People may not even——'

Lalita had been glaring at her and broke in angrily, 'Speak English. I not allow you make talk I not understand, so you make plan to cheat me.'

Fleur shrugged. 'My bank account is rather low at the moment. I was only asking Mr. Van Ryn whether he could arrange before he leaves tomorrow to have some money paid into it, so that I could do as we suggest for you until my next dividends come in.'

'How much you pay me, How much each month?'

'I think I could manage five hundred rupees.'

'Not enough.'

'I can't make it more. If I did my bills would pile up until someone sued me. Then my husband would insist on going into my affairs and everything would come out.'

'Not so. You say Mr. Van Ryn help you, so you make it more.'

Fleur then realised that the explanation she had used to cover what she had said in French had made her vulnerable to the blackmailer's demands, and she looked unhappily at Truss.

He nodded. 'Only fair that I should help out. Let's say a thousand a month.'

Lalita remained silent for nearly a minute, then he said, 'Money sweet but revenge sweeter. Seventy-five pounds English once month not to be thrown away. But with Colonel's pay I not hard-up. To see lawyer Rajapakse made mocking stock for all Colombo very pleasant for me. But possible to have revenge on him quite different way. I have to think.' Staring at Fleur through his thick glasses he asked, 'When you plan go back to Colombo?'

'It all depends what time the aircraft leaves tomorrow,' she replied.

'Soon I search. Find jewels with one of you and aircraft not leave. You all put in prison. If no stones here my men search aircraft very thorough. Just possible they already in it. Not likely but possible, and search take all day.'

'Then, unless you arrest me, I should get back to Colombo on Tuesday night.'

'O.K. I get back jewels, then revenge better than money. If not per'aps I take money. For few days I think over. By Saturday I decides. Mrs. de Mendoza, she ring you in morning to tell place for meeting. You come with first thousand rupees. Either she take, or tell you I make your husband mocking stock of Colombo. All peoples point and jeer—your wife Scarlet Woman.'

Having paused for a moment he went on, 'Now we make search. No need I find for spare blushings of Mrs. Rajapakse. Not knowing I bring Mrs. de Mendoza. She do this room. Mr. Van Ryn, he come with me.'

If there was any blushing to be done it was now for Truss to do it, as he was naked and had to get out of bed to put his pyjamas and dressing gown on in front of Lalita and Mirabelle. She had remained a silent listener, regarding them the whole time with mild amusement. As Truss saw her fine brown eyes now fixed on him he angrily turned his back and hurriedly pulled on his clothes. Then raising a smile to cheer Fleur he said, 'Don't fret, honey. Be seeing you,' and left the room with Lalita.

Three of the Colonel's armed police were standing outside in the passage. The Sergeant was one of them and spoke to him in Sinhalese. He made an angry gesture, which suggested to Truss that they had already searched his father's and Simon's rooms and failed to find the jewels. Knowing that they would not find them in his room either, he hid a smile and led the way along to it.

For the next twenty minutes they ransacked it, throwing everything in his suitcases out on the floor, searching in every likely and unlikely place and making a thorough examination of the bedding, while he stood watching them indifferently, his mind still on the wretched situation in which he had unintentionally landed Fleur.

A few minutes before they had finished Mirabelle de Mendoza came in and, although she spoke in Sinhalese to Lalita, it was obvious from the spate of curses he let fly that she was reporting to him that in Fleur's room she had drawn a blank.

Rounding on Truss, Lalita exclaimed, 'No jewels! This I not believe! I think my men careless in the rooms of your father and Mr. Aron. They search again, this time while I watch on. You to remain here. Understand. No communication with others till come morning.' He then stalked from the room followed by Mirabelle and his men.

For a time there came the occasional slamming of doors and the muffled sound of voices; then, some while afterwards, quiet fell again. Cautiously, Truss opened the door of his room with the intention of talking matters over further with Fleur. Outside in the passage the lights were full on and about twelve feet away a security guard was standing. At the sound of the door opening he turned, said something in Sinhalese and lifted his Sten gun.

Truss promptly shut the door, gave a tired sigh, slipped out of his dressing gown and got into the now much disturbed bed.

After turning restlessly for a while he dropped off to sleep, but as soon as he woke in the morning the events of the night flooded back to him. Getting up he put on his dressing-gown, meaning to go along and see his father. But the policeman was still lounging in the corridor and, rousing from a doze, waved him back.

Lalita appeared soon afterwards. He had a breakfast of tea and fruit brought up to each of them in their rooms, then ordered them to pack under the supervision of himself and his men. When they had done he had their baggage despatched ahead of them to the airport and told them that he intended to search the aircraft, which would take some hours; so they were to remain in the hotel until he sent for them. In consequence it was not until about half past nine that they at last found themselves free to get together downstairs in the lounge.

While the party discussed the raid to which they had been subjected, Truss and Fleur could do no more than exchange glances of commiseration. Rex and Simon laughed together about the blustering threats with which Lalita had opened the proceedings and his angry disappointment when he had had to call off further search as useless; but the two younger people were in no laughing mood and, as soon as Truss decently could, he said that he would like to have a private word with his father in the garden.

As soon as they were out of earshot of anyone in the hotel Rex said, 'Well, son; you're looking pretty gloomy. What's eating you?'

'Plenty,' replied Truss unhappily. 'I'm sorry, Dad; but I won't be able to accompany you on this trip.'

Rex came to an abrupt halt and a frown crossed his face. 'I don't get you. For why?'

'I've got to stay in Ceylon on account of Fleur.'

'So that's boiled up again, has it?' For a moment Rex was silent, then as he walked on he said not unkindly:

'Look, son. I know you fell for her when you were a youngster, and although I've never mentioned it I was given to understand that the two of you got pretty close together some years back when you were in Corfu. You know I've never been given to moralising, but I'm not giving you any marks for having started your affaire with her again this past week. Douglas Rajapakse is a very decent guy, and it's hard on him that you should have risked breaking up his marriage. But if you're still in the clear with him you'd best pull out while the going's good. For you to stay on here as Fleur's boy friend could lead to a fine packet of trouble for all concerned. And, anyway, it's important that you should meet our business contacts in the Far East.'

'I know, Dad, and I'm sorry. But I'm not in the clear. That little bastard Lalita caught us in bed together last night.'

'Hey! What's that?' Rex came to a sudden halt again. 'Lord Almighty! And he hates Rajapakse's guts. This will properly put the cat among the pigeons.'

'You're telling me,' said Truss bitterly. 'Anyway, that's the way things are.' He then went on to tell his father how matters stood between himself and Fleur, and of the way in which they had tried to induce Lalita to hold his tongue. To end up with, he said:

'So you see I've simply got to stay on here. It's not as though he were blackmailing us with letters, or anything we could buy from him, and he'd make no promise that he would accept these monthly bribes from Fleur to keep quiet. His pay as a Colonel must be pretty good, so he may prefer to get his own back on Douglas and spill the beans next week. I can't possibly leave her here on her own with this thing hanging over her head and the possibility that life will be made hell for her till I can get back. I must be here to stand by her if the balloon does go up and get her out of Ceylon just as soon as I can.'

'You're right, son,' Rex agreed. 'That's what you must do.

This is a lousy business, and we can only hope Lalita takes the bribe so that you'll get a breathing space to save poor Rajapakse's face. I'll put Uncle Simon wise later to the real reason why you're not coming with us. And at least I can say one thing. I'm glad that you and Fleur have not just been having a roll in the hay, but have really settled for one another. She's a lovely girl, and has far more individuality than most. I will be real glad to have her for a daughter-in-law.'

'Thanks a lot, Dad,' Truss smiled. 'You've always been a tower of strength to me. Fleur and I are both old enough now to know our own minds, and once we're through this trouble I'm sure we'll make each other happy.'

When they returned to the lounge Rex said to Simon, 'Truss has been talking to me about last night. He feels that since Lalita showed such vindictiveness to all of us, and he hasn't got his jewels, he is more than ever likely to make trouble for Greyeyes; and that our old friend ought to have someone with him better able to get him immediate Diplomatic protection, if need be, than that Dutch policeman or old Max. I think Truss is right; so I've agreed that he shall stay behind.'

Simon's eyes flickered for a moment, then he said, 'Wouldn't be going myself if I hadn't thought Douglas capable of calling in the heavy guns. Still, the more friends Greyeyes has on the spot the better. And Truss will be company for him.'

Fleur made no comment; but she guessed what really lay behind Rex's announcement, and shot a grateful glance at Truss.

It was not until the late afternoon that Lalita's Sergeant arrived in a small police bus to escort them to the airport. There, Lalita had the whole party stripped in separate rooms and searched once again. Then, having no legal grounds for detaining them further, he had to give a surly consent to the travellers' going out to the aircraft. The good-byes were said and a quarter of an hour later Rex and Simon were airborne on their flight across the Indian Ocean.

Truss and Fleur went to the garage to which her car had been towed in, and learned to their satisfaction that the repairs to it would be completed by the following morning. Then, as there was little of interest to see in the town, they made their way to the end of the peninsula on the neck of which it is situated, and climbed the height whereon, before its destruction by the Portuguese, had stood the great Tamil 'Temple of a Thousand Columns'.

From there they had a splendid view of the two bays that constitute one of the finest harbours in the world. Therein, over a period of a hundred and fifty years, mighty British fleets had ridden at anchor while maintaining the freedom of the Eastern seas. Now it was nearly empty, its tall cranes were rusting and its great naval arsenal of barracks, stores and workshops falling into decay.

That night they dined quietly in the hotel. Reluctantly they decided that it would be wiser for them not to risk sleeping together, as there was always the possibility that, in a fit of rage and spite, Lalita might have telephoned Douglas that morning; and if he arrived by car to find them actually together in bed that would turn an already bad enough situation into an intolerable one.

Their run next day was uneventful, and they reached Colombo a little before dinner-time. Truss was not expected back at the American Embassy and intended to stay at the Galle Face; but, instead of asking Fleur to drop him off there, he accompanied her to her home in case Lalita had already given them away. With considerable trepidation, they went into the house. Douglas was there and, greatly to their relief, gave them a cheerful welcome. Then they exchanged news.

On the Saturday, Douglas said, soon after Lalita had learned that his contract was valueless, he had gone to the Galle Face with a party of his men and made a thorough search of the Duke's apartments, but, of course, quite uselessly; and de Richleau had suffered no more than a certain amount of inconvenience. Douglas then asked Truss to stay to dinner but, as he was anxious to see the Duke, he declined and, after he had had a drink, a taxi was telephoned for to take him to the hotel.

There, he secured the room Simon had occupied, had a quick bath, and was just in time to surprise de Richleau by joining him for dinner. Over the meal he gave an account of the fascinating trip from which he had just got back and of Lalita's abortive search for the jewels at Trincomalee; but it was not until they had adjourned to the sitting room upstairs that he divulged the real reason for his unexpected return, together with all that had led up to it.

As Truss described how Lalita had caught him in bed with

Fleur, de Richleau began to chuckle, then laugh, until holding out his glass, he burbled, 'For God's sake, boy, give me some more brandy, or I'll choke.'

Truss swiftly complied, but said a little stiffly, 'There wasn't anything at all funny about it, Grandad.'

The Duke wiped the tears from his eyes. 'There never is at the time. But to hear about it is better than a French farce; and later you'll laugh about it yourself. One comes to realise how ridiculous one must have looked.'

'D'you mean . . .?'

'Oh yes. My hair wasn't always white, you know.'

Truss smiled. 'Then, anyhow, you can sympathise.'

'I do; with your predicament. I only hope that Lalita gave you time to assure yourself that the beautiful Fleur is as admirable a bed companion as you found her when staying with me on Corfu.'

'Eh!' Truss exclaimed, his eyes going round and his mouth dropping open.

'My dear boy, you must not imagine that because I am now a very old man that I have altogether lost my powers of obsevation, and I'm happy to say that my hearing is still pretty good.'

'Hell's bells! I hadn't an idea! Did Fleur's father and mother know about us?'

'I don't think so; although your Uncle Richard, knowing Miss Fleur better than her mother does, may have had his suspicions. However, that is beside the point. If I had not assumed what you now confirm to have happened in Corfu I should be inclined to censure you severely. Douglas Rajapakse is a fine man and, as far as we know, a devoted husband. For you to have come between him and his wife would have been inexcusable, even if Fleur has become dissatisfied with the marriage that she insisted on making against the advice of her parents. But the fact that you have loved her since you were a boy, that for a short time two years ago she became your mistress, and that she had decided to leave Douglas in order to marry you, does justify your conduct. Her wish to save her husband's face does her credit; but it now looks as if Lalita's malice may bring that to naught. This offer to him of money seems the only likely way of stalling him off, and we must do our utmost to protect Douglas; so if you need further funds you have only to let me know.'

'Thanks, Grandad,' Truss said feelingly. 'I'm mighty grateful to you, but I'm O.K. for money at the moment.'

With the aid of his malacca cane de Richleau got to his feet. Patting Truss on the shoulder, he said, 'I must get to bed now. We will hope that things will turn out all right and that Douglas may be spared. So far my inheritance in Ceylon has brought me nothing but trouble. Neither Olenevka nor the jewels have ever really meant anything to me. I've dug my toes in about holding on to them only because I'm a pigheaded old man who won't allow a rogue to get the better of him. But age does not prevent one from making mistakes, and in this matter I fear I have been foolish.'

Throughout Wednesday, Thursday and Friday Truss and Fleur spent their time much as they had before they had set out on their trip to the ancient capital. But while they lazed on the beach they could no longer derive their former enjoyment from the hours they spent together. Always the fear lay on them that when Fleur returned home she might have to face a bitterly reproachful Douglas, utterly shattered by the knowledge that it was now being put about all over Colombo by Lalita that he had actually come upon her naked while playing the wanton in bed with her American lover.

So depressed were they by thinking hour after hour of this sombre possibility that at times they were tempted to go to Douglas and make a clean breast of everything. But as the seemingly interminable days dragged past they gradually became more confident that Lalita would, at least, hold his hand until the end of the week.

On Friday after lunch Fleur drew the thousand rupees from her bank; then on Saturday morning, silently praying that Mirabelle would not ring up before Douglas had gone to his office, she hovered near the telephone. After two false alarms, which proved to be friends calling her, at half past ten Mirabelle rang up. She said:

'You will come, please, to the Khan Clock Tower. I will meet you there at three o'clock this afternoon.'

Fleur agreed and well before time she was at the appointed place. A few minutes later Mirabelle appeared, walking with extraordinary grace and looking as though she were a Princess who had stepped out of a Persian miniature. With a smile, she asked:

'You have the money?'

On receiving a nod from Fleur she went on, 'I chose this place, Mrs. Rajapakse, because at this end of the city no one is likely to recognise you, and tell afterwards that we are seen together. Please walk with me as far as the canal. There is a shop there that make good ices. We enjoy one while we sit quite alone and have a little talk.'

The canal lay only a hundred and fifty yards away. Outside the shop they took a table in the shade and when they had given their order, Mirabelle said:

'For the time being Lalita decide not to talk while you pay up; so give me the money.'

Fleur had the notes in an envelope in her bag. With considerable relief she took it out. As she slid it across the table Mirabelle thanked her, then went on:

'Now you permit I tell you a little about myself. I am an orphan and married, as they say, from the cradle, very young, as is often the case here in Ceylon. When I am twenty-one my husband run away. Not because he like me no more but because he lose all his money through bad speculation and fear to be sent to prison. Where he goes I have no idea. Perhaps he is alive, perhaps not. I still do not know. What shall I do? I have no money, no close relative who will keep me, and I cannot marry again. For job in office I have no training. To go as a servant or shop girl thank you very much not at all. I could become good whore but such a life is harder than many suppose. Also it is very uncertain.

'Ukwatte d'Azavedo I already know. He says, "Become my mistress." Well, why not? Old man's darling is easy life. I agree and go to live with him as his housekeeper. Then Lalita. A woman like myself needs more of sex than an old man can give her. I take him too as lover and we have good times together. Eight years are gone since my husband disappear so now I can marry again. We plan that when old Ukwatte dies and Lalita inherits fortune we get married. Now, perhaps yes, perhaps no. I can no longer regard as certain.

'Lalita no longer has fortune. He make many enemies, and if present Government be one day thrown out he is finish. On other hand if it goes on for a long time he perhaps become rich through it. But either way perhaps he decide one day to finish with me. It now happens that I have good chance to make fortune for myself. But to do so I must betray him. I ask now your advice. Shall I let things go on and risk future with

Lalita, or make break with him and give help to his enemies?'

Having been made this unexpected confidence, Fleur hardly knew what to reply. She had no cause whatever to speak in Lalita's favour and possibly save him from disaster, but she felt that she ought to give an honest answer; so after a moment's thought she said:

'It depends on how much you love him. If you do and you think that even if he doesn't marry you he means to stick to you, I should have thought you would want to remain his mistress.'

Mirabelle shrugged her slim shoulders. 'As Colonel of the Security Service he has many opportunities to make woman give themselves to him. Of that he makes no secret to me. And for myself I would just as soon live with another man. This is not question of love but how I act best for my future, and I now come to point. It is you who can secure it for me. If you will agree. . . .'

'I!' exclaimed Fleur. 'But there is nothing I can do.' Then fearful that she was about to be subjected to another blackmail, she added hurriedly, 'I've already agreed to pay Lalita a thousand rupees a month. I couldn't possibly find more to pay you a sort of pension too.'

'Pension,' Mirabelle repeated with a low laugh. 'That is nice word but not very descriptive in this case. Now I shall tell you something. I was educated in a convent school, and there I learn French. Enough, anyhow, to understand what you say to your American boy friend when you are in bed with him. You say you mean to leave Rajapakse, go to America and soon afterwards you stop payments to Lalita. This you cannot deny.'

Fleur went a little pale. 'Yes,' she admitted in a whisper. 'I . . . I did say that.'

'Very well. I have not yet tell Lalita. But if I am to remain with him I must. Directly he learn you mean to double-cross he will blow your husband up. I give you chance to save him but you must pay my price.'

19

Of Mirabelle and Murder

Fleur had stopped eating her chocolate sundae. With her thoughts racing she stared at the beautiful coffee-coloured face and sleek dark hair of the woman opposite her. The big, widely spaced eyes held neither greed nor malice. They were quite expressionless; yet their owner had become a potential menace.

Although Lalita had decided to accept a monthly bribe to keep silent, it was certain he would not remain so when he learned that Fleur intended to get a divorce, then cut off his payments. She felt no doubt that, enraged by her plan to cheat him, he would vent his spite by giving full publicity to her adultery at once; so that she as well as Douglas should be shamed and have to bear being ostracised by his family and friends until she could leave the country.

Humiliating as that, and the covert sneers of the lower-caste Sinhalese with whom she had dealings, must prove, with the prospect of marrying Truss in front of her she felt that she could, somehow, manage to face it. But she knew that if there was still some way in which she could protect Douglas, and she failed to take it, she would never forgive herself. Drawing a deep breath, she said:

'Well. What is your price?'

'You give me Olenevka,' Mirabelle replied quietly.

'I can't,' Fleur protested. 'How can I? You heard me say to Colonel d'Azavedo the other night that it would be impossible for me to sign it away without giving my husband a reason. What reason could I give him except by making a clean breast of everything? And if I did, I'm certain he wouldn't let me.'

'He need never know. I have a friend who is lawyer. He would write deed for me and keep quiet. You sign it in secret.'

'Deeds like that have to be registered. It would be bound to come out.'

'Not so to harm you. I think of that. We make deed for transfer to be in six months' time. By then you perhaps have your divorce. Anyhow, you are in America. Whatever comes out will then be old tale and you say yourself not much harm your husband.'

Fleur was quick to realise that Mirabelle's plan could save the situation, but she recalled Truss's indignation when Lalita had tried to get her to part with Olenevka. He had declared it outrageous to demand a property worth fifteen thousand pounds as blackmail. She shook her head:

'No. I am anxious to save my husband from this scandal; but you are asking too much. Far too much.'

'Only what I must have if I make break with Lalita,' Mirabelle countered. 'Even if the mine does not again pay very much Olenevka is pleasant property. I like it there, and if I am owner I can make good marriage. I can choose as husband a man I like, live with respect of everybody, and my future is secure. For you who are to marry the rich American, what is Olenevka? A nothing. Besides you give it me and I become your ally. It is not just to stop scandal that I ask so much. If you still have fondness for your husband you will wish to save him from much worse things.'

'What do you mean by that?' Fleur asked.

Mirabelle gave a pitying shake of her smooth dark head. 'You do not know the half. Lalita is most vindictive man. He never forgive your husband for starting all this trouble about the will. That he finds you in bed with the American is only icing for the cake he bakes. On your old Duke too, for having stole his jewels, he is determined to be revenged. But first old Duke's defences must be broke down. His clever lawyer must be got out of the way. Soon now Lalita springs something on your husband so that he is arrested. Then he shatter him by telling how he find you and the American in bed, because he prefer this pleasure of humiliating to more money, and he mean then to finish with him. Among prisoners there is often fight and riots. Many bad men in prison glad to do whatever Lalita say and earn quick release. Easy for him to fix big dust up in which your husband receives a terrible injury, or perhaps killed. Who does it no one will give away. Next act, Lalita ensnares your Duke. Perhaps by planting papers on him to show that he conspire against the Government. Then he too is arrested and go to prison. For a man so old that means death anyway.'

As Mirabelle revealed these plans of Lalita's, Fleur became more and more alarmed. Her hand trembling slightly she took another spoonful of her now runny ice as she asked, 'Could you . . . is it really possible that you could prevent all this?'

Picking up an ice wafer Mirabelle snapped it between her slender fingers and replied, 'Yes. You give me Olenevka and I break Lalita like this.'

'But how . . . how could you?'

Mirabelle leaned forward and said in a low voice, 'Lalita is a murderer, I know it. I can tell you how to get proof, and when you have it I give evidence. Once he is arrested on charge your husband and the old Duke have no more to fear. He is finish.'

Fleur's eyes opened wide at this revelation, but she instantly grasped its implications. 'Very well,' she said, 'if you can do that I'll do as you wish.' Then caution caused her to add quickly, 'That is, if my friends agree. I must tell them what we have arranged before I . . . actually sign anything.'

'If you feel you must I make no objection,' Mirabelle replied. 'But you must give decision very soon. Lalita makes move against your husband as early perhaps as end of next week. We have to work fast if we are to stop him. When can you let me know with handshake that all is settled?'

'Tomorrow. I could meet you here tomorrow at the same time.'

That being agreed they beckoned the waitress over, paid the bill and parted. Knowing how anxious Truss would be to hear the result of her talk with Mirabelle, Fleur had arranged for him to meet her outside the Dutch Belfry; so she hurried off in that direction. It was barely half a mile away and ten minutes later she found him sitting there in a self-drive car that he had hired. While he drove her slowly back past the lake towards her home, she told him about Lalita's vicious intentions and the possibility of Mirabelle putting a stop to them if Olenevka were made over to her.

Having heard her out, he shook his head. 'It's one hell of a price to pay, honey, just to stop these people talking; and the rest of it may be lies for all we know.'

'I don't think so. I really don't,' Fleur asserted in an agitated voice. 'It is the sort of thing one might expect from Lalita; and

Mirabelle's anxiety to make her future secure is very understandable.'

'Sure; sure. She's got brains, that dame; and she's seen the chance to cash in on our troubles. But her story that she can prove Lalita to be a murderer calls for a lot of believing.'

'She seemed quite confident that she could, and we can't possibly afford to ignore the chance to put an end to this whole awful business.'

'We'll certainly go into it. At all events she was right in one thing; as you are marrying me, giving up Olenevka need cause you no pain and grief. We'd never go there, the income from it is problematic, and there's more money in the Van Ryn settlements than you could spend in a dozen lifetimes. I don't think Grandpa Greyeyes would object to your giving it up either. Not if that's going to put us all in the clear and Lalita gets no part of it. The old boy's dug in his toes only because he was determined not to let a rogue get away with what is rightly his. But this inheritance has proved a pain in the neck for him, and I think the time has come when he'd be glad too hear the last of it.'

'I hope you are right about that, because I couldn't give Olenevka away without his consent. We must talk it over with him as soon as possible.'

Truss nodded. 'After dinner tonight would be best, but if you dined with us I don't see how we'd manage to sidetrack Douglas You'd better look in at the Galle Face for a drink at around six.'

'I can't, unfortunately. We are going out to drinks at the home of one of the High Court judges. For me to cut that is out of the question, and I couldn't come on to the Galle Face afterwards unless I brought Douglas with me. It will have too be tomorrow. Douglas was brought up as a Buddhist, so he never goes to church with me. Instead of attending the morning service I'll go to the hotel. I'll be there at about half past ten.'

'I had no idea you were a church-goer, honey.' Truss turned on her an interested look. 'Somehow I wouldn't have thought that to be in your line.'

'It wasn't during my hectic youth,' she told him a little sombrely, 'but for the past year or so I've made a habit of it here. Nostalgia for something English perhaps. I don't know.

But I've found it rather comforting. Have you anything against it?'

'No, ma'am; indeed not,' he assured her quickly. 'In the States good families keep up with religion these days more than yours do in Europe. I'd come with you if we hadn't made a more important date.'

That night Truss told de Richleau about the new situation that had arisen and when Fleur arrived at the Galle Face on Sunday morning the three of them settled down to discuss it.

To Fleur the Duke said, 'Olenevka is your property, my child, to do with as you wish; but I should be sorry to see you part with it unless you could get something very well worth while in return.'

'I'd look on giving it up as a small price to pay if that will save you and Douglas from Lalita's malice,' she replied at once.

'I am sure you would. But the question is, has this Mendoza woman really got it in her power to rid us of him? My advice is that you should sign nothing until she has produced actual proof that he is a murderer.'

'And she'll have to be quick about it if it's to be of any use,' Truss added. 'That is, if she's right in believing that Lalita may put a fast one over Douglas come the end of the week, and if that's to be prevented.'

'Yes, she herself stressed the necessity for acting quickly,' Fleur agreed. 'That's why I am meeting her again this afternoon. When I do, what do you think I ought to say?'

'Much the best thing would be if Truss and I could take these negotiations out of your hands, my dear,' de Richleau replied. 'Do you think she would be willing to come here this evening to talk to us?'

'I can't say. I doubt it. She might be afraid that one of Lalita's spies would see her and tell him.'

'Yes, I thought of that. But as things are I am most averse to leaving the hotel, particularly at night. It occurred to me that she would run very little risk of Lalita learning about her visit if Truss met her nearby on the sea front, say by the lighthouse, and brought her through the garden entrance to the swimming baths. They are always deserted by dinner-time.'

'Well, I'll ask her.'

'If she refuses, arrange for her to meet Truss and me at the Zoo any time tomorrow morning in front of the monkey cages. There won't be many people about and we could talk there in low voices while looking at the animals without appearing to know one another. But as we have to work against time a meeting tonight would be preferable.'

The Duke knocked an inch of ash carefully off his cigar, then went on, 'I have been considering very seriously what may happen should she fail to produce this evidence. Whether she can or cannot I feel that we would be foolish to ignore her warning regarding Lalita's intentions, and that the time has come when discretion may prove the better part of valour. Loath as I am to deny myself some further weeks of sunshine a price to pay for them. And whatever precautions the good van Goens may take to prevent any incriminating documents being planted here I prefer not to risk that happening. Therefore, instead of waiting for your Uncle Simon's return at the end of the month I should like to leave Ceylon soon, while I've still got the better of Lalita.'

'But, Greyeyes, darling,' Fleur protested, 'you really ought not to risk making such a long flight alone.'

'No, my child; but I was coming to that. Have you quite definitely made up your mind to leave Douglas?'

'Yes, definitely. All I am anxious to do now is to save him the humiliation of it becoming public that I have been unfaithful to him and am running away to marry Truss. And, of course, to protect him as far as I can from Lalita.'

De Richleau nodded. 'How far you will be able to do the latter depends on Madame Mirabelle. But as Lalita has accepted your first payment you should be on fairly safe ground about the former for the time being. Your plan, as I understand it, was to tell Douglas that you feel you must have a holiday in England and leave with myself and Uncle Simon when he gets back?'

'Yes. Then when I got home I'd write to Douglas and ask him to let me divorce him. With luck, if Mirabelle plays up, it won't get out then about me and Truss until Douglas has had a chance to save his face by leading people to believe that I left him only because he was having an affaire with another woman.'

'Exactly. Now, I am sure you will appreciate that it is only with great reluctance that I am prepared to assist in a conspiracy to deceive a man like Douglas, whom I regard as a friend. But you have taken me into your confidence and, naturally, I am anxious for your happiness. Moreover, in this instance, it seems that only by deceiving Douglas can we spare him great pain. I therefore propose to tell him that, owing to Lalita having become a serious menace, I should like to leave Ceylon towards the end of this week, but that I hesitate to make so long a journey on my own. Then, I suggest, you could cover your real reason for wanting to get away by offering to accompany me.'

Fleur hesitated a moment. 'I'd love to do that, anyway. But to explain knowing about Lalita's intentions you would have to tell him about Mirabelle.'

'Of course, my child. But we need not tell him that this situation has arisen because she was with Lalita when he found you in bed with Truss, and that you are being blackmailed by them both. I shall leave you out of this and lead him to believe that she has approached me direct with a view to double-crossing Lalita and getting Olenevka for herself as the price of securing Douglas and myself from his malice. Of course, as Truss has remained in Ceylon only with the ostensible object of looking after me, Douglas may ask why he should not accompany me back to Europe; but Truss can say that unless it is impossible for you to do so, he feels it to be his duty to join his father in the Far East as soon as possible. In the circumstances, it's hardly likely that Douglas will refuse to let you go. Then you and Truss will be able to make your own arrangements about your future without further delay.'

'Oh, Grandpa, how clever you are!' Fleur's eyes were dancing with happiness. 'That's a wonderful idea!'

'Very well, then,' de Richleau returned her smile. 'This afternoon you must do your utmost to persuade Madame Mirabelle to come to the swimming baths here for a talk with us at about eight o'clock this evening. Then, if she agrees, bring Douglas along for a drink after dinner. When I have given him my version of what is going on, all you have to say is that if he has no objection you would love to be my companion on the flight, and see your mother and father again. Then leave the rest to me.'

At three o'clock that afternoon Fleur kept her appointment with Mirabelle down by the canal. The market there had been over for some hours, but as it was a Sunday there were still quite a number of people about; so instead of having another ice together they had their talk while walking along some of the less frequented byways.

At first Mirabelle proved very loath to risk going to the Galle Face. But Fleur declared that she would not assign Olenevka to her unless she was prepared too give de Richleau grounds for believing that she really could spike Lalita's guns; so eventually Mirabelle agreed to meet Truss by the lighthouse at a little before eight o'clock.

After leaving her, Fleur telephoned from a call box to let Truss know that she had been successful, then she went home and, with an uneasy conscience, told Douglas that a new development had arisen with regard to Lalita about which the Duke wished to talk to them at the Galle Face after dinner that night.

Although Truss and Mirabelle had met only once under decidedly unusual circumstances, they recognised each other at once, and she accompanied him through the sea-front garden entrance of the Galle Face to the swimming baths. There, alone and in semi-darkness, de Richleau was sitting at one end of the baths in a canvas-backed chair. With the aid of his malacca, he stood up, greeted her cheerfully and gallantly bowed her to another chair. Then he said:

'Madame; as age prevents me from going far from my quarters in these days, I am most grateful to you for coming here. As I am in no position to offer you any refreshment I will not detain you longer than need be. Therefore, let us go straight to business. Mrs. Rajapakse has told me of your reasons for wishing to become the owner of Olenevka, and I sympathise with them. But only a few years ago that property was said to be worth half a million rupees and even today its value is estimated to be two hundred thousand. Please be kind enough to inform me precisely what you could do for myself and my friends in return for the equivalent of such a considerable sum?'

'I will tell, my lord, how a charge of murder can be made against Lalita d'Azavedo,' Mirabelle replied without hesitation. 'And I will stand in court to be witness for you.'

'Then, as good citizens, apart from any private interest we may have in this matter, it is our duty to investigate this. Perhaps now you will be so good as to tell us how we should proceed.'

Mirabelle took a pack of cigarettes from her reticule. Truss promptly lit one for her and, when she had puffed at it, she said:

'This goes back to time when the firm Rajapakse first declared the will of Count Plackoff to be a forgery. You recall that is due to Pedro Fernando making confession that it was so on his death-bed. Other witness was his wife Vinala. They were for some years retired and living in bungalow on the estate. The Rajapakses write to her asking her to make a statement. She was much worried and fearing trouble for herself does not know what to reply. The d'Azavedos learn of this and are frightened that she confirm her husband's confession. If so they are lost; so they decide to kill her. They do not say this to me, but I know of the will being contested and what hangs to that. One evening father and son get a little drunk. Later they go out and when they come back they are in shocking state. Next morning I clean clothes. There is blood and muck on those of both. Then I learn that old Vinala has gone, left her home, disappeared. It is said that she ran away from fear she has to show herself in court and admit to witnessing will she know to be forged. But I know better. She never again show herself anywhere.'

'Most interesting,' remarked the Duke, 'and I have very little doubt, Madame, that your guess about what happened to her is correct. But her disappearance and your finding bloodstains on the clothes of the two men are no proof of murder.'

'No, my lord. But I make it possible for you to tie all ends up.'

'How will you do that?'

'Soon after Vinala disappears, Ukwatte says her bungalow no good; beams rotten, so dangerous for anyone else to make a home in. He has it pulled down. For why? Because he do not want anyone else to live there. For why? Because somewhere near is buried Vinala and he fears that it be discovered. Where is her body? I tell you. The muck I clean from the clothes of Ukwatte and Lalita was pig manure. They bury her in the pigsty. I am certain of it. Go there and you will find I am right.'

'Now we're really getting some place,' Truss exclaimed. 'If her skeleton is there, with your corroborative evidence we can put Lalita on the skids.'

'Yes,' agreed the Duke. 'Motive, opportunity, and the remains of the body will enable us to bring a charge. But only your evidence about the bloodstains, Madame, will secure a conviction. May we count upon you to give it?'

Mirabelle lit another cigarette from the one she was smoking. 'Yes, my lord. As showing good faith I will sign a statement and exchange for deed giving me title to Olenevka.'

'Nothing could be fairer,' smiled the Duke. 'But I think it would be advisable for the deed to be drawn up by Mr. Rajapakse. He will not, of course, be told about the . . . er . . . possible scandal from which it is part of our understanding that he should be protected; only that you have approached me with this proposal for preventing Lalita from making a great deal of trouble for all of us. If Rajapakse draws up the deed we can be quite certain that no knowledge of it will get back to Lalita; whereas if your lawyer friend acts for you I feel there is some risk that it might. Do you agree?'

'I think I could trust my friend, but he is also friend of Lalita; so perhaps, my lord, what you propose is best.'

'Good. Then there remains only one other point. We need directions as to how to find the ruin of the Fernandos' bungalow, so that someone can be sent to look for the remains of the body.'

Mirabelle gave them. It was not far from the house, and de Richleau was satisfied that anyone who knew the property should have no difficulty in finding it. Having thanked her, he stood up and said:

'May I congratulate you on your good sense in coming to us, Madame. For the assistance you are rendering us you have well deserved the future security you seek. Once we have found the remains of the body and have your signed statement I pledge you my word that the deal shall go through.'

'I thank you, my lord.' Mirabelle came to her feet and bowed. 'But how long will this take? You must hurry. You have only a few days. Perhaps as soon as this week Lalita springs trap for Mr. Rajapakse, and once he is in prison he perhaps never come out alive.'

'I appreciate that; so I shall send someone to Olenevka tomorrow. By Tuesday night, or Wednesday at the latest, we should know where we stand.'

After a further exchange of compliments they parted. Truss saw Mirabelle to the side entrance of the hotel grounds, then went in with the Duke to dinner. As soon as the waiter had taken their order, Truss asked:

'What did you think of her?'

'I was decidedly impressed,' de Richleau replied. 'She is a pleasant creature, honest, I should say, according to her lights, and decidedly attractive.'

'She certainly is that. From what I've heard of old Ukwatte it's surprising that a woman with her looks should have been willing to tie up with a man like him; or anyhow to remain with him for so long. And as for Lalita!'

The Duke smiled. 'My dear boy, in such matters women are entirely unpredictable. Physical attractions do not weigh with them nearly as much as they do with our sex. According to Fleur, Madame Mirabelle is lazy by nature, and she evidently liked being the mistress of Olenevka, even if only an unofficial one.

'What do you think the chances are that she's telling the truth?'

'Very high. She may be exaggerating Lalita's powers to do us harm but the intentions she has attributed to him are plausible. And she is no fool. She must know that she would stand to gain nothing by telling us this story of the murder if it were simply invention.'

'I take it you'll send van Goens up there to investigate?'

'No. That was my first thought; but he used to be a police inspector in that area and, having lived at Olenevka for so long, Lalita is certain still to have friends in the neighbourhood. If one of them tipped him off that an ex-policeman was snooping there, his guilty conscience would alert him to his danger. He would be up there within a matter of hours to destroy any evidence that may remain of the crime. He might even tumble to it that Mirabelle has suspected him all along and is now selling him out. If so he's quite capable of killing her; and we must not risk that.'

'Then I'll go up if you like, sir,' Truss volunteered.

'Thank you, Truss. I was about to suggest it; and I have thought of a way to explain your visit to de Zoysa, the manager there. He may not yet know that I have made the property over to Fleur, but I will ring him up tomorrow morning and tell him. I shall add that she wants to sell it and that she has been lucky enough to find a possible buyer almost at once. That will be you. And that both of you are on your way up there so that you can see the present state of the mine and get a better idea of its possible value. Even if that does get back to Lalita, as he already knows that the place belongs to Fleur, the reason for your visit will appear quite natural to him.'

Truss laughed. 'Grandad, you're a marvel. That will give me two days on my own with Fleur; and, after the end of this week we won't be seeing one another for quite a while, so I couldn't be more grateful.'

'I don't know that you deserve them,' de Richleau remarked dryly, 'and but for this other business I certainly would not aid you to deceive poor Douglas. But love as well as war has its casualties, and as you are the victor one cannot blame you for wishing to enjoy the spoils.'

An hour later they were upstairs in the Duke's sitting room with Douglas and Fleur. As de Richleau told them of the latest development regarding his unlucky inheritance, brought about by, as he said, Mirabelle's approach to him, Fleur contrived to show the same surprise and concern as her husband; but when the Duke disclosed that Mirabelle had demanded Olenevka as the price of her alliance, their reactions were quite different. Fleur at once agreed, but Douglas proved most averse to her giving it up, on the grounds that he thought Mirabelle was probably lying and had been put up to this move by Lalita in the hope that by some new trick or other they could between them get hold of the property.

It then fell to the Duke to put on an act. Had his old companions Simon, Rex and Richard been present they would have seen through it at once, because they knew that while he was always cautious when threatened with danger he had never been known to panic or show fear. But now he gave the impression that he was really scared. He insisted that Mirabelle had given him ample grounds for believing that unless Lalita could be stopped both Douglas and he would become his victims and lose their lives. He then insisted that their only chance of saving themselves lay in agreeing to her terms.

Infected by this display of fear Douglas was persuaded to agree; upon which the Duke said, 'You will appreciate that this must be done with the utmost secrecy. Should one of the clerks in your office chance to be in Lalita's pay and report to him that a Deed of Gift to Mirabelle is being drawn up, the fat will be in the fire and he will take steps to render her useless to us; so you had better draw it up yourself at home.'

Douglas promised to do so and the Duke then spoke of his wish to make a speedy return to Europe. Truss made difficulties, as arranged, about going with him; then Fleur stepped into the breach, adding what a treat it would be for her to see her parents and spend Christmas with them if Douglas could spare her for six or seven weeks.

While doing so, although she knew that the object of her deception was in part to save her husband from a most harmful scandal, her conscience was so stricken that she wished she could have dropped through the floor; and she felt even more guilty when he, without the least hesitation, generously agreed.

That settled, de Richleau produced his plan for finding out if Vinala Fernando's remains were really buried in the pigsty near her bungalow. This was new to Fleur and she at once protested:

'But, Greyeyes, dearest; if I'm to leave with you for Europe at the end of the week, I must have time to pack and make all sorts of arrangements.'

To that he replied firmly, taking Douglas's consent that she should go to Olenevka with Truss for granted, 'My child, this is an emergency. The lives of your husband and myself may depend on verifying the fact that Lalita is a murderer. It would be unwise for you to arrive unexpected by de Zoysa, and I may not be able to get him on the telephone until the siesta hour; so you need not leave until after lunch tomorrow. And you should be back by Tuesday evening. I shall get seats for us on the plane for Friday; so that will give you Wednesday and Thursday. In those two and a half days you must do the best you can.'

There remained little more to discuss. They speculated for a while on Lalita's machinations and, should Vinala's skeleton not be found, the possibility of paying Mirabelle generously to warn them about his plans; then the visitors took their departure.

When they had gone de Richleau drew his hand wearily over his forehead, and said to Truss, 'My God, what a party! It's the first time in my life I've had to pretend to be a coward. But we pulled it off, and instinct tells me that Mirabelle is right about Lalita having it in for Douglas and myself. I can get out, but he can't; so praise be to the Lord that we persuaded him to agree to our plan. Open a bottle of champagne, dear boy; open a bottle of champagne. I need something to revive me, and we can easily manage a bottle between us.'

Next morning, after three abortive attempts, the Duke got through to de Zoysa. Meanwhile Truss had secured three seats on a plane calling at Athens, from where there was a connection to Corfu, for Friday the 18th and one for himself to Manila, where his father should be on that date. After lunch he picked up Fleur in his self-drive car and they took the road to Ratnapura, arriving at Olenevka at a little before six o'clock.

They were made most welcome by de Zoysa and his wife: a large, smiling lady who was a little flustered at entertaining rich Anglo-American guests, but determined to do the honours of her house to the best of her ability.

After dinner de Zoysa produced toddy, the national drink of Ceylon. He explained that the ordinary brew is made from pressed coconut flowers. It is said to be very good for one but should be drunk within eight hours of being made. This was Ambassador toddy, and much superior to the ordinary type, its fermentation having been stopped by the addition of lime juice. Later he brought out a bottle of Arrack, a distillation of coconut which when new is sheer firewater but after keeping for twenty years can be very good, and resembles the Slivovitz made in the Balkan countries from plums.

On the way up, Truss and Fleur had been hoping that they would be able to sleep together. But the rooms they were given in the rambling old house were so far apart that they reluctantly decided that to do so might result in discovery and precipitate the scandal Fleur was so anxious to avoid; so they resigned themselves to becoming half muzzy on the potent Arrack and retiring to sleep the night through in their separate rooms.

Next morning there was no escape for them from making a tour of the mines with de Zoysa. On reaching the valley in which they lay Fleur's mind was filled with vivid recollections of the time when, with de Richleau and her parents, she had been trapped there, and she pointed out to Truss the cave in the hillside in which they had taken refuge.

De Zoysa, evidently with the hope that Truss, if he became the new owner, would take him on as manager, or Fleur retain him, spared no effort to impress them with his activities and persuade them that the mine would soon again be a paying concern. That he might make it so if he could increase his labour force certainly seemed possible, as he had made good most of the sabotage that Ukwatte had carried out in the mines before leaving them; but the thoughts of Truss and Fleur were upon whether they would find anything in the Fernandos' pigsty; so they could only feel sorry for the wasted eagerness of the thin, nervous mine manager.

After the midday meal, when their host, hostess and the servants settled down for the siesta, their impatiently awaited opportunity came. They met by arrangement at the back of the house, Truss found a spade and shovel in a shed and, following Mirabelle's directions, they set off towards the bungalow, which lay only a quarter of a mile away.

They found it without difficulty and saw that the jungle had encroached on the ruin; several sizable trees sprouted from its interior and creepers covered the greater part of the structure that had not been eaten away by white ants and termites.

The pigsty, too, was half buried in lush greenery; but Truss set to work with a will, cutting at it with the edge of his spade. Under his powerful slashes, with Fleur pulling great armfuls of cut creeper away, after a quarter of an hour's intensive labour they had the greater part of it cleared.

Truss then remarked that if there had been pigs in the sty at the time the murder took place, the d'Azavedos would have had to bury the body several feet deep or the pigs would have rooted it out to eat the flesh; so by just turning up the earth he would not be likely to come on Vinala's skeleton.

With the sweat pouring from him under the scorching afternoon sun, he dug down into the hard, baked ground. Pausing only now and then for a minute to get his breath, he stuck doggedly to his task while Fleur shovelled aside the tightly packed earth he turned up. For three-quarters of an hour they laboured and panted with growing depression. By then Truss had dug a pit in the centre of the sty about four feet across and three feet deep without coming on any indication that a body had been buried there.

Had Truss been a frailer man he would have been nearly exhausted and inclined to accept that further exertion would prove futile; but after a short rest, determined not to give up until he was convinced that Mirabelle had been mistaken, he began to attack the corners of the sty. He had dug out only a dozen spadesful from the second corner that he tried when

Fleur gave an excited cry and, stooping, seized upon a small bone.

It might well have been part of some dead animal that had been thrown to the pigs, but Truss continued to dig with renewed energy and his efforts were soon rewarded. Two minutes later he turned up a larger bone that looked as though it might have come from a leg; then, with a gasp of triumph, he heaved clear of the hole a human skull.

For a full minute they both stood back, their thin shirts drenched with sweat, striving to recover their breath while they stared with mingled horror and satisfaction at the earth-clogged ball that had been Vinala Fernando's head. Then Truss rasped out:

'We've got him! This will put paid to Lalita all right. Now to take some pictures for the record.'

Picking up the camera he had brought with him, he took a dozen shots: first close-ups of the skull and leg bone, then others showing the sty in relation to the ruins of the bungalow. When he had done, he rolled the gruesome remains into the deep hole in the middle of the sty and began to shovel earth back to fill it up. As soon as he had levelled the surface and stamped it down Fleur trailed over the sty all the nearby creepers that had not been cut, so that only anyone coming close to it would notice that it had been disturbed.

By the time they got back to the house over two hours had elapsed, but they succeeded in reaching their rooms without being seen by the de Zoysas or any of the servants and, utterly worn out, threw themselves down on their beds to sleep. So exhausted were they from their labours that they both slept until after six o'clock. When they had cleaned themselves up and put on fresh clothes it was seven and close on time for dinner; so, although, after finding the skull, they had hoped to return to Colombo that night with news of their success they decided against making the long drive in the dark.

Anxious, nevertheless, to let the Duke know as soon as possible that the object of their mission had been accomplished, Truss went to the telephone but, to his annoyance, found that it was out of order. De Zoysa, with a smiling apology, told him that in such remote places the line was broken every few months by wild animals, and might not be mended for some days; but as they did not use the telephone much they never worried about this minor inconvenience.

Next morning, when they got up they saw that the sky was overcast and at breakfast the de Zoysas urged them to postpone their departure for Colombo until the next day, predicting that a heavy storm was about to break. Truss thanked them but would not hear of it, pleading urgent business in the capital; so, having said good-bye to their friendly hosts, shortly before ten o'clock they set off.

Had they known what a storm could be like in the 'wet' zone of Ceylon they might have heeded the de Zoysas' warning. They had been on the road for only half an hour when flashes of forked lightning began to streak a now black sky and peals of thunder like the explosions from the broadside of a battleship echoed round the jungle-clad hills. Five minutes later the rain came down.

It struck the car like a cataract, a solid sheet of water reduced visibility to a few yards and Truss was compelled to pull up at the side of the road. For three-quarters of an hour the rain sheeted down and now and then, between the crashes of thunder, they caught the sharp crack of trees felled by lightning. When the storm eased a little they went on but now with caution as, every half mile or so, big branches partly blocked the road.

Twenty minutes later there came another cloudburst but this time, luckily, they were just entering a small town, and a white man, already drenched to the skin, who had been shopping there, very decently ran out of a store to tell them that there was a rest house only a few hundred yards' distant.

Nosing the car slowly through the veil of descending water, they managed to reach it then, soaked through in a moment, ran inside. As it was now after midday they decided to have an early lunch, then for another hour or more they sat impatiently watching the downpour.

By half past two it had ceased, and with extraordinary swiftness the black clouds rolled away to be replaced by blue skies and brilliant sunshine. But the heat of the sun on the sodden jungle soon caused steam to rise almost with the density of fog. Added to which, for several hundred yards in some of the valleys the road lay under a sheet of water, in places a foot deep; while now and then rushing streams eddied and gurgled from one side of the road to the other. In consequence a journey that they should have done in three hours took them over eight, and it was half past five before they reached Colombo.

On arriving at the Galle Face, still damp and tired from their frustrating drive, but brimming over with excitement at the good news they brought, they went straight up to de Richleau's sitting room.

With him he had Nicholas van Goens, and the Duke said at once, 'You may speak freely in front of our friend here, because I have taken him into our confidence. But I have bad news for you.'

His face was so grave that for a moment they feared to ask for it, then he added, 'Lalita has struck sooner than we expected. Douglas was arrested yesterday afternoon.'

'Oh no!' exclaimed Fleur.

'Yes, my child. This is a wretched business. But, of course, his father is doing everything possible to get him released.'

Truss nodded. 'Yes, that's bad. But not so bad as it might be now we've got the goods on Lalita. Mirabelle was right about Vinala Fernando having been buried in the pigsty. We found her skull and I photographed it. We're all set now to have Lalita charged with murder.'

De Richleau shook his head. 'No, Truss; we've lost the game there, too. I don't doubt that he and his father murdered her, but there's not one scrap of evidence to prove they did, except that Mirabelle de Mendoza could have given about the blood-stains on their clothes. She——'

'Could have!' Fleur interjected sharply.

'Yes. Van Goens has just been telling me that her dead body was found in the lake this morning.'

20

Well Planned, but . . .

Fleur and Truss stared aghast at de Richleau. After a moment he said:

'It's a tragic business. That poor woman: such a pleasant creature both to talk to and to look at. Only yesterday, full of life and with high hopes that she was about to win for herself a happy future. Then last night stabbed in the back and thrown in the city lake to become food for the fishes.'

'How awful,' Fleur murmured. 'And with her has gone our one chance to get the better of Lalita.'

'Surely there's still a case against him?' Truss argued. 'We can produce the photographs I took, and it's obvious that Vinala was murdered. The motive stands out a mile. If the d'Azavedos hadn't done her in she might have endorsed her husband's confession that the will was a forgery. And living so near her they had ample opportunity.'

It was van Goens who answered, 'That's not enough, sir. We wouldn't have a hope of getting a verdict.'

'But Douglas,' said Fleur quickly. 'Tell me about him.'

'He was arrested in his office soon after lunch yesterday,' the Duke replied. 'Then they went to your house, turned it upside down and took away all his papers. We can't be certain, of course, but it seems highly probable that it was that which led to Mirabelle's death. You will recall my fears that one of Douglas's clerks might be in Lalita's pay, and my asking him to draw up the deed of gift himself at home. All the odds are that Lalita found it among Douglas's papers. A glance at it would have been enough to tell him that Mirabelle was double-crossing him. Being the villainous devil he is that would have been quite sufficient to make him decide to pay some thug to put her out of the way.'

'And now . . . and now,' Fleur choked with tears in her eyes. 'Now he has Douglas in prison he will have gloated over him about . . .' She had been going to say 'Truss and me', but realising that van Goens was present, hastily checked herself.

'I doubt if he will have had time to interrogate your husband yet, Madame,' van Goens said. 'He will have been too occupied with a bigger fish and a number of other people that the Government are out to get.'

'D'you mean that Lalita's excuse for roping him in is that he has taken part in a conspiracy?' Truss asked.

'Well, not exactly. This concerns smuggling. Some time ago two ships of the Royal Ceylon Navy were sent out on a cruise to the Far East, to show the flag, so to speak. Since their return there have been rumours that they brought back a large quantity of dutiable goods and have been gradually bringing them ashore. The senior officer on the cruise was Rear-Admiral Royce de Mel. He is reputed to be an efficient man, and it's very probable that any smuggling that did occur was done without his knowledge. But as he is a Roman Catholic the Bandaranaike crowd have got it in for him. He and six of his officers were interdicted this morning and since then, I gather, Lalita and his Security boys have been hard at it searching the two ships from bridge to keel for any contraband that may still be in them.'

Truss frowned. 'But what could Mr. Rajapakse have had to do with a racket of this kind?'

'I don't suppose he had anything at all to do with it, sir. But he is accused of receiving some of the smuggled goods. I expect d'Azavedo bribed one of the servants to plant them in the house. He has used this affair only as a means of pulling in Mr. Rajapakse.'

'Well, anyway, it's not a very serious charge.'

'But that's not the point!' Fleur burst out. 'You know what Mirabelle said Lalita meant to do to him once he got him in prison.'

De Richleau nodded and said to van Goens, 'We have reason to fear that d'Azavedo may use his powers to induce some of the hardened criminals among the prisoners to set on Mr. Rajapakse and do him a serious injury. What do you think the chances are of that happening?'

'It could happen, Your Grace. Of course, until he has been brought to trial and convicted he will be kept in a separate cell and, short of an organised riot, as long as he is in it he should be safe. But the prisoners are taken out for exercise every day and in the yard there are sometimes nasty scrimmages. I wouldn't put it past d'Azavedo to arrange one and have him got at that way.'

'Oh, this is too terrible!' Fleur cried, dabbing at her eyes with her handkerchief. 'We must get him out! Somehow we must get him out. Why hasn't his father done anything?'

'He has done all he can,' de Richleau said. 'I went to see him this morning and asked him what hopes there were of securing Douglas's release. But it seems that the Security Police have special powers to veto the release on bail of anyone they have arrested until they have completed their investigations.'

Looking miserably at him Fleur declared, 'I can't go home with you on Friday now. I can't! To desert Douglas at a time like this would be an awful thing to do. I've simply got to remain here as long as he is in prison.'

'Of course, my child. And while you are in this trouble nothing would induce me to leave you.'

'But, Greyeyes; you ought to go. You are threatened, too. Truss joining his father in Manila, or somewhere, must give way to your safety, and he can see you back to Europe.'

'Have a heart!' Truss protested. 'As though either of us would run out on you at a time like this.'

'But it's Greyeyes' safety that matters. He must go.'

The Duke smiled at her and laid a hand on her arm. 'Thank you, my dear, for your concern for me. But in my long life I have been threatened many times without coming to grief. And I don't think that my ability to look after myself is likely to fail me now. What we have to worry about is how we can get Douglas out of prison; and very quickly, before harm comes to him.'

Turning to van Goens, he went on, 'As an ex-Inspector of Police you must be well informed about conditions in the prisons of Ceylon. How frequently are escapes made from them?'

'Fairly often, Your Grace,' van Goens replied. 'The prison system here is nowhere near as efficient as it is in Europe. The warders are a poor lot, ill-trained and lacking discipline. Many of the prisoners are desperate men and hold their lives cheap, so some of the warders will turn their backs rather than risk their own lives when a cut-throat makes up his mind to break out. And, of course, as is the case in all Asiatic countries, many of the officials are open to bribery.'

'That is what I had in mind. But I am in no position to handle such an affair. You know the ropes; and money is no object, either for bribes or for any reward you care to ask, if you could enable Mr. Rajapakse to escape.'

Van Goens hesitated for a moment. 'It might be done, Your Grace; and it would be a pleasure to help you, because the Bandaranaike Government most unfairly put an end to what was for me a promising career. But I have to think of my future. My present prospects are not very bright, but at least they are better than if I were caught aiding a prisoner to escape. You must allow me to think it over.'

'But time is so important,' Fleur said quickly. 'If you could, now that I can still dispose of the Olenevka property, I'd willingly make it over to you.'

Raising his eyebrows van Goens exclaimed, 'But, Madame, I understand it to be worth two hundred thousand rupees. That is an enormous sum to an ex-Inspector of Police. Too much; much too much for any service I can render.'

De Richleau laughed and said, 'Only a few years ago it was said to be worth over five hundred thousand rupees, and it may become so again. But I am heartily sick of this damnable property I inherited, and Mrs. Rajapakse has the right to dispose of it as she wishes.'

'Whatever its worth, you're welcome to it,' Fleur declared, 'if only you can arrange my husband's escape. Once he is free I . . . we, that is, will probably go to live in another country; so I'll not be able to get any money from it. But you might, and I'd wish you luck.'

'Madame,' van Goens said gravely, 'you are now under the stress of great emotion. So I would not hold you to this. I ask only the assurance of His Grace and yourself that should I get into serious trouble through attempting to aid Mr. Rajapakse you will see to it that my wife is adequately provided for, and when the trouble is past take steps that will give me a good chance to earn a decent living.'

'Nothing could be fairer,' said the Duke, 'and you have my word on that.'

So far, since the arrival of Fleur and Truss, all of them except de Richleau had remained standing. Now the others sat down while Truss provided them with drinks, then they set about discussing possible ways in which Douglas might be aided to escape.

Having been stationed in Colombo for some years before he had been transferred to Ratnapura, van Goens knew the prison well and the methods by which the most daring prisoners had succeeded in getting out. But even if instructions could be smuggled in to Douglas, which van Goens thought would not be very difficult, they did not feel that he was the type of man to take big risks readily. It was, moreover, probable that as de Richleau had told him of Lalita's evil intentions towards him, he would suspect such a message to be a trap designed to lead him to expose himself, so that he might be shot while trying to escape.

In consequence, they came to the conclusion that their best hope lay in the classic method of sending someone in to see him, with whom he could exchange clothes then walk out.

Van Goens said that Douglas, not yet having been convicted, would be allowed to receive a limited number of visitors in his cell and that, in the case of high-class prisoners, it was not unusual for their visitors to bring a servant with them, carrying a big basket containing food and clean clothes. The plan that emerged was, therefore, that someone known to Douglas should visit him, and be accompanied by a man, acting as a servant, who would be willing to remain behind.

Truss immediately volunteered to be the visitor.

At that Fleur took alarm and cried, 'No, no! You owe nothing to Douglas, and if you were caught you would be imprisoned too. I'm his wife. That will be my job.'

He smiled at her. 'If anyone is going to be imprisoned I'd rather it were me than you. And you're wrong about my owing nothing to Douglas. I've never forgotten that time in Corfu when we all went for a midnight swim. It wasn't my fault he didn't drown. I've had that on my conscience for a long time and I'd like the chance to even things up. No arguing now. If you're a good girl I'll let you row in to the extent of waiting in a car outside ready to aid our getaway.'

De Richleau nodded. 'Yes, my child. That would be much the best way. Asiatics have no great opinion of women as their companions in dangerous situations, and a man who would otherwise be willing to act as a substitute for Douglas might well refuse to go into the prison with you.' Turning to van Goens he asked, 'What do you think the chances are of your being able to secure such a man during the next twenty-four hours?'

'He will have to face a prison sentence for abetting an escape,' van Goens replied, 'but if he were tied up and gagged before Mr. Rajapakse left his cell it should not be a very long one, and he might even get off. There are plenty of ne'er-do-wells in Colombo who would be willing to do that for, say, two thousand rupees. The difficulty will be to find one who resembles Mr. Rajapakse in height and build. But my knowledge of the criminal classes here is fairly extensive and I have two men in mind either of whom, if he is still about, might serve our purpose. I will go round the dock area tonight and see if I can run one or other of them to earth.'

'Good. The next thing is, how are we to proceed should the escape prove successful?'

'The attempt should be made as late as possible in the evening. That, I think, could be arranged by a bribe to one of the senior warders. You will appreciate that whoever gives it to him is liable afterwards to be connected with the escape. Naturally, I wish to avoid that if possible, but Mr. Van Ryn would be suspected in any case because he is to introduce the substitute, so I suggest——'

'O.K.' Truss put in. 'If you get me his name and he is fixable, I'll fix him.'

'Then, if you can make a clean get-away in Mrs. Rajapakse's car, you should have all night before the substitution is discovered and the police are warned everywhere to keep a look-out for you and Mr. Rajapakse. That should enable you to get to some sparsely populated jungle area. At some suitable place you would be wise to abandon the car. As you have plenty of money you should be able to find some lonely dwelling where for a good payment the peasant owner would take you in and keep you there in hiding for some weeks until the hunt for you has died down.'

'No,' said the Duke. 'That will not do. Given suitable clothes, Mr. Rajapakse could pass himself off as a peasant; but not Mrs. Rajapakse nor Mr. Van Ryn, even if they stained their faces and hands. After a while it is certain that it would get about in the neighbourhood that two white people were in hiding there, and a little later it would reach the ears of the police. Again, they could not walk very far after abandoning the car, and if it were found and identified that would lead to a search of the whole area. No. Somehow they must leave the country.'

'That would be next to impossible, Your Grace. All the ports will be watched.'

'We could go to the far north,' Fleur suggested, 'and get away across Adam's Bridge.'

'What's that?' Truss enquired.

'It almost connects Ceylon with India. Long narrow capes run out from both into the Palk Strait. The twenty miles between them is impassable by all but ships of shallow draught, and they are dotted with rocks and little islands. If we could buy a small boat up there we ought to be able to make the crossing.'

'You might, Madame,' van Goens agreed. 'But even at night you would be taking a big risk. It is the age-old road of invasion from India, both in war and peace; and the Government here does its utmost to prevent illegal immigration; more so than ever now that they are so strongly averse to letting Tamils into the country. A score of guard-boats are always on watch there and as it is illegal to leave Ceylon without a permit one of them might very well pick you up and require to see your papers.'

'To go out by air is the only thing then,' the Duke said with a frown. 'I did not wish to involve Truss's father and your Uncle Simon in this, in case you all got caught. But we shall have to. We will cable them urgently to return at once. If the escape fails they will have had their flight back for nothing; but that cannot be helped. If it succeeds we will arrange a rendezvous in some desolate place where the plane can land and pick you up.'

Truss nodded. 'That's by far the best idea yet, sir. And I'm sure my old . . . my father would come hustling back here the moment he hears we're in trouble. I'll get a code cable off to him this evening through our agent here.'

'Good. We must now decide on a suitable place for the rendezvous. There is a map of Ceylon in the bookcase, Truss. Be good enough to get it for us.'

When the map was spread out van Goens said, 'The east coast would be best as it is both flat and sparsely populated. As there is no point in your going further north than you have to I suggest somewhere about half-way between Batticaloa and Trincomalee.'

'The plane must have some easily identifiable object to home on,' said the Duke, 'and I see there is a railway from

Polonnaruwa to Batticaloa. They could pick that up easily enough, and it reaches the coast at a little place called Kalkudah, about twenty-five miles short of completing its run. Somewhere in that area seems a good possibility.'

Putting his finger on the map, Truss added, 'There's a useful little cape jutting right out for four or five miles north of Kalkudah. With the railway just south to help them they couldn't miss that. It . . . yes, it's called Elephant Point.'

'Couldn't be better,' De Richleau looked at van Goens. 'That is, if the terrain is suitable for a plane to land.'

'I can't say for certain, Your Grace, because I haven't been there. But along most of the north-east coast there is a deep belt of sandy waste, so it should be.'

'Very well then. We will settle for Elephant Point. And, Truss, you had better buy bright red headscarves for the three of you to wear. Then when the plane comes over your father will not mistake a group of peasants for you and make a landing to no purpose. Now; is there anything else?'

For a further ten minutes they discussed the situation with which they were faced but no other points arose; so van Goens went off on his search for a crook whose build suited him to take Douglas's place and soon afterwards Fleur and Truss went down to his car together.

As he turned it in the direction of her home, she said, 'Aren't you going to your agent to send that cable? It ought to go off as soon as possible, and I can sit in the car outside while you send it.'

He shook his head. 'They'll not get it till tomorrow morning anyway, and my agent's office will be shut by now. I'll have to dig him out at his home and take him along to produce the code book. Time enough for that after dinner, and I know you must be anxious to see what Lalita's thugs have done to your house.'

When they arrived the servants met Fleur with doleful faces. They had done their best to put the place to rights, but every cupboard had been ransacked and every drawer emptied of its contents; so much tidying up had yet to be done. The head boy told them that the seized contraband had been hidden under the raised wooden floor of the summer house, and had consisted of some large rolls of Thai silk, cases of spirits and several Japanese miniature radio sets. Going out into the garden, they found that the summer house floor had been ripped to pieces; but Truss consoled Fleur a little by saying that the place chosen to plant the contraband made it less likely that one of her servants was in Lalita's pay and spying on her, as the stuff could have been put there any night without their knowledge.

The shock of the news with which the Duke had greeted them, and the urgency of the conference that had followed, had temporarily taken their minds off the fatigue they had felt after their eight-hour journey. But now it came upon them again and they were both longing for a hot bath to revive them; so Fleur said:

'You can have one in the guest bathroom and I'll have one in my own; meanwhile the servants can be getting ready some dinner for us.'

Truss gave her an uneasy look. 'Is that wise, honey? I mean, it may look to them as though you're taking advantage of your husband being in prison to bring home a guy.'

She shrugged unhappily. 'I don't give a damn what they think. By now that fiend Lalita has probably done his worst on poor Douglas and will put it all over Colombo tomorrow that he came on you and me in bed together. Besides, with luck, this will be the last night I'll ever spend here.'

Accordingly Truss stayed on, but throughout dinner he adopted a very formal manner, and left immediately afterwards, to drive to the home of the head of the firm that in Colombo acted as the agents for his bank. It was only on the other side of the Race Course, so not far away, and his acquaintance proved eager to render any service to the heir to the Van Ryn millions. A quarter of an hour later they were in the firm's office and Truss encoded the following telegram to his father:

In serious trouble. Stop. Please return Colombo with utmost urgency in own aircraft. Stop. Repeat own aircraft. Stop. On arrival communicate with Duke immediately. Stop. Truss.

As the Post Office was closed he took it along to the American Embassy and had it despatched from there. By ten o'clock he was back at the Galle Face getting ready for bed. Soon afterwards, with the health of the young, he was sound asleep.

There followed an anxious day of conferences and visits. In

the morning Fleur went to see her parents-in-law. In his office old Mr. Rajapakse, believing that she was still in love with Douglas, received her with the deepest sympathy and did his best to console her; although he admitted that he saw little hope of securing Douglas's early release. When she left him she was almost weeping at the thought of the blow it would be to him when he learned that she had betrayed and made a laughing stock of his son. At the Rajapakse home she found her mountainously fat mother-in-law in tears, but the old woman quickly dried them and began to reproach her bitterly. Quite illogically, as it was her husband's firm that had initiated the dispute about Count Plackoff's will, knowing only that her son's arrest was in some way connected with it, she laid the blame for his misfortune on Fleur and her English friends. Having paid this duty visit, Fleur left her with increased loathing and the hope that she would never see her again.

Truss, meanwhile, had been waiting impatiently with the Duke at the Galle Face to learn if van Goens had been successful. He was not in his room and an enquiry at the desk produced the information that he had not come in till four o'clock in the morning and had gone out again at nine.

He did not return till nearly midday, but when he did he was smiling. During the night he had traced a pickpocket named Wira Banda, but succeeded only at a second meeting that morning in persuading him to do what was required for two thousand rupees—the equivalent of a hundred and fifty pounds. Van Goens said that he meant to provide Banda with a long, loose gown and a soft hat to pull down over his eyes; and that, if his face was partly bandaged as though he had an infection in one of his eyes, Douglas Rajapakse coming out in the same rig should have a good chance of passing for him. He was to receive half the money before the job and the other half when he was released.

The Duke had arranged with the hotel cashier that morning to provide him with a considerable sum against traveller's cheques; so he handed over the money with an additional five hundred rupees to van Goens for expenses. Van Goens then gave Truss the names of the Chief and second warders at the prison and directions how to get there. It was situated behind the city over two miles from the sea front, which Truss learned with satisfaction, as that meant they would be able to drive straight off into the country without the delay caused by going through crowded streets.

While they were lunching, a cablegram was brought to de Richleau. It had been handed in at Manila at 9.40 that morning and said only *On our way stop rexsimon*. Laconic as it was, it cheered them greatly to know that, at latest, the aircraft could be expected to arrive in Colombo by the following morning and so be able to make the short hop up to the rendezvous on the east coast in the afternoon.

As soon as they had finished their meal, Truss went out to his car and drove to the prison. There, he slipped a twenty rupee note into the hand of the clerk at the enquiry desk and no difficulty was made about his seeing one of the senior warders. To him he explained that, as a friend of Mr. Rajapakse, he wanted to bring him some food and a change of clothes; but that he had had no time to get them that morning and business engagements that he could not put off would not make it possible for him to visit the prisoner until between eight and nine o'clock.

The warder told him gruffly that five in the afternoon was the latest hour at which visits were allowed, upon which Truss produced his gold cigarette case to offer the man a cigarette. Out of the case there fluttered to the floor a hundred rupee note. Truss made no attempt to pick it up but regarded the warder with a quiet smile. The warder returned the smile and said:

'Exceptions can be made. America has been good friend to Ceylon. Very much against old Colonial system; so helped to push Britain into giving us independence. For American business man I make exceptions. I give your name at gate, Mr. Van Ryn, to be admitted any hour up to nine o'clock.'

Owing to the wide knowledge of the world that Truss had acquired from his father, it was his private opinion that his country had let the side down by coercing Britain into giving self-government to many peoples who were not yet fitted for it, and exposing them to Communism. But he naturally refrained from saying so and, much relieved, shook the official warmly by the hand.

On leaving the prison, he drove his hire-car to its garage, had it fully serviced and filled to capacity with petrol. While this was being done he went into a nearby grocer's, had a good supply of drinks and provisions packed into two cartons, carried them back to the garage and put them in the boot of the car.

Before returning to the Galle Face he went again to his agent's and drew five hundred dollars' worth of rupees, then to Cargill's big store and bought three large bright-red handkerchiefs. When he got back to the hotel he had a bath, packed his suitcases and paid his bill, then he went in to de Richleau.

Fleur was there, slumped in a chair, looking very gloomy; and although Truss was able to report that he had arranged matters satisfactorily at the prison, he was far from sanguine that this attempt to rescue Douglas would prove successful.

By then it was the cocktail hour and, observing their depression, the Duke rallied them upon it.

'Come, my children,' he smiled. 'Why such long faces? Your parents would be ashamed of you. In the old days the prospect of getting the better of a pack of rogues always stimulated us; and to have confidence in yourselves is half the battle. I only wish I were still young enough to join you in tonight's undertaking. But at least I can put some stimulant into you. God alone knows how it got here, but they have some of Môet and Chandon's special cuvée, the Dom Perignon, down in the cellar. There are no magnums; but ring down, Truss, and order up a couple of bottles.'

While the wine was still in the ice buckets van Goens came in to make final arrangements. He said that he had provided Banda with everything necessary and, when Truss told him about his visit to the prison, that he would meet them with the pickpocket at the crossroads where Campbell Place and Baseline Road met, about a quarter of a mile south of the prison, at ten minutes to nine. They were to drop him a few hundred yards short of the prison gate. He would remain there to observe how things went; and, as soon as the attempt was over, one way or another, return to report to the Duke.

The superb wine put new heart into Fleur and Truss and, when van Goens had drunk good luck to them and left, they went down to dinner with de Richleau. During the meal he kept their thoughts from the danger they were going into by recounting past exploits in which he, with the aid of their fathers and Uncle Simon, had tricked and brought to grief their enemies.

At half past eight, a frail white-haired figure, leaning on his malacca, but with glowing eyes beneath his 'devil's' eyebrows, he blessed them and waved them away in their car.

They had left well ahead of time to cover the three miles to the crossroads, but found van Goens and Banda already there. The latter proved to be a smarmy little man who had a smattering of English, but his height and general appearance gave the impression that, unless seen face to face, he might pass for Douglas.

Three hundred yards short of the prison van Goens asked Truss to pull up, again wished them luck and got out. Truss then drove on to the main entrance to the building. Fleur took over the wheel of the now stationary car, and murmured a prayer as Truss left it followed by Banda carrying a big basket. As they approached the iron-studded door a sentry who had been lolling against it took up his rifle and challenged them. Truss produced a piece of paper with his name written clearly on it and that of the senior warder with whom he had arranged his visit.

The sentry took it, stared at it upside down for a good minute, then jerked down an iron bell pull. A bell clanged dismally somewhere in the distance. They waited several minutes, then the door was opened by a short, thick-set man with long gorilla-like arms. The sentry handed him the paper and, after looking at it, he beckoned them inside. Truss slipped him twenty rupees and he nodded. Without a word said they followed him down a succession of dimly lit corridors. Halting at last, he jangled his bunch of big keys, selected one, opened a cell door with it, and motioned them to go inside.

Truss was now feeling on his mettle but, even so, his heart gave a nasty lurch as the iron door clanged to behind him and Banda, and he heard it relocked.

Douglas was sitting disconsolately on a truckle bed, but the moment he recognised Truss he came to his feet with an exclamation of surprise and delight. In a low voice Truss made his explanations as briefly as possible, and they set to work without delay. Banda took off his gown and hat, and unwound the bandage round his face. Douglas put them on, then helped to tie Banda up and gag him with cords and a strip of cloth that had been brought in with other things in the big basket. Then they laid him on the bed and covered him up with his face towards the wall.

There followed an anxious ten minutes, as it would have appeared unnatural for a friend of the prisoner to have cut his visit short before he had to by banging on the door for the warder.

Douglas's greeting had been so spontaneously friendly that Truss thought it improbable that he had yet learned about Fleur and himself. But he felt so ill at ease while not knowing for certain that he asked a leading question:

'I suppose Lalita's been here to gloat over having got you. Was he particularly offensive?'

To Truss's relief Douglas replied, 'I've been expecting a visit from him any time; but so far the little swine hasn't been near me.'

Soon afterwards the warder unlocked the door, and with a jerk of his head signified that the time had come for the visitors to leave the cell. With a word of good night to the figure in the bed, Truss led the way out, followed by Douglas, with the brim of the felt hat pulled well down over his bandaged face and carrying the now empty basket.

With heavy, echoing footfalls, the gorilla-like warder conducted them through the long corridors, then let them out. As Truss felt the fresh night air on his face he sent up a silent prayer of thanksgiving. Then he saw that another car had driven up behind that in which Fleur was waiting for them. From it there had just emerged a Security Guard and a civilian. A moment later, with Douglas still behind him, he was within a few yards of the approaching men.

The light above the door of the prison shone directly on their dark features and it struck Truss that those of the Security Guard were vaguely familiar. Next moment the man displayed his white teeth in a broad grin, and said, 'Hello! You not with pretty girl tonight, eh?'

Suddenly Truss recognised him as the Sergeant who had entered Fleur's room at the hotel in Trincomalee with Lalita and Mirabelle, and next day escorted them all to the airport. His heart had begun to hammer violently, but he managed to raise a laugh, and reply, 'I don't always have such luck.'

Ignoring his crack, the man was now staring past him at Douglas. Suddenly becoming suspicious, he demanded:

'Who with you? Who you bring out of prison?'

Taking a step forward, he grabbed Douglas by his gown

and swung him round so that he could see his features in the light.

'Devils!' he exclaimed. 'It is Rajapakse who I help arrest day before yesterday!'

Next moment he had sprung back and unslung his Sten gun.

21

A Desperate Bid for Freedom

Truss had only seconds in which to decide. Should he surrender or make a fight for it? If he allowed himself to be arrested he would be charged with aiding a prisoner to escape. That would mean a prison sentence of several months. And worse: Douglas would remain at the mercy of Lalita. Yet if he tackled the Sergeant and failed to get away he would receive a much heavier sentence. Still worse, during the scuffle, he might be riddled with bullets from the Sten gun.

These possibilities flashed through his mind with the speed of lightning, to be followed by a sudden memory. It was of the Duke's mesmeric, grey, yellow-flecked eyes glowing with delight in those past exploits that he had recounted over dinner. Truss knew then that he would never be able to look 'Grandpa Greyeyes' in the face again if he tamely gave in.

The Sergeant had lost no time in unslinging his Sten gun from round his shoulders, but before he could bring it up Truss sprang forward and seized it with both hands.

'Run, Douglas, run!' he shouted as he gave the weapon a violent twist. 'Get in the car! Don't wait for me!'

Spitting curses, the little Sergeant clung to his gun gamely. But Truss was a head and shoulders taller than the puny Sinhalese and too strong for him. Another violent wrench and the gun was torn from his grasp. Having got possession of the weapon Truss swung it round and jabbed its barrel hard into his adversary's stomach. With a grunt the man doubled up, swayed sideways and, clasping his belly, collapsed on the ground. The civilian who had accompanied him from the car had remained standing a few yards off, watching the struggle with frightened eyes. The moment he saw the Sergeant collapse he turned and ran.

During the bare minute the struggle had lasted it had fully engaged Truss's mind. Now he became aware of slithering footsteps and heavy breathing behind him. Douglas had not, as urged, made a bolt for the car. He had swung round and, before the slothful sentry could raise his rifle, struck him a blow under the chin that had temporarily knocked him out. But the warder had not, as Truss had thought, closed the door of the prison after them. Seeing the Sergeant and his companion approaching, he had kept it open. Then, as Truss sprang at the Sergeant and Douglas knocked down the sentry, the warder had run out to take Truss in the rear. Douglas had barred his path and they had gone into a clinch. But the warder was much the more powerful of the two and now, as Truss swung about, he saw that Douglas was being dragged back into the prison.

At that moment the man who was running away looked over his shoulder. Seeing that Truss's back was now turned, he grabbed up a large stone, swung round, and threw it. Either his aim was good or it was a lucky shot. It caught Truss on the back of the neck just as he was about to go to Douglas's rescue. He stumbled, pitched forward and went down on his knees. The big stone had struck him squarely at the base of the skull, rendering him temporarily sick and dizzy. With an effort he pulled himself together and stumbled to his feet. But by then the warder had pulled Douglas inside the door and, despite his continued struggles, had nearly succeeded in closing it.

Lurching forward, Truss managed to get his foot and knee in the door. For a short time a trial of strength then took place between the gorilla-like man inside and the tall, muscular young American. Truss dared not step back to throw his whole weight against the door in a charge, as the pressure on its other side would have snapped it shut, but the warder was handicapped by having to cling on to Douglas. Gradually it inched open, then suddenly gave a foot or more. Greatly encouraged, Truss redoubled his efforts. Next moment he realised to what he owed his temporary advantage. His opponent had relaxed only for long enough to press a nearby switch. Alarm bells shrilled inside the prison.

Desperate now at the thought that within another few minutes the game would be up, Douglas again a prisoner and himself a fugitive with nothing to show for it, Truss reacted in a way only excusable by the heat of the moment. Thrusting the Sten gun in above his knee, he pressed the trigger sharply once, sending two bullets into the warder's foot.

Letting out a howl of pain the man staggered back, and the door flew open. With one huge hand he still held his prisoner by the collar, but the strength of his grip had lessened. Douglas tore himself free, pushed him back and stumbled outside.

All this had occupied only a few minutes, but they were sufficient for the Sergeant to have partially recovered and he was on his feet again. He made a grab at Douglas as he ran towards the car but Douglas dodged him and ran on. Pointing the Sten gun at the Sergeant, Truss yelled, 'Out of the way, you; or you'll have had it.'

The man threw up his hands and backed away. Truss, keeping him covered for another half-minute, shuffled swiftly crabwise towards the car. Fleur had opened both doors ready for them. Douglas scrambled in beside her, then Truss dived into the back. She let in the clutch and they were away. But by then the sentry had regained his senses. Grabbing up his rifle he sent two shots clanging into the back of the car.

As soon as they had partially regained their breath, Douglas panted, 'Thanks, Truss; thanks. In there . . . I was constantly in fear they'd . . . find some way to kill me. For getting me out I can never repay you.'

'We'll be mighty lucky if . . . soon we're not back in there,' Truss replied between gasps for air. 'I'm in it too now . . . up to the neck . . . for having shot that warder. It'll not be months but years if they get me.' Then he added to Fleur, 'Drive like hell, hon . . . Fleur. Take no notice of traffic signs or anyone who tries to stop us. They'll be after us in that damn' car any moment now. That Sergeant will have waited only to get a couple of other men with weapons from the prison.'

In his preoccupation with their danger he had momentarily forgotten the delicate situation between the three of them, and had nearly said, 'honey'. But Fleur was far from having forgotten it. To rescue a man from prison does not excuse taking his wife, and, like Truss, for the past half-hour she had been on tenterhooks to know if Lalita had disclosed her infidelity to Douglas. Able to bear the suspense no longer, she said to him:

'While you were in prison did . . . did Lalita come and question you?'

'No,' he replied. 'I haven't seen him since he arrested me.

I'm charged, you know, with having received a lot of smuggled goods from the ships that Admiral de Mel took on a cruise. One of the warders, who was quite a friendly fellow, told me that de Mel and several other officers were interdicted yesterday; and I imagine Lalita was too busy with them to bother, for the time being, about me.'

Fleur had hardly given a silent sigh of relief before her thoughts were brought back with a jolt to the immediate present. Truss was kneeling on the back seat of the car peering out of the window; and she had just slowed a little to take the corner out of Baseline Road into that which led east, away from the city when he shouted.

'Step on it, Fleur! I can see their headlights and they're gaining on us.'

At that hour there was little traffic and they were running through a suburb of scattered tumbledown buildings. Fleur put on all the speed she could, but half a mile further on a horse and cart emerged from a side turning. She was forced to brake sharply and reduce speed almost to a crawl before they could get by. The police car came streaking up behind them. Truss felt that, knowing him to be armed, the men in it would not have dared press the chase without first arming themselves. At any moment he expected them to open fire. Swiftly he decided that the only chance of escape now lay in firing first. With a heavy blow from the butt of the Sten gun he bashed a big hole in the triplex glass of the rear window, thrust the barrel of the gun through it and fired a long burst.

Fully conscious of what a terrible thing it would be if he killed one of the police, he aimed low. The spray of bullets smashed into the radiator, tore open one tyre and the car lights went out. The car swerved to one side, mounted a low bank and came to a halt half-way through a croton hedge.

By then Fleur was regaining speed and after another two miles they were out in the country which surrounds Colombo, where patches of jungle alternate with plantations of coconut, paddy fields and many small villages. Lights were still burning in the villages and quite a few people moving about. In spite of the necessity for speed, while running through the villages, Fleur had to drive carefully; so it was past ten o'clock before they had covered the fifteen miles to the considerable town of Gampaha.

By that time orders to stop them could have been telephoned ahead; so they feared that here they would be faced with an attempt to do so. As they ran through the town they peered anxiously ahead. Then as they approached the main crossroads they saw that their fears were only too well founded.

A line of six policemen barred their way. But they had not had time to make a road block; so Fleur charged straight at them. They held their ground until the car was within twenty feet, yelling and waving for it to halt. Then, as they realised that the driver was not slowing down, they leaped aside, two of them rolling into the gutter. Two of the others pulled out their revolvers and sent shots after the retreating car. But their aim was poor, and none of the shots took effect.

It was when they were about five miles past Gampaha that Fleur noticed that the petrol gauge was unexpectedly low. The tanks had been full when she had started out; now they were four-fifths empty and the car had done only something over twenty miles. Alarmed at this she brought it to a halt; then Douglas and Truss got out to see if they could trace a leak.

By the light of a torch they found that, although the tank had not been pierced by the bullets fired at the car, it had been scored by one of them. In the middle section of the furrow it had made before ricocheting off, the metal was paper thin and the petrol seeping through minute holes in it. As they had no putty or anything which, when the car was in motion, would serve to stop the leak, they decided that the only way they could continue their journey was somehow to get hold of another car.

At a reduced speed Fleur drove on until they came to the outskirts of a big village. There she pulled up at the side of the road, then Truss got out and walked on.

Douglas, too, got out and kept an anxious watch on the road behind them; for since leaving Gampaha they had feared that a police car would be sent in pursuit and, if it was, their only course would have been to try to get away in the jungle. But it seemed that the Gampaha police were either too lacking in initiative to come after them or, having learned that the fugitives were armed and had already shot to disaster one police car, were too scared for their own skins to give chase.

After a quarter of an hour, their fears that they would have to take to the jungle while still separated from Truss gradually lessened but, as they waited impatiently for his return and the time of his absence lengthened, they began to be afraid that while attempting to steal a car he had been caught.

Over an hour elapsed before an old Ford drew up beside them and Truss got out of it. 'Best I could do,' he said a shade unhappily. 'In these parts people don't run to slap-up autos, and I had to go for one parked in a lean-to. Still, it's more than half full of gas. Come on, let's transfer our things to the old jalopy and get going again.'

On opening the boot they found that another bullet had embedded itself in one of Truss's suitcases; but he raised a laugh by saying he wished both bullets had made holes through his clothes as then he would be able to go about looking like a real gangster. Within five minutes they had moved their baggage and stores over to the Ford, and while doing so discussed what should be done with the car they were abandoning.

When found, it would give away that after leaving Gampaha they had continued on the main road to the north-east and had not attempted to throw off pursuit by taking a side turning. But for one of them to have run the car some distance down a jungle track, left it there and then walked back, would have cost precious time; and it might, anyhow, have been discovered there quite early in the morning.

Having decided to leave it where it was, they piled into the old Ford and, with Truss at the wheel, set off again. For some two and a half hours the ancient vehicle banged and clattered along, at no great pace but a fairly steady speed, passing now through unlit villages and long stretches of impenetrably dark jungle. At about half an hour after midnight they were approaching Kurunegala, much the biggest town on their route, so certain to hold great danger of capture for them. Feeling sure there would be a police block on the main road Truss took a turning to the left soon after entering the suburbs. Twice they lost their way in rambling lanes but, after twenty minutes of anxious twisting and turning, found their way back on to the highway to the north of the town.

Then at about a quarter to two in the morning, soon after they had left behind them a small town that Douglas said he thought was Galewela, while they were going up a short but steep gradient the engine suddenly conked out. By the light of the torch Truss and Douglas examined it, but could not discover what had caused the break-down. Perhaps the old bus might have been good for another year or two, doing only short runs at a moderate speed, but it seemed that the pace at which Truss had driven for over thirty miles had proved too much for her.

They were now some sixty miles from Colombo as the crow flies and estimated that Dambulla, the half-way point of their journey, lay not much more than twelve miles ahead. But that was small consolation, as they should have reached it hours earlier; and in darkness with a car travelling at high speed they would have stood a much better chance of getting through a police cordon there, as they had at Gampaha, than they would have now they had to walk and could not hope to reach the town before dawn. To add to their depression there was no alternative to abandoning their luggage and stores.

Truss would have liked to leave some money in one of the pockets of the car as compensation for its owner; but Douglas said that whoever found the Ford, or the police when they searched it, would be certain to pocket a banknote; so, after they had fortified themselves with a drink from one of the bottles of red wine in the boot, Truss took Fleur's beauty case from her and they set off.

When Truss, as a boy, had been at summer camps he had often gone on long hikes; so he made them march in step and join him in singing favourite choruses, as the best means of delaying fatigue and keeping up their spirits. After they had covered eight miles the sky began to lighten and the jungle on either side woke to life. Through the thick foliage below the tall palms, bread-fruit and mango trees, they caught glimpses of animals large and small. Once they had to step over a procession of giant ants that was crossing the road; at others monkeys, performing a variety of acrobats, frequently gibbered at them from the tree tops.

On the last hour of their trudge they fell silent, as both Fleur and Douglas were unused to the strain of such continued exertion; although she stood up to it better than he did, because frequent swimming and tennis had kept her muscles in better trim.

It was about half past four when they came to the first scattered houses of Dambulla. Although it was by then fairly light their occupants were not yet stirring, and as they passed the third house Douglas came to a sudden halt.

'I've had an idea,' he said. 'We have already stolen a car——'

'I know,' Truss interrupted, 'and I'm keeping a look-out. With luck we'll come on another, parked by some bungalow, and be able to make off in it before its owner is about.'

'No, no. Not a car.' Douglas pointed to a thatched lean-to that stood near the house. 'Why not a cart? And there's one over there. I'll drive and you two could travel inside it.'

'It would be terribly slow,' Truss demurred. 'Unless there's some hitch the aircraft will be coming to pick us up this afternoon. We'd never make it to Elephant Point with a horse and cart.'

'We must chance that,' said Fleur quickly. 'What matters at the moment is to get past the police in Dambulla. Douglas is right. In a cart we'd stand a much better chance than in a car or on our flat feet.'

'That's true,' Truss agreed, 'and maybe we'll be able to pick up a car later. Come on, then.'

Moving quickly to the side of the road, Fleur kept watch on the house while Truss and Douglas got out the cart and harnessed to it a small shaggy horse from an adjacent stall. The cart was a small one on two high wheels with a tattered canvas cover supported by hoops. When sitting on its floor, Fleur and Truss were concealed from view, and as Douglas was wearing the outer garment and old hat that Banda had brought into the cell he did not look conspicuously unlike a Sinhalese peasant. Within six minutes of their decision to take the cart they were jolting off down the road.

When they entered the town proper it was still deserted, except for a few market people beginning to arrange their stalls for the day; but as they neared its centre Douglas saw that preparations had been made for their reception. Ahead lay a road block composed of poles and trestles. Between them was sufficient space only to allow a single vehicle to pass and that could have been closed swiftly with another pole by the group of police who were lounging nearby.

Now, Douglas had good reason to thank his stars that he had thought of the cart for, otherwise, there would have been little chance of their escaping capture. Even as it was, if the police looked inside the cart their number would be up. But to have turned back at the sight of the barriers might have aroused suspicion. Endeavouring to suppress his fears, he hunched his shoulders, so that his chin nearly touched his chest, cracked his whip and drove on.

When he reached the barrier he had to hold the reins tightly to stop his hands from trembling, and perspiration was beginning to break out on his forehead as he thought of the wretched fate that was in store for all of them if they were arrested. But he managed to call a cheerful 'good morning' to the policemen.

One of them stepped into the road and asked him what he had in his cart. With his heart in his mouth he replied, 'My poor wife. She's gone down with a typhoid and I'm taking her to hospital.'

As he did not know where the hospital was, and it might have been in the direction from which they had come, he had taken a desperate gamble; but he was hoping that from fear of infection the policeman would refrain from pulling aside the back curtain of the cart.

Inside it, crouching in the semi-darkness, Fleur and Truss knew only that the cart had come to a halt and that Douglas was being questioned. Clasping hands and holding their breath, they waited for a few minutes in awful suspense. Then the whip cracked and the cart moved on. Yet for some while they continued to fear that at any moment it might be halted again.

It was not until a quarter of an hour later that Douglas pulled aside one of the front flaps of the hood to tell them that they were safely out of the town. By then it had become very stuffy inside the cart so, greatly relieved, Truss was able to tie back the rear curtains, enabling Fleur and himself both to look out and to get more air.

As had been the case on their trip up to the ancient cities, at Dambulla they had left the main highway for the road east to Polonnaruwa, and were now entering a sparsely populated area of jungle. When they had been in the 'dry' zone before, the annual rains had only recently started; so many of the trees still had bare branches or were clothed in grey beards of lichen and such leaves as remained had been baked an apricot colour. But that had been a fortnight back. Now their life had been renewed, they were sprouting with every shade of tender green, the creepers were sending out new tendrils and the young fronds of giant ferns were unfolding.

Through occasional breaks in the forest, away to the south-east of Dambulla they could see range after range of mountains rising to six thousand feet, a lovely misty blue against the brighter blue of the sky. But, fortunately, the country through which they were passing was the beginning of the great eastern plain; for the little horse, although he seemed game enough, had quite a load to pull and even here on the flat could manage only about five miles an hour.

To while away the tedium of the journey Truss and Fleur began a competition to see which of them could first spot the greater number of wild animals, giving extra points for rarity. Monkeys were two a penny as there were colonies of them every half mile or so. The deep-voiced wanderoos barked at them as they passed, small mischievous ones chattered excitedly and threw nuts. Some swung rapidly from tested branch to tested branch along roads among the tree tops that they knew well, the females often carrying their young slung below their bodies; others would remain perched aloft absorbed in the friendly task of picking the fleas from a companion. There were many squirrels, jackals and now and then a mongoose; also herds of the little spotted Mouse deer and the common Moutjac. Fleur won good points by sighting a big cow elephant with her cherubic little calf hanging on to her tail, but Truss evened up with a twenty-foot python coiled in the fork of a tree.

There were, too, a great variety of birds: kites, falcons and serpent eagles sailing high overhead, green pigeons, jungle fowl and partridges rooting among the undergrowth for grubs, occasionally a strutting peacock and, dashing in and out among the branches, green bee-eaters, parakeets, Paradise fly-catchers, red-backed woodpeckers and brown-headed barbets; all lovely to watch, and, for a time, pointing out the beasts and birds to one another took the minds of Fleur and Truss off their anxieties.

But not for long. In spite of their ill luck in Douglas being recognised when escaping from the prison and their having had to abandon two cars, they had thrown off the pursuit, evaded the police net spread for them and, for all the police knew, they might now be anywhere in central Ceylon; so for the time being, they were in little danger of capture. Yet that meant only putting off the evil day unless they could leave the country; and from Dambulla they had still the worse half of the journey to do. Unless they could find a much swifter form of transport it was certain that they would not be able to reach the rendezvous on the coast that afternoon.

Occasionally a car passed them and, as they drove through each of the infrequent villages in the area, they looked eagerly from side to side in the hope that they might see one in front of a bungalow or shop, temporarily unoccupied, with which they might make off. But now full day was come, the villagers were going about their business and very few of them were well-off enough to own even a rattle-trap car.

By half past seven, having been up all night, they were both tired and hungry, and mosquitoes had begun to trouble them. To pull up and sleep was out of the question, but they halted in a village while Douglas went into the general store to buy honey-cakes, chocolate, fruit and soft drinks.

While he was absent, a group of small boys believing the cart to be empty attempted to raid it. They were naked and their protruding stomachs, due to enlarged spleens, showed that the poor little wretches were already the victims of malaria. Fleur and Truss would have liked to give them money, but to do so would have revealed themselves as whites; so Fleur drove them off by shouting at them in Sinhalese, and swiftly drew the back curtains of the cart that they had pulled apart before they could have had more than a glimpse of its dim interior.

In addition to a supply of food Douglas had bought a tin of quinine pills which, having seen the malaria-ridden children, they took eagerly as a precaution against the mosquitoes infecting them with the disease. He had also bought maize for the horse so, half a mile beyond the village, they pulled up again, beside a stream, where the little animal could be watered and fed and given half an hour's rest while they picnicked.

By a quarter past eight they were on their way again. From time to time, to ease the load, Truss and Fleur got out and walked, and during the morning they made two more half-hour halts to rest the horse. By midday they entered the great area of creeper-draped ruins and moribund waterworks that had once been Polonnaruwa.

In recent years some of the 'tanks' had been reclaimed by the Government; while the bottoms of others, since the rains had come, were now shallow lakes from which trees were protruding. On them the bird life was fantastic in its variety and abundance. Pelicans, egrets, spoonbills, herons and kingfishers were to be seen by the score. Flights of rose and white flamingoes skimmed patches of giant red water lilies with bluish leaves. The upper branches of many of the trees about them were solid with the nests of weaver birds; sandpipers, bitterns and jacana pheasants picked for worms on the shores.

As they continued on their way they now had much more time than they had when covering the stretch of road by car in which to appreciate the magnitude of Ceylon's second oldest capital. Weed-choked canals criss-crossed it in every direction, huge mounds of rubble were scattered among the tall trees. Peering through leafy screens or down occasional open vistas, they saw broken gateways, monolithic headless statues and fallen pillars covered with intricate carving: a vast paradise for future archaeologists.

With the horse and cart it took them another half-hour to reach the squalid modern shanty town and there they halted only to buy more food and drink. Beyond it there was an equally long stretch of road through acre after acre where for seven hundred years trees and creepers had striven to obliterate the temples, monasteries and palaces that had been the glory of the ancient city.

Although it was November, as central Ceylon is only eight degrees north of the Equator, for the past two hours they had had no protection from the blazing midday sun except, at intervals, the protection of the covered cart. The clothes of all three of them were soaked through with sweat. Truss, less used to such exposure than the other two, knew that he was getting badly sunburnt, and the whole party had been for so many hours without sleep that it had become imperative that they should have a really long rest.

About five miles east of the outskirts of the new Polonnaruwa they chose a ruined culvert through which, centuries ago, the flow of water into a 'tank' had been controlled. In the shade cast by one of its tall stone sides, they took off most of their clothes, and, taking their little horse with them, on a rein, went down to refresh themselves with a dip. But they dared not go much further out than knee-deep and, even then, had to keep a sharp look-out, for the 'tank', as had been the case with all the others they had seen, was inhabited by many crocodiles.

Even in hollows that had so far accumulated only shallow

pools several of these voracious beasts lay, apparently somnolent but watchful, in partially submerged, scaly heaps. Here, from the deeper water, every few minutes an ugly snout and great gaping jaws emerged, either holding a big fish or to seize an unwary teal that had landed on the surface intending to snap up smaller fry.

Douglas said that even elephants and buffaloes were frightened of crocodiles, so would come down to the 'tanks' to bathe in the evenings only in herds; but if a crocodile attempted to snatch one of their young, as often happened, both breeds of animal would charge their foes and most terrible battles would ensue. He then pointed out a number of big pits along the foreshore as elephant hip baths, for the great beasts, and buffaloes too, love nothing better than almost to bury themselves in mud.

Not wishing to leave the shade of the culvert, but aware of the danger that a crocodile might come up out of the water and attack them while they slept, they tethered the horse between the water and themselves, knowing that he would remain alert enough to act as a sentry and give a loud neigh if he found himself threatened. Then they made themselves as comfortable as they could and fell into a sleep of exhaustion.

It was as well that they had taken precautions, for they were roused from their deep slumber by a terrified whinnying. Jumping up they saw that two big crocodiles and one small one had left the water thirty yards away and were already half-way up the foreshore.

Grabbing his Sten gun Truss fired a burst at them. The foremost lashed out wildly with its powerful tail for a moment then rolled over dead, exposing its white belly. The small one, evidently wounded, turned and slithered awkwardly back towards the water. The third gave a furious hiss and, with surprising speed, continued to thrust its way forward. Fleur screamed. Douglas seized her arm and began to drag her up the bank. But Truss stood his ground and fired a second burst. The brute's great jaws with their saw-like teeth had opened wide to seize him. From its mouth there came a sickening stench that almost caused him to vomit. Then, as the bullets ripped through its upper jaw and down its throat, it halted, threshed furiously for a moment, curled up and died.

By then it was half past four and, allowing for the curves the road might take, they estimated that they were still some forty miles from the coast, so they had long since abandoned hope of reaching the rendezvous that day. But they were hoping that Rex would have landed his aircraft and be waiting for them and, as the heat of the day had declined, refreshed by their three-hour sleep, they decided to push on while daylight lasted.

Soon after leaving the Polonnaruwa area they entered that known as the 'parklands'. These, between belts of jungle, were large, open spaces said to have once been agricultural land. They were dotted with large single trees and for the greater part of the year were barren deserts; but now the rains had come the grass which grew as tall as a man was already a foot high, and herds of deer, buffalo and buck were grazing peacefully on it.

Halting to rest their little animal and themselves from time to time they covered another ten miles along the lonely road until at about half past six they came to a branch that led off it. Truss consulted the large-scale map that he had brought with him from his car and decided that they ought to turn off, as the main road they were on led south-east to Batticaloa, whereas to reach their rendezvous they should keep in sight the railway that ran due east to the little town of Kalkudah. It proved to be no more than a track and some way along it they passed another 'tank' at which, now that evening had come, many larger animals were watering; so they called another halt there and watched them.

A score of elephants, belly-deep in the water, were drawing it up with their trunks then sluicing themselves, and their frequent trumpeting mingled with the weird laughter of a flock of hornbills. A herd of buffalo were wallowing in the mud, there were several bears and a couple of sleek handsome leopards drinking delicately from the water's edge. Every few moments a crocodile surfaced and, with an awful yowl, a pariah dog that had swum too far out was snapped up by one of them.

After eating and drinking again the little caravan resumed its wearisome march along the pitted stony track only, half an hour later, to meet with a disaster. Having bumped over a big flat stone lying at the bottom of a gully, one of the big wheels of the cart came off with a loud crack. As the wheel spun away that side of the cart hit the ground with a crash and the axle snapped. Fortunately both Fleur and Truss had been walking behind the cart; so neither was injured, and Douglas only rolled off the driver's seat to regain his feet quickly. But the old cart had not been meant for such rough service and, even had they had the tools, it would have been no easy task to repair it.

Unharnessing their shaggy little horse, they converted the canvas hood of the cart into rough panniers to go on his back, and put into them their remaining food and bottles of soft drink; then, with him on a lead rein, resumed their way.

By this time they were in jungle again, but one of a type that differed greatly from the dense lush jungle of the highlands. Here there was much outcrop with, at times, piles of rock rising to fifty feet; and mingled with the deciduous trees, such as wild figs, there were many cacti. Big groups of aloes thrust up innumerable grey spikes and here and there tall euphorbia trees reared up like great hands, their fingers covered with sharp needles.

With twilight the jungle again came to life, as it had in the early morning. Here, it being some distance from the nearest 'tank', the animals were making for their water-holes, which were generally deep, canoe-shaped depressions in the rock, some of them as much as forty feet in length and half that in width. Elephants came to them by the age-old roads that for countless centuries their progenitors had used to travel, often great distances, through the jungle; deer approached the holes with caution, sniffing the air in case one of their enemies, the leopards, chanced to be in the vicinity; brown, woolly bears shambled with their black snouts nosing from side to side across the rocks; a sudden rustle of quills heralded the arrival of a family of large, spiky porcupines and sometimes a cowardly jackal was to be seen, slinking by.

While on the road to Batticaloa now and then a car, lorry or cart had passed them; but since they had left it, only an occasional glimpse of the railway line gave evidence of man's existence. The animals were so tame that even a leopard a few yards off paused in his seeking only to stare with unblinking eyes at them for a moment through a gap in the foliage, then moved on about his business.

Darkness fell but stars soon lit the heavens, giving sufficient light for them to see the rough places on the track; so they continued on until nine o'clock, when they came upon further evidence of Ceylon's ancient civilisation. This was a great mound of rubble which, perhaps, had once been a monastery; for on its summit a row of skeleton walls that had enclosed small spaces suggested monks' cells. At the base of the pile there were several caves which had later probably been inhabited by hermits. Nearby there gurgled a shallow stream.

They were very tired again now, so Truss suggested that the caves would make a good place to doss down in for the night; but Douglas would not hear of that, saying it was certain they would be the homes of vampire bats, tarantulas and centipedes, or perhaps even a leopard. However, he agreed that they were unlikely to find a better place to sleep than on the mossy bank beside the stream.

Having tethered the horse, they ate again, then decided to freshen themselves up with a dip. Some twenty yards away from the place where they were sitting a dam made by otters had formed a deep pool; so, with Fleur setting an example which she felt to be justified by the semi-darkness, they stripped and, with little exclamations at the comparative coldness of the water, went in.

Suddenly Truss gave a shout, and went over backwards. He had stepped on something that moved beneath his foot. The water broke and churned as a four-foot-long reptile broke the surface. For a moment they thought it was a small crocodile and scattered in confusion. But the beast was as frightened of them as they were of it and swiftly slithered away into the undergrowth. Douglas, on getting a better sight of it, said that their fears had been groundless; it was only a giant lizard known as the armour-plated cabaragoya.

On resuming their bathe, they found their legs being deliciously tickled. Truss stepped out, fetched his torch and shone it down into the water. It showed that Douglas's dark legs, as he stood waist deep, had become powdered in a film of what looked like flour by some substance that was being carried downstream. Fleur's legs were also covered with it, although on them it did not show so distinctly, and hundreds of minute fish were feeding on it.

The night air had become a little chilly so, on emerging from the water, they ran up and down to dry themselves, then got into their clothes and made themselves as comfortable as they could for the night. But they were destined to sleep for less than two hours.

They were woken by a neigh that mounted to a scream. The

moon had risen and, starting up, they saw by its light that, thirty feet away, a leopard had sprung on to the haunches of their little horse. Fleur was nearest this heart-rending sight. With a courage inspired by mingled horror and excitement, she grabbed a big stone that lay near her, jumped to her feet, ran forward and hurled it at the leopard.

The stone struck the great spotted cat on its flank. Instantly it dropped from its prey, bounded forward and crouched to launch itself at her. Douglas was immediately behind her. He gave her a violent push that sent her reeling into the stream, then tensed himself to spring aside. He was too late. Its yellow eyes gleaming in the moonlight, the lithe, twelve-stone streak of muscle and sinew came hurtling through the air. Burying its claws in his shoulders it knocked him like a nine-pin to the ground.

Truss was only a few feet away. He raised the Sten gun but for a moment did not fire from fear of killing Douglas. Then, as the leopard's claws tore his muscles, Douglas screamed. Taking the only chance to save him, Truss pressed the trigger. The barrel of the weapon spurted flame but only two bullets issued from it. After the other burst that Truss had fired they were all that were left in the magazine. The bullets smacked into the leopard's back and one broke its spine leaving it far from dead and only partially paralysed. Snarling fiercely it twisted about, continuing to maul the screaming Douglas. Clubbing the gun Truss ran forward and beat the animal on the head with all his strength until it lost consciousness and sagged motionless upon its victim.

Panting and horrified, Truss and Fleur rolled the great beast off Douglas and into the stream to drown. Either from shock or agony Douglas had been rendered incapable of coherent speech and remained writhing on the ground. As gently as they could they got his clothes off. Both his shoulders and his thighs had been badly lacerated and he was whimpering with pain.

The only possession that Fleur had been able to retain was her beauty box. It was still in one of the panniers that they had left beside the horse when they had tethered him. The terrified animal was making the night hideous with almost human wails and trembling as though it had the ague, but she could not now give time to soothing him. Snatching her beauty box from the pannier, she ran back.

Truss had pulled off his shirt and was attempting to staunch the blood that was seeping from Douglas's wounds. Fleur quickly looked through the contents of her box. The only things that might be of use in it were a mild disinfectant and a soothing cream. When the flow of blood from the deep rips in Douglas's flesh had eased, they washed them carefully with the disinfectant and applied the cream. Then, with strips from their undergarments and his, they bound up his wounds as best they could.

The little horse was still whinnying pitifully, but they succeeded in calming him and found that, although there were nasty lacerations on his haunches, made when the leopard had leapt upon him, the brute had not had time to tear the flesh severely.

The hour that followed was an agony for all of them. Douglas remained *non compos mentis* and continued to groan and twist where he lay. Fleur and Truss, all thought of sleep gone from them, sat beside him, made desperately unhappy by the knowledge that they could do nothing to ease his pain. Round about midnight Truss could bear it no longer, and said to Fleur:

'We can't stay here. We've got to get him to some place where he can be attended to. Even one of those groups of mud huts we've seen now and then in clearings of the jungle would be better than nothing. The jungle folk are used to this sort of thing and have their own remedies for wounds inflicted by wild beasts. I don't think his injuries are fatal by a long sight; but I've heard that leopards return to their kills to eat putrefying meat, so their claws become infected and can cause gangrene to set in.'

Fleur had been quietly crying but she at once agreed that it would be better to move on than to stay where they were, as even when morning came it might be hours before a vehicle came along the infrequently used jungle track.

Strong as he was, Truss could not have carried Douglas any great distance, but they thought the little horse was in good enough shape to bear such a burden. To have slung the injured man over the animal's withers would have caused the blood to run to his head as it hung down on one side and, perhaps, brought about dangerous congestion; so they mounted him and used a cord from the canvas cart cover to attach his feet under the horse's belly and another to link his hands round its neck, with his head resting on its mane. With Fleur leading the horse and Truss holding Douglas in position they then began to make their way through the jungle, now lit by eerie moonlight.

After a while Douglas lapsed into unconsciousness. The others were kept constantly on the alert by rustlings in the undergrowth as the animals there pursued their nightly hunting. More than once, when such sounds came near, their hearts were gripped with the fear that they were about to be attacked by another leopard attracted by the smell of Douglas's blood. Twice bears lumbered across their path yet took no notice of them, but Fleur was badly scared by a big eagle-owl that swooped down and circled round their heads.

Resting now and then, they had been going for about two hours when, at the side of the road, they came upon a clearing in which there were some half-dozen low wigwams made from branches and palm leaves. With mingled hopes and fears about the reception with which they might meet, they made their way towards the camp. Suddenly dogs began to bark and four skinny mongrels came rushing at them.

For a moment it looked as though they were about to be badly savaged, but Truss had hardly beaten off the attack of the first with a stick he had been using occasionally to keep their horse moving, when a little crowd of natives came scrambling out of the huts and called off the dogs.

They were very dark, lean, long-haired, dressed in rags and tatters and, but for the fact that silver bracelets jingled on the skinny arms of the women, might have been a prehistoric people. Jabbering excitedly and brandishing spears, they surrounded the newcomers. But their Headman, a wizened-faced elder whose untidy locks were streaked with grey, waved back his followers and Fleur spoke to him in Sinhalese.

By a shrug of his shoulders he showed that he did not understand her; but when they untied the still-unconscious Douglas and lowered him to the ground the natives at once realised what had befallen him.

They carried him over to a camp fire, the embers of which were still glowing, then examined his wounds. Going into one of the wigwams, the Headman returned with the leaves of some healing plant, laid them on Douglas's injuries, then bound them up again. Meanwhile Fleur said to Truss:

'I think these people must be Kuravars, the gipsies of Ceylon. Unlike the other jungle dwellers they lead a roving life and never build mud huts, but live almost like animals in these roughly-made bivouacs. They never farm or keep herds, but earn enough money for their few wants by charming snakes and training monkeys and other animals to perform, then taking them into the towns. But they are said to have a great knowledge of herbal medicine and keep remedies that will cure all sorts of ills; so there is a good hope that those leaves they are putting on Douglas will prove effective.'

When the old Headman had finished treating Douglas he had the wounded man carried into an empty hut; then two of the women brought their visitors a calabash, in which there was a cold, mealy mush, some pieces of dried meat and several coconuts, the eyes of which had been pierced. As they ate they could not tell whether the meat was pig or venison, and it was very tough; but they found the fresh coconut water delicious.

During their five-mile tramp their legs had pained them badly, but they had put that down to tiredness. Now, the fire having been made up, they saw that between their ankles and knees there clung a number of repulsive leeches, some of which were over four inches in length. With an exclamation of disgust, Fleur made to pull one of the slimy brutes from her instep, but with it the skin began to come away and a native standing nearby swiftly stopped her. Taking a glowing brand from the fire he applied it to one after the other of the leeches and, sizzling up, they dropped off.

When they had finished their meal and smiled their thanks the Headman signed to them to go into the wigwam into which Douglas had been carried. It was no higher than Fleur's head and had only a hole for entrance. Having crawled inside they found it did not contain even a mattress; but the flooring consisted of leaves several inches deep, so was comparatively soft. In the close, hot darkness they at once heard the infuriating whine of mosquitoes, but they were so utterly weary that, after slapping ineffectually for a few minutes at their foreheads, wrists and ankles, they settled down on either side of Douglas who, although breathing stertorously, was sound asleep.

Some hours later they were roused by his suddenly becoming delirious, shouting nonsense and striving to tear off his bandages. While Truss restrained him, Fleur crawled out to see if she could find the Headman. By then dawn had come and the natives were already moving about their camp. The Headman had their patient carried out into the open, forced him to swallow some sort of potion that quietened him and, soon afterwards, sent him off to sleep again.

Only then did Fleur and Truss have a chance to take proper stock of themselves. Being young and healthy sleep had somewhat restored their vitality, but during the night the mosquitoes had made a fine meal off them and their legs were dotted with big, black ticks. Truss produced the tin of quinine tablets from his pocket and they swallowed a few, then they set about removing the ticks, which had swollen from the size of pinheads to that of peas. Fleur had met with ticks before, when making trips up-country, and knew that if the head of a tick is left in it continues to suck blood; so they again resorted to a burning brand which, when applied, made the ticks drop off, but their legs were now semi-raw and their faces and arms puffy from stings.

For breakfast they were given the same fare as before, and, while they ate it, the Kuravars provided them with an entertainment of snake charming and a dancing bear. They also had some performing loris—small monkeys which resemble humans more nearly than any other species, and have big, pathetic eyes that are almost blind in daylight.

Fleur and Truss clapped, smiled and did their best to show appreciation to their good-natured hosts, but their minds were occupied with worrying about Douglas and the problem of securing proper medical attention for him. It therefore came as a most welcome surprise when they saw two of the natives emerge from the forest with a rough stretcher made from intertwined branches, and two others carry Douglas from the wigwam to lay him upon it.

The Headman signed to Truss to untie the little horse. Swiftly he decided, as they had no further use for it, to leave it as a token of their gratitude, and conveyed his meaning by a gesture of refusal then pointing at the Headman. There being nothing further to detain them, the Headman led the way from the camp, followed by the four bearers carrying the stretcher, with Fleur and Truss bringing up the rear.

The Headman did not take the road, but a narrow path which, after a quarter of a mile, debouched into a much broader way. Here and there torn branches, six to ten feet up, and the heavily trampled appearance of the track showed it to be an elephant road along which a herd had recently passed and fed. They followed its windings for the best part of two hours without halting, then emerged into another clearing where there was a fair-sized bungalow and several long, leaf-thatched sheds. By then, for some time past Douglas had again become delirious, his forehead was almost burning to the touch and it was obvious that he was in a high fever.

The barking of a dog brought out from one of the sheds two men, both naked to the waist but wearing big turbans and colourful cotton skirts. The elder conferred with the Headman in his own language then turned to Truss and Fleur and gave them a courteous welcome in Sinhalese. She told him that they had been on their way to Kalkudah when their car had broken down, that when trying to find help they had become lost in the jungle and benighted there, then been attacked by the leopard.

He had Douglas carried into the house and, after an exchange of many friendly expressions in dumb-show with the Kuravars, the gipsies took their departure. Having examined Douglas's wounds, their new host put some ointment on them and gave him a soothing drink, but it was clear that he was far from happy about the state of the injured man. When Fleur asked if there were any means by which Douglas could be taken to a hospital, he shook his head and said gravely:

'This man has suffered much from having been carried so far. To move him further would prove fatal. It is not only the blood he has lost, but he now has fever of the brain. His only hope lies in rallying his strength by rest, so he must remain here. I will do what I can for him but his fate lies in the hands of Allah, the Merciful, the Compassionate; Blessed be His Name and that of his Prophet. By midday we should know if it is decreed that your friend is to live or die.'

When Fleur translated this to Truss, he protested, 'But we can't just leave it at that. If he can't be moved we must fetch a doctor to him. One can tell from the sun that we've been moving north-east this morning; so we can't be a great way from the coast. Ask this guy how far it is to Kalkudah and if he has any transport.'

For some minutes Fleur talked to their turbaned companion, then she said in English, 'These people are Moormen, Indian Mohammedans, most of whom live on the east coast. The younger man we saw was this man's son and he has another. They earn their living by hunting the big lizards, like the one you trod on in the pool, and get good money for the skins because they are in great demand for making women's shoes. He says it is about fifteen miles to Kalkudah, and no transport is available because they have only one horse and cart and his other son set off there with a load of dried skins this morning just before we got here.'

'If it's only fifteen miles I can walk it,' Truss declared, 'and I'll bring a doctor back with me. Ask him to draw me a map so that I can find my way there.'

'No!' Fleur replied firmly, with a quick shake of her head. 'I'll not let you. There can be very few white men in a little town like that. It would be as good as giving yourself up, and after all you've done that would mean several years in prison.'

With an unhappy frown, Truss said, 'I know that, honey. But you'll have not forgotten there was a time when I left Douglas to drown. I'll not have it on my conscience that a second time I failed to do all I could to save him. If I'm caught that will just be too bad; I'll have to risk it.'

Fleur grasped his arm and he felt her fingernails dig into it. 'I tell you I won't let you go. I'd feel I just might have to if there were a real chance of your doing any good. But it would take you the best part of four hours to walk into Kalkudah; then you'd have to find a doctor and, even in a car, six or seven hours would be gone before you could bring him back here. The Moorman says that by midday we'll know if Douglas is to live or die; so by the middle of the afternoon a doctor won't influence the outcome either way.'

Giving him an angry shake, she hurried on, 'And there is another thing. If you are arrested I will be soon afterwards. I may not get as long a sentence as you, but if you insist on this quixotic act you will be sending me, too, to prison.'

Her first argument was based on sound sense; her second loaded with feminine guile. Combined, they weighed so heavily with Truss that he reluctantly agreed to abandon his plan and resign himself to inactivity.

After listening to their fierce argument without understanding it, the Moorman treated their faces, arms and legs with another ointment that considerably relieved the heat and pain from which they were suffering; then he left them with Douglas.

The room was clean but had only the mattress on which Douglas was lying and some bearskin rugs and cushions on the floor. Still in bad need of sleep after their appalling night, they lay down on the rugs and dozed through the morning, dropping off now and then, but rousing each time Douglas was seized with another bout of delirium.

At midday the Moorman came in again, examined the patient and, as he was neither better nor worse, said there seemed a fair chance that he might now pull through. He then took Fleur and Truss into another room, where a shy-eyed youngish woman, wearing a yashmak, served him, his son and the visitors with a meal of rice, plovers' eggs, vegetables, fruit and tea, which they ate sitting cross-legged on the floor.

Soon after Fleur and Truss had returned to sit beside Douglas, someone switched on a radio in the next room. For a few minutes it played music, then the announcer started the daily two o'clock news summary. As there was no door to the airy room they could hear the Sinhalese words quite clearly. Suddenly Fleur looked across at Truss in dismay, for she had realised that one of the first items was about themselves.

'The search continues,' the voice box blared, 'for Douglas Rajapakse, who escaped from prison on Thursday evening with the aid of his wife and a young American named Van Ryn. After abandoning their own car, and later a stolen Ford which was found thirteen miles south of Dambulla, it is now believed that they were responsible for the theft of a horse and covered cart from a bungalow in a suburb of the town and continued their journey in it. During the past twenty-four hours no further information has been released to indicate the road that the fugitives have taken but the police are pursuing several promising lines of investigation.'

There followed descriptions of Douglas, Fleur and Truss, and the offer of two thousand rupees reward for information which would lead to their capture.

When Fleur told Truss what the announcer had been saying, he exclaimed, 'This is bad, real bad, honey. If these people tumble to it that it's us the police are after they'll surely turn us in.'

'I don't think they would just to please the Government,' Fleur replied. 'Like the Hindus and Christians, the Mohammedans have become the victims of Buddhist fanaticism, and they naturally resent it.'

'Maybe, but two thousand rupees must mean a lot to them.'

'It would certainly tempt them,' she agreed. 'But we've come a long way from Dambulla, and there are thousands of white people in Ceylon; so there is a good chance that they won't connect us with the announcement.'

Truss remained uneasy. He would have liked to get Fleur out of the house and slip away with her along some jungle track that led towards the coast, rather than risk the possibility that the Moorman had realised that they were the fugitives and might send his other son in to Kalkudah to fetch the police. But they could not leave Douglas.

During the long hours of the afternoon he continued to alternate between long spells of coma and brief ones of delirium, but during each of the latter his ramblings grew weaker.

Fleur frequently bathed his temples and from time to time gave him a drink, but his handsome face gradually became a putty colour and his cheeks seemed to be falling in. On three occasions the Moorman came in to have a look at him and on the last only shook his turbaned head, then went out again without saying a word. As he left them Fleur burst into a passion of tears and continued to sob for many minutes, as though her heart would break.

All Truss's efforts to comfort her having failed and fearing that she would exhaust herself, he said at last, 'Come, honey, I know how you're feeling; but if you continue to carry on this way I'll begin to think you love him more than you do me.'

As he had hoped, his implication took immediate effect. Choking back her sobs she turned a tear-stained face to him. 'It's not that. You know it's not. But he is such a fine person. It's terrible to see him like this. And I owe him my life. If he hadn't pushed me aside and taken my place, I'd be lying there now instead of him.'

At a little before six o'clock Douglas opened his eyes and they suddenly realised that he had regained consciousness. Fleur took his hand and he pressed it feebly. Recognising her, he lifted his head a little and murmured with a smile, 'Fleur, my sweet Fleur. You . . . have been my life's blessing.' Then his head fell back and he was dead.

Burying her face in her hands, Fleur sobbed, 'He never knew. Oh, thank God! He never knew.'

Truss nodded. 'Yes; at least he was spared that, and I feel a heel beside him. But he's out of all his troubles now.'

It was at that moment that the Moorman again came in. After one glance at Douglas, with the resignation of an Oriental, he said:

'It was decreed. The fate of every man is bound about his brow. My elder son has just returned from Kalkudah. The three of us will make preparations for the burial.'

Less than an hour later they stood beside a three-foot-deep grave, that the Moorman and his sons had dug while Truss did his best to comfort Fleur. As Douglas's body was laid in it there could be no ceremony, but in their different ways all five of them sent up silent prayers for him.

Sunset had come, so it would have been madness for Truss and Fleur to leave that evening and again risk becoming lost at night in the jungle. But they continued to be acutely worried; not only by the possibility that the Moorman might, while they slept, again send off his elder son in the horse and cart, this time to fetch the police, but also because for the second day they had failed to arrive at the rendezvous; so by now Rex might have given up hope that they would reach it and have taken the aircraft back to Colombo.

Next morning, immediately after they had breakfasted, as Fleur could not say that they wanted to go to any place other than Kulkudah she told their host that they wished to start at once for the town and asked him to give them directions to it. As she made her request she felt unhappily sure that he would offer to send them in by his cart, which meant that either they would have to go there, or be faced with the difficulty of providing a reason—for which they had already racked their brains in vain—for leaving the cart some miles before it reached the town.

That, it was certain, would arouse the suspicions of the driver about their intentions. Then, when further announcements were made that the police were searching for them, the Moorman would put two and two together, belatedly realise that he had harboured the fugitives, and the hunt would be up in the immediate neighbourhood. It was, therefore, a considerable relief when, instead, he replied:

'I should have been happy to send you in with one of my sons, but unfortunately on its return journey yesterday afternoon our horse fell lame; so I fear you will have to walk. But

I will draw a map for you of the jungle trails that lead back to the road.'

Feeling certain that their host would consider it an insult if he were offered money for the trouble to which they had put him, Truss asked, through Fleur, if he might buy some lizard skins to be sent to him in Colombo. To that the Moorman readily agreed and they went out to one of the long sheds where the skins were hung to dry and selected half a dozen. But, instead of his own name, Truss gave that of the First Secretary at his Embassy, while wondering a little pessimistically when, if ever, he would be able to let his friend know what had led to his receiving a parcel of skins.

After covering Douglas's grave with flowers and receiving the sketch map and a supply of provisions from the Moorman with grateful thanks, they once more proceeded along a jungle trail, speculating uneasily whether, after a delay of two days, they would find the aircraft still at the rendezvous.

As the elephant road by which the Kuravars had brought them to the Moorman's clearing had led north-east, and Elephant Point was some miles north of Kalkudah, Truss believed that they were nearer the rendezvous than the town, and estimated that they had only ten or twelve miles to go. For the first hour they followed the directions they had been given then, instead of taking a trail that led south-east, they took one that led east.

In spite of the emotional strain they had been under the previous day, sitting quietly throughout it, followed by a night's sleep, had restored their vigour and done much to relieve them of the soreness inflicted by leeches, ticks and mosquito bites; so they made good going and hoped to reach the rendezvous soon after midday. But during the third hour of their journey they began to fear that, although the position of the sun should have provided a reliable guide, they had lost their way. According to van Goens, for several miles inland on that part of the coast the country was barren, consisting of sand-dunes with, beyond them, splendid beaches; yet the jungle was as thick as ever.

During one of their halts to rest they anxiously discussed the situation and decided that it must be further to the coast than they had thought, so they continued to head east. Then, a mile further on, it was suddenly proved that neither their estimate of distance nor direction had been wrong. Through a break in the trees they saw the sea only a hundred yards away.

Hurrying forward in dismay they found there were no sand-dunes, no beach. The trees ran right down to the water and ended in a tangle of naked mangrove roots upon which the waves were breaking. From where they stood they could see, only a mile or so away to the south, the land curving sharply out in a way that made them feel sure it must end in Elephant Point; but that was no consolation. It, too, was covered with jungle, so no aircraft could possibly have landed there or anywhere along the coast on which they stood.

Bitterly disappointed they stood staring about them in silence for a few moments, then Truss said, 'Hell's bells! This has put us in a pretty fix. Van Goens said he had never been to this part of the coast, but he seemed certain that the terrain here would serve the purpose. Still, perhaps the country's different on the south side of the point and there's a good beach there. We'd best go and see.'

That was easier said than done, as there was no track running along the shore, nor at a little distance from it; and the mangroves were so thick and tangled that, even with machetes, a way could not have been cut through them at a greater rate than a hundred feet an hour.

Disconsolate and now acutely worried, they retraced their steps for nearly a mile before they found a track leading south and another two hours elapsed before they succeeded in reaching the extremity of the Cape. It ended in a rocky spot below which there was a sandy beach but it was much too narrow for an aircraft to land on and, as soon as they got a view of the coast south of the peninsula, their last hope was dashed. As far as they could see and nearly up to a small harbour, behind which lay a cluster of buildings that must be Kalkudah, the jungle came right down to the sea.

'Whatever shall we do now?' Fleur asked in a despondent voice.

'God knows!' Truss replied unhappily. 'What a bloody awful let-down. We'd better sit on the rocks here and think a while.'

They sat and thought in vain. To go into Kalkudah would amount to giving themselves up, and that they were determined not to do. To go back to the Moorman was equally out of the question; for a few more broadcasts from the accursed radio would almost certainly lead to their identities being discovered and, even if that did not happen, what were they to do then? At length they came to the conclusion that their only hope now was to remain where they were and pray that the aircraft might come over again that afternoon, spot them on the point and drop them a message giving them a new rendezvous further along the coast.

That such a happening would mean at least another day, or perhaps several, tracking through jungle without a guide, no food other than such fruit as they could find, and further exposure to such dangers as snakes, tarantulas, poisonous centipedes and leopards at night, was an unnerving prospect; but they took comfort from one thing. The more they thought about it the more certain they felt that if Rex had returned from Manila to Colombo in his aircraft he would, having seen the Duke, find some way of getting in touch with them at the agreed rendezvous.

Until they had reached the Point they had been protected from the blazing sun by the shade from the jungle trees, and out there in mid-afternoon it was no more than pleasantly hot owing to a gentle breeze blowing from the sea; so Fleur, who was beginning to recover from the worst effects that watching Douglas die had had upon her, suggested that they should bathe.

Going down to the little beach they found on it many lovely crustaceans, nautilus, cowries, conches, fan-shells and corals. Then they stripped and went in hand in hand. Truss as usual kept in the shallows and Fleur went only a little way further out for fear of sharks and barracudas. The dip revived their spirits considerably and afterwards, lying embraced on the warm sand, for a time they managed to forget the further perils they felt sure they would have to face.

Nevertheless, subconsciously they continued to listen hopefully for the drone of an approaching aircraft, and when they had dressed they climbed the rock again so as to be able to scan the sky in all directions. Time moved on and the sun gradually got lower behind them until the afternoon merged into early evening, and with it their hopes sank again. Yet there was nothing they could do. Having eaten the last of the food with which the Moorman had provided them, they took such poor comfort as they could from the fact that by passing the night out there on the headland they would not be exposed to leeches and other horrors of the jungle.

It was just on six o'clock when Truss first noticed a low vessel coming up from the south. During the course of the afternoon they had seen several native dhows and other small sailing craft leave and enter Kalkudah harbour. Some had come fairly close, which had led them to speculate on the possibility, in the last event, of attempting to steal one from the harbour at night, and trying to reach India in her. They had also seen a small tramp some way out and, on the horizon, a ship that looked like an oil tanker. But this, they saw as it rapidly approached, was a large, sea-going motor launch. When she was almost level with the point, and still about a third of a mile out, turning in a graceful sweep, she headed for the little beach from which they had bathed.

Suddenly they were seized with apprehension. The crew of one of the fishing boats that had passed close in might have reported seeing two unusual-looking figures up on the headland, and the authorities in Kalkudah sent the launch to find out who they were. Then, just as they were about to run for cover in the jungle, a flag was run up on the single mast of the launch. There, fluttering in the breeze, was the Stars and Stripes.

'God be praised; she's flying "Old Glory"!' Truss cried, tears starting to his eyes. 'It's them! We're saved, sweetie! We're saved! Look! I can see my old man standing in the stern, and there's Uncle Simon with him.' Snatching off their red head-scarves they waved them wildly.

Ten minutes later, a dinghy having been put out to take them off, they were being hauled on board. Forgetting for once to be undemonstrative, father and son fell into a clinch, Simon embraced the half-crying, half-laughing Fleur, and the crew of four Sinhalese looked on with happy grins.

The dinghy was hauled in, the launch's engine started up and she sped out to sea, while the rescuer's and rescued all tried to talk at once in their endeavours to tell each other of their experiences and anxieties during the past three days—days that now seemed like weeks.

After a while Rex said, 'But you must need a drink. Come into the cabin.' As he spoke he had turned and glanced aft. Pausing, he remarked to Simon. 'There's that little ship again that we sighted not far behind us early this morning. I expect she's on her way up to Trincomalee. But she's put on speed. Just look at her bow wave.'

For some minutes, forgetful of their drink, they continued to watch her. She was overhauling them fast and now less than a quarter of a mile away. Then, pointing to her, one of the sailors cried:

'Ceylonese Navy. Gunboat.'

Rex snatched up a pair of powerful binoculars and focussed them on her. 'That's what she is,' he agreed. Then suddenly he added, 'That fellow standing in the bow? God help us; it's Lalita!'

22

Meanwhile in Colombo . . .

At half past eight on the previous Thursday evening, when the Duke had waved Truss and Fleur away from the Galle Face, although he had not shown it he was a very worried old man. As he turned away from the entrance and went up to his sitting room he wondered if age was at last impairing his judgment and sense of values; for he had the honesty to admit to himself that he, and no one else, was responsible for Douglas being in danger of losing his life, and for Truss and Fleur now being about to risk their freedom.

From the beginning the Plackoff inheritance had meant nothing to him financially. It could not buy him a better bottle of wine or a better cigar than those he bought already, or anything else that might conceivably have added to the comfort or the quiet pleasures of old age. He realised now that he should have left it to the lawyers to handle and then, when Fleur had decided to marry Douglas Rajapakse, made her a wedding present of it.

But it had tempted him to see beautiful Ceylon again and, once there, it had led to his becoming personally involved with the d'Azavedos. Their attempt to murder him and his friends had aroused in him the old iron-willed determination to get the better of an enemy; yet when he had left Ceylon after his first visit that had been anything but satisfied, and he had had to resort to sending the most respected handwriting experts out from Europe to secure a verdict that deprived them of Olenevka.

Even then, it had proved a Pyrrhic victory; for they had partly sabotaged the mine before giving it up, and robbed him of its major asset—the very valuable stock of gems held in reserve to sell at times when the market was most favourable.

Then, when Simon had spoken of his intention to meet Rex in Ceylon, he had again been tempted to pay a visit to the island. At the time he had told himself that it was to enjoy warm sunshine in winter with his two old friends, but he admitted to himself now that, partly at least, he had been influenced by the thought that, somehow or other, he might find an opportunity to make the d'Azavedos pay for having sabotaged the mine and, if they still had the reserve of jewels, take them from them.

The d'Azavedos had themselves reopened the game, by proposing a settlement that would have restored Olenevka to them yet have been of advantage to him; but it had proved to be a trap in which he had very nearly lost his life. After that he had gone into the battle with, in his view, no holds barred. He had killed the father, robbed the son of the jewels then, by two clever tricks, wiped out the expectations Lalita had had of getting back the estate.

All this, in spite of the warnings of his friends that ill would come of it, had made de Richleau as happy as a sand boy. But his friends had proved right. Had he not tricked Lalita out of both the estate and the jewels, his enemy would have had no cause to seize on the chance to retrieve a part of his losses when he had had the good luck to catch Fleur in bed with Truss. That had brought Mirabelle into the game, and led directly to her being murdered.

Her death had been the first fruit of the Duke's obstinate and, to his mind, justified determination to let Lalita retain no part of the Plackoff inheritance. And her death had saddened him because, although she had been planning to betray her lover, he felt that, intrinsically, she was a decent woman who, as an orphan and deserted wife, had been the victim of circumstances, so deserved a happier future.

But worse had befallen as far as the interests that really touched him were concerned. Douglas Rajapakse had been thrown into prison and, still worse, Truss and Fleur had felt in honour bound to risk their own freedom in an attempt to get him out.

Their attitude in the matter had his full endorsement and warmed his old heart. Yet that Douglas should be in prison at all was due not to them, but to him. And that age should have rendered him incapable of undertaking Douglas's rescue himself distressed him greatly. Moreover, he was now plagued with an awful fear that they might bungle it.

He endeavoured to reason with himself that it was only

because he was an old fogey that he lacked confidence in the two young people. But that would not work. His long experience in wars, and with Richard, Rex and Simon in many desperate situations, had made them most formidable antagonists; used to assessing chances, cunning, dangerous and ready instantly to put aside all scruples if it came to saving themselves from capture: whereas Truss had never even experienced the hazards of war and had been brought up as a law-abiding citizen. How could he be expected to keep a cool head in an emergency, or deal swiftly and ruthlessly with any opposition with which he might meet? And, game as Fleur might be, he had only a girl to aid him.

For once, as the Duke thought of these things, his big cigar remained unlit between his long, almost transparent fingers.

At half past nine, a knock on the door caused him to start up in his chair and call, 'Come in.' Van Goens entered, took a few paces and came to a halt in front of him.

'Well?' asked de Richleau with apparent calm. 'How did it go?'

The ex-Inspector shook his head. 'Not too well, Your Grace. They got Mr. Rajapakse away but not without trouble. He was recognised when coming out. I was standing in the darkness about fifty yards away, so I don't know exactly what happened. But there was a fracas and shots were fired.'

'That's bad,' said the Duke. 'Do you know whether anyone was wounded?'

'No. By the most infernal luck a police car pulled up behind Mrs. Rajapakse's just as they were leaving the prison. There was enough light for me to see that one of the man who got out of the car was carrying a Sten gun, and it was he who challenged the escape party. Mr. Van Ryn tackled him and got the gun, then used it on someone just inside the prison doorway.'

De Richleau smiled. 'At all events that shows that the boy has resolution. And you say they got away?'

'Yes, Your Grace. But the prison alarm was sounded, the sentry fired two shots from his rifle after their car as it drove off, and two minutes later the police car went in pursuit of them.'

'May the Powers protect them,' murmured the Duke. 'What chance do you think they have of evading capture?'

'I can't say. As soon as the two cars had disappeared I ran

to the place where I'd left my own. But it was some way off; otherwise I would have been here sooner.'

'You have proved a good friend, van Goens, and done all you could to help us. Get yourself a drink from the tray, then come and sit down and tell me in detail all you saw.'

The ex-Inspector was still mixing a whisky and soda when, after a quick knock, Rex and Simon entered the room.

De Richleau came to his feet, his face wreathed in smiles, 'How happy I am to see you so soon. I had thought it more likely that you would not be here until tomorrow morning.'

'I've good friends in QANTAS at Singapore,' Rex replied. 'They cut the usual delays that affect private aircraft and refuelled us right away. There's a gain of three hours on the clock, too, coming from Manila. We got in at seven-forty and would have been here an hour ago if the jacks in office at the Katunayake airport hadn't held us up about one damn' thing after another.'

Simon was not wearing his glasses. Craning his narrow head forward he peered short-sightedly at the Duke. 'Tell us about the muddle. Must be a nasty one for you to have sent for us.'

'It is indeed. Van Goens here knows the whole story and he has been most helpful. He was just about to give me details about the latest development. But that can wait now until I've told you what has been happening during the past ten days. First, though, help yourselves to drinks.'

As soon as they had full glasses de Richleau gave them an account of Lalita's recent activities and their result, then van Goens described all he had been able to see of the escape.

When they had done, Rex's usually smiling face was set in a grim frown, and he said, 'Then young Truss has gotten himself in one hell of a mess. It'll be prison for him if he's caught, and it's a dollar to a dime that he will be. It's certain that the police will telephone ahead and have road blocks put out.'

'Um,' Simon nodded. 'And it's not even as if they'd got a good start. Full marks to them, though, for making the attempt. Poor little Fleur. She seems fated to get herself in muddles.'

The Duke looked at van Goens. 'When do you think we can hope to get any news?'

'I expect there will be an announcement over the radio in the first news bulletin tomorrow morning,' the ex-Inspector replied. 'But I've still a few good friends in the police; so I thought I'd go out and see if I can pick up anything.'

His suggestion was accepted gratefully, and when he left them the Duke had some cold supper sent up for his friends. While they ate it he told them in more detail about the part that Mirabelle had played and the finding by Truss and Fleur of Vinala Fernando's remains.

'If only we could have hooked that on to Lalita,' Rex sighed. Then, after a moment, he added, 'I'll tell you what, though. If we put every private dick in Colombo on the job we might get him for having done in his mistress. If we could, and seeing we could show his motive, that would put Truss and Fleur in better case as having enabled Douglas to escape only because they had grounds to believe that Lalita intended to have him murdered, too.'

'Um. Well worth trying,' Simon agreed.

The Duke nodded. 'We will talk to van Goens about this, when he gets back. If we succeeded, with strong representations from the American Ambassador and British High Commissioner, we might even get our young people off.'

It was midnight by the time van Goens returned. Momentarily their faces brightened as he said, 'They got clear of Colombo,' then fell again when he added, 'but only by shooting up the police car that was following them. The incident occurred out in the suburbs. Apparently Mr. Van Ryn blazed off through the back window with the Sten gun he snatched.'

'Oh, God! Did he kill anyone?' gasped Rex.

'No, sir. I think he did his best to avoid that by firing low at the radiator and tyres. But the car ended up in a hedge and the two men in it were badly injured. One was a sergeant in the Security Service. He was cut about the face and may lose an eye. The other was a clerk at Police Headquarters. He's got a broken arm and two smashed ribs. To that we have to add that the shots I heard when I was outside the prison were Mr. Van Ryn putting two bullets through the foot of a warder.'

Rex groaned, 'May the Lord deliver us. How'll we ever get him out of this?'

There was no comfort that his friends could offer the unhappy father, and nothing they could do but wait for a radio announcement in the morning. De Richleau then put up the idea of making the utmost efforts to trace Mirabelle's murderer.

Van Goens shook his head. 'The police will be treating it

only as a routine case, Your Grace; and in the bad part of the city such murders occur with some frequency, so they are rarely solved. I'll put all my own men on the job and instruct the other agencies if you wish, but I can't hold out much hope of success. It's a hundred to one that d'Azavedo paid some criminal to kill her for him, and even if the man were traced I doubt if we'd get any further. If he could be persuaded to give away who employed him, directly an investigator learned that it was Colonel d'Azavedo he would drop the enquiry like a hot brick. He'd be too scared for his own skin to get himself into a tangle with a senior officer of the Security Service.'

'Nevertheless, I would like you to do all you can,' replied the Duke. 'And put an advertisement in all the papers as soon as possible, offering a reward of five thousand rupees for information leading to the murderer.'

Next morning they waited impatiently for the news. The papers carried only brief stop-press statements, but it ranked as second item in the radio bulletin. From its earlier part they learned nothing new, but it went on to state that after scattering police who had endeavoured to halt the escapers' car in Gampaha, the car had been found abandoned at the entrance to a village eight miles beyond the town, and that from the village the car of a Mr. Nissanka had been stolen; so it was assumed that the fugitives had continued their journey in that. The number and make of the car were then given, followed by descriptions of Douglas, Fleur and Truss with an urgent appeal to the public to acquaint the police at once with any information which might lead to the arrest of these dangerous criminals.

Why they should have abandoned their own car for a 1954 Ford the listeners could not imagine, but they took considerable comfort from the knowledge that the fugitives had succeeded in evading capture during the night. Given sufficient petrol, even in an old Ford they should have had no difficulty in covering the hundred and forty miles to the neighbourhood of Kalkudah while darkness lasted; so, unless they had met with an accident, they should by then have been at the rendezvous for some hours.

The Duke produced his map and Rex agreed that Elephant Point being such a prominent feature on that part of the east coast, with the aid of the railway line from Polonnaruwa to

Kalkudah he should have no difficulty in locating it. Then he said:

'I'll not take the Captain of my aircraft because if trouble arises out of this he could be charged with taking an active part in an illegal operation. But I've had plenty of practice landing my big new kite; so you need have no worries about that.'

Knowing that he had been a member of the Eagle Squadron —that gallant band of Americans who had volunteered for service with the R.A.F. long before the United States had entered the war—the others did not doubt his capabilities for a moment, as he went on:

'My crew can't be held responsible for anything I do, and in case you wanted to make a quick get-out I told them last night that they must stand by for a take-off any time. But there'll be formalities to go through at Katunayake even though I'll say I'm only flying up to Trinco', and some of those surly bastards there may create delays; so I'll get off right away.'

Soon after they had wished him luck and he had left them, Mr. Rajapakse was announced. The elderly lawyer was both agitated and angry. Very naturally he was greatly distressed about Douglas but he held Truss and Fleur to blame for having greatly intensified the trouble his son was in, through having organised his escape. With good reason he contended that, whereas Douglas had been arrested only for a very minor offence, his having broken prison with companions who had fired upon the police had both ruined his career and laid him open to the most serious penalties.

Unless they confided to him the whole of their dealings with Lalita and Mirabelle, he could not be given the imperative reason for getting Douglas out of prison; and that de Richleau was averse to doing. Much, too, as he would have liked to comfort the distraught father, to let him know that there was a good chance that his son might be picked up and flown out to Madras that afternoon would have been to risk his telling his wife and other interested parties, so have jeopardised the security of the operation. In consequence the Duke took the blame on himself for having organised the escape and, for some ten minutes, showed considerable forbearance in listening to a diatribe of tearful reproach from his visitor.

Mr. Rajapakse having taken his departure, van Goens came in to report that he had engaged every 'private eye' available in Colombo to investigate Mirabelle's murder and that he had put his own staff on to check up on Lalita's movements for the whole of the Tuesday, in the hope that should the murderer be run to earth it could be shown that Lalita had been in communication with him.

As a precaution against the fugitives being captured, the Duke and Simon sat down to compose a note of warning for Richard. When they had agreed upon it, the cable ran:

Regret to tell you Fleur in serious trouble. Stop. Rex and Simon with me and hope to deal with situation. Stop. Will keep you informed of developments. Stop. Love to you both from us all de Richleau.

Simon went down to send it off and they then waited anxiously for the midday news. After a repetition of the gist of the earlier announcement it was stated that the Ford had been found abandoned thirteen miles south of Dambulla and it was believed that the fugitives had taken to the jungle in that neighbourhood. An intensive search was in progress for them and it was not expected that they could for long remain untraced. A reward of two thousand rupees was offered for information that would lead to their capture.

As they listened de Richleau and Simon looked at one another in dismay, then Simon said, 'This is bad! Oh, very bad! unless they've managed to pinch another car they'll never get to Elephant Point by this afternoon.'

'No,' the Duke agreed, with a heavy sigh. 'And if those three poor children have taken to the jungle, Lord help them. Douglas may know something of it, but being a townsman I doubt that. I do, of course, from my travels in many places; but I have always gone on safari with the best weapons, trackers who knew their work, and a score of porters bearing tents, food and other necessities. Without such aids they are certain to lose their way, and become exposed to all sorts of dangers—wild animals, snakes, blundering into morasses, not to mention the leeches and mosquitoes.'

They lunched with little appetite and spent a miserable afternoon. At half past five Rex returned angry and disgruntled. Having said that the airport people had made no trouble about his taking off, he went on:

'But that bloody fool van Goens has let us down. Elephant Point is no more than a rocky promontory and for miles on either side of it the jungle comes right down to the sea. Even a helicopter couldn't land anywhere near. He ought to have proposed a rendezvous north of Trinco', somewhere on the Vanni coast. It's all sandy desert up there. I passed over it three weeks back when we flew down from Delhi.'

'See any signs of them on the Cape?' Simon asked. 'They should have been wearing bright red handkerchiefs on their heads.'

'Not a thing. And I hadn't much hope I would after having learned about the noon broadcast, though I flew up all the same. Seems they're bogged down in the jungle some place short of Dambulla. All we've got to hang on to now is that they're still free. But how long they'll remain so, God alone knows.'

'Then you missed the news summary that is put out at two o'clock every afternoon,' said the Duke. 'From it we learned that early this morning a horse and covered cart was stolen in the southern outskirts of Dambulla and the police think it probable that the fugitives have continued their journey in it. That at least improves their chances. In a day and a night, even allowing for half that time being given to resting the horse, a light cart might cover the seventy or eighty miles between Dambulla and Elephant Point.'

'Then there's a hope they'll make it!' Rex declared with sudden optimism, 'anyhow by tonight. I'll fly up again tomorrow.'

Simon shook his head. 'What's the good if you can't land and pick them up?'

'I could drop a message,' Rex suggested. 'Give them a date to pick them up some place north of Trinco'.'

'Ner. That would mean another eighty-mile trek for them and nights sleeping in the jungle. Doubt if they'd ever make it. Got to think of another way. Now, wait a minute; I'll tell you. We'll hire a motor launch. Go up and take them off in that. Then go on to some little port in southern India.'

'Crossing the island to Kalkudah by road is only about a hundred and forty miles; but to go half-way round it by sea is a very different matter,' the Duke demurred. 'I think it very unlikely that you would be able to get there that way by tomorrow afternoon.'

Getting out the map, they made a rough assessment of the distance and estimated that for a launch keeping in fairly close to the coast it would be about three hundred and sixty miles.

'Not a hope for tomorrow afternoon, then,' Simon muttered. 'Should be able to get there next day, though—sometime Sunday. If they do manage to reach Elephant Point, it's unlikely they'll leave it. Not till they decide there's no hope of their being picked up, anyhow.'

'Simon's right,' said the Duke. 'Both about going up in a sea-going launch and that they will remain there until they despair of your coming to their rescue. Where else could they go? They are utterly unfitted to maintain themselves for any length of time in the jungle; and on Truss's performance so far I don't see them giving themselves up.'

'O.K.' Rex stood up. 'I'd best go out and set about hiring a suitable vessel. If I'm to make the rendezvous by Sunday I'll have to have her put to sea first thing tomorrow morning.'

Simon stood up too. 'Think I'll come with you. Wouldn't have been any use in your aircraft, and I've never been much good in a boat except . . .' he tittered into his hand, 'an electric canoe on the Thames in the reaches above Maidenhead. But you'll have a Sinhalese crew. May make trouble when they tumble to what we're up to. You show me how and I might help to read the Riot Act.'

For the first time in hours, Rex grinned. 'That's true. I'd be glad to have you along, Simon. Let's get going.'

While they were absent the evening news broadcast took place. The Rajapakse escape had become Number One news item. But it was clear that the police were baffled. They asked the public to keep a look-out for the fugitives, either in a covered cart or on foot, in all parts of central Ceylon. So evidently they had no idea whether their quarry had continued on to the north, turned east or west, or possibly turned back south into the jungles of the highlands.

When Rex and Simon returned, de Richleau gave them this good news and, somewhat cheered, they all went down to dinner. Over the meal the others told him that they had succeeded in chartering a sea-going launch with a crew of four, ostensibly for a trip up to Trincomalee, and had arranged with her captain to go on board at six o'clock next morning. They had then gone to the American Embassy and Rex had borrowed, through one of his friends there, two pistols and ammunition, in case the crew of the launch had to be coerced into obeying orders, and a Stars and Stripes to show if they entered any port. Later Simon got hold of the head waiter and gave him a handsome tip to have a hamper full of food and drink packed up to take with them.

When they had returned to the sitting room, de Richleau asked Rex, 'If you succeed in picking them up and reaching southern India, what do you intend to do then?'

'We'll make for the nearest city that has an airport. That will probably be Madras. Then I'll cable the Captain of my aircraft to bring her over. You and Max can come in her. Then, after dropping you all off in Europe, Truss and I'll head for home.'

The Duke nodded. 'Thank you, Rex. I only pray that we may all meet in India in a few days' time. What I had in mind, though, was that the attention of the police might be drawn to a cable from Truss's father and they would think it very queer that you should have left Ceylon while your son was still a hunted man. If they then communicate with the Indian authorities at the place from which the cable was sent they will learn that Truss, Fleur and Douglas are with you, and out of malice may impound your aircraft.'

'Yes; I suppose that is a possibility.'

'We could avert it if instead of a cable to your Captain, in which you would have to use your name, you sent one to me. Simply the name of the city you wish your plane to go to with the spelling reversed and signed . . . well, let us say Porthos. But you will have to give me a note for your Captain telling him to act on any instructions I may give him.'

'Um! Excellent idea,' Simon nodded. 'Can't be too careful.' So, sitting down at the desk, Rex wrote the note. Then, as they had to be up very early in the morning, de Richleau wished them luck and they went off to bed.

Next day the papers splashed the Rajapakses' escape. There were long articles about it, a photograph of Douglas with an account of his career, another of Fleur, with particulars of her social activities and work for the Family Planning Association, others of the warder who had been shot, the injured sergeant and the wrecked car.

Van Goens busied himself all day with the attempt to trace Mirabelle's murderer, so the Duke spent the long hours alone, a prey to alternate hopes and fears. There was no fresh news until the evening broadcast, when it was given out that the stolen covered cart had been found with one of its wheels off at the side of the road from Polonnaruwa to Kalkudah. On hearing this, de Richleau's gloom increased as he thought of the three young people now, presumably on foot and faced with the dangers of the jungle.

After an almost sleepless night, he sent early for the Sunday papers. They again contained many columns about Douglas and Fleur. Photographs of their marriage had been dug up, and enlargements made of Richard, Marie Lou and de Richleau himself. He was stated to be Fleur's grandfather and Truss to be her cousin. About Truss, Rex and the millionaire banking family to which they belonged there were also pieces.

The tone of many of the articles caused the Duke additional worry; as it was clear that for Douglas, having been a well-liked and respected man, there would have been considerable sympathy had he remained in prison only on a charge of receiving smuggled goods, and it was implied that he had foolishly allowed himself to be persuaded into making his escape; whereas Fleur and Truss were condemned for having made it possible and the injuries that had been inflicted on their victims had aroused public indignation to a point which made it certain that any court would deal harshly with them if they were captured.

An hour later a cable was brought to him. It read:

Away from home when yours arrived. Stop. Comforted that you are coping but greatly worried. Stop. Have booked seats on Tuesday's aircraft will fly out if you advise. Stop. Our thoughts are with you all. Stop. Richard Marie Lou.

For the time being he could send them no word of comfort, and if the pick-up planned for that afternoon proved successful there would be no point in their making the long, expensive journey. So he decided not to send a further cable until he had definite news.

There was nothing fresh in the radio bulletins that morning or evening. Somehow he got through the day, from time to time studying the map and calculating roughly how near the launch had got to its destination. Then when he came up from dinner he turned on the radio for the nine o'clock news in English and the blow fell.

It was only a brief statement giving a report received by wireless from a Government gunboat. Information had reached Colonel d'Azavedo that Van Ryn's father and a Mr. Aron had left Colombo in a sea-going launch early on Saturday morning. Suspecting that they intended to pick up the fugitives at a previously agreed place on the coast, Colonel d'Azavedo had shadowed the launch in the gunboat. His assumption had proved correct. The fugitives had been taken off from Elephant Point a few miles north of the town of Kalkudah. They, and their rescuers, had then been arrested.

'And I,' thought the Duke, 'am responsible for this. It was my egoism and vanity, my senseless pride in never having admitted defeat, that has brought grief and ruin to those I love. And here am I, aged and feeble, unable to lift a finger to help them.' Sadly he went to bed.

Yet that was still not the worst. When he opened his paper the following morning its banner headlines shouted at him:

LALITA D'AZAVEDO DEAD: PRISONERS TO BE CHARGED WITH MURDER.

23

The Duke Plays His Last Great Hand

De Richleau forced himself to read as much of the shattering story as had so far been released. After praising Lalita's astuteness in trailing the launch, the account described how, at twenty past six the previous evening, Fleur and Truss had been taken off the point in a dinghy and the launch had then continued on its northerly course, presumably with the intention of landing them in India. Within half an hour the gunboat had overhauled its quarry, forced it to heave to and taken on board the two Van Ryns, Simon and Fleur. They had been locked in cabins and the gunboat had put about on the order of Lalita to head for Batticaloa. Two hours later the three men had broken out of their cabin, attacked Lalita and killed him. By ten o'clock the gunboat had reached Batticaloa, and the prisoners were being brought to Colombo by road.

No mention at all was made of Douglas, which the Duke found puzzling; but he was so overwhelmed with distress at the fate that now awaited his friends that, for the moment, he gave it little thought. As soon as he had pulled himself together he telephoned the High Commissioner and Ambassador, and both gave him appointments for that morning.

After hearing the nine o'clock news the previous evening he had handed in at the desk a cable to Richard, for despatch as soon as the telegraph office was open, which had said only: *Situation deteriorated your presence required urgently*, and he wondered how he could break the appalling news—which was so infinitely worse now than it had been then—to Fleur's parents.

Getting up, he rang for Max, dressed and sent for van Goens. The ex-Inspector could tell him no more than was in the papers, and had had no success in tracing Mirabelle's murderer. Impatiently they waited for the news bulletin. It told them no more than had the papers, except for solving the mystery of there having been no mention of Douglas. The prisoners, it said, had stated that on the Friday night he had been savaged by a leopard in the jungle and had died the following day.

When the time came de Richleau made his calls at the High Commission and Embassy. Both the High Commissioner and the Ambassador expressed their deep sympathy. The American said he would do his utmost for the Van Ryns and the Englishman promised to do his utmost for Fleur and Simon; but neither could offer the Duke much comfort.

De Richleau then went to see Douglas's father and found the poor man in tears. Having expressed his heartfelt contrition at having in part been responsible for Douglas's death, the Duke asked him whether he was willing to undertake the defence of the others. The lawyer then said that he had always been very fond of Fleur and, that apart, it was his duty to do everything possible for her as his daughter-in-law. De Richleau instructed him to engage the best Counsel in Colombo, whatever the cost, and said that he would pay twenty thousand pounds to any barrister who could save his friends from being condemned to death.

On returning to the Galle Face, he asked van Goens whether he could arrange for him to see the prisoners, but the ex-Inspector shook his head. 'Not today, Your Grace. They can't have left Batticaloa much before eleven o'clock last night. From there it is a long run and a tricky one, especially at night, as it means going right through the mountain country. They won't have got in till this morning, and most of today will be taken up with interrogations. But I'll try to arrange something for tomorrow.'

There was nothing else the Duke could do so, really feeling his age for the first time, he mooned about in abject misery until the following afternoon. Van Goens then took him to the prison and introduced him to a Colonel Talawa of the Security Service, who had stepped into Lalita's shoes and, happily, proved to be a very different type of man. He was courteous, helpful and, believing de Richleau to be the grandfather of the two younger prisoners, expressed his sympathy for him. But he said that he must be present at the interviews and the prisoners were brought one by one to a grille through which the Duke talked to them in turn.

From them he learned the truth about what had happened.

When Rex had sighted Lalita in the bows of the gunboat, he had ordered the launch to her maximum speed and endeavoured to get away. Then, as the gunboat was catching up with them, he had turned her in to the coast, hoping that they would be able to land and escape into the jungle. The crew of the launch had mutinied, and while he and Simon, with their pistols, were forcing them to keep the launch on her course, the gunboat had put a shot across her bows. There had then been no alternative but to surrender.

On board the gunboat, after submitting to Lalita's insults and his gloating over their capture, the three men had been locked into one cabin and Fleur into another, opposite. Fleur's contribution to the story was that at about nine o'clock Lalita had come into her cabin, reminded her that she had refused his kisses during her first visit to Olenevka, taunted her with being a whore because he had found her in bed with Truss, then declared that now she was at his mercy he was going to take, with interest, the kisses she had denied him. He had then said that he had no time to waste, as in an hour they would dock at Batticaloa, and told her that if she did not take off her clothes he would tear them off. There had followed a struggle in which she had had the worst of it and, when near defeat, she had started to scream.

The men told de Richleau that on hearing Fleur's screams they had guessed what was happening and at once decided that they must go to her help. Rex, being much the most powerful of the three, had thrown himself at the door of their cabin and burst it open, but tumbled head foremost into the passage. Truss had jumped over him; so had been first in the other cabin where Fleur and Lalita, with him uppermost, were struggling on a lower bunk. Seizing Lalita, Truss had dragged him off, then broken his neck. Hearing the rumpus, Lalita's men had arrived on the scene with guns in their hands, so to put up a further fight had been out of the question. Truss, Rex and Simon had been trussed like chickens for sale and thrown back into their own cabin where they had passed an hour in agony before being taken off the gunboat at Batticaloa.

The Duke told each of them that everything conceivably possible was being done on their behalf and assured them with a confidence he was far from feeling that the true story of what had taken place was certain to be accepted. He then offered a handsome *pourboire* to Talawa, but the Colonel refused it with a smile and said he would ensure that the supply of good food and wine that de Richleau had brought with him should be enjoyed only by the prisoners.

Next morning the Duke saw the High Commissioner, the Ambassador and Mr. Rajapakse again and gave them the true facts. All of them agreed that the killing of d'Azavedo had been morally justified, but shook their heads over the difficulty of proving it in the face of the evidence that would be brought by his men, who were certain to swear that he was innocent, and the prejudice of an angry public imbued with anti-colonialism, who would howl for the blood of the white man who had killed him.

De Richleau's only hope now lay in van Goens tracing Mirabelle's murderer and linking him with Lalita; but another black day passed without the ex-Inspector being able to produce even a clue that held hopeful possibilities.

On the Wednesday morning the Duke had ordered Max to call him early. He would have given anything to postpone the awful task of having to tell Richard and Marie Lou that Fleur was in prison faced with a charge of having incited Truss, Tex and Simon to murder Lalita, but it was against his life-long principles to shirk his responsibilities. With the unfailing support of van Goens he was driven out to the airport to meet them.

They met in the Customs shed and, while Marie Lou was having her luggage examined, he managed to get Richard aside. Leaning heavily on his malacca cane he told him first that Fleur was in prison, then with what she was charged. Richard took it well, and said:

'I thought it must be something pretty grim for you to send for us; but not so grim as this.'

When they had settled down in the car to return to Colombo, there was no evading Marie Lou's anxious questions. Richard took her hand and told her the worst. Then de Richleau gave an outline of what had led to Fleur getting into such a terrible situation.

While they were speaking Marie Lou stared straight ahead of her, dumb from shock and distress. Then before bursting into tears, she cried, 'It will be all right! I know it will be all right! You'll save her, Greyeyes. I know you will. You've never yet failed in anything you've undertaken.'

Her futile confidence in him caused de Richleau to close his eyes in an agony of spirit, but he could not bring himself to disillusion her.

When they reached the Galle Face, he gave them chapter and verse, then they went to lie down and attempt to rest after their long flight from England.

In the afternoon he had arranged for them to visit Fleur and he accompanied them. Again Colonel Talawa showed them every consideration; but when Marie Lou got back to the hotel she went to bed prostrate with grief.

That night the harrowed Duke, who seemed to have aged ten years in the past few days, came to the conclusion that he could no longer hope that van Goens stood much chance of bettering the prisoners' case by producing evidence that Lalita had been responsible for Mirabelle's murder; so if anything were to be done it lay with him to do it. For hour after hour he racked his wits then, at about two o'clock in the morning, he conceived the nucleus of a plan.

When he got out of bed six hours later he was a different man. Once again he was going into action. The years had fallen from him and he was his old authoritative determined self. Sending for van Goens he told him to go out and buy several things and ask no questions. Three-quarters of an hour later the ex-Inspector returned with them. They were a woman's wooden-backed hairbrush, a slab of what looked like kitchen soap about four inches square and two deep, a thing that looked like a ball-point pencil, a coil of thin wire, a roll of cottonwool and a string shopping bag.

Having cut the bristles off the hairbrush with a pair of scissors, the Duke inserted the pencil carefully into the slab so that only its pointed end showed, then bound the slab to the hairbrush with the wire, wrapped the whole contraption in the cottonwool, and put it carefully into the string carrier.

Next he sent for the Captain of Rex's aircraft, showed him the note of authority Rex had left with him and said, 'I wish you to have your aeroplane ready by nine o'clock tomorrow morning to fly to London. The route we take I leave to you. It is quite possible that we may not be able to leave in her. But I am in hopes that we shall, so you must be fully prepared.'

At first the Captain protested, on the grounds that Rex was in prison. But he could not ignore his master's written order and, eventually, agreed.

The Duke then affixed five seals with his signet ring to a piece of paper and had himself again driven to the American Embassy, asked for the jewels that Rex had deposited there, and was given them.

Returning to the Galle Face he said to Max, 'I wish you to pack all my things and be ready to leave at seven o'clock to-morrow morning. I shall not be with you because shortly I am going on a mission that none of my friends can undertake. But Mrs. Eaton will still be here and you are to take your orders from her.' Then he laid his hand on the old valet's shoulder and added:

'I may not come back, Max. If not, don't grieve for me. I thank you now for your many years of faithful service and you may rely on it that you are well taken care of in my will.'

Tears sprang to Max's eyes. 'But you must come back, Your Grace! You must! I am many years younger than you, but without you I'd be lost and die too.'

Tears then came to de Richleau's eyes as he replied, 'No, Max. You must live on and enjoy a happy old age. And, after all, you have known me to come through many dangers. Take heart. It may be the will of the Lords of Light that I should also survive this one.'

Over lunch, to the amazement of Richard and Marie Lou he talked with his old animation of happy times that they had enjoyed together in the past, his yellow-flecked grey eyes were sparkling and his hands no longer trembled a little from age as he refilled their glasses with wine.

Afterwards, upstairs in his sitting room, he said to them, 'You, my beloved Marie Lou, are to remain here. I desire you to pack your things and Richard's and be ready to leave with Max and van Goens at seven o'clock tomorrow morning for the airport. I hope that Richard and I will be able to join you there. The two of us are going on a mission. More than that, for the moment, I cannot say. But I think it most unlikely that any harm will come to him.'

'But you!' Marie Lou exclaimed. 'Oh, Greyeyes, what are you about to do?'

'Make a bid to better the situation of Fleur and the others. That is all I can tell you,' he replied. 'Now, Richard, put in a bag just the things you'll want for a night and we'll be off.'

Knowing de Richleau so well, Marie Lou accepted what he said without further argument. Richard collected his things;

ten minutes later she embraced them both fondly, and let them go.

Outside the hotel, in accordance with an order de Richleau had given him that morning, van Goens was waiting with a car. To him the Duke said, 'I may not see you again. If so, I thank you for your loyal service. I have already made arrangements with the elder Mr. Rajapakse that you will be well rewarded. There is only one thing more I wish you to do. Be here at seven o'clock tomorrow morning and drive Mrs. Eaton and my man, Max, to the airport.'

Van Goens looked a little surprised but agreed without question to do as he was asked. The Duke shook hands with him then got into the car beside Richard, who had already taken the wheel. The car rolled away and, two minutes later, de Richleau told Richard that he wished him to take the road to Kandy.

They arrived there in the early evening and had a meal at the Queen's Hotel. After it, de Richleau said, 'I want you to book yourself a room here, then drive me along to the Temple of the Tooth and drop me there. I expect to be away all night. If there is any sort of commotion, you are to drive straight back to Colombo. That is an order. It will be useless for you to come in search of me because I shall be dead. Is that clear?'

Richard stared at him, then burst out, 'God knows what you intend to do! But surely, surely, I can do something to help?'

'No, my son. Nothing. I alone can handle this affair. All the Queen's horses and all the Queen's men could not aid me in it. You must do as I say, and no harm should come to you. If I fail it will be your job to return and stand by poor little Fleur and the others, and do your best to comfort our dear Marie Lou. But if things go well I shall send for you in the morning, perhaps even as early as four o'clock. But it may be midday before you hear from me.'

Obediently, Richard made no further protest, but drove de Richleau along to the Temple and, after a long handclasp, left him there.

The Duke went in and sent up his card with the request that the High Priest would receive him. After only a short delay, he was taken to that dignitary's sanctum. To de Richleau's considerable relief he found the High Priest to be the same with whom he had had a long conversation over two years previously, was remembered by him and given a warm welcome.

When they were seated the Duke said, 'Serenity, I am in grave trouble. Would you be so gracious as to bear with me while I tell you of it?'

'Certainly, my son,' the High Priest replied courteously. 'It is to receive such confidences that I hold my office. You will, I hope, permit me to call you "my son"; for I recall that in our previous conversation we found ourselves at one in certain fundamentals.'

'Gladly, Father,' replied the Duke. 'We agreed that all true beliefs spring from the same root, and while I, too, am a Priest of Light in my own right, although a very humble one, you are my superior.' He then launched into an account of the terrible consequences that had resulted from his claiming the Plackoff inheritance. When he had done, he said:

'Now, Father, can you aid me to extract my friends from the terrible situation in which they are, mainly owing to my egoism, and only to a much lesser degree to their own impetuosity?'

The High Priest shook his head. 'I regret, my son, but that is not possible. Man-made Law and the Logos of Eternity are things apart. They must pay the physical penalty for their crime, and you must make restitution in your lives to come for having brought them to it.'

De Richleau gave a heavy sigh then produced the flat case of jewels, unzipped it so that they glittered in the light and said, 'At least, Father, I am in a position to make this offering to the Lord Buddha and ask his intervention on behalf of my poor friends.'

'You have a small fortune there,' the High Priest said quietly. 'It is indeed a handsome offering, and it may be that your intercession with the Lord Buddha will not go unanswered. My prayers shall join your own.' Rising from his ebony elbow-chair, he added, 'Come, and you shall present it at the shrine.'

Following him, the Duke showed no hint of his satisfaction that matters were going as he had expected, and in silence they walked the short distance along a balcony to the Holy of Holies.

It was a lofty room but only about fifteen feet square. It contained no furniture, but the central area was taken up by a glass case, also square, about eight feet wide and deep. In it at chest level stood a gold pear-shaped casket on the surface of which were hung many strings of big pearls and precious gems. Under it there were six other golden caskets, in the last of which reposed the Sacred Tooth.

Accepting de Richleau's jewels with a low bow, the High Priest turned, genuflected three times in front of the shrine when offering them and said a long prayer in Sinhalese. While he was so engaged and his back was turned, the Duke sat down on the floor in a corner of the room that could not be seen from outside the doorway. When the High Priest had finished his prayer he looked round and, raising the eyebrows below his shaven skull in surprise, said:

'In your present life you have many years behind you, my son. It is understandable that you should be weary; but accompany me back to my room to rest in comfort. Or, if you wish, we shall be happy to receive you here as our guest and provide you with a room of your own for the night.'

'I thank you, Father,' the Duke replied, 'but it is necessary that I keep a vigil here, perhaps for many hours. And the time has come when I must tell you that, besides my jewels, this evening I brought another thing to this illustrious shrine.' As he spoke he opened the string bag that he had been carrying all the time, took out the package it contained, carefully removed the cottonwool, held up the hairbrush, and went on:

'I doubt, Father, if, in your secluded life, you have ever seen anything like this; so I must tell you about it. In the first World War, soon after trench warfare started, there were no such things as Mills grenades, so we made our own bombs to throw into the trenches of the enemy. We did so by tying slabs of gun cotton, with a fuse inserted, to pieces of wood. This is a similar contraption, but instead of gun cotton, the square slab you see attached to this hairbrush back is of modern plastic and a much more powerful explosive.'

The High Priest stared at him. 'I do not understand, my son.'

'Then I must enlighten you, Father,' the Duke replied with a smile. 'I seek your aid to restore my friends to liberty. Either you will give it or, with great reluctance, I shall feel compelled to blow this Temple, the Sacred Tooth, yourself, and all else that is in it straight up to Heaven.'

'My son, my son, you have taken leave of your senses,' said the High Priest quickly. 'To do as you threaten would be the most terrible sacrilege. A devil must have entered into you.'

'No, Father. Believe me, I am as sane as you are. I realise, too, that it would take me many lives to redeem myself from such a crime. But that is the price I am prepared to pay, rather than allow my friends to be arbitrarily deprived of their present incarnations.'

'But in that, my son, there is nothing I can do to help you.'

'Yes, Father, there is. You can speak on the telephone to those in temporal authority over us. You will tell them that unless they grant the prisoners a free pardon and provide them with all facilities for leaving the country at nine o'clock to-morrow morning, the most sacred relic in the whole Buddhist world will have ceased to exist. It has been the symbol of truth and righteousness for over two thousand years. Your people succeeded in preserving it from the fanatical Portuguese, and the Dutch, the British in their wisdom, having captured it, restored it to you. Is it now, after all these centuries, to be destroyed because your Government will not release four prisoners who have not yet been proven guilty of the crimes of which they are accused? I trust not.

'And may I add, Father, your government can save its face by making public the story of myself and my friends as I have told it to you—the d'Azavedos' incitement of the Tamils to kill us at Olenevka, the lies by which they illegally retained those jewels for a year after they should have been handed over, their plot to bring about my death by their cobra, the finding of Vinala Fernando's remains, and the murder of Mirabelle de Mendoza. Regarded in sequence, all this provides such a damning chain of circumstantial evidence that no one could doubt Lalita d'Azavedo to be deserving of death, and a justification for a clement Government to refrain from pressing the charges against my friends.'

'I must retire. I must think on this,' said the High Priest. Then, carrying himself with dignity, he walked out of the shrine.

It was over an hour before he returned and said, 'I have spoken on the telephone to Colombo. They will not agree and have instructed me to send for the police to arrest or, if need be, shoot you.'

'That is regrettable,' said the Duke, 'and I beg you, Father, to save yourself by leaving the vicinity of the Temple before the police arrive; for I must tell you what will happen.' Lifting the hairbrush he pointed to the protruding point that looked like that of a Biro pencil. 'This is the detonator. It contains fulminate of mercury. It will go off if it receives even a slight jar. In my corner here the police cannot seize me and, should they shoot me, I shall automatically drop this hand-made grenade. No trace of myself, the police, you if you are sufficiently ill-advised as to remain here, or the Sacred Tooth, will ever then be recovered.'

While the High Priest appeared to consider this, he held the Duke's eyes with his. But de Richleau guessed at once that he was now trying to hypnotise him and, fearing that the priest might prove the more powerful, averted his gaze.

After a few minutes the High Priest gave up and said, 'Then I shall leave you here until you come to your senses.'

'For both our sakes, and that of this, the most sacred of Buddhist relics in the whole world, I pray that you will not,' the Duke retorted swiftly. 'You must be aware, Father, that at my age and with my infirmities there must come a time when I can no longer remain a menace. This compels me to give you a time limit. Unless by three o'clock you can give me an assurance that the Government agrees to my requests I shall have no alternative but to blow up myself and the Temple.'

Again the High Priest left him, and this time was away for very much longer. During his absence de Richleau became terribly tired, but he summoned all the resources of his will to keep his eyes wide open.

When the High Priest at last returned he said, 'The Lord Buddha smiles upon your courage; and in Colombo those young in incarnations bow to his will. It is to be assumed that you have confided your intentions to others, and for it to become public that the Government had allowed the Sacred Tooth to be destroyed rather than agree to release four criminals would bring about a revolution in which its members would perish. At a special meeting of the Cabinet, called an hour ago, it was agreed that your friends should be set at liberty.'

De Richleau gave a heavy sigh of relief, which hid the upsurge of triumph that ran through him, and replied, 'Father, for your aid in this I can never thank you sufficiently, but I will remember you in my prayers. May I now suggest that you should again telephone and ask for it to be arranged that the prisoners, with papers in order to permit of their departure, should be taken to the Katunayake airport by eight o'clock this morning. And that you will also telephone Mr. Richard Eaton at the Queen's Hotel here and ask him to bring his car round for us.'

'For us?' The High Priest raised his eyebrows.

'Yes, dear Father,' de Richleau smiled. 'I would trust Your Serenity without limit, but not the Government of this island. Yet, having saved the Tooth, I can hardly think that they would be willing to risk its High Priest being blown to fragments. If I travelled alone to the airport they might be tempted to assassinate me. You will, I am sure, see the wisdom of informing them that you are doing me the honour to see me and my friends take our departure from your country.'

The High Priest returned his smile. 'My son, it shall be as you wish. And I count you wise to require this very sensible precaution.'

Again the Duke was left for a long time on his own, from which he rightly judged that the authorities had counted on dealing summarily with him as soon as he and his bomb were a safe distance from the Temple, and that the High Priest was having difficulty in persuading certain people in Colombo that in this matter they must resign themselves to defeat.

Time drifted on, but at last the High Priest returned and said, 'Those young in incarnations were very loath to allow discretion to dominate anger in their discussions. I regret that so long has elapsed before they made up their minds and telephoned their decision to me. But all is agreed and I have just sent to the Queen's Hotel for Mr. Eaton. You must now, my son, be greatly fatigued. I beg you to accept from me some refreshment.'

Suppressing a groan as he tensed his muscles the old Duke struggled to his feet, and said, 'I thank you, Father; and I would be grateful for some fruit and a mild stimulant.'

They left the shrine together and went along to the High Priest's sanctum. An attendant novice was sitting there cross-legged in contemplation while awaiting the return of his master. He was sent outside to watch for the car. Then the two old gentlemen shared one of those gloriously-scented pineapples that can be grown only in Ceylon, and drank a brew of superlatively fine tea.

When the novice announced the arrival of the car, the High Priest put on an outer robe and they went down to the street. There de Richleau presented Richard to him and said, 'His Serenity's intercessions have saved those we love, and he is doing us the honour to accompany us to the airport.' Holding up the hairbrush he added, 'But this is a bomb that will explode if it is dropped, so it would be well for you to drive with care lest in an accident we are all blown to Kingdom Come.'

Richard could only marvel, and stammer his thanks to the High Priest, as he and the Duke got into the back of the car. Two minutes later they were on their way. With great caution Richard drove them through the darkness until dawn came up, and soon afterwards they arrived safely at Katunayake.

The others were not yet there, but the High Priest was received with great deference. Richard sat in silence, still wondering what had taken place, while the two old men placidly carried on a discussion that lasted for nearly two hours about the true meaning of 'Nirvana'. At last the prisoners, accompanied by a police escort, were brought in. Then Marie Lou, Max and van Goens arrived. De Richleau only smiled at them, told them that they must refrain from questioning him and continued his discussion with the High Priest about the hereafter.

There were no formalities and a few minutes later they were led out to the aircraft. The Duke, still nursing his bomb, said to the High Priest, 'You will oblige me, Father, by telling these people that should any attempt be made to machine-gun the aircraft as it leaves the ground, our pilot will have had instructions to bring it round, so that my bomb can be dropped on the airport building.'

The ready smile of the High Priest came again. 'I will do so. You deserve your triumph and I rejoice in it. Now, as we part, it should not be as father and son, but as brothers who walk side by side on the path upwards towards the Eternal Light.'

Solemnly the two old men kissed one another on both cheeks, then de Richleau and his friends went on board the aircraft.

Five minutes later they were airborne and on their way to England. The Duke was in a forward seat with Marie Lou next to him. Turning his head he said to Fleur, who was sitting behind her mother, 'Do not forget, my child, to make over

Olenevka to Nicholas van Goens. He has been a good friend to us, and I am happy to think that in this way we shall at last be rid of my disastrous inheritance.'

After his long day and night he was utterly exhausted. He had used up every ounce of the energy that remained to him. Now that he had saved those he loved reaction swiftly set in. He gave a groan and his chin fell forward on to his chest.

In alarm Marie Lou cried, 'Oh Greyeyes, are you all right?'

He roused himself to say a little thickly, 'Yes . . . my dear. But I am . . . again about to set out on . . . on the interesting journey. All . . . all of us will meet again because . . . because we are bound by love.'

As he spoke Simon saw that the hairbrush was slipping from his grasp. Reaching forward he clutched it.

De Richleau roused again and gave a faint chuckle. 'Don't . . . don't worry, my son. It . . . it's only a piece of soap . . . and a pencil.'